No Red Lines

ALSO BY MICHELLE KIDD

DI JACK MACINTOSH MYSTERIES
Book 1: Seven Days to Die
Book 2: Fifteen Reasons to Kill
Book3: Sixteen Carved Pieces
Book 4: Twenty Years Buried
Book 5: Three Broken Bodies
Book 6: The Twelfth Floor
Book 7: No Red Lines

DI NICKI HARDCASTLE SERIES
Book 1: Missing Boy
Book 2: The Trophy Killer
Book 3: The Hardwick Heath Killer

NO RED LINES

MICHELLE KIDD

DI Jack MacIntosh Mysteries Book 7

JOFFE BOOKS

Joffe Books, London
www.joffebooks.com

First published in Great Britain in 2025

Cover art by Nebojša Zorić

ISBN: 978-1-80573-089-7

CHAPTER ONE

Time: 11.25 p.m.
Date: Thursday 9 April 2015
Location: Cadogan Buildings, Wheeler Street, London

He hadn't realised until this moment just how much he missed the taste of death.

Seventeen years.

It was a long time to go without the very thing that fed your soul, but he was back now; and the taste was just as sweet as it had been all those years ago.

Seventeen years.

Seventeen *long* years.

He'd put a lot of thought into selecting this particular spot. Research was everything — he remembered that much from before. And although no sound could possibly escape her lipsticked mouth, he'd gagged her all the same.

Just like he had with all the others.

The others.

The memory made him smile as he tightened the cable ties around her slender wrists. He remembered each and every one of them with startling clarity — every scream that clogged in their throats, every tear that dripped from their eyes. He remembered them all.

Just like he would remember this one.

He'd been methodical, taking his time — now wouldn't be a good moment to get caught in the act.

The offices used to be home to a multinational corporation and the building stretched skywards for the best part of fifteen floors. It had lain uninhabited for the last nine months, the previous occupants packing up and shipping out to seek more financially attractive premises in the tax haven of the Cayman Islands. It was always the same — those that made the most money seemed to know the way to accumulate even more. Money talked, especially in this city.

With no one else clamouring to fill the cavernous office space now on offer, the empty floors suited his purposes, and he had his pick of the entire building. Getting inside had been no issue — a handy narrow access road led around to a car park at the rear, out of sight of the main street. And with no cameras on site, he was virtually invisible.

The delivery entrance was easy enough to penetrate — nothing that a crowbar and a little brute force couldn't deal with. As he stepped over the threshold, the welcome sound of silence enveloped him.

The building was just as stark on the inside, with each floor stripped down to the bare walls, and as the previous inhabitants had left nothing of value behind, the cost of surveillance seemed to outweigh the desire to protect an empty shell. Shiny metal signs on the outside advocated that the site was under twenty-four-hour surveillance, giving the impression the building was impenetrable. But that was all it was — an impression. It was quickly and easily overcome.

The girl had been beautiful once, there was no doubt about that, which was why he had chosen her; why he had chosen them all. Her soft brunette hair cascaded down over her shoulders like a waterfall, masking the ligature marks scored into her delicate neck. Her porcelain skin made the purple contusions stand out all the more.

It made him smile.

The flash from the camera bounced off the empty walls. Another one for his collection.

When he was satisfied that he had positioned her just as he wanted — hands tied behind her back, legs forced together at the ankles — he slipped the rope around her limp neck. The company had thoughtfully left behind curtain poles above each window — sturdy metal cylinders securely fastened to the concrete walls. It would be more than enough to support the woman's petite frame.

Hauling her up wasn't difficult either, and it didn't take long to deftly secure the rope to leave her hanging. And with the large expanse of glass in front of her, the scene was perfectly staged.

He hadn't chosen a window at the front of the building for obvious reasons — he wasn't daft. A schoolboy error like that would get him arrested before he'd even left the premises. London was a city that never slept — parts of it would slumber on occasion, but it was never fully asleep. Eyes and ears twitched at any hour of the day and night — somebody, somewhere, watching and waiting. *Listening.* He likened London at night to a napping cat — ears pricked for even the slightest noise.

The windows at the rear looked out over the disused car park. Beyond that, he could see a brick wall with presumably an alleyway on the other side. A line of terraced houses backed onto the alley, but they were far enough away to still afford him the cover of darkness.

There was always the risk that some nosy neighbour would be looking out of their back window, maybe glancing across at the disused offices right now. The familiar thrill of danger bubbled inside.

But his senses told him he was safe for now — and his senses had done him proud in the past. Leaving the woman swinging from the curtain pole, he quickly swept the area with a well-trained eye for any sign of his presence. There was none — just as he expected.

He was careful.

He was meticulous.

He'd done this before.

* * *

Time: 5.15 a.m.
Date: Friday 10 April 2015
Location: Rougham Street, London

The note had been pushed through Lorna Henshaw's letterbox sometime during the night — for it certainly hadn't been on the mat when she'd gone to bed at a little before ten o'clock, heading upstairs with her usual mug of hot chocolate and a book. Retirement was suiting her just fine these days and she didn't miss the cut-throat world of investigative journalism for a single second. Many a TV company had headhunted her before she'd finally hung up her notepad, wanting her skills for their hard-hitting and probative documentaries, but the thought hadn't appealed to Lorna in the slightest. She was tired of the reporting game, both in mind and body, and she felt she had served her time more than generously over her twenty-five-year career. It was time to take a step back and focus on herself for once, hence the early night with a hot chocolate.

People told her forty-eight was too young to retire, and maybe they were right. So, she placated them by saying she was on a 'career break' — but it was a career she had no intention of returning to.

But along with retirement came the inevitable onset of ageing. When she was working fourteen-hour days, she hadn't had the time to think about the passing years. It was only when she'd stopped, forced herself to lead a less hectic

4

lifestyle, that the years began to make themselves known. First came the generalised aches and pains, usually first thing in the morning, but it didn't take long for them to creep into the rest of the daylight hours, too. Early-onset osteoarthritis ran in her family, so it wasn't exactly unexpected, even if unwelcome. And then there was the insomnia — if she did manage to fall asleep, she would wake up at the crack of dawn or even before.

So, here she was, with the sun not yet up, standing by the front door with an empty mug in her hand. She had been on her way to the kitchen when she saw it — the small, square envelope resting on the doormat. Her initial intrigue was very soon replaced by an all-too-familiar sinking feeling sloshing in the pit of her stomach.

It might have been seventeen years, but she instinctively knew what it was.

And who had sent it.

Placing the empty mug on a side table, she bent down as much as the emerging arthritis in her hips allowed and scooped up the envelope. Hands trembling, she slid open the gummed seal.

At forty-eight, Lorna thought she'd seen it all. She'd covered any number of human tragedies in countless war zones around the world; witnessed, first-hand, the carnage left behind by terrorism, both at home and abroad; stood by helplessly as famine consumed entire communities in some of the poorest nations on earth. But none of that compared to how she felt when she opened the envelope.

She grabbed hold of the wooden banister behind her, nausea threatening to overwhelm her while her legs threatened to give out.

It was him.

There was no mistake.

And he was back.

* * *

Time: 7.30 a.m.
Date: Friday 10 April 2015
Location: London

The printer whirred into action, soon spitting out the series of colour photographs. He smiled as he scooped them up, marvelling at how easy it was now. Before, he'd had to teach himself how to develop his own films, studying the basics of how to operate a hastily improvised dark room. But it had been the only way to do it back then — he couldn't exactly send his films to the local camera shop or pharmacy and have them developed alongside someone's snaps of their annual summer holiday in Benidorm.

His films were of an entirely different nature.

The smile deepened as he pinned the latest images onto the wall.

Keeley Saul — she fitted in so perfectly.

He always made a point of finding out their names before he ended their lives; it was important to him, an essential part of the killing process. None of them were faceless or nameless to him; they were real people, and he wanted to get to know them a little during the short period of time they were held at his mercy.

She looked divine, lying there with her hands and feet bound, the rope tied around her neck. As usual, he had taken several before and after shots, the *before* pictures clearly showing the fear in her widening eyes as she lay helpless in the back of the van. It was something that never failed to excite — the way they looked at him, the way they *pleaded* with him. Towards the end some of them even started praying.

And then there were the *after* shots — the pictures he always took of them strung up by the window. It brought him a sense of accomplishment — maybe even pride. Satisfaction, definitely.

Content with his latest work, he stepped away from the wall and switched his focus to the map spread out on the table

6

behind. Where to next? He let his finger trail over the map's surface, a familiar ripple of anticipation teasing his skin. It was showing some wear now, the edges beginning to split and fray — but he couldn't bear to part with it. He smiled again and picked up a marker pen, moving in to slowly circle one of the stations.

He knew which one would be next.

And where.

He just needed to be patient and wait for the when.

CHAPTER TWO

Time: 8.00 a.m.
Date: Friday 10 April 2015
Location: Metropolitan Police HQ, London

Detective Inspector Jack MacIntosh eased himself into his chair and surveyed his desk. The usual carnage and chaos that littered it was curiously absent. The in-tray was empty, except for that month's Police Federation magazine, and so was the out-tray. There were no towers of files threatening to spill onto the floor, no Post-it notes stuck to the front of his computer monitor demanding his attention.

Instead, he could see the wood of his desk, not a sight he had witnessed in a very long time. Even the circular stains from the countless mugs of coffee that had been left to go cold over the years had been polished and eradicated from existence.

Sniffing the air as something flowery assaulted his nostrils, he lowered his gaze to the floor. The carpet tiles had been recently vacuumed, the filing cabinets and shelving opposite dusted.

House elves, it had to be. The Met didn't usually stretch to this level of cleanliness, not with budget constraints the way they were.

Relaxing back into his newly polished leather chair, Jack savoured the quiet. His first day back on the job — officially, anyway — since an improvised explosive device had sent him tumbling through debris three months ago, resulting in a fractured metatarsal and a perforated eardrum. He'd been lucky to escape with such minor injuries, so various members of the hospital staff had repeatedly informed him. Very lucky, indeed. Lying in his hospital bed, with pain raging like a torrent through his battered and bruised body, Jack hadn't felt all that lucky, to be honest — but he understood their point.

If Jack had hoped for a quiet and unobtrusive reappearance on duty, this was dashed when the office door creaked open and a familiar face peered around the frame. Despite the interruption, he couldn't help but smile as all thoughts of house elves giving his office a spring clean in his absence disappeared in an instant.

"Welcome back, guv." DS Amanda Cassidy edged into Jack's office, armed with a takeaway coffee cup and a grease-proof paper bag. "I called in at Isabel's on my way in and got you these." She waved the cup and bag in Jack's direction before depositing both on the empty desk. "And I had a bit of a tidy-up while you were off, too."

Jack reached for the paper bag. "I thought you might have." Peering inside, he saw his favourite sandwich — toasted cheese and ham — and felt his stomach rumble in appreciation, having left the flat that morning in true Jack MacIntosh style with just a black coffee inside him. The welcome aroma of melted cheese hit his nostrils. "Thanks for this." He nodded towards the sandwich and coffee cup. "And for the cleaning too, obviously."

Cassidy's face brightened. "No problem. I thought the place could do with a spruce up — goodness knows how long ago it was since that desk had been polished. And the floor vacuumed."

Jack knew.

Never.

9

Just then a whooshing sound burst into life from the window ledge and Jack's gaze flickered across to see an addition to the office that had so far escaped his attention.

Cassidy giggled. "I thought it needed a bit of a freshen up, too — so I got you one of those new motion-sensor air fresheners. I think it's meant to be orchids or lilies or something."

"Thank you." Jack sank his teeth into the toasted sandwich. "Again."

"And how have you been getting on with your step count while you've been off?" Cassidy perched herself on the edge of Jack's spotless desk and nodded towards the Fitbit on his wrist.

As he chewed and swallowed, Jack tilted the charcoal-grey wristband towards himself. Initially sceptical of the birthday gift the team had bestowed on him at the beginning of the year, he had to confess that it was growing on him and had actually proved useful during his recovery. The physios had told him to gradually increase his exercise tolerance as the fracture healed, and keeping track of his step count each day had gone some way to helping with that — to the point that he'd now become quite attached to the thing.

"All good, Amanda. It's been useful."

Cassidy's smile widened. "Good. I knew you'd love it." Pushing herself off the desk, she headed for the door. "Well, everything's under control here, so you've got nothing to worry about. We've got a spate of burglaries on commercial premises on the go, possibly linked, then a robbery at a building society and two stabbings — all keeping us busy. Obviously, the Hatton Garden investigation is dragging a lot of resources away. It's mind-blowing how they managed to get away with so much. It sounds like something out of a film. Anyway, when you're ready, we'll update you."

Jack waved a hand in acknowledgment as Cassidy stepped out into the corridor and disappeared from sight. The Hatton Garden jewellery heist had been one of the reasons he had requested to return to work. With the robbers working through the four-day Easter Bank Holiday weekend, the burglary had only come to light on Tuesday morning. Although they'd done their best to keep some aspects of the case out of the media, the press soon got wind of the fact that items worth some fourteen million pounds had been stolen. Jack was aware his team would be unlikely to get involved in the investigation, but it didn't stop the familiar stirrings of excitement creeping in at such a huge case landing on the station.

Jack turned his attention back to his sandwich and coffee, savouring both. As far as first days back at work went, this was turning out to be a relatively pleasant one.

But no sooner had he scrunched up the greaseproof paper bag and swirled a glug of coffee around inside his mouth than the desk phone rang.

* * *

Time: 8.30 a.m.
Date: Friday 10 April 2015
Location: Rougham Street, London

Lorna spread the photocopied images out across the dining room table and sighed. Just pulling them out of the bureau where they had been stored for the last seventeen years was bad enough, but now she was looking at them all side by side, her skin began to crawl. She had hoped that chapter of her life was over — dead and buried — and as the years passed, she slowly allowed herself to start to forget. Shutting the images away in the bottom drawer of the bureau had gone some way to helping with that. But she hadn't quite been able to take that final step and get rid of them entirely.

Maybe it was her deep-seated investigative training that prevented her from destroying them. Even though she had given up the reporter's life some time ago, she still felt it bubbling away beneath the surface every now and again — the need to shock, the need to thrill. And it wasn't a feeling she particularly welcomed.

But she had begun to forget about the envelopes.

Until now.

Since making the call to the police, she'd spent the last three hours just staring at them. She couldn't recall why she'd made so many photocopies — it was almost as if she couldn't bear the thought of losing them. But that was crazy, wasn't it?

The first envelope had landed on her doorstep on 8 February 1998 — it was a date she would never forget — the victim later identified as Gail Colman. Lorna hadn't known back then just how many more would follow, and just thinking about it now made her shudder as her gaze shifted towards the next image.

Cindy Benham had been victim number two.

When the second envelope had landed a month after the first, she could recall with startling clarity the unease that accompanied it, quickly followed by intense frustration when nobody was prepared to take her seriously.

The arrival of the third envelope — the victim being named as Sadie Bloomfield — changed all that, but it hadn't made them stop. After that came Lynn Jaggard, Christine Gooch and Becky Scott. She remembered each name without needing to try, the women imprinted on her brain like brands from a searing hot poker. She would *never* forget. But in November of that year, they had stopped — just like that. Almost as abruptly as they had started.

Lorna let a finger trail over the photocopied papers. It had taken many months for her to stop shaking every time she walked past the doormat, her heart jumping every time the letterbox rattled. She hadn't kept any of the newspapers that flooded the shops at the time, attention-grabbing headlines and salacious news articles giving more than the usual fifteen minutes of fame. She didn't need a visual reminder — her own memory was good enough for that.

But all she could think about now was, if they *were* starting again, how many more would there be?

* * *

Jack squinted up at the fifteen-storey building, each window reflecting the pale morning sunshine back at him. The start of April had been unseasonably warm so far, temperatures nudging confidently towards twenty degrees accompanied by balmy breezes. The weather forecasters were unsure how long it would last, warning of thunderstorms on the horizon, but the capital was enjoying an unexpected early taste of summer. Jack wasn't sure he particularly enjoyed summer in the city — the inevitable influx of tourists clogging up the streets made everyone's nerves a little more frayed, their tempers a little more brittle, or maybe that was just him.

"We're to go in the front entrance, boss." DS Cooper gestured towards the front of the building. "They think whoever did it went in through the back, so it's sealed off awaiting forensics."

Jack followed Cooper towards a door that was standing open wide, a lone uniformed PC on guard outside. After entering their details in the attendance log and donning protective suits and overshoes, they were allowed inside.

The journey up to the second floor didn't take long, guided by a series of metal stepping plates. Jack was thankful they didn't have to climb any higher — although his fitness was returning after the explosion, he hadn't been exactly match fit to begin with, fractured foot or no fractured foot. Easing on a pair of protective gloves, the detectives approached the inner cordon, where the familiar figure of Elliott Walker met them.

"Good to see you, Jack. You too, Chris. We're just through here."

Jack and Cooper followed the crime scene manager along the corridor towards the rear of the second floor. As they walked, Jack noticed how empty the place looked — everything stripped back to the core including the light fittings, leaving only bare wires protruding from the plaster.

13

Faded square outlines hinted where picture frames had once been displayed, and a circular outline suggested there had once been a wall clock.

But time was now standing still — both for the building and also for the poor soul found hanging from a curtain pole in an abandoned office that was now a crime scene.

"You just missed Dr Matthews," continued Elliott, snapping his elasticated cap back into place. "He sends his regards, but he had to shoot off somewhere. He'll be in touch once we get her off to the mortuary. Said he hoped to rejig his list so he can squeeze the post-mortem in later today."

"Who called it in?" Jack followed the crime scene manager into the open-plan office. "Who found her?"

"Well, here's the thing." Elliott came to a halt a few metres away from the body of a young woman lying face up on the carpet tiles. He stepped to the side, allowing the two detectives space to see the woman's bloated face, a deep ligature mark around her neck obvious even from a distance. She was dressed in a pale blue vest top and denim jeans, her feet bare. "It was a journalist."

Jack tore his gaze away from the body, a frown forming on his brow. "A journalist? Who?"

Elliott shrugged beneath his protective suit. "That I don't know, I'm afraid. Your chaps over there might be more help." He waved a gloved hand towards two uniformed officers standing by one of the far windows. "I understand they were the first on scene."

Jack nodded, making a mental note to do just that. "Anything you can tell me so far?"

Elliott made a face. "On a cursory initial sweep, the whole place appears quite clean — there's not much here — but we'll go through it meticulously and see if our killer left any traces behind. The rear entrance has been sealed off, as that appears to be how they gained entry."

"No cameras?" Jack knew the answer before the words left his mouth. Of course there wouldn't be cameras.

Elliott gave a confirmatory shake of his head. "No cameras, despite the signs out front, which are obviously just for show. The rear door was forced open, maybe a crowbar or something similar. But I doubt anyone in the area heard much, especially if it was during the night. This place is quite tucked away."

"Dr Matthews have much else to say?"

Another shake of the head. "Only that the rope she was found hanging from probably wasn't the one that killed her." Elliott squatted by the side of the body and pointed a gloved finger towards the woman's exposed neck. "He said the ligature mark was too narrow. With a rope the thickness of this one, he would have expected a much wider imprint."

"So, strangled before she was strung up?"

The crime scene manager shrugged again. "Not my place to say, but I think that's what he was getting at."

"So, all this was just for show." Jack stepped closer towards the body. "All staged." Glancing up, he saw DS Cooper had made his way over to stand by the nearest window. "Anything of much interest out there, Cooper?"

The detective sergeant hesitated before turning around. "Just an abandoned car park, boss. But there is a row of houses a way over there." He nodded back towards the window. "Maybe someone saw something?"

Jack went to join Cooper and followed the man's gaze. A line of terraced houses with small back windows — presumably bathrooms or spare bedrooms — backed onto the scene. They were still some distance away, so it was a long shot, but even a long shot hit home once in a while. "We'll get a team out there and do a house-to-house."

"Do you think he — or she — wanted someone to see them?" Cooper gestured towards the floor-to-ceiling glass. "Why else would they string the poor lass up right in front of a window?"

It was a thought, Jack had to concede, but a killer who *wanted* to be seen? It wasn't an obvious conclusion. "Maybe.

Let's see what the lads over there have to say, being first on the scene as they were." Jack started to walk towards the uniformed officers. "In particular, I want to know why a newspaper reporter called it in."

Jack's question was met with two blank expressions.

"No idea, sir," replied one of the officers. "That's all we were told. A call came in via 999, telling us that we needed to search abandoned businesses and empty buildings close to the Underground at White City."

Jack frowned. "That was it? Just abandoned buildings near White City? Nothing more specific?"

PC Paddy Harper shook his head. "That's all we were told. To be fair, there aren't that many empty buildings in this area. This was only the second one we looked at. Saw the rear door had been jemmied open, so we called it in."

"You have the name of this journalist? The one that called it in?"

Another shake of the head. "No name was given to us — we didn't even know it was a journalist until later. All we were told was to get out and start looking. It'll be logged in the system somewhere, I'm sure."

Jack nodded his thanks and then waved at DS Cooper to follow him out. "We're done here, Cooper. Let's get back to the station and see if we can't track down this mysterious journalist."

Jack just hoped to God that it wasn't the one he was thinking of.

CHAPTER THREE

Time: 11.15 a.m.
Date: Friday 10 April 2015
Location: Rougham Street, London

Jack's prayers were answered when the name of the reporter was traced through the call system.

Lorna Henshaw.

Jack had heard of the woman by reputation but, as far as he was aware, their paths had never crossed. Until today. And when the journalist opened the door to them, she wasn't quite what Jack had been expecting.

Her face was soft, her eyes sparkling with good humour — although they were now clouded with a heavy dose of apprehension. But she didn't seem to have that raw, abrasive edge that most of the other investigative journalists he'd come across would wear like body armour.

"It's good of you to see us, Miss Henshaw."

The woman nodded and stepped back to let Jack and Cooper cross the threshold. "Not at all, come on in — and call me Lorna."

The interior of the semi-detached house was just as well kept as the outside, with warm recessed lighting giving it a

17

homely feel. "Thank you. We'll try not to take up too much of your time."

The journalist led the detectives along the hallway towards the kitchen at the rear of the house. "Take up as much as you want, Inspector. My time is my own these days."

Jack and Cooper entered a spacious kitchen — dining area, a flood of light passing in through a pair of patio doors that led out into an equally spacious and airy conservatory. Floral-patterned wicker furniture made it look like they were stepping into the pages of a homes and gardens magazine.

"Take yourselves through and I'll bring us a pot of coffee."

Jack was about to wave away the offer of refreshments when he decided he could probably do with a pick-me-up. The takeaway coffee and toasted sandwich DS Cassidy had brought him earlier that morning was a distant memory now. "Thank you, that's very kind."

Jack and Cooper seated themselves in two armchairs, the padded seats soft and comfortable.

"Jenny says she wants a house with a conservatory next." Cooper gazed out the window at the small patch of luscious green grass and expertly tended raised flowerbeds. "And a garden. She wants dogs."

Although Jack admired anyone who kept a garden, and Lorna Henshaw's looked especially neat and well-cared for, all he saw was the extra work involved — cutting the grass, planting and pruning bushes, weeding and caring for flower beds. It was a time-consuming headache he could do without. He liked his flat on the second floor without so much as a window box to look after.

"You best get the overtime in then, Cooper. These places don't come cheap."

Lorna soon arrived with a tray laden with three mugs and a tall coffee pot. Jack saw Cooper's eyes light up when he spied the plate of chocolate biscuits that accompanied it. Once the coffee was poured, Jack asked the question they had come all this way to ask.

"What led you to make the 999 call this morning?"

Although Lorna Henshaw looked harmless enough, Jack's experience told him it was wise to be on guard from the very beginning, and to never make assumptions. Here was someone who had tipped the police off about a dead body — and Jack wanted to know why.

The journalist hesitated, her coffee mug clasped in her hands. She had taken the seat opposite Jack and Cooper, her eyes straying over their heads to the garden beyond. Jack was just about to ask the question again, wondering if the woman had heard him properly, when she spoke. "He's back," she said simply, her voice hushed. "I know he's back."

"Who's back, Miss Henshaw?" Jack left his coffee mug untouched on the wicker table. "Do you have a name for us?"

Lorna shook her head, a solemn look ghosting her eyes. "No — I just know he's back."

Jack watched DS Cooper reach for his first chocolate biscuit, then switched his gaze back to the journalist. "Why don't you start from the beginning?"

Lorna took a mouthful of coffee before getting to her feet and crossing over to a small bureau in the corner of the conservatory. Reaching inside the top drawer, she pulled out a small white envelope and headed back to the detectives.

"This came through my letterbox sometime overnight. I can't be sure of the exact time — somewhere between ten o'clock last night and five fifteen this morning."

Jack reluctantly took the envelope, eyes wary.

The journalist gave a forced smile. "You don't need to worry about ruining any fingerprints or other forensic detail, Inspector. He's far too clever for that. His missives are always scrupulously clean."

Jack's eyes widened. "You mean you've had more than one of these?"

Lorna simply nodded and gestured towards the envelope. "Once you see what's inside, I'll explain."

Confusion mounting, Jack did as he was told, opening the envelope to reveal a folded map of the London Underground. The only annotation was a red circle around White City Tube station. The frown on his brow deepened. "I don't understand." Flipping the map over and peering back inside the envelope, he noted there was nothing else to see. "How did this lead you to ring 999?"

"Inspector, the person you are looking for is the Central Line Killer. I think that was what he was dubbed in the newspapers at the time."

Jack frowned. "The Central Line Killer? I'm not sure I . . ." Slowly the cogs inside his head started connecting and realisation dawned. It hadn't been his case at the time, he'd been away on secondment to another force when it had hit the headlines, but it had saturated the news for months.

The Central Line Killer.

"You think *this* is from the same person?" Jack gestured towards the Tube map and envelope still in his hands.

"I *know* it's from the same person."

"Forgive me, Miss Henshaw — Lorna — but that case is what . . . twenty years old?"

"Seventeen, it was 1998."

Jack nodded, slowly. "OK, 1998. Seventeen years ago. It's still a stretch to suddenly jump to the same conclusion. It wasn't my case, so I'm not sure I know all the facts . . ."

"Well, I do, Inspector." Lorna Henshaw's voice took on an icy edge. "And you have to believe me when I tell you it's him — *again*." Pausing, her face relaxed a little, the hardness in her eyes softening. "Sorry. I apologise for my terseness. I don't mean to be rude, but I'm telling you the truth. It's him."

Jack went to hand the envelope to Cooper, who was busy licking his fingers after his second biscuit, chocolate smearing his lips. "Wipe your hands before you handle this, Cooper." He turned back to the journalist. "I think you need to tell me what you know — right from the start."

Over the next fifteen minutes, Lorna did just that, telling Jack and Cooper all she knew about the Central Line Killer.

"In February 1998, I received an envelope identical to the one you see here. It contained a London Underground map. The Tube station at Stratford was circled in red ink. It didn't mean anything to me — I was working for one of the big tabloids at the time and we often got strange items sent to us through the post, so I didn't pay too much attention to it. That was until the following day, when a woman's body was found in a building close to Stratford Underground. I still wasn't quite sure what to make of it but, a month later, I received another envelope with another map — and another Tube station circled. The following day another body was found."

Jack was starting to remember bits and pieces about the case. "I recall it, yes. Go on."

"I immediately took both maps over to the police and explained what had happened. I was convinced I was being sent them on purpose, as if the killer wanted to give me clues for some reason."

"And what response did you get?" Jack already had an idea. There was nothing in his albeit fractured memory that recalled anything about Underground maps being sent to a reporter.

"To begin with, nothing much. I recall that the team dealing with it tried to put the whole thing down to coincidence, maybe someone playing a trick on me. But then the third envelope arrived, with another map — and it didn't take the investigation team long to change their mind and start taking me seriously."

Took their time, though, Jack wanted to add but didn't.

"The media then started to dub him the Central Line Killer, because of the location of the bodies. I got six envelopes in total."

Hands now clean, Cooper flipped the Tube map over. "I'm no' sure I remember this one, boss. But in 1998 I was still up in Glasgow."

"It was big news down here, Cooper. Six women were killed over a ten-month period — the country hadn't seen anything like it since the days of the Ripper. And then, towards the end of the year, I believe, it simply stopped. Am I right, Lorna?"

The journalist nodded. "Yes, the envelopes stopped coming."

"Do you remember who was handling the investigation back then?"

"Yes, it was a Detective Inspector Tyler. Nice man."

Jack nodded. Frank Tyler had been well respected within the force for many years, eventually retiring not so long ago after serving some ten years as a DCI. "Why wasn't any of this made public? Unless I'm wrong, I don't recall your connection to the case appearing in any of the press reports back then."

"It was kept away from the media on purpose. The only ones who knew about my involvement were the investigation team themselves — nothing wider than that as far as I know. I wasn't allowed to tell anyone — no one at work, no one within my own family. I think the idea was that by keeping the details about the envelopes and the Tube maps out of the public domain, it would be easier to identify the real killer if they surfaced."

"Which they didn't," added Jack. "Did you ever discover why you were being targeted? Why the killer chose to send the maps to you?"

The journalist shook her head. "No, we never got to the bottom of that one. I seem to remember DI Tyler and his team looked into my past cases — checking out articles where I might have trodden on one too many toes." She gave a short laugh. "I suspect there were too many to count, in the end. I have no idea why the killer chose me, Inspector — maybe it was a random thing, he just needed a name from the newspapers."

"Maybe." Jack wasn't a great fan of random. "But that then begs the question, why involve you at all — if none of it was ever made public? What was the killer hoping to achieve?"

The blank look on the journalist's face told Jack maybe this wasn't the time to dive down that particular rabbit hole.

"And this envelope definitely came by hand?" He had already noted the absence of a stamp or postmark on the front.

"Definitely. Just like the first three in 1998."

"What happened after the first three?"

"After the third one, DI Tyler arranged for surveillance to be put outside the house — but the rest of the envelopes arrived in the regular post. It was as if the killer knew."

Jack nodded. "It certainly appears that way. He either knew or was very astute. You mind if we take this with us?" He gestured towards the envelope still in Cooper's hand. If what the reporter had told them was correct, it wouldn't have much forensic value — especially after the pair of them had had their grubby mitts all over it — but it wouldn't hurt to check it out.

"Of course. And I can give you copies of the others from 1998 if you want? I made several of each." She nodded towards a large envelope on the coffee table. "I never got the originals back — not that I would ever want them — so I assume they must still be in storage somewhere."

"That would be great, thanks. And I'd also like you to come in and make a formal statement, if that's OK?" Jack got to his feet. "In the meantime, we'll get access to the paperwork from the previous investigation. And, for the time being at least, I need you to keep this to yourself." He took the envelope from DS Cooper. "We don't want this getting out into the media until we know exactly what we're dealing with. Your discretion would be appreciated."

"Of course."

"And it's likely that we'll want to set up some kind of surveillance on your property again."

Lorna nodded. "Thanks. I'd feel a lot better if you did." As Jack and Cooper started to head back towards the front door, Cooper ramming another chocolate biscuit into his mouth as they went, she handed over the A4 envelope. "It's all in there."

Taking the envelope, Jack stepped out onto the porch. "Thanks, we'll be in touch."

As they made their way back towards the Mondeo, Jack grimaced. His Fitbit told him he hadn't walked particularly far that day, but his foot was beginning to ache already. He rummaged for his keys and threw them at Cooper. "You fancy driving us back so I can take a look at this lot?" He waved the envelope in the air. "But wipe those hands of yours before you touch my steering wheel."

***

Time: 12.30 p.m.
Date: Friday 10 April 2015
Location: Blackfriars Road, London

Stuart "Mac" MacIntosh pulled the motorcycle helmet from his head, grateful for the feel of fresh air on his face. Not that the air was particularly fresh, more cloying and clammy, but it was better than nothing. It was halfway through his day, and he was due a break, but he just wanted to get one more delivery completed first.

As he wiped his brow, about to replace his helmet, he knew he would have to ring Isabel back, make some sort of grumbling apology for his terseness before leaving for work that morning. She'd been fretting over Jack again — saying they both needed to go over and visit him, check that he was all right.

"*He could have died in that explosion, Mac — and he's your brother.*"

Mac had made some smart-arse response along the lines of, "*He's already died about a million times before, Isabel, the man's indestructible.*" It hadn't gone down well, something Mac realised the moment the words had left his mouth, and his wife of eleven months had shot him one of her increasingly familiar looks over the steam from the café's coffee machine. Isabel owned and ran Isabel's Café, a quirky little coffee shop on the Horseferry Road, offering an eclectic mix of coffee, pastries and books.

Mac was immensely proud of how she'd managed to build up the business from scratch in a matter of three years, and repeatedly had to pinch himself that someone like her wanted to be with someone like him. He knew he was punching above his weight. Stuart MacIntosh hadn't inherited his brother's good fortune — if you could call it that. They'd both had the same rocky start in life — placed into foster care after the death of their mother — but Jack's path had ended in a good career while the younger MacIntosh had followed an entirely different path of his own choosing, a path that led to a stint in youth detention and then prison.

But he hoped he was making up for his wayward days now — holding down a decent job with the motorcycle couriers and helping out at the café when he could. He was also working hard at cementing his newly resurrected relationship with Jack, after years of separation. It made Mac smile the way Jack still called him Stu — refusing to adopt the widely used nickname Mac had acquired during his teenage years.

Rubbing the sweat from his eyes, he pulled the motorcycle helmet back on. He knew he still needed to apologise to Isabel; maybe a bunch of flowers from the garage on his way home would be a good place to start. And although he knew his brother was fine — Jack was a resilient bugger and more than happy to look after himself — he made an additional mental note to give him a call, too. Just to check in and suggest a beer one night.

Turning the bike back into the traffic, Mac set about the rest of his day. Family dynamics would have to wait — he still had work to do.

* * *

Time: 1.00 p.m.
Date: Friday 10 April 2015
Location: Metropolitan Police HQ, London

Jack pulled out one of the vacant chairs and sat. "This morning's discovery means we have a live murder investigation which needs to be our priority for the foreseeable." He took in the range of expectant faces looking back at him and knew he could count on each one of them to give it their best.

DS Chris Cooper was his most experienced officer — a bundle of ginger-haired energy with a deep-seated love of food, especially bacon sandwiches. DS Amanda Cassidy, not long promoted to sergeant, was also an exceptional officer and just three months ago had put her life on the line during an unauthorised undercover operation to catch a serial killer. Escaping from a crashed vehicle with a head injury and concussion, luck had been on her side that night. Always on a health kick of some sort, every so often she would try and tempt Jack away from his sugar-laden coffee but, as yet, she had been unsuccessful. And then there was DC Trevor Daniels. Daniels had joined the team eighteen months ago and it hadn't taken long for the young officer to win a place in Jack's heart. Originally labelled the station "nerd", with a brilliantly quick mind and a love for anything historical or supernatural, he was now an invaluable part of the team.

"I appreciate you all have a lot on already, but we need to make this one our main focus." Jack turned to the first whiteboard, where several crime scene photographs had been tacked already, courtesy of Elliott Walker. "Operation Quicksand. We have an as-yet-unidentified female, found at the Cadogan Buildings on Wheeler Street earlier this morning. She was hanging in an open-plan office in front of one of the rear windows on the second floor. Cooper and I took a look at the scene before the body was moved to the mortuary. The building was last inhabited by a multinational corporation and I'm reliably informed that it's been empty for the last nine months. The perpetrator is thought to have gained access via the rear entrance, and other than a row of terraced houses some distance away on the far side of the car park, it isn't overlooked."

"A clever choice, then." Cassidy unwrapped a cereal bar and took a bite. "Sounds like they know what they're doing."

"Indeed. Dr Matthews has suggested that the victim was most likely dead before she was strung up, so this may not be our actual murder scene." Jack paused. "I'm not sure if that makes it any better or not. The post-mortem will hopefully be held sometime today, and I'd like Amanda and Daniels to head over for that one." He gave Cassidy an apologetic look. "Sorry, Amanda. Can't be helped."

"No problem, guv." Cassidy tried a smile as she placed the cereal bar back in its wrapper. "I'll give them a call in a minute, see when it's scheduled."

"We also need to investigate a potential link to a series of unsolved murders from 1998 — an offender dubbed the Central Line Killer. You youngsters probably won't recall, but it flooded the headlines for most of that year and the killer was never caught."

"So, it's just a *potential* link?" DC Daniels looked up from his keyboard. "It's not definite?"

"At the moment, that's the official line — until we know more, of course. Certain information was kept out of the media at the time, standard stuff these days, but it's the involvement of an investigative journalist that suggests it has to be the same killer."

"A journalist?" Cassidy took a sip from her peppermint tea. "Who?"

"Woman by the name of Lorna Henshaw. She was very high-profile back in the day — her articles were used in any number of hard-hitting documentaries both in print and on TV. Cooper and I have just been to see her and the link appears to be genuine — I don't think we're looking at a copycat here. The killer sent her maps of the London Underground before each killing, marking the area where the body would later be found." Jack waved the A4 envelope in his hand. "She's given us photocopies, but the originals will be kicking around here somewhere. The important thing to note is that the number of people who knew about her involvement back in 1998 was limited to the immediate investigation team and no one else."

"Which is why we think it must be the same killer." Cooper sank his teeth into a freshly prepared bacon roll from the staff canteen. "No one knew about the maps."

"Perhaps not a true copycat, then — but it could still be someone connected to the previous case." Daniels nudged his spectacles a little further up his nose. "Not necessarily the original killer."

Jack gave an unenthusiastic shrug. "We'll look into it, of course, but something tells me that's not what we're looking at here. I really don't think it's one of us." He broke off, taking a moment to digest what he'd just said. If it *wasn't* the real killer emerging again, then the only other logical conclusion would be a member of the investigation team. It wasn't a particularly nice thought, and he hoped he was right to discount it. "Before you head over to the mortuary, Amanda, can you do the necessary with Missing Persons? We need to get an ID as soon as possible."

"Will do, guv."

"And Cooper — you're a tech wizard when it comes to CCTV and such like. Pull as much as you can from around Wheeler Street and also from around White City Underground. Flag up anything that looks out of place. He must have brought her to that location somehow, dead or alive." Jack got up from his seat. "Daniels, help Cooper out with the camera footage until it's time to go to the mortuary. Fixed cameras, too. I'll be heading down soon to take a look at the papers for the 1998 investigation. If these cases are linked, then we'll need to pick it apart piece by piece to see if anything was missed the first time around. I'll be in my office for a while yet if anyone needs me."

"The chief superintendent's PA called down earlier." Daniels waved a Post-it note in the air. "Second time today."

Jack tried to hide the smile on his face. "I'm sure she did, Daniels. Just file it away for now — I'll get around to checking in with the chief just as soon as I get a spare moment." Making his way over to the door, he knew that the young detective constable had been part of the team for long enough now to know what "file it away" meant. Before stepping out into the corridor, he took a brief look back over his shoulder, just in time to see Daniels deposit the Post-it note in the bin.

CHAPTER FOUR

Time: 2.15 p.m.
Date: Friday 10 April 2015
Location: Westminster Mortuary, London

The mortuary wasn't DS Cassidy's favourite place in the world. It was somewhere she would try to avoid, if at all possible, but today that wasn't an option. The boss was busy accessing the cold case files, and Chris was bogged down with CCTV, so it fell to her and DC Daniels to attend the post-mortem. To give him his due, Trevor had offered to go it alone, having none of the misgivings about the recently deceased that Cassidy did. If anything, he seemed to be looking forward to the experience.

"I don't mind if you want to sit this one out." Daniels pulled on his rubber wellington boots. "You can just sit in here, if you like. No one needs to know."

Cassidy glanced around the changing room, temptation biting. But, as much as she might want to, she knew she couldn't do it. Trevor would be true to his promise and wouldn't utter a word to a single soul, she was certain of that. But *she* would know. She would know that she'd ducked out and left him to shoulder the responsibility alone. Although more than capable, it wouldn't be fair on him.

"It's OK, Trevor. Sitting in here wouldn't be all that much better anyway." She wrinkled her nose as she pulled on the rubber apron and fitted the elasticated cap to her head. The unique aroma from the examination room had already managed to infiltrate the walls of the changing room. Swallowing past the ever-increasing lump in her throat, she headed for the door. "Let's get this over with."

The room was already laid out when they stepped inside, Dr Philip Matthews taking up his customary position at the side of the steel examination table. He afforded both detectives a warm greeting.

"Welcome, welcome. Good to see you both again. DS Cassidy. DC Daniels." The pathologist's smile was genuine. "If you'd care to step a little closer, then we'll begin."

Dr Matthews was well aware of Cassidy's aversion to his examination room but admired her spirit in attending when it was called upon. He could see by her pale complexion that she still found the experience a daunting one.

Reaching up to switch on the digital recording device above his head, the pathologist began the external examination.

"Today's date is Friday the tenth of April, and before us we have a Caucasian female, approximate age range between twenty-one and twenty-nine years of age. I will now document the external injuries as follows." The young woman's clothing had already been cut from her body prior to the examination, and it now sat in a series of plastic evidence bags at the side of the room, which left her pale and lifeless body exposed on the table. Dr Matthews gave a small cough to clear his throat. "Starting with the feet and lower legs, there is little by way of injury — some minor bruising and abrasions to the right ankle which look to be at least forty-eight hours old. Moving on to the upper legs, again nothing concerning but some mild bruising once again to the right knee. This looks to be more recent."

The pathologist paused, stepping out of the way to allow the mortuary technician, introduced as Perry, to take a series

30

of close-up photographs. Once completed, he continued. "The lower abdomen and pelvic areas show no sign of injury, but swabs will be taken to check for any sexual assault. There is evidence of a Pfannenstiel incision indicative of a previous caesarean section."

Cassidy would often try to tune out much of what was said during a post-mortem, usually training her eyes on the tiled floor for the duration of the proceedings, but she wasn't quick enough this time and clearly heard the word "caesarean". She felt her stomach flip — a caesarean meant there was most likely a child out there somewhere, and one still young enough to be missing its mother.

"Moving up, the upper abdomen and thorax show no sign of injury. There are several skin lesions that look like benign naevi on the left breast, but otherwise the examination is unremarkable." Dr Matthews edged along the table. "Both upper limbs show significant recent bruising. The left upper arm has a four-centimetre contusion on the anterior surface, with several less-defined contusions on the posterior side. The right upper arm has a slightly longer contusion on the anterior surface at six centimetres, with similar less-defined markings on the posterior aspect. Both could be consistent with manual handling." Once again, the pathologist stepped to the side to allow the injuries to be photographed, raising his gaze to meet that of DC Daniels. "If you would care to step a little closer, detective, you'll see that the pattern of bruising on the anterior surfaces of each upper arm could suggest the imprint of a thumb."

Daniels didn't need asking twice. "So, he grabbed her by the arms?" The detective's gaze remained fixed on the lifeless body. "With both hands?"

Dr Matthews gave a small shrug and resumed his position by the table. "It's possible. Both forearms have also sustained significant bruising, many of which in my opinion could be considered defensive wounds. They look recent — I would estimate all occurred within the immediate twenty-four hours prior to death. There are also more marked abrasions around each wrist, consistent with a restraint of some kind."

Together with the mortuary technician, Dr Matthews then turned the body onto its side. "Detectives, you'll see the signs of lividity here, most prominent on the backs of the thighs, the buttocks and the upper torso." The pathologist pointed towards the widespread purplish-blue discoloration. "The areas of blanching suggest where the body was in contact with a hard surface." Noticing that Daniels had taken another step forward, he smiled and continued. "Lividity begins thirty minutes to four hours after death, detective, most pronounced at around twelve hours. It can help determine the position of the body at the time of death — once the heart stops beating, gravity helps the blood pool at the lowest point."

"So, she was on her back when she died?"

Dr Matthews slowly inclined his head. "Most likely. Or at least was moved onto her back shortly afterwards. And remained there for some time."

Daniels' eyes gleamed behind his glasses. "This is fascinating."

The pathologist's mouth twitched into a smile. "If you're interested in this kind of thing, I have a number of textbooks back in my office that might be of use. I'm sure Perry here will be more than happy to show you."

Daniels nodded enthusiastically. "I am, yes. That would be great."

"In the meantime, let's move on to the head and neck."

Cassidy felt the ground sway slightly beneath her feet. She had already caught a glimpse of the poor woman's face as they'd entered, not quite able to avert her gaze quickly enough. She didn't need the pathologist to inform her that the woman had been strangled.

"Clear ligature markings to the neck." Dr Matthews gently turned the woman's head to the side. "From the intensity of the bruising to the anterior aspect of the neck, I would suggest your perpetrator was behind the victim at the time of applying pressure. Furthermore, the width of the contusions lends itself to the ligature being no more than 1.5 millimetres in diameter."

With a final set of photographs completed, Dr Matthews gestured towards the technician. "If you would be so kind, Perry, as to pass me an examination bowl?"

The technician placed the camera down onto the steel bench behind him, then selected a freshly sterilised bowl from the rack above while Dr Matthews picked up a scalpel and pair of tweezers from the instrument trolley. "DC Daniels? You may want to witness this."

Cassidy sensed Daniels edging closer, but her own gaze remained fixed to the floor. Part of her wanted to know what the pathologist was about to show them, another part of her definitely didn't. Eventually her curiosity overcame her fear, and she slowly raised her eyes to witness Dr Matthews starting to gently tease the woman's lips apart.

Once open, the pathologist used the stainless-steel tweezers to reach inside the woman's mouth, slowly pulling out a piece of crumpled paper which he deposited into the waiting bowl. He then turned his attention back to the two detectives, a pensive look on his face.

"You'll both be far too young to remember, I'm sure, but if I'm not very much mistaken . . ." Using the tweezers to carefully prise apart the crumpled paper, Dr Matthews tipped the bowl towards Cassidy and Daniels. "What we have here is a London Underground map."

* * *

Time: 2.15 p.m.
Date: Friday 10 April 2015
Location: Metropolitan Police HQ, London — Cold Case Unit

Jack liked the basement. He liked the coolness of the air the lower you descended; and he liked the quiet. But most of all

33

he liked the fact that it was a place where you could disappear. Halfway down the first flight of steps, his phone signal cut out. Smiling, he slipped the handset back into his pocket. One of the major advantages of the subterranean world that housed the Cold Case Unit was that no one knew where you were.

He liked that a lot.

The unit was home to a series of narrow corridors and surprisingly roomy offices buried deep in the lower bowels of the station. As Jack descended the final flight of steps, he was met by a familiar face.

"Hello, Jack. Good of you to pop down." To Jack, Detective Inspector Jane Telford always seemed to have a sly, mischievous glint in her eye — and today was no exception. "How's the foot?" She gestured towards Jack's leg.

Jack placed a well-practised smile on his face. "Never better." It wasn't a complete lie — the fracture had healed well thus far, so he was told anyway, and he could do just about everything he used to do before it happened. It would ache if he stood for too long or walked that bit too far — but that could just as easily be his ageing body as much as anything else. Every morning, he seemed to wake up with a new ache or pain.

Jack knew Jane well enough by now to know she would realise the stock answer was all she was going to get. Waving for him to follow, she started heading back along the corridor. "Come on through."

Jack did as he was told and followed the detective inspector deeper into the burrows beneath the building. He liked Jane; she seemed to "get" him when so many other people didn't. She had been his plus-one at his brother Stu's wedding last year and the tongues around the station had only just stopped wagging. The thought that Jack MacIntosh, lifelong bachelor, could have somehow snared himself a woman — and a woman as highly regarded as Jane Telford — was the talk of the station for some considerable time. Jack had remained predictably tight-lipped about the whole thing, amused and not a little bemused at other people's apparent interest in his personal life. Once everyone had eventually got the message that there was no juicy gossip to be had, no delicious secrets to unravel, the whispers had slowly petered out.

Jack soon recognised the layout of the cavernous Cold Case Unit's main office, with its racks of metal shelving hugging the walls, numerous boxes and crates piled on top. Nothing much seemed to have changed since his last visit. By the look on Jane's face, she'd read his thoughts remarkably well.

"Not a lot changes down here, does it?" She waved towards two chairs by the side of a large wooden table. "Take a seat. I've got everything out from the 1998 investigation — there's quite a lot to sift through, as you can see."

Jack eyed the boxes stacked neatly to one side of the table, the rest piled up on the floor. "Isn't there just."

Jane proceeded to pull out one of the chairs and sat down, then pointed toward two takeaway coffee cups. "I took the liberty of getting us some decent coffee in. You won't be surprised to hear that the vending machine is still spewing out tepid dishwater." She grinned and nudged one of the cups towards Jack. "Let me know how I can help with this lot."

For the next hour, Jack sifted through box after box, file after file. The investigation had been extensive and, although not on the investigation team himself, he had still heard enough to understand that the Met had been chasing their tails for much of the time, trying to find an elusive offender who quickly became dubbed the Central Line Killer. Jack wasn't usually a fan of nicknames — and especially not ones that had been dreamed up by the media — but this one seemed fairly apt, with each victim found close to a Central Line Tube station.

Jane had already established a timeline for the 1998 attacks, which began in February of that year and ended abruptly that November.

"As part of the cold case review a few years ago, we started looking at earlier offences." Jane reached for one of the boxes on the floor. "Looking for similar patterns in other unsolved cases."

Jack nodded. It was exactly the route he would have taken himself. Offenders rarely started their careers with cold-blooded murder. There would be one or two, obviously, who bucked the trend, but most would begin with some lesser crime, building up their repertoire from there. He watched as Jane extracted a series of folders from the box.

"The offences in 1998 were clearly sexually motivated. If the victim wasn't raped before being murdered, then they were seriously sexually assaulted. We then found a group of offences in late 1996, and the first part of 1997, which were loosely tied to the investigation at the time." Jane placed two buff-coloured folders in front of Jack. "The 1996 ones are on top."

Jack proceeded to open the folder while Jane continued with her summary.

"The first victim was a Mandy Steed, sexually assaulted in Halifax on the sixteenth of September. From her statement, it appears the attacker fled the scene after the assault. He wasn't disturbed, had ample time to kill her or at least attempt to kill her if that had been his plan — but he didn't. He just left."

Jack flicked through Mandy's statement, making a mental note to read every word later. For now, he was happy with a résumé.

"The second attack came in November 1996. Kristel Turner was on her way home from work when she was attacked in Huddersfield. She was beaten around the head, then raped. Again, the attacker fled the scene. There was one more assault in 1996 — in early December. Colette Burgess was attacked in Hebden Bridge. Again, she was beaten around the head, before being sexually assaulted."

"Was there any thought given as to the choice of location? First thing that springs to mind is that they all begin with the letter H."

Jane shook her head, peering over the top of her wire-rimmed spectacles. "Not that I remember seeing, no."

"And all the attacks were linked forensically?"

Another shake of the head. "Not exactly. There wasn't too much by way of forensic detail at any of the crime scenes, and unfortunately the techniques used in the late nineties weren't advanced enough to obtain any DNA profiles. But the offences were linked by the victims' description of the attacker. All three described an overweight man of average height. Two mentioned a 'beer belly'. He was said to have a southern accent, possibly London. All three women described him having a stale alcohol and cigarette smell about him, as well as body odour. They also all mention a smell of stale urine and that the offender was always dressed in black with a balaclava and a distinctive light grey bandana around his head."

Jack opened the second folder.

"Then there was a break until February 1997, when a young woman — Trace Manning — was abducted from just outside Harrogate. She was taken to a disused warehouse, beaten and raped. This was the first time the offender had abducted his victim, taking her somewhere else. All the 1996 attacks were on the street, the women dragged into nearby alleyways or dense bushes. This was the first change in his methodology."

"And there was no doubt that it was the same offender?"

"Again, no DNA profile was able to be extracted from the forensic evidence, but the victim gave an almost identical description of her attacker, even down to the bandana around his head. She likened it to one of those cartoon characters — the ninja turtles."

Jack's interest was piqued. Assuming it was the same offender, serial attackers like this would normally work to a pattern — any deviation would most likely be due to some outside force, or a change in circumstances. So, just what had made this offender change his MO?

Jane continued. "With this victim, for the first time, he also made some attempt to strangle her."

"An attempt?" Jack looked up, sharply. "Was he disturbed?"

Jane shrugged. "That's not too clear from the evidence gathered. Trace Manning lost consciousness, so she has no

37

recollection other than coming round to find the attacker was gone."

Jack gestured for the detective inspector to continue.

"There were three more attacks in 1997, two in Ripon and then one a bit further afield in Whitby — similar scenarios, abducting women from the street at night, taking them to a disused building, raping and then attempting to strangle them. The last attack was at the end of July before he then went quiet."

Jack felt a shiver run up his spine. Suddenly the usual welcome cool of the Cold Case Unit was starting to feel uncomfortable. "Well, that puts paid to my theory about the locations all beginning with the letter H. So, what are we saying here exactly? That he was practising in '96 and '97? Before he later went on to kill in '98?"

Jane could only shrug once more. "From what I can gather, the sex assault cases were looked into at the time, to see if there was a potential link to the murders in the capital. Remember I said that Trace Manning was the first assault victim where the attacker attempted strangulation?" Jack nodded. "A length of 1.5-millimetre wire was found close to the scene — it couldn't be linked forensically to the attack, but it obviously flagged up once the Central Line Killer murders started. In addition, at the scene of the first 1998 murder victim, a piece of grey material was found close by. It's hard to tell, as the documentation is a bit sketchy, but I assume this also raised the possibility of a link. Although, I'm not sure it went anywhere and any potential link seemed to fade into the background. Maybe it was the change of location — London as opposed to Yorkshire. And, of course, the crime scenes themselves were different — the 1998 murders clearly linked to the Underground network."

"The potential link to the sex assaults is interesting and I agree, the involvement of the Underground system is a puzzle. I went to see Lorna Henshaw this morning. I take it her involvement is mentioned in the case notes?"

Jane nodded. "The originals of the envelopes and maps that were sent to her will be in one of the boxes. It's very different to what happened in '96 and '97. Maybe that was why a definite link wasn't made."

"Do you think the cases *should* have been linked?" It was a fair question. No one was infallible, and that included the police. Jack had made enough mistakes of his own over the years to know that it happened and, as much as the media might not want to admit it, detectives were only human.

"Difficult to say. I get the feeling the possibility of a connection was investigated — what with the finding of the piece of wire and grey material — but, as I said, the documentation isn't great in that regard. But if Frank Tyler and his team seriously considered the cases were connected, it looks like they discounted the idea, or at least didn't pursue it."

"What does your gut instinct tell you, Jane?" Jack respected the detective inspector's ability to sometimes see through the crap and locate the golden nugget that had otherwise been hidden from view. That was what made her ideal to head up the Cold Case Unit. "Are we looking for the same offender?"

Jane's brow furrowed. "The forensic evidence was patchy at best, on all three investigations. There were some fibres found in several of the 1998 cases — investigations at the time likened them to carpet or rug fibres. But nothing similar for the sex assault cases. We have to acknowledge that this was the late nineties and techniques have moved on immeasurably since then — as has crime scene analysis. But the more I read into it, the more I think there has to be a connection. I'm just not sure what that connection is."

"Did you order any re-testing of the evidence when you did your case review?"

Jane's face took on a sad look. "I wanted to, believe me. It would have been the only way to find out if our suspicions held any weight. But we had huge budget constraints at the time, and it just wasn't authorised."

Jack turned his attention back to the files for the London murders. "What do you make of the offender in 1998 stringing his victims up at the window? In each of those cases, the victims were all found hanging at or near a window. The same with our case this morning. Is he an exhibitionist of some kind?"

"I'm not so sure of that. If he really wanted to show off, then there are plenty of other locations that would have suited him better. Instead, he chose disused buildings that weren't overlooked. To me that doesn't sound like someone who wants others to see what he's doing."

"And what about the journalist angle? Why contact her? That was new for the 1998 cases, and it's not something I've heard of before."

"Me neither. It certainly adds another layer of complexity to the killer. He might not want to be seen or caught in the act, but he definitely wants you to find out what he's done afterwards."

Jack moved his empty takeaway cup to the side. The coffee had been consumed a long time ago now and the caffeine was beginning to wear off.

"Should I go and get us another round?" Jane nodded towards the cups. "If you're staying, that is?"

Although sorely tempted, Jack glanced at the wall clock and reluctantly shook his head. "As much as I'd like to, I'd better raise my head above ground and check in with the team." He started to gather together some of the paperwork. "Can I take this lot upstairs with me?"

"Of course, help yourself. You'll need a hand if you want to take it all, though. There's far too much for one person to carry."

Jack gave a mischievous wink. "It's fine. I know just the person."

* * *

Time: 3.25 p.m.
Date: Friday 10 April 2015
Location: Westminster Mortuary, London

"You OK?" Daniels handed Cassidy a polystyrene cup of water from the dispenser in the changing room. "You look a bit pale."

Cassidy managed a smile before grabbing the cup and downing the water in a series of gulps. "Better now, thanks." She wiped her lips with the back of her hand. "That poor woman."

Daniels slipped out of his rubber boots and pulled the elasticated cap from his head. "It's never nice to see — what one human being can do to another."

After the external examination was complete, Dr Matthews had turned his attention to the internal organs, which was the part that tested Cassidy's resolve to the max. Seeing the organs of the human body on display like that — removed from their darkened cavities, then examined, weighed and measured — would often tip her over the edge.

She managed to catch some of the pathologist's commentary, but eventually tuned a lot of it out. She knew Trevor would be listening for them both, hoovering up every detail into his sponge-like brain. Sometimes, she wished she was more like him — eager to digest every detail, always hungry for more. But another part of her was glad she wasn't like him at all. Quite how he got through each day and then to sleep at night with such images circulating his brain, she couldn't even begin to fathom.

"And how are you — after the crash, I mean? Any lasting damage?" Daniels slipped his feet into his shoes. "I know it's been a while, but something like that must stay with you."

Cassidy gave a slow nod, kicking off her own rubber boots and heading once more for the water dispenser. Whenever anyone asked her about that night, she always tried a smile and assured them she was fine. Which was true up to a point — she was alive, after all.

"I'm OK, thanks, Trev. It's all part of the job." She poured herself another cup of cool water and downed it in one.

It was only when she stopped to think about what had happened, allowed herself to be transported back to that cold, drizzly night in January, that the memories really started to resurface. She was acutely aware that it could all have gone horribly wrong and ended very differently, but the same could be said for life in general. Take a wrong turn, make a bad decision — life could turn on a pinhead. She'd been lucky, that was all it was. Luck.

"I try not to think about it too much, if I'm honest." She gave another weak smile and decided to change the subject. "Anyhow, enough about me, how's the marathon training going? It's not long until the big day, is it?"

Daniels made a face. "Twenty-seven days. To tell you the truth, I'm not really looking forward to it at all. For some reason I decided to upgrade and enter the full marathon, instead of the half. I'm kind of wishing I hadn't now."

"But I thought you loved running?"

"Oh, I do — the running isn't the problem. I even like the training. I'm just not so sure I'm going to be any good at the racing part of it."

Cassidy tossed the polystyrene cup into the bin and shrugged into her jacket. "It doesn't necessarily have to be a race, though, does it? You could just go out and enjoy yourself, not worry about the time?"

"Hmmm." Daniels followed Cassidy to the door. "It's not really the time that bothers me either."

"It's the people, isn't it?" Cassidy knew the quiet and unassuming detective didn't really "do" people at the best of times — and certainly not when there were several thousand of them all running in the same direction. Noting the uncomfortable look on his face, she linked her arm through his and steered him out into the corridor. "Why don't we call in at Isabel's on the way back and get ourselves something nice?"

CHAPTER FIVE

Time: 4.40 p.m.
Date: Friday 10 April 2015
Location: Westminster Mortuary, London

Dr Matthews tipped exactly half a teaspoon of sugar into his coffee and stirred. He didn't normally take sugar, didn't normally drink coffee in the afternoon either, but today he felt in need of both.

The last post-mortem had unnerved him more than usual, having seen the very same thing some seventeen years ago. And now here it was again. Taking a tentative sip of the sweetened coffee, he glanced up as the office door opened.

"I've rejigged the rest of the day's caseload, moving two to first thing tomorrow. This just leaves us one more for today." Perry Musgrove slipped the amended list onto the pathologist's desk. "I can come in extra early in the morning and get started."

Dr Matthews nodded, gratefully, taking a quick look at the amended list. "Thank you, Perry. Give yourself a half-hour break before we start again."

Dr Matthews liked Perry, and was in no doubt there was an excellent pathologist in the making. The lad had a cool

43

and unflustered demeanour, and an unwavering, meticulous eye for detail — not to mention an extremely steady hand. All were essential attributes if you wanted to succeed in the post-mortem room.

After Perry had closed the door behind him, Dr Matthews leaned back in his leather chair and let a small sigh escape. Some cases touched you more than others, refusing to leave you alone no matter how hard you tried to block them out — and their last examination had been one of them. The art of being a successful pathologist was the ability to detach yourself from the horrors that presented themselves on the mortuary slab, being able to separate what you saw at the end of the scalpel from the life around you — you wouldn't last five minutes unless you did. But there were always those cases that bucked the trend and remained with you, despite your best efforts to banish them.

For Dr Philip Matthews, the Central Line Killer was one such case.

It might have been seventeen years ago, but it felt like hardly anything had changed in the interim, that time had stood still. He could recall each victim with a crystal-clear clarity and, if he wasn't very much mistaken, here they had another.

Pushing the china cup and saucer to the side, neither wanting nor needing the caffeine fix any more, the pathologist reached for his phone.

* * *

Time: 4.45 p.m.
Date: Friday 10 April 2015
Location: HMP Wandsworth, London

He didn't really know why he kept them. It wasn't through any misplaced sense of loyalty, that was for sure. Maybe it was because he didn't have much — only the letters. Ellis Magee

44

had spent most of his adult life locked up in one establishment or another, courtesy of Her Majesty, with only the occasional brief spell on the outside. But with every change of scenery, and every change of cell, the letters still came with him.

Stretching out on the top bunk as much as the cramped conditions would allow, the thin mattress beneath not offering much by way of comfort for his sixteen-stone frame, he continued to stare at the bundle of letters. His cellmate was out at court and had been gone for much of the day. Magee envied him. Even a trip to court was better than being holed up in here for twenty-three out of every twenty-four hours.

But he knew the six-foot-five ex-wrestler would be brought back to the cell before long — there was no chance of freedom for him today, not that the man would be too bothered by that. Already serving a lengthy stretch, he'd been charged with violent disorder after yet another prison uprising over in Belmarsh at the beginning of the year. The best he could expect was a few more years tagged onto the end of his sentence.

But it was a day out, nonetheless.

Magee had shared cells with far less worldly-wise prisoners in the past, and the night before any court appearance, especially when a jury verdict was due, would find them tossing and turning on their mattresses, anxiety eating away at their insides. Their stomachs would be so tied up in knots that even an experienced Boy Scout would be hard pressed to untangle them. On more than one occasion, Magee had to refrain from taking matters into his own hands, just to get a few moments peace and quiet. But thumping a cellmate in the mouth just to shut them up would earn him a stint in solitary, maybe even worse.

As each one left for court, he would see the glimmer of hope in their eyes — hope that the next words they heard echoing around the courtroom walls were "not guilty". Magee sniggered beneath his ragged beard.

Not guilty.

It wasn't a phrase he'd been lucky enough to hear himself at his own trial. Not that it mattered all that much to him. He *was* guilty, and guilty of a lot more besides — more than the twelve upstanding members of the jury had been led to believe, anyway.

Stretching his arms above his head, the prisoner heard his shoulders crack. The wing was on another lockdown because some numpty had decided now was a good time to stage a dirty protest for some reason or another. It wouldn't have been so bad if that was it — but this time it had escalated into several other inmates then deciding anarchy was the best way to entertain themselves on a Wednesday afternoon. Magee had seen it all before, swiftly returning to his cell the moment all hell broke loose on the landing outside.

To give them their due, it hadn't taken the prison officers long to regain control of the wing. So here they all were, some forty-eight hours later, on a self-induced lockdown for their trouble, banged up in their cells all day with just an hour for exercise if you were lucky. Magee knew that some of it might be a result of the prison break not that long ago, from which the prison was still reeling. Escapes from prison were never something to be lauded, but this one had been audacious to say the least. James Quinn, someone Magee hadn't really had much interaction with, had managed to escape in the back of a prison laundry van. It had been the talk of the prison for some time — and as far as Magee knew, the man had yet to be recaptured.

Good luck to him, Magee had thought, as time ticked on. Given half a chance, would he do the same? It was a question he wasn't fully able to answer.

But, overall, Magee didn't mind lockdowns all that much. They happened from time to time, for one misdemeanour or another, and mostly he would just use the extra solitude to think. Contrary to what people on the outside might believe, prison didn't give you the opportunity to think all that much — you were too busy watching your back. Tempers could flare at the slightest insult, everyone's nerves permanently on a knife edge; so you needed your wits about you 24/7. You even learned to sleep with one eye open.

Which didn't leave a lot of time for reflection.

Once more, Magee's gaze flickered across the six-by-eight-foot cell to the desk fixed to the wall opposite. His cellmate wasn't much of a reader, or a writer come to that, so the desk space was mostly Magee's to do with as he pleased. He owned a few tatty paperbacks, but his preferred reading material — the porn mags and other X-rated publications — never made it past the security checks.

He usually kept the bundle of letters tucked away on the left-hand corner of the desk, stacked up against the wall. His cellmate had made the mistake of moving them once, not long after he'd been transferred across from Belmarsh — he hadn't made the same mistake a second time. The man's nose had eventually healed, although it looked a little bent now.

The letters.

Magee swung his legs over the side of the top bunk. He probably should get rid of them; they served no real purpose any more, weren't of any value inside, either emotionally or financially. But there was always something that stopped him destroying them.

The man had been persistent, Magee would give him that. He would write letter after letter, week after week — continuing even when Magee decided it was time to put an end to their correspondence. He'd been encouraging to begin with, but the missives had soon begun to irritate. On the whole, Ellis Magee admired persistence. He admired loyalty. Admired commitment. It was a pity he didn't have anything resembling those attributes himself. Prison knocked most things out of you if you were inside long enough — grinding you down into a shadow of your former self until it spat you back out onto the streets.

Would their paths ever cross again? Magee strongly doubted it — so why was he keeping the letters? With a renewed vigour from somewhere, he jumped down from the bunk and swiped the bundle up, sliding them into the solitary desk drawer.

Just like he had the last time.

And the time before that.

And the time before that.

They would spend a few days, maybe even a week, buried in the drawer until he felt the need to bring them back out again. But maybe this time he meant it.

Just then, the sound of heavy footfall on the landing outside disturbed his thoughts. Then there was the unmistakable clanking of the prison officer's keys.

His cellmate was back.

* * *

Time: 4.50 p.m.
Date: Friday 10 April 2015
Location: Metropolitan Police HQ, London

Shit.

It hadn't come as much of a surprise, but it still wasn't exactly what Jack had been wanting to hear. "You're sure?"

"Absolutely," replied Dr Matthews. "I've seen it before, Jack. And although I'm no detective, in my humble opinion you've got yourselves the same killer."

Jack sighed. The pathologist's deep yet soft tone didn't make the words any easier to hear. "You worked the other cases, didn't you? Back in 1998? I've only managed to get a quick look at the paperwork so far, but I skimmed through some of the post-mortem reports and saw your name."

"I did. All six of them. It may be seventeen years ago, but I remember every one like it was yesterday."

Cassidy and Daniels had returned from the mortuary not long before, bearing fresh delicacies from Isabel's Café. Jack had waved away the Danish pastry and retired to his office once they had filled him in on what happened during the post-mortem — and notably what had been pulled from the poor woman's mouth. No post-mortem could ever be called a pleasant experience, but this one seemed all the more sickening for it. "Cause of death?"

"Same as for the others. Strangulation leading to asphyxiation. A thin 1.5-millimetre-diameter ligature was used. There is also evidence of some degree of manual compression of the neck, either before or soon after death. On the detailed internal examination, I found evidence of the hyoid bone being fractured, as well as soft tissue injuries to the larynx and trachea. Your perpetrator exerted a good deal of force, Jack — certainly more than was strictly necessary to kill. There were also extensive external contusions on both upper and lower arms, with some breaks to the skin."

"Defensive wounds?"

"Quite possibly. I think the poor woman could well have put up quite a fight at the end."

"What about evidence of sexual assault?" Jack knew the victims in the 1998 murders had all been raped or seriously sexually assaulted, and he heard the pathologist sigh.

"Clear evidence of that, yes. Bruising and lacerations to the vagina. I've taken the necessary swabs to send to the lab. I've also taken the usual scrapings from beneath the fingernails, with additional samples from the site of the other injuries. The usual blood work has been sent off, too."

"What about time of death?" Jack knew an exact time was impossible — the best he could hope for was a general window.

"I don't believe it was too long before the body was found, between twelve and twenty-four hours is my best estimate. The lividity tells me that she was lying on her back for quite some time after she died, and then she was moved."

"And with the ones before, from 1998 — was it always in the mouth?"

"The Underground map? Yes, a map was always found in the mouth. Never pushed in too far, and never swallowed. My guess has always been that it was inserted post-mortem, before rigor mortis set in. You might want to pick DI Tyler's brains on that one — or *DCI* Tyler, as I'm reliably informed he became before he retired. I'm sure he'll still remember the case well."

I'm sure he will too, grimaced Jack. This wasn't a case you would be able to forget in a hurry. "Cheers, doc. I plan to do just that."

"He was a very astute detective, as I recall. I certainly had a lot of time for the man — pass on my good wishes when you catch up with him."

"I will. Thank you."

Jack cut the call and rubbed his bristly chin. First day back and he should really have shaved.

Just as Jack replaced the handset of the desk phone, the office door swung open and DC Daniels' head appeared. Jack was half hoping it would be Cassidy again, returning with one of the leftover Danish pastries from Isabel's. Despite the nature of his conversation with Dr Matthews, Jack's stomach was rumbling. Instead, he waved the young officer in and gave him a genuine smile.

Jack had a lot of time for DC Trevor Daniels. They'd met eighteen months ago when Daniels was a newly qualified detective constable, seconded to the team in their hunt for the crazed serial killer dubbed the Bishop. With Daniels' quick mind and talent for chess, he'd played an important role in the killer's eventual capture. From that moment on, he had secured his spot in Jack's incident room. "Thanks for attending the mortuary earlier. Was Amanda OK?"

It was no secret that DS Cassidy harboured a distinct lack of love for visiting the mortuary, but Daniels merely gave a curt nod. "She was fine, boss."

Jack smiled again. He had no doubt that Cassidy hadn't been fine at all, and may even have passed out at some point, but he admired Daniels' attempt at discretion. It was what made him such a valued and trusted member of the team. "Did you want me for something?"

Daniels nudged his spectacles higher up onto the bridge of his nose. "The chief superintendent's PA called down again. Third time today — quite insistent this time. He *really* wants to see you."

I bet he does, mused Jack. "Did she say anything else?"

"Only that it should be sooner rather than later."

CHAPTER SIX

Time: 5.00 p.m.
Date: Friday 10 April 2015
Location: Metropolitan Police HQ, London

Chief Superintendent Douglas "Dougie" King gestured for Jack to take a seat. "So, how has the first day back been, Jack? I hear you've caught a big case?"

Jack slipped into the vacant chair, grateful for a chance to rest. He didn't want to admit it, but being on his feet for much of the day had taken its toll. As he eased himself down, the slight grimace that crossed his face didn't go unnoticed.

"And how about that foot?"

"The foot's good, sir. Never better." The chief superintendent was no fool, but Jack told the lie anyway and Dougie King seemed to swallow it with good grace.

"I'll take your word for that, Jack. But go easy."

On arrival, Jack had waved aside the offer of coffee, his head scrambled enough without the added caffeine shot. There was also a large part of him that hoped the lack of refreshments would bring a swifter end to the meeting. As much as he liked and admired the chief superintendent, and often enjoyed their good-natured banter over a strong Colombian coffee, there were any number of tasks he really needed to get on with before finally calling it a day — so the less time he spent in here the better.

"Tell me about the case."

For the next ten minutes Jack did just that, watching the senior officer's expression grow graver by the second. "And you're sure?" Dougie King's gaze narrowed. "We're definitely looking at the same killer?"

Jack nodded. "In my view, yes. And Dr Matthews echoes my thoughts. I really don't see how it can be anyone else."

"You've pulled all the previous papers for the Central Line Killer, I take it?"

Another nod. "I've already had a brief look through but I'm getting them brought up from the Cold Case Unit. There's a lot more to analyse and I'm about to arrange a visit to see Frank Tyler."

"Good. Frank's a decent man. I'm sure he'll help where he can." Dougie King paused, then asked the question Jack knew was coming. "And what about the media, Jack? How are you planning to include them?"

Jack gave a small laugh. "I wasn't planning to include them at all, sir, not until I know exactly what we're dealing with here." He wasn't aware of how much the chief super-intendent knew about Lorna Henshaw's involvement in the 1998 investigation, seeing as it wasn't made public at the time, and he wasn't about to dive in headfirst right now.

"Well, you know you can't keep them in the dark for too long, Jack. They're not mushrooms. These things have a habit of getting out into the public arena, no matter how tightly closed you think everyone's lips are. History should tell you that much."

"I'll brief them when I think it's necessary." Jack avoided the senior officer's penetrating gaze, knowing his tone was a little terser than he'd intended.

Dougie King seemed to accept the response was as good as he was going to get and moved on to slightly safer ground.

"Well, when you take a more detailed look at Frank Tyler's investigation, I want to know the minute you find something that could come back to bite us. And I mean anything at all. I'm not saying you will — and I'm praying that you don't — but I need to be forewarned on this one."

Jack gave another nod, fully aware of what the chief superintendent was getting at.

Mistakes. Errors. Things that weren't done but should have been.

Fault.

"You'll know the minute I do, sir."

Dougie King sighed. "I won't lie to you, Jack, you know me better than that by now, but this has come at an awkward time. You being in charge of what will no doubt turn out to be a high-profile investigation will make some people very nervous."

By "some people", Jack knew exactly who the man was referring to.

Those upstairs.

Dougie King continued. "They're still very twitchy, Jack, and your last case almost sent them into orbit. I'm still not quite sure how I managed to keep you in your job, but they're unlikely to forget what happened in a hurry. They might look old and set in their ways, but they're an astute bunch with a very long reach — and even longer memories. Not much gets past them, if you catch my drift, so don't treat them like fools."

"Sir."

"I need you to be upfront with me at all times. I want to know the minute things start going south. Daily updates, understand?"

Jack nodded again. "Of course, sir. I'll be the model of transparency."

A smile twitched at Dougie King's lips. "No need to go overboard, Jack. Just keep me up to speed. No surprises."

Jack's own mouth twitched. For reasons Jack was never quite sure of, Dougie King always seemed to have his back.

Whenever Jack strayed over the procedural white line, which was probably more often than the senior officer would like or indeed knew about, the man was always there to bail him out.

Jack had tested the man's patience on many an occasion, but none more so than earlier in the year. Video footage showing Jack paying cash to sex workers in a notorious red-light area was released by a newspaper reporter intent on destroying Jack's career — and he had very nearly succeeded. Dougie King had worked miracles to douse the resulting flames. But Jack was acutely aware there may come a time when the man considered enough was enough — and Jack wouldn't blame him in the slightest when that day finally came.

Dougie King made to get up from his chair. "Well, I won't keep you, Jack. But you need to keep your nose clean this time. Stay out of trouble. No cock-ups. Think you can manage that?"

"It's what I do best, sir."

Dismissed, Jack made his way along the corridor, then down the stairs towards the incident room. The paperwork from the Cold Case Unit should have arrived by now and time was marching on. Reaching the bottom step, he winced as a jolt of pain stabbed him across the top of his foot.

What he wouldn't give for a decent shot of single malt right now.

Thoughts of an evening spent in the company of a smooth Macallan were soon pushed aside as he entered the incident room and saw DS Cooper heaving the last box up onto one of the tables, his face flushed red and his breath coming in short, sharp gasps.

"That's the last of it, boss."

"Good man." Jack tried to hide his emerging smile. "What would I do without you?"

A withering look crossed Cooper's still reddened face. "Those stairs are a killer. I think I might have pulled something." He started rubbing the backs of his thighs.

"And there's me thinking I was doing you a favour — you're always telling us how Jenny wants you to get fit, join the gym or some such nonsense. Here, you've just had a work-out for free!"

"Thanks — remind me to repay the favour sometime, boss."

Jack surveyed the table and sighed. Above ground, the boxes somehow looked bigger than they had when buried down in the Cold Case Unit. "There's no easy way of saying this, but we're going to have to go through each piece of evidence for the 1998 murder cases, pull the whole thing apart. And then we need to do the same for the sexual assault cases in '96 and '97." He saw the look of trepidation crossing both Cassidy and Cooper's faces. DC Daniels, however, merely looked intrigued. "I suggest you go and stock up on some snacks — this could take a while."

"We staying on tonight, boss?" Cooper collapsed into a chair. "Jenny's working late, so I don't mind the overtime."

"Fill your boots, Cooper. It's not compulsory, but the sooner we tackle this lot, the better the understanding we'll have of who we're looking for. Those that are staying tonight, I'll send out for pizza for us all, how's that?"

Cooper's face lit up. "Count me in."

"Then I'll leave you to make a start. I've got a few things to catch up with in my office, but I'll join you in a bit." Jack turned for the door. "I want to arrange to go and see Frank Tyler first thing in the morning, if he's free. Amanda, I'll need you with me. I've a feeling he's moved out of the city, so be prepared for an early start."

Cassidy nodded and got up from her seat. "Before you go, guv, I've been in touch with Missing Persons like you asked — but it's not very good news. Nothing they have fits the description of our deceased."

Jack's shoulders sagged. "Thanks. It was worth a shot. Anything else while I've been gone? How about the CCTV, Cooper?"

"Not much yet, boss. Just getting started really. I've got recordings from around the crime scene and the Tube station. Which should be the priority? That, or—" he gestured towards the table stacked high with boxes — "this?"

Jack paused by the door, his foot throbbing. "For tonight, probably the cold case paperwork I'm afraid. Crack on with the CCTV tomorrow."

With that, Jack left the team to it. With a shot of whisky still looking as though it was a while away yet, he decided a search for painkillers would have to do.

* * *

Time: 5.35 p.m.
Date: Friday 10 April 2015
Location: HMP Wandsworth, London

The bottom bunk creaked as Lindsay Jenkins heaved his six-foot-five frame onto the pathetic excuse for a mattress. His day in court had been uneventful, but he hadn't expected it to be any different. He was well aware that his not guilty plea to the charges of violent disorder and criminal damage while at Belmarsh were unlikely to convince any jury worth their salt, but it gave him something to do. And some valuable days out of prison.

The day had been long — countless hours of just hanging around as the legal teams argued over one minuscule point of law that probably wasn't even relevant — but he didn't mind. At least the grub in the courthouse was better than it was in here.

He yawned and stretched back against the thin pillow. He wasn't due back in court until Monday now, the weekend affording a brief respite. He'd noticed the difference the minute he'd set foot back inside the cell. Having spent a good number of years inside, the one thing it taught you to do was notice things, little things.

Little things like his cellmate moving those sodding letters again.

Jenkins wasn't a big reader and hadn't been all that interested when he'd first seen the bundle stacked up on the desk, bound together with a cheap rubber band. Each to their own, he'd thought, hardly giving it a moment's further consideration.

But now they had disappeared.

Again.

Jenkins knew he would find them tucked away inside the drawer where they hid the sugar, if he bothered to take the time to look. Again, it didn't concern him one way or another — but it certainly seemed to bother his cellmate.

Jenkins heard the man turn over on the mattress above. They were both big men, but Jenkins thought he outweighed Magee by at least two stone. Which didn't mean the man couldn't be handy, of course — he definitely had some weight behind him, something Jenkins had first-hand knowledge of. His nose still felt blocked on occasion, as if the bones weren't knitting together as straight as they should be.

Sighing, he rolled off the bottom bunk and lumbered across the confined cell to the kettle, not taking his eyes from the desk drawer. Hiding the letters like that made him want to read them all the more; it surprised him it had taken him this long to realise. But he would bide his time a little longer — eventually he would get the chance to find out exactly what the letters contained.

And why Magee was so intent on keeping them.

* * *

Time: 6.05 p.m.
Date: Friday 10 April 2015
Location: Metropolitan Police HQ, London

Jack leaned back in his chair. With the team now knee-deep in the paperwork from the 1998 investigation, he knew he would have some peace and quiet for a while. Frank Tyler had indeed moved out of the city after his retirement, heading out to the coast. A quick call had secured them an early morning appointment to pick the former DCI's brains.

The prospect that their current case was linked to not just the 1998 Central Line Killer case, but potentially two other sexual assault investigations, caused Jack more than a little unease. If it turned out to be true, he would need extra bodies at the bare minimum, and extra bodies would cost extra money. And that was before all the forensic re-testing he intended to order along the way. The cost of the investigation would quickly spiral, and Dougie King's hair would turn even greyer as the pound signs mounted up.

With his desk still curiously tidy, very little having landed in the in-tray during the course of the day, Jack knew he should go back to the incident room, roll up his sleeves and get stuck into the paperwork alongside the team. It wasn't the most thrilling of tasks at the best of times but, just as he was about to get up from his seat, a good excuse came knocking at the door.

"Hey, Jack — how's the foot?" DS Robert Carmichael closed the office door behind him and slid into the only other chair in the room. "No crutches, I see." The detective sergeant's eyes swept Jack's office for any lurking orthopaedic equipment. "That's good."

"No crutches required, Rob. I don't even have to wear that bloody boot any more, either." Jack swung his leg out from underneath the desk. "Footloose and fancy free."

Carmichael settled back in his chair. "You'll be back dancing again soon, then?" He raised his eyebrows mischievously. "Word tells me you've been down to see the delightful Jane Telford. Anything to report that I should know about?"

Jack made a face. "It was related to work, before you get carried away. You remember that Central Line Killer case from the late nineties? Well, we think he's back."

Carmichael didn't attempt to hide the surprise on his face. "Back? Wow. I thought that case was long since forgotten."

"I think a lot of people did, Rob, but you know that call we got this morning? It has all the hallmarks of the previous killer. It could be a copycat, of course, but somehow I don't think so." The envelope delivered to Lorna Henshaw flashed across Jack's mind. The extracts he'd managed to read from the 1998 paperwork so far had backed up the journalist's claim that her involvement had been kept out of the media. If it *was* a copycat, then it had to be someone close to the case — a thought that was not particularly palatable. "Anyhow—" Jack brushed the thought aside — "what's new with you?"

Jack had seen Carmichael several times during his convalescence, on one occasion the detective sergeant bringing with him a bottle of Jack's favourite single malt and a punnet of grapes. And then there had been the trip to Knowles Farm.

They hadn't spoken much about what Jack had discovered at the farm that day — there weren't really words to describe it. It wasn't often you stumbled, almost literally, across what looked to be the remains of your mother's murderer being eaten by a group of pigs. Jack hadn't revealed the events of that day to anyone other than Rob.

Just another secret to bury along with all the others.

"What about searching for your sister? You had much luck with that?" The last time they'd spoken, Carmichael had divulged his intentions to try and locate his sister, Genete — someone he hadn't seen for the best part of thirty years since they were removed from their mother's care as young children. Having been raised in the foster care system himself, Jack felt a unique kinship with the detective sergeant.

Carmichael shifted in his seat. "Well — that's kind of why I stopped by."

"Oh?" Now Jack was intrigued. "A development?"

Carmichael shook his head. "Not as such. I've made a few enquiries back in Liverpool, to see if I can find out where she went when she left foster care. It's a bit of a minefield, though. She might have moved to the other end of the country, or even abroad, for all I know."

"True."

"But before I got too bogged down in it all, I thought I'd better tell Mum what I'm doing. I don't want to do it behind her back."

Jack nodded. Carmichael's mum was his adoptive mother, Barbara Tindleman. Jack had had the pleasure of meeting her several times during the last couple of years, warming to her immediately. Widowed five years ago when her husband, Charles, was blown up along with his car on Westminster Bridge, she had bounced back from tragedy to found the Tindleman Trust, a charity supporting children and parents as they negotiated the tricky waters of fostering. Consequently, Jack had a huge amount of respect and admiration for the woman.

"Do you think she knows where Genete might have gone?"

Rob grimaced. "I doubt it. As far as I know, once we were separated that was it."

"Well, like you say, it wouldn't hurt to let her know that you're looking — but I'm sure she'll be fine with it. If I know your mum like I think I do, she'll probably even offer to help you."

"Good, that's what I hoped you'd say." Carmichael's mischievous look returned as he got to his feet. "Because we're both going round there for dinner tonight."

"We are? What's the occasion?"

Carmichael merely shrugged. "Of that, I'm not quite sure, mate."

Jack's gaze strayed back to his still neat and uncluttered desk. He couldn't exactly use the "I'm too snowed under" excuse this time, but they did have a new investigation that needed his attention. And he'd promised the team pizzas that evening to keep them all going as they worked. But Carmichael was already one step ahead.

"There's nothing here that can't wait." The detective sergeant waved a hand towards Jack's empty desk. "And I'm sure the rest of the team can spare you for one night. You still need to eat, remember — and I have a feeling Mum's making your favourite. I know it's short notice, but we'll be two hours, tops, and then you can wallow in as much paperwork as you want — push on through till dawn, if that floats your boat."

Jack couldn't help but mirror Carmichael's grin. The man had a point. He did need to eat — he hadn't managed anything all day, apart from the toasted sandwich from DS Cassidy, which seemed like a lifetime ago. "Sure," he eventually replied. "I'll be there."

CHAPTER SEVEN

Time: 7.30 p.m.
Date: Friday 10 April 2015
Location: 7 Palace Mews Road, London

Jack ran a finger around the inside collar of his shirt. Having dispensed with his tie much earlier in the day, he hadn't had time to go home and change, instead coming straight from the station. As he'd left, he saw the team were about to tuck into the stack of pizzas he'd ordered, his parting instruction being not to stay all night.

Deciding that he would drive rather than get a lift with Rob — taking the Mondeo would stop him drinking and he needed a clear head for the trip to see Frank Tyler in the morning — he pulled up outside number seven at bang on seven thirty. Rob's car was already parked on the drive.

With a quick glance in the rear-view mirror to flatten down his hair, he rubbed a hand over the three, maybe four days' worth of growth on his chin. Scruffy or not, he would have to do. Exiting the Mondeo, he made his way up the garden path. On the drive over he'd passed a petrol station, stopping to pick up a bunch of flowers for Barbara. Jack wasn't a gardener and had no idea what they were, but they looked and smelled nice.

Carmichael opened the door and ushered Jack inside. "Mum's still cooking up a storm in the kitchen. I feel it's best we stay out the way — too many cooks and all that."

Jack hung his jacket on a coat rack by the front door then followed Carmichael into the Tindlemans' living room. Having been to the house several times in the past, everything looked familiar — even down to the photographs decorating the mantelpiece. Jack immediately noted that centre stage, once again, was the photograph of Rob at his graduation ceremony at police training college, the arm of his adoptive father Charles Tindleman draped around his shoulders.

Jack took a seat on the floral two-seater sofa just as Barbara Tindleman breezed in, an apron sporting red poppies tied around her waist, her hair pulled back into a loose ponytail. Strands of fair hair fell down onto her shoulders. She blew another wayward wisp from her eyes.

"Gosh, it's hot in there!" She flapped a tea towel in front of her face as she crossed the living room carpet. "Good to see you, Jack. I hope you're hungry." A warm smile broke out across her flushed cheeks, her eyes crinkling at the corners. "I've made so much it looks like I'm feeding the five thousand!"

Jack returned the smile. "Starving, Barbara." He got to his feet and handed over the flowers. "These are for you."

Barbara Tindleman beamed, draping the tea towel over her shoulder and wiping her hands on her apron before taking hold of the carefully wrapped bunch of carnations. "Thank you, Jack. They're lovely. You shouldn't have, but it's much appreciated." She then turned to Carmichael, flicking the tea towel towards her adopted son. "See, Robert. Some gentlemen have manners!" With a good-humoured wink, she hurried back out towards the kitchen, calling over her shoulder, "I'll just put these in water and then I'll be ready to dish up in about fifteen minutes."

While they waited, Carmichael went in search of drinks — coming back with a beer for himself and a shandy for Jack. After a couple of mouthfuls, Jack asked, "You found out what the occasion is yet? Have I missed a birthday?"

Carmichael shrugged and shook his head at the same time, sinking a third of his beer before responding. "Still no idea, mate. Mum just asked if I wanted to come round for dinner, and to bring you with me — and when I say *asked*, it was more of a command. Then I thought it might be a good opportunity to tell her about looking for Genete. Other than that, I'm as much in the dark as you are."

Great. Jack managed a tired smile as he swallowed some more shandy. He could do without getting involved in a family drama right now; he had enough to contend with back at the station. He still felt a little guilty at leaving the team to plough through the paperwork alone.

Twenty minutes later, they were all seated around the Tindlemans' dining table. Large patio doors gave a view of the garden, which was now bathed in a deepening dark, the sun having gone down, with just the occasional solar-powered light giving a warming hue. The dining table was heaving with plates and dishes, and Jack's nose twitched. As he took his seat, he remarked, "You weren't wrong when you said you were feeding the five thousand, Mrs T."

Barbara's eyes sparkled as she handed round the dinner plates. "Well, the pair of you are still growing boys. And I'm sure you don't eat properly, living on your own the way you do."

Carmichael immediately started digging into the pot of roast potatoes, spooning a healthy portion onto his plate. "I've tried my best to get him married off, Mum, but he's a resilient bugger."

"I wasn't just talking about Jack, Robert." Barbara took the lid off the broccoli and sprouts. "You could do with settling down yourself."

Carmichael popped a roast potato into his mouth and grinned. "We're modern men, Mum. We're more than capable of looking after ourselves these days, no one else required."

The look on Barbara Tindleman's face suggested she didn't quite believe it, but she let it pass. "Help yourself to the beef wellington, Jack. Don't let my greedy son eat it all."

Jack selected a large slice and transferred it to his plate. He couldn't remember the last time he'd eaten beef wellington — most probably the last time he was invited to dinner at the Tindlemans' — but the aroma was intoxicating. He then added a decent pile of roast potatoes and vegetables before tucking in. His stomach growled in anticipation as the first mouthful melted on his tongue.

"This beef is delicious, Mrs T. Truly delicious."

Barbara beamed again, tucking another stray hair strand back behind her ear. "Nothing is too much trouble for my two favourite boys."

They ate for another twenty minutes, Barbara asking how work was going and listening intently to the replies. After second helpings of the beef wellington and the last of the roast potatoes were dished out, Carmichael put down his knife and fork and broached the as yet unasked question.

"What is it you really wanted to talk about, Mum? I'm intrigued. Why are we here?"

Barbara had opened a bottle of red wine to accompany the meal and took the opportunity to top up both her glass and her adopted son's. Jack had politely declined, happy to stick with sparkling water for the meal.

"What makes you think there was something I wanted to talk about? Can't I just invite my lovely son and his best friend round for dinner?"

Carmichael gave a snort behind his wine glass. "I can see right through you, Mum. You're no good at this. There's obviously something you want to say — so just come out and say it. We're both big boys now, we can take it."

Barbara rested her knife and fork against her plate and reached for her wine glass. Jack noted that the pinkness of her cheeks had faded a little now, and so had the sparkle in her eyes. Pausing momentarily, she took a sip of wine before reaching to pull open one of the drawers of the sideboard behind her.

"I wasn't sure what to do with it — it came last week." Barbara pulled a white envelope out of the drawer. "I got a similar one at the same time, so I've a pretty good idea what yours is going to say." She leaned across the dining table and passed the envelope to Carmichael. "I'm sorry, but it's not very good news."

Interest piqued, Jack swallowed the last of his beef wellington and speared his last potato. As the envelope passed by in front of him, he noted the postmark and stamp on the front.

Messrs. Houghton and Sandford Solicitors, Liverpool.

Not very good news.

What did that mean?

For a split second, Jack thought about Carmichael's sister, Genete. Had Rob's initial enquiries borne fruit already? And if they had, the fact that it wasn't "good news" didn't exactly bode well. Jack saw his friend and colleague's brow crease.

Judging by the look on Barbara's face when he looked across the table, Jack would bet his last pound that someone had just died.

* * *

Time: 7.30 p.m.
Date: Friday 10 April 2015
Location: Metropolitan Police HQ, London

Cooper broke open the third pizza box and scooped up a slice of pepperoni.

"Where on earth do you put it all, Chris?" Cassidy wiped her hand on a serviette, frowning towards the pizza that was being quickly devoured before her eyes. "Honestly — the guv is spot on when he calls you a human dustbin."

Cooper grinned and swallowed. "I'm a growing boy, Amanda. And my brain works better with a bit of fuel."

"A bit? You've had a whole pizza to yourself already!"

Cooper grinned again, reaching for another slice. "Well, the boss seems to have over-ordered, don't you think? So, what can I say? I'm preventing waste."

It was true. Cassidy looked at the stack of pizza boxes that sat in the middle of the table, almost dwarfing the paperwork they were meant to be trawling through — almost, but not quite. Six large pizzas between the three of them.

"You *can* eat cold pizza, you know, Chris. It's not against the law. Take some home with you and have it for breakfast."

Licking tomato sauce from his fingers, Cooper laughed. "Jenny would kill me if I brought pizza into the house. And she'd kill me all over again if I ate it for breakfast."

"You still on a diet, I take it?"

Cooper patted his belly. "Can't you tell?" A glum look clouded his eyes. "It's all superfoods and low carbs in our house at the moment. I don't remember the last time I even saw a slice of bread or a potato."

"Well, I seem to recall you tucking into at least one bacon roll this morning — unless I was seeing things, of course." Cassidy pushed the pizza box away. "And what about that stash of Easter eggs you have in your desk drawers?" With the Easter weekend having just passed, various boxes of chocolates had appeared in the incident room, most of them centred on Cooper's desk.

Cooper waved a fresh pizza slice in Cassidy's direction. "Yeah, well — that's different. It doesn't count when it's here."

For the next forty-five minutes, the team worked in near total silence, the only sound being the rustle of paper as each file was opened and digested. They had already spent two hours sifting through the case files, putting everything into some form of order, but there was still plenty to do.

"I don't know about you, but I could do with another coffee." DC Daniels rose from his chair and crossed over to the hot water urn. "Green tea, Amanda?"

"Please, Trev."

Drinks poured, Daniels handed them out, then placed his own coffee mug down on top of a pile of witness statements.

"Anyone else struck by how far forensics have advanced since the nineties?" He gestured towards the paper stack. "It's not really that long ago — seventeen years isn't much in the grand scheme of things — but the advances made in both the collection of evidence and the techniques used to process them is nothing short of astounding."

Cassidy murmured her agreement through a mouthful of green tea. "I was just about to say the same thing. The number of samples taken at the crime scenes is nowhere near what would be taken today. And with those that were taken, there's a real risk of contamination or degradation. I can't find a single sample that took any of the cases forward."

Daniels shook his head. "We rely on forensics so much these days, it's easy to forget how new it all is."

"Agreed. I'm looking at the last victim from the 1998 investigation — Becky Scott. There was semen found on pieces of her clothing, but at the time they couldn't get a full DNA profile from it."

"Same here." Cooper tapped a pile of paperwork on his desk. "Several of the victims had semen stains on their clothing — but none of them gave up a DNA profile. I'm guessing the boss will want to re-submit it all, get it all re-tested."

"And have you seen how poorly the victims were treated in the sexual assault cases?" Cassidy made a face. "It's practically out of the Dark Ages. I thought that kind of thing had been stamped out a long time ago."

Daniels pulled a piece of paper out of one the files on his desk. "I found exactly the same thing. So much was said in the media at the time and, I hate to say it, in the investigation papers themselves, about how the women shouldn't have been walking home at that time of night, alone in the dark. How they should have dressed more modestly, not had so much to drink."

"That kind of thing makes me so angry." Cassidy took another gulp of her tea. "You don't hear men being told not to walk home alone at night, or to dress differently. It's not right that it seems to be so acceptable for women."

"I hear you," agreed Daniels. "It's not acceptable, but it is accepted. That's the issue. It's a societal thing and I really don't know how we go about changing it."

"Do you think they missed anything?" Cassidy's voice took on a sombre edge. "DI Tyler and his team? Did they really make a mistake in among all this?" She gestured towards the mound of paperwork.

Cooper started to shake his head. "Forensics aside, I'm not sure they put a foot wrong. They worked with what they had at the time, and I can't see a step that wasn't followed up, to be honest. Not so far, anyway. No leads that weren't investigated. It's also understandable how they dismissed the connection with the 1996 and 1997 sexual assaults — on the face of it, they're entirely different."

Cassidy sighed. "I'd hate for one of our cases to be pulled apart like this. For someone to be searching for a mistake we might have made. It's like someone trampling all over your grave."

They continued trawling through the paperwork until eventually Cooper's phone trilled. His face lit up as he answered. "Jenny? How are you getting on? You heading home yet?" Listening to the reply, he reached for the final slice of pepperoni pizza from the box on his desk. "I'm almost done, too. No, I've not eaten yet, either."

Cassidy and Daniels exchanged a look. "Not eaten yet?" Cassidy nodded towards the empty pizza boxes. "What would you call that, then?"

Cooper grinned as he ended the call and reached for his jacket, swallowing the last of the pizza. "Like I said — nothing here counts. She wants a low-carb Chinese."

"Is there such a thing?"

"I guess I'm about to find out!"

Cassidy pulled another set of paperwork towards her as Cooper shuffled to the door. She didn't have the energy to argue, and Cooper's eating habits were really none of her concern, as bizarre as they may be. She yawned and stretched, hearing her neck click. The guv had already told her about the early start in the morning, so she could do with getting going herself.

"I think I'll call it a day, too. You coming, Trevor?"

DC Daniels nodded, closing the folder he'd been looking at. "Ready when you are."

Filling an empty pizza box with some of the leftover slices, she scooped it up and headed for the door. "Let's go — we can pick this up again tomorrow. Chris has a low-carb Chinese to eat."

* * *

Time: 8.35 p.m.
Date: Friday 10 April 2015
Location: 7 Palace Mews Road, London

Carmichael let the letter fall onto his plate. "So, she's dead, then?"

After seeing the sadness in Barbara Tindleman's eyes, Jack flashed a look of genuine concern across the table. He felt the need to say something but wasn't quite sure what that something should be. Before he could come up with anything, Carmichael continued.

"My mother is actually dead."

A strange sensation bordering on relief flooded Jack as the words sank in. It wasn't Carmichael's sister after all. It wasn't Genete. But it was still his mother. "I'm sorry, mate." He couldn't think of what else to say.

Carmichael stared at the letter on his plate for several more seconds before looking up. "Don't see why. She didn't mean anything to me — hasn't done for years."

Jack gave a tired smile. "Even so."

Picking up the bottle of red wine, Carmichael poured himself another glass. "I don't really see why they needed to let me know — why they thought I might be interested."

Barbara reached across and gave Carmichael's hand a squeeze. "I got a similar letter. If you keep reading, you'll see that your mother left a will naming you and your sister as sole beneficiaries — but, unfortunately, it doesn't look like she had anything of value to leave behind. So, I think the estate is worthless."

Taking a mouthful of wine, Carmichael gave a rueful chuckle as he re-read the letter. "So I see. And why doesn't that surprise me?" Bitterness began to edge into his tone which he silenced with another gulp of wine. "Sounds like the same old Sheila to me."

Barbara persevered. "You'll see that the letter goes on to give the funeral details. It's on Monday."

"Not interested." After a pause, Carmichael softened his expression, flashing an apologetic smile towards his adoptive mother. "Sorry. I didn't mean to sound so rude, but she doesn't mean anything to me any more. She never did really. She's virtually a stranger." He slotted the letter back inside the envelope, then frowned. "So, if she left everything she owned to me and Genete, does that mean they might know where my sister is?" He tapped the front of the envelope. "The solicitors?" He caught Barbara's eye. "Do *you* know where Genete might be?"

Barbara gave a sad smile. "No, sorry, I don't. I didn't hear anything more about Genete after we brought you home." She paused and gestured towards the envelope still in Carmichael's hand. "But you're right — the solicitors might know something. Do you think you might want to try and get in touch with Genete? Try and find her?"

Carmichael gave a slow nod. "Maybe."

Putting down his knife and fork, Jack could almost see Carmichael's brain whirring inside his head, the cogs churning. If Rob wanted to find his sister, then the solicitors could be a good place to start. He made to get up from his chair, detecting that the earlier convivial atmosphere had dampened somewhat with the arrival of the subject of death.

"I'll take these through to the kitchen, Mrs T. Maybe make a start on the washing up." He gestured towards the plates. "Then I think I'll make a move and leave you to it."

"You'll do no such thing, Jack." Barbara wiped the sad smile from her face and stood up. "You sit yourself back down, young man — there's cheesecake to come yet."

CHAPTER EIGHT

Time: 10.30 p.m.
Date: Friday 10 April 2015
Location: Kettle's Yard Mews, London

Marmaduke wound his furry body around Jack's ankles and mewed.

"Just coming, don't panic." Jack ripped the lid off the tin of tuna and tipped a good portion onto a china saucer, feeling the cat's tail thumping against his calf as the mewing increased. "Jesus, you're acting like you haven't been fed in a week." Bending down to place the saucer on the floor, he stroked the ginger tabby's head as it guzzled down the fishy treat. "Steady on — don't you go throwing up on my carpet, sunshine."

Leaving Marmaduke to devour his tuna, Jack padded back to the sofa. The TV in the corner was tuned to a twenty-four-hour news channel, the volume on mute. They'd had to release a press statement about the discovery that morning, but the details given to the media were intentionally sparse, making no mention of the suspected link to the 1998 cold case. But Jack knew it wouldn't take the hacks long. They were generally an astute bunch with long memories — they would connect the dots in a heartbeat.

He just hoped Lorna Henshaw would be true to her word and keep her mouth shut. He had no reason to suspect that she wouldn't — she seemed sensible enough and clearly wasn't thrilled about being involved once again. She hadn't so much as spilled a single bean when the original investigation was at its height, so there was no reason to suggest things would be any different this time around.

But all it would take would be one careless word in the wrong ear.

Keeping an eye on the scrolling headlines, Jack turned his attention back to the evening at Barbara Tindleman's. It had been pleasant enough, the meal exceptional as always, and Jack was glad that Rob had talked him into it; at least it meant a decent dinner, instead of his usual repetitive diet of takeaways. The revelation that the detective sergeant's birth mother had died, however, had caused a somewhat subdued end to the evening. Jack knew Rob wasn't exactly close to his birth mother but, when he'd caught his friend's eye, Jack could see it was a wound which hadn't fully healed.

Abandonment.

It was well documented as being the root cause of many cases of psychological trauma over the generations. Jack and his brother may have grown up without a mother — Jack finding her swinging from a light fitting when he was just four years old — but at least she hadn't abandoned them. For more years than he cared to remember, they had both been under the illusion that Stella MacIntosh had killed herself — but the painful truth had emerged not that long ago that their mother had, in fact, been murdered.

Murder.

An unlawful killing created its own sense of unease, but at least they knew their mother hadn't given up on them. It had to hurt when the person who brought you into this world — the one who's supposed to love and care for you, no matter what — happily turned their back on you without so much as a backward glance, which was what had happened to Rob and Genete. On the outside, Rob appeared to have escaped unscathed from his childhood abandonment, but there was every possibility he was just burying that hurt — hurt that could now resurface in spades. Jack made a mental note to keep an extra close eye on his friend.

Pushing thoughts of Rob and his estranged family to one side, Jack surveyed the paperwork still stacked up on the coffee table. Logistically, he couldn't bring home every page of the 1998 cold case — Cooper would surely have had something to say about lugging the files and boxes back out of the incident room and into Jack's car — so he'd only copied a few of the most pertinent pieces to bring home, managing to get it all into three box files.

He had no doubt that the team would have made a good start on the paperwork that night, putting everything in order ready for tomorrow. To be fair, Jane Telford would have done most of the donkey work beforehand when conducting the cold case review, so now it was really a case of ploughing through the detail and seeing if anything unusual jumped out.

The murders had been horrific, of that there was no question. And, apart from the obvious link to the London Underground, in particular the Central Line, there didn't seem to be anything linking the victims to each other.

But there would be.

There *had* to be.

No serial killer was that random in their thinking.

Jack had learned a few things over the years, one of which was that serial offenders liked routine. They liked repetition. They liked to work to a pattern. It was just a case of finding out what that pattern was.

He reached for the first box file, which housed the bundle of post-mortem reports — and it made for grim reading. Taking each report out one by one, he lined up the photographs on the coffee table, each one annotated by Dr Matthews in meticulous detail.

The beef wellington from earlier had, until now, been sitting quite comfortably in Jack's insides. Although not particularly squeamish, the sight of so many innocent lives being ended so cruelly — and so barbarically — made his stomach begin to churn. Maybe he shouldn't have had that second serving of cheesecake after all.

Even from a brief look through the paperwork, Jack knew Dr Matthews was right when he'd said the 1998 cases were linked to the body discovered that morning — the similarities were unmistakable. Back in 1998, each of the victims were strangled with a thin wire ligature, one with a narrow 1.5-millimetre diameter. Additional bruises suggested they were restrained, with contusions evident around the wrists and ankles, and also the upper arms. The body from this morning was almost identical.

Although the 1998 cases had been hindered by an almost complete lack of forensic evidence, apart from a collection of carpet or rug fibres on some of the victims, and some unidentified semen stains, Jack knew that was largely down to the techniques available at the time; whether they would be more fortunate with the body found that morning, only time would tell. If not, then they were either dealing with a killer who was extremely lucky, or one that knew exactly what they were doing.

Jack didn't know which was worse — a lucky killer, or a clever one.

As he sifted through the post-mortem reports one more time, Jack took a closer look at the images of the Underground maps that had been crumpled up inside each victim's mouth. That part of the puzzle unnerved him. The motivation behind the murders appeared to be sexual — but what was the relevance of the maps? It was something that had toyed with the minds of the initial investigation team too, but they never seemed to come to any satisfactory conclusion.

Were the maps the key to it all? Or just a time-consuming red herring? They were clearly left for a reason — they just had to try and find out what that reason was. Jack knew it would be a question Frank Tyler and his team would have wrestled with. The 1998 team had looked extensively at disgruntled Underground staff, following up and interviewing anyone who had been sacked or left suddenly in the months before the attacks started. But it had all ground to a halt; there was nothing tangible to work with.

Picking up a pen and notepad, Jack started to make a list. *Tube worker.*

The angle had already been explored before, but there was always a chance that maybe they hadn't been looking in the right places. It would be worth looking at again, with a fresh eye, even if just to rule it out.

Stations.

Did the choice of Tube stations mean anything to the killer? Again, it had been something the previous investigation had looked at, but Jack considered it worth another shot.

Forensic evidence.

Techniques had moved on rapidly since the Central Line Killer was last active. Forensic analysis and testing back in 1998 was completely different to the techniques used today and many a cold case killer had been caught since by evidence being re-tested, sometimes decades down the line. Jack underlined the entry twice. *This* was where they had to start.

Yawning, he placed the pen back down on the coffee table just in time to see Marmaduke leap up onto the sofa beside him. Instinctively, he reached out and gave the cat a scratch behind the ears. As Marmaduke settled down on top of one of the cushions, Jack couldn't help but smile. Who would have thought Jack MacIntosh would end up bonding with a cat? Not Jack, that was for sure. The loud purring coming from the ginger tabby made Jack's smile widen.

Marmaduke had landed in Jack's flat in the middle of January as a happy accident. Mrs Constantine from the floor below was going into hospital for a planned operation and needed someone to keep an eye on the cat while she was gone. Being the good neighbour that he was, Jack had volunteered. Originally only meant to pop down morning and night to replenish the cat's food bowl, he soon found that Marmaduke had other ideas. Jack would often find the cat waiting for him on his doormat when he came home from work at night, and it wasn't long before Marmaduke followed him inside . . . and made himself at home.

The ginger tabby changed position, curling up and tucking his head between his front paws. He was meant to go back to Mrs Constantine as soon as she'd recovered from her operation, but on the day she was to be discharged from hospital, she'd suffered a stroke. The decision had been taken to move her to a nursing home. When the old woman's family had arrived at the flat to go through her things, Jack found himself volunteering once again — this time to look after the cat on a more permanent basis. Quite where those words had come from, he still couldn't fathom.

Casting an eye over the scattered paperwork, Jack was acutely aware he was unlikely to achieve much more tonight — and knowing there were beers in the fridge, he was sorely tempted to break one open. But he also knew he needed a clear head for tomorrow morning, and to be at Frank Tyler's house bright and early, which meant he should really try and get some sleep.

Sleep.

Jack and sleep had an unconventional relationship at best, but he was used to it now. It no longer concerned him if he found himself sitting up, night after night, watching the dawn break; once you accepted insomnia it became a comfortable companion of sorts. And at least he had a full stomach tonight — he might have a decent shot at a few hours' sleep, if he was lucky.

Yawning, he gave Marmaduke a final tickle under his chin before sloping off to the bedroom. He felt buoyed at the prospect of picking Frank Tyler's brains in the morning — it could be just what the investigation needed to get it off on the right foot.

* * *

Time: 10.45 p.m.
Date: Friday 10 April 2015
Location: 7 Palace Mews Road, London

Robert Carmichael closed the door to his childhood bedroom and glanced around. The internal decoration may have changed over the years — gone was his single bed and wardrobe; gone also were the posters of movie stars and motorbikes that had once been pinned to the walls; and gone were the mounds of dirty washing piled up in the corners, but it was still the same room.

His room.

There might be a brand-new sofa bed beneath the window, and a fresh coat of paint on the walls, but it was still the room he remembered, a safe cocoon protecting him from the world outside. He would be the first to admit to being a bit of a handful when he was younger. Fostered at the age of five, he went off the rails a little — and if the Tindlemans hadn't stepped in quite when they did, then who knew where he may have ended up. Not as a detective sergeant, that was for sure. For a while, there was a distinct possibility he could have landed on the other side of the police cell door entirely. He knew he owed Barbara and Charles a lot — unable to have their own children, the couple had happily opened their hearts, and then their home, to the wayward eight-year-old Robert Carmichael.

Sinking down onto the sofa bed, he momentarily closed his eyes and let the events of the evening sink in. It hadn't gone quite as he'd planned. Having fully intended to tell Barbara about wanting to search for Genete, and the steps he

79

had already taken, all that had been shot down in flames by the revelation contained in the letter.

He still wasn't quite sure how he was meant to react to the news of his mother's death. Was he meant to feel sad? Maybe he should at least have shown some emotion, perhaps even shed a tear? Or felt his heart ache at a good life lost? She was his mother, after all.

The answer was a resounding no.

How could he mourn the loss of someone he barely remembered, much less cared about? The woman calling herself his mother had given up that right the moment she'd chosen the bottle over bringing up her own kids.

It wasn't that he disliked her. If he took the time to think about it, he didn't even hate her — hate required an emotion, a *feeling*, and he had no feelings for the woman who gave birth to him and then went on to abandon him. He wasn't even interested in how she had died. The letter didn't say, and he wasn't about to ask.

His first reaction was to bin it, maybe even burn it, but instead he'd stuffed the envelope into his back pocket and finished his dinner. Pulling the envelope back out, he smoothed the creases and teased the thick piece of A4 paper out once again.

We regret to inform you that your mother Sheila Carmichael passed away at Liverpool City Hospital on Saturday 21 March.

We regret.

It was a strange phrase. Regret suggested there was some choice in the matter, that her death might have been avoided in some way. Or alternatively, it assumed that the news would evoke some feeling of sadness on his part — which it clearly didn't. Instead, he felt nothing except a void. Well, maybe that wasn't strictly true. Whenever he did think about his mother — which wasn't all that often — it wouldn't take long before a bitterness started to creep in. Reading the solicitor's letter only served to stoke the fire. The woman had cheated him out of the childhood he was entitled to, and now she was cheating him out of mourning her death, too.

Sighing, Carmichael kicked off his shoes and loosened his tie. That he was letting her get to him after all these years rankled him. She had no hold over him now, and what he really needed to do was focus on finding Genete. Tonight's news only made him want to do that even more.

The letter from the solicitors had stated his mother passed away at a hospital in Liverpool, but didn't go on to give any further detail.

Liverpool.

It looked like she hadn't moved far — so it was possible Genete hadn't either.

Carmichael had stopped short of divulging his plans to find his sister over the dinner table — somehow it hadn't felt quite right. Barbara had suggested he might want to, and he knew she would support him every step of the way, but the unexpected news had rather taken the wind out of his sails. There would be time enough to come clean about Genete later.

He took another look at the letter.

Funeral to be held at Parkland Crematorium, Liverpool on Monday 13 April.

Before he could talk himself out of it, Carmichael grabbed his phone and began searching for trains to Liverpool.

CHAPTER NINE

Time: 9.30 a.m.
Date: Saturday 11 April
Location: Herne Bay, Kent

Jack pulled the Mondeo to a stop outside a detached house at the end of a quiet street. After killing the engine, he turned towards the passenger seat.

"Do you remember our little trip out to the wilds of Essex, Amanda? When we went to visit the delightful DCI Hobbs?"

Cassidy peered ahead through the windscreen, then turned to meet Jack's gaze. "How could I forget? You called the man a twat."

"Well, Graham Hobbs was a twat. Still is a twat." Jack pulled the keys from the car's ignition. "Today we are visiting another retired DCI — DCI Frank Tyler — but this one will be a far more enjoyable experience, I promise you."

"He's not a twat, then?" Cassidy followed Jack's lead in getting out of the car.

Jack gave a chuckle as he slammed the driver's door. "Not even close. Frank was a good man. A decent copper back in the day, and he made an excellent DCI."

"Thank goodness for that." Cassidy tailed Jack towards the Tylers' front door. "I don't think I could handle you making any more enemies."

"You make it sound like it's a daily occurrence, Amanda."

Cassidy sniggered. "No — just weekly, maybe."

Jack's knock at the stout wooden door was answered quickly by a pleasant-looking woman in her mid-fifties. Her skin had a natural-looking healthy glow, suggesting she spent a good deal of time outdoors, and her eyes sported a warm sparkle. Jack liked Irene Tyler the moment he saw her.

"Mrs Tyler," he greeted. "I'm Jack MacIntosh, and this is my colleague Amanda Cassidy. It's very good of Frank to make time to see us."

The woman smiled warmly. "No problem at all. Come on in, he's out the back."

Irene led Jack and Cassidy through the hallway and towards the kitchen at the rear. Attached to the kitchen was a spacious conservatory not unlike the one Jack and Cooper had seen at Lorna Henshaw's home yesterday.

The day had dawned bright and clear, promising more unseasonably warm temperatures — but the forecast also suggested heavy downpours and thunderstorms would arrive by lunchtime. For the moment, however, the conservatory was bathed in a warm, comfortable light.

"If you go and take a seat, I'll bring through some tea. Or coffee if you'd prefer?"

"Either is fine, Mrs Tyler." Jack gestured for Cassidy to walk ahead of him. "Whichever is easiest."

Frank Tyler was sitting in a recliner on the far side of the conservatory, facing the open patio doors. A gentle breeze greeted them as they approached.

"Morning, Frank. Good to see you." Jack came to a stop by the retired DCI's side and regarded one of the very few men that he'd looked up to in his career. His first role model, Graham Hobbs, had shown himself to be a narcissistic liability — someone who repeatedly cut corners and refused to take responsibility for his own shortcomings — but Frank Tyler was an entirely different animal altogether. When Jack had joined CID as a detective constable, Frank had been a detective inspector who was renowned for handling the big cases, the ones that hit the headlines — and solving many of them, too. Everyone wanted to work with Frank, and that had included the young DC MacIntosh; but it was never to be. Graham Hobbs got his claws into Jack first, and by the time he spat him out the other end, Frank Tyler's team was complete. But their paths would cross from time to time, and Jack's respect for the man only grew as the years went by.

Frank turned in his chair, the same warm eyes that Jack remembered met his own. For a man dying of metastatic bowel cancer, he looked remarkably well. Appearances could be deceiving.

"Jack MacIntosh, as I live and breathe. How the devil are you, my boy?"

Jack grinned. He hadn't been called "boy" for many years — but somehow it sounded right coming from Frank.

"Everything's good, Frank. It's been a while."

"It certainly has. When Reenie told me you were popping by, I tried to recall when it was that I last clapped eyes on you. I seem to think it was old Bernard Thorpe's leaving do back in 2004."

Jack's eyebrows hitched a notch. "Wow, that's some memory you've got there. But you could be right."

The retired DCI returned Jack's grin. "The body might be giving up on me these days, but my brain cells are working just fine — for now, at least." He gestured towards the wicker furniture. "Have a seat, the pair of you."

Jack went to sit on one of the armchairs. "This is Amanda, Frank. One of our best sergeants."

Cassidy's face coloured as she took the armchair next to Jack's. "Nice to meet you, Mr Tyler."

"Oh, call me Frank — everyone does." Frank pressed a button on the remote control he held loosely in his hand,

and the recliner slowly tipped him upright. "While we wait for Reenie to come through with the refreshments, let's get down to business." Jack noted that the warm, almost jovial expression that had been on the retired detective's face since they arrived had now clouded over. "And it's a bad business, I'll say that much."

Cassidy brought the thick folder she had tucked under her arm down onto her lap. Taking a moment or two to flick through the contents, she passed Jack a selection of the paperwork.

"It's good of you to do this, Frank." Jack took hold of the papers. "I'm really grateful."

"I want to help." Frank sat up straight and reached for the spectacles that hung on a chain around his neck. "If I can."

Jack picked out a good handful of A4 sheets and passed them across. He'd already outlined a little about the case to Frank's wife when they'd spoken yesterday, so Frank would have an idea what was coming — and its potential link to one of his own cases. As he settled back against the cushions of the armchair, Jack watched the retired detective put his glasses on and lower his gaze to the brief summary the team had prepared for the new investigation. As well as the summary, Jack had copied each post-mortem report for the 1998 victims of the Central Line Killer, plus the crime scene photographs. None of it would be anything the former detective hadn't seen before, but that wouldn't stop it from being unsettling.

While Frank digested the paperwork, Irene Tyler entered with a wooden tray laden with a tall coffee pot, several china mugs and a plate of individual apple pies dusted with sugar. She bent down and slipped the tray onto a wicker-framed coffee table, proceeding to pour freshly brewed coffee into three mugs.

"Frank takes his black these days, but there's milk and sugar there — help yourselves." Irene waved towards the small milk jug and bowl of sugar on the tray. "And please help finish off those apple pies. They're far too tempting for me — all they do is go straight to my hips!" She gave a soft chuckle as she straightened back up. "I'll leave you in peace."

As Frank's wife left, Cassidy leaned forward to deposit a splash of milk into two of the mugs, and then a generous teaspoon of sugar into Jack's. After looking up briefly and catching his inquisitive gaze, she grinned and deposited another large spoonful.

Jack mirrored the grin and took hold of the mug. "Cheers, Amanda."

A comfortable silence descended on the conservatory, the only sound coming from the garden, where a pair of cooing pigeons were flapping around in one of the trees that flanked the Tylers' back garden. Neither Jack nor Cassidy felt the need to fill the silence, instead letting Frank carry on reading from the pile of paperwork on his lap.

Once he'd read enough, Frank sighed and swung his legs from the recliner, swapping the paperwork for his mug of cooling coffee. After a fortifying mouthful, he spoke. "This is the one case that has always haunted me, Jack — the one case that I really wanted to put to bed before I retired." Another sigh. "Alas, it wasn't to be." The sadness in his voice and regret in his eyes deepened. "I don't think I've ever had a full night's sleep since — not even after they pump me full of drugs, which they have a habit of doing more and more these days." He tried a smile. "It's always there — you know what I mean, don't you? Those cases that refuse to leave you alone. For me it was this one — the one that got away. The *killer* that got away."

"I've already read a lot of your investigation, Frank. The whole team have. And the Cold Case Unit will have studied it from start to finish. There's nothing in there that you overlooked. Nothing you didn't follow up." Jack knew the words would sit emptily in the air, even though he meant every one of them. As far as he could see it had been a textbook investigation, on paper at least. Impeccable. They just hadn't found the killer. "You did nothing wrong."

"That may be so, Jack, but sometimes these cases have a habit of haunting you."

Jack nodded. He knew all about those cases. One of his own experiences as a wet-behind-the-ears, greener-than-green detective constable had stuck with him throughout his career. Little Carrie-Ann Dixon. Although the mistakes made in that case weren't of Jack's doing — those were laid fairly and squarely at the feet of Graham Hobbs — he had personally shouldered the responsibility of failing to find the little girl's killer, wearing it like a millstone around his neck for the best part of a quarter of a century. When the case was finally solved last year, he had made a peace of sorts with himself and, more importantly, made peace with Carrie-Ann's memory — but it was still something that refused to leave him. So, he knew exactly what Frank Tyler must be feeling right now.

"I spoke with the Cold Case Unit yesterday. There were a series of unsolved sexual assaults in 1996 and 1997 which could have been connected to the Central Line Killer. And that means potentially to our case from yesterday, too."

Frank Tyler's eyebrows hitched. "That rings a bell. Were they the same MO?"

"Not exactly. The assaults were up in Yorkshire for a start, and they seemed to be more random in nature. Obviously, no links to an Underground network or other transport system."

Frank took another gulp from his coffee mug. "Yorkshire, you say? I think I recall it now. I certainly remember looking at some unsolved cases. Do you think there might have been a connection after all?"

Jack shrugged. "I really don't know, Frank. It's just an angle we plan to look at."

The retired detective's face dropped. "If we dismissed the idea too quickly, then I'm sorry. That's my bad."

Jack instantly shook his head. "Not at all. Like I said, there's no criticism of your investigation here — and there's no real concrete evidence that the cases are linked. It's just a line of enquiry we'll be opening up again. It could very well come to nothing. I plan to get all the forensic evidence reassessed for both the 1996 and 1997 sexual assault cases, plus the 1998 murders. Techniques have come on a long way since the nineties. It might give us something to work with."

Frank nodded. "That's a good plan. I heard all about you cracking that cold case last year — that poor wee mite found in the attic of her own home. As I recall, it was one of Graham Hobbs' many spectacular cock-ups."

Jack felt a smile twitch at the corners of his mouth. This was one of the reasons why he liked Frank Tyler. The man despised Hobbs just about as much as he did.

"It was. And it might have taken twenty-five years or so to get Carrie-Ann the justice she deserved, but we got there in the end."

"And I heard what you called him, too." The smile on Jack's face was mirrored on the retired detective's. "But I think 'twat' is somewhat tame for the likes of him. I'd have gone for something a bit stronger."

"You forget, Frank — you've already retired. I still have to watch my mouth these days." Jack heard a snigger coming from the armchair next to him, something that didn't seem to escape Frank Tyler either.

A genuine warmth entered Frank's eyes. "I think your detective sergeant here has got the measure of you, Jack. I can tell she's a smart one. I may be retired and put out to pasture, maybe not even long for this wonderful world of ours, but I still get to hear things from time to time. You've crossed so many lines in your career, I think you could make hopscotch an Olympic event. And you must have an entire drawer to yourself in Dougie King's filing cabinet by now, documenting each and every complaint levelled against you over the years. How many grey hairs has the poor man got now?"

Jack grinned behind his mug. "Maybe one or two."

Frank's voice took on a more serious tone. "All I know is, I recognise a decent copper when I see one. You keep doing what you're doing, Jack, and don't let the buggers grind you down.

Step on as many toes as you need to if it gets you a result with this one. These women deserve that at the very least. If anyone can finally crack this case, I know you can."

Jack accepted the compliment with a slow nod. He just hoped Frank was right. "I plan to bring in a forensic profiler — they might want to come and talk to you, if that's OK?"

"Anything to help, Jack. If you want me to talk to your mind doctor, just send them my way."

Jack had a feeling Frank was as sceptical as he had once been on the role of psychology in criminal investigations. Back in the nineties, profiling was still in its infancy — and, with some spectacular errors in some very high-profile investigations, cases had understandably hit the headlines for all the wrong reasons, dragging the reputation of psychology deep down into the mud. Consequently, many in the force distrusted its use entirely. Jack had been firmly in that particular camp for quite some time, but after using Dr Rachel Hunter, a clinical psychologist specialising in criminal behaviour, in some of his more recent investigations, his opinion had slowly, and a little reluctantly, begun to change.

"We have a very good profiler, Frank. She's as straight as an arrow, and her profiles do sometimes help."

Frank gave a conciliatory nod. "Then send her to my door. I meant what I said — I want to help. I want to see you catch this bastard, preferably before I start pushing up the daisies."

"I'll do my best."

After a few more minutes' general chit-chat, Jack eventually caving in and demolishing one of the apple pies, he and Cassidy rose to their feet. "We'll see ourselves out, Frank. Thanks again for your time."

The retired detective made no attempt to get up, instead waving a hand in the detectives' direction. "No problem at all. I'll take another look through this lot." He pointed towards the pile of paperwork on the coffee table. "And if you want to send me through anything for the 1996 and 1997 cases, I'll take another look at those, too. See if I remember more about whether we seriously considered a link or not."

Jack made a mental note to do just that. With a final wave, and after passing on Dr Matthews' good wishes, he and Cassidy headed back out towards the hallway. Irene Tyler appeared in the door frame, a small box in her hand. "You'll take some of these away with you, won't you?" She thrust the box of Mr Kipling apple pies towards Jack. "They're not really Frank's favourites any more — his taste buds have changed, and he doesn't have the same appetite for sweet things that he once did. You'd be doing me an enormous favour."

Jack was about to refuse, even though the pie he'd eaten had gone down very nicely with a second cup of coffee, but then he thought again. Taking the box, he gave a wink towards Cassidy. "Thank you, Mrs Tyler. I think we both know someone back in the incident room who will be most appreciative of them."

Back in the Mondeo, Cassidy snapped on her seatbelt and turned towards Jack. "He was nice."

Jack pulled away from the kerb and took the main road back to London. "He was, *is*, one of the good ones, Amanda. I have a lot of time for people like Frank Tyler."

"So, what's next?"

Jack ran through his mental checklist. "When we get back to the station, we need to send everything we have on the 1996 and 1997 sexual assault cases through to him."

"I'll do that."

"And all the evidence needs to be looked at again. I want *everything* re-tested from the Yorkshire assault cases, plus the 1998 murder investigation, too. Techniques are changing all the time. We might get lucky."

"I'm sure Chris will ask Jenny to put in a favour or two at the lab for us — if you ask him nicely."

Jack flashed Cassidy a grin. "I don't need to ask nicely, Amanda — I have pies." He nodded towards the box on the dashboard. "Cooper will be like putty in my hands."

* * *

Time: 11.00 a.m.
Date: Saturday 11 April 2015
Location: Herne Bay, Kent

Frank Tyler's tired gaze came to rest once again on the pile of paperwork stacked up on the coffee table — he wanted to scrutinise it all again and see if he did, after all, miss something back in 1998. Although Jack had been most complimentary about the investigation, he needed to check for himself. Mistakes happened, everyone knew that, but when mistakes happened in cases like that of the Central Line Killer, they had lasting consequences. And, if the killer had now started killing again, Frank wanted to do all he could to help bring the man down. An unsolved case like this wasn't something he wanted to take to his grave.

Irene had been in to clear away the coffee tray, replacing it with his morning fortified milkshake and another round of painkillers. The shake was meant to be strawberry flavour, but Frank's taste buds were so shot to bits now that it could have been anything. He dutifully swallowed the drink and the tablets, then settled back to close his eyes.

Talking about the Central Line Killer with Jack had resurrected all manner of memories that Frank had considered long since buried. And the problem with memories like these was, once reactivated, they stubbornly refused to leave you.

* * *

Time: 1.20 a.m.
Date: Friday 22 May 1998
Location: The Hungry Traveller Snack Bar, Silver Street, London

The crime scene was horrifyingly similar to the two that had come before, and if Detective Inspector Frank Tyler didn't realise they were dealing with a serial killer back then, he certainly did now. Three dead women in three months.

He scratched the thin beard that clung to his chin.

The call had come in at just before midnight, when Frank was still in the incident room trying to piece together the evidence generated in the case so far. One by one the rest of the team had packed up and gone home, sighing as they switched off their computers and put their notepads away, leaving him to stare at the pin boards, searching for inspiration. He knew the team were feeling the strain just as much as he was, saw it etched into their faces every day — dullness swamping their eyes, dark circles quickly appearing beneath. Everyone had been working solidly for the last three long months, pulling extra shifts where they could and overtime at weekends, all annual leave cancelled.

And they had piss all to show for it.

Except an overtime bill that even made Frank shudder.

Although he knew exactly what he would find, he'd decided to come and see the crime scene for himself. The body had already been cut down from where it had been found hanging, now lying on the cold tiles of the abandoned restaurant.

He didn't need to get that close — he could see from where he stood the dense purple contusions around the girl's neck. *Just like the others.* Her face also sported impressive-looking bruises across the cheekbones, plus a laceration above her right eyebrow. Blood had circled around her eye and then trickled down her porcelain face — it clung to her skin like a dried-up river of scarlet-red tears. He noted the girl's hands were tied behind her back, her legs secured together at the ankles.

Number three.

The call had come in from a well-known and well-respected investigative journalist by the name of Lorna Henshaw. She worked for one of the better class of rags, if there was such a thing. Quite what her involvement in all this was, Frank didn't quite know. But he was determined to find out.

She first contacted them back in March, after the second body had been found. Frank remembered the exchange, talk of two envelopes containing Underground maps arriving at her home address. The team, including Frank, had dismissed her as a possible crank at the time, putting the missives down as nothing more than coincidence.

But now they had a third body.

Crank or no crank, this woman clearly knew something, and Frank was going to make a point of finding out just what that was.

With a heavy sigh, he took a step back. With the time well into the early hours, he knew he wouldn't be going home anytime soon. He had already phoned home to let Reenie know he was working late, and she knew Frank well enough by now to appreciate that "late" often meant he wouldn't make it home at all. To give her her due, she never complained or suggested he was working too hard. She understood the job and his unswerving commitment to it. She would merely leave him a plate of dinner in the fridge and go to bed.

He was well aware he'd struck gold the moment he'd met the petite Devon-accented woman on a night out in Pimlico. Unsure that she'd been all that impressed with his schoolboy attempts at chat-up lines, he'd consoled himself that she had at least taken his number. Three years later they were married, and not a day went by when he didn't remind himself of just how lucky he was.

Having seen enough, Frank made his way towards the exit, pulling a cigarette packet out from his pocket but waiting to light up until he got outside. He would leave the forensics team to do their thing; there was nothing he could really add by hanging around — and he would only get in their way if he stayed. Inhaling deeply, he felt the hint of drizzle hitting his face as he walked. The shit would no doubt hit the fan when the news of the latest murder leaked — the powers that be were getting restless, wanting results. But Frank and his team were already working night and day, so he wasn't quite sure what else they were meant to do. The papers had latched onto the story in their usual feeding frenzy, quickly labelling the offender the Central Line Killer as soon as the second body was discovered.

Frank wondered which idiotic journalist had dreamed that one up.

Even though the killer had been on the streets of London for the last three months, once the initial shock and awe of the front-page headlines had worn off, the story was slowly relegated to the inside pages. Instead, the Millennium Bug was on the tip of everyone's tongue. The impending slip into the next millennium was still eighteen months away, but everyone it seemed was already getting the jitters. Frank couldn't really see the sense in it all. He was more concerned about finding a killer than worrying about whether his computer would turn on properly when the calendar flipped to the year 2000, or whether he would be able to get any money out of the cashpoint.

People's priorities were strangely skewed sometimes.

Taking another long drag from the cigarette, he headed away from the Hungry Traveller — now a crime scene — to where he'd parked the car. The road was a narrow side street, the restaurant hidden away from prying eyes, and the girl's body had been strung up in the front window, next to an advert for the restaurant's latest meal deal. Ironically, it was offering two-for-one on vegetarian options. Frank noted that unless you were taking a walk out this way, you wouldn't necessarily see it. And at this time of night, not a lot of people were out and about in any case.

Arriving at his Honda, Frank dropped the cigarette butt to the ground and crushed it with his shoe. The nicotine had sharpened his senses and, despite what he'd just witnessed, his stomach growled. He was hungry.

He knew Reenie would have a delicious healthy meal waiting for him back at home in the fridge — all he needed to do was whack it in the microwave for a few minutes when he got in — but delicious and healthy wasn't what he craved right now.

Knowing there was an all-night burger van a few streets away, he bypassed the Honda and headed in its direction.

* * *

Time: 11.35 a.m.
Date: Saturday 11 April 2015
Location: Herne Bay, Kent

Frank Tyler stirred at the sound of the lawn mower starting up. Pulling open one heavy eyelid, then the other, he saw Irene starting to methodically stride up and down their modest expanse of grass. She was a keen gardener, even before Frank became ill, and Frank was particularly glad about that. He had no interest in anything horticultural — could barely tell a hydrangea from a rhododendron — so happily let her have free rein in the garden.

But he worried that the house was becoming too much for her now. Even before the cancer started to take its hold, they had begun to rattle around the three-bedroomed house and had spoken several times about downsizing again. They had moved out of London to Herne Bay on Frank's retirement in 2010 and, in hindsight, it had been a mistake; they should have gone for something smaller. But any thoughts about moving on were shelved after his diagnosis eighteen months ago, and Frank was all too aware that the next time he downsized, it would be into a wooden box. It was one of life's cruel and painful ironies.

Reenie never complained about staying on top of the upkeep of the house and garden, even saying that she enjoyed it. Frank hoped it was true and that she wasn't just doing it out of duty, quietly wishing to herself that he would just hurry up and die.

Knowing he was being morbid, he tore his gaze away from the garden and focused again on the paperwork still sitting on the coffee table.

Sadie Bloomfield.

That had been her name.

Taking a slow breath in, he could almost smell the greasy burger he'd devoured only moments after leaving the Hungry Traveller. It was an aroma that had stayed with him for weeks afterwards, maybe even months. And now, when he smelled a burger frying, covered in lashings of onions and cheese, it instantly took him right back to that day — that fateful night on Silver Street and the Hungry Traveller Snack Bar.

Seeing his own investigation again in black and white had transported him back to 1998, each victim resurrected in his mind and seared onto his brain. He'd never forgotten them, not for a single day. And if he could help put past mistakes right, then he would die trying. The irony wasn't lost on him.

He just hoped he had enough time left to do it.

CHAPTER TEN

Time: 1.15 p.m.
Date: Saturday 11 April 2015
Location: Metropolitan Police HQ, London

Jack threw the packet of apple pies in Cooper's direction. "There you go, Cooper. Don't say I never give you anything."

The detective sergeant deftly caught the box, eyes shining. "Wow! Cheers, boss."

Jack headed across to the whiteboard where the details of the current investigation were listed. "Like everything in life, Cooper, there's a condition or two attached." Picking up a marker pen, he stepped towards a second whiteboard and proceeded to write *THE CENTRAL LINE KILLER — 1998* across the top in capitals.

Cooper looked longingly at the box of pies. "What do I need to do?"

Jack suppressed a smile. "Nothing too onerous, Cooper. First, arrange for all the forensic evidence from the 1998 murder investigation to be sent to the lab for re-testing." He tapped the second whiteboard with the marker pen. "And then do the same for the '96 and '97 sexual assaults. All available evidence

97

is to be looked at again. And if you can have a little word in Jenny's ear and see if she can prioritise it for us, I might just stretch to some Bakewell tarts next time."

Cooper grinned, already ripping open the box and taking a bite out of one of the apple pies, pastry crumbs tumbling down the front of his shirt. "Consider it done, boss."

Jack continued annotating the second whiteboard, adding *Yorkshire sexual assaults* — *'96 and '97*. "As you know, Amanda and I went to see Frank Tyler this morning and, as expected, he's more than happy to help us in any way he can. I've reassured him we haven't found anything yet to suggest he missed something back in 1998, but we'll obviously keep looking. I've promised to send him the '96 and '97 sexual assault cases — he vaguely remembered considering them, but for some reason dismissed them as unrelated. We need to look at that again and find out why that decision was made."

"I'll get the extra documentation copied, guv," volunteered Cassidy. "Get it sent over later today."

"Thanks. Have we had much joy from the CCTV around Wheeler Street or White City Underground?"

DC Daniels shifted in his seat, nudging the mouse on his desk to activate the computer screen. "Not really, boss. Chris and I have looked at everything available so far and we've taken note of any vehicle registrations seen close to the scene, but as there aren't any cameras in the vicinity of the building itself it's a bit of a shot in the dark."

"Run the plates anyway. Flag up anything that doesn't feel right. He had to transport her there somehow." Jack rummaged in his jacket pocket, pulling out the list he'd made the night before. "And I want to revisit the Tube worker angle, too. What, if anything, do we know about that from the previous investigation?"

Daniels tapped his keyboard. "The 1998 investigation made a list of people who had either been sacked or left under a cloud in the three months before the first murder. All were traced, interviewed and, as far as we can tell, ruled out."

Jack grimaced. "Do it again while we wait for forensics to get back to us. Something might have been missed."

Daniels gave a curt nod. "Boss."

"In the meantime, I'm sending everything we have across to Rachel Hunter. This case sounds like something she might be able to help with." Jack caught an all-too-familiar look crossing each of the team's faces. Sending all the evidence back to the lab to be re-tested, and now employing the services of the force's criminal profiler, wouldn't come cheap. But Jack didn't care about the money.

"Before any of you ask, no, I haven't cleared it with anyone. If we're going to catch this person, then it needs doing — money shouldn't even come into it. I'll take the flak if, and when, the complaints come in." He gave what he hoped was an encouraging smile. "Just keep your heads down if the shit begins to fly." After throwing the marker pen back down, he started heading for the door.

"Before you go, guv, there's been a few calls coming in about a potential ID for our victim." Cassidy scooted her chair back towards her desk. "I'm starting to collate them, but it could take a while."

Jack nodded. "Well, we need an ID if this case is going to move forward. Can I leave that with you, Amanda? I appreciate you'll have to wade through a lot of crap first, but assess the calls and follow up on any that sound promising."

"Sure, guv. I'll get onto it as soon as I've sorted out the papers for DCI Tyler."

"Good. I'll be in my office if you need me."

* * *

Time: 1.30 p.m.
Date: Saturday 11 April 2015
Location: Herne Bay, Kent

Irene Tyler plunged her hands once more into the bowl of hot, soapy water, welcoming the scalding sensation on her skin. Rinsing Frank's milkshake glass, she watched the soap suds drip back into the sink as a tear slid down her cheek. She didn't cry in front of him if she could help it; the last time had probably been a few weeks ago when they'd been poring over the photo albums again. She'd poured them both a glass of wine — Frank barely touching his — while they immersed themselves in the past. With page after page of memories assaulting them, it had been an emotional evening. By the end of it, their cheeks were damp with tears.

Seeing snaps of the children growing up had reminded them all too clearly about the steady, relentless march of time, and that there was nothing they could do to stop it. But since Frank's diagnosis, it was as if someone had accidentally pressed the fast-forward button, the days now whizzing by in a flash.

At least that was how it felt for Irene. She often wondered if Frank felt the same. With his days peppered with bone-gnawing pain and stomach-churning sickness, maybe time was actually dragging for him and he craved a swifter end to it all. The thought made her feel ill. The idea of losing Frank caused her to wish with all her heart that the days would never end, and although she knew it would just prolong his suffering, she wanted it all the same. An end to his pain would mean an end to *them* — something she hadn't quite come to terms with yet. She knew how selfish it all sounded.

Another tear dripped from her cheek and splashed into the soapy water. She didn't ever want to be without him, not for a single second, but equally knew she would have to face that particular harsh reality one day, and probably a lot sooner than she wanted.

But just not today.

Plunging her hands back down into the water, she scooped up Frank's milkshake glass and placed it on the draining board. He'd dozed off again in the recliner while she'd finished mowing the lawn and would most probably be out for the next couple of hours, maybe more. He was tiring more easily these days, his stamina slowly declining. Not that he would admit it; the man was still too proud for that.

She'd noticed the wind picking up while putting away the lawnmower, thunder clouds gathering overhead, so she'd hurried inside to close the patio doors and pull a blanket over Frank as he slept. She'd taken the empty milkshake glass from his hands, then spied the pile of paperwork on the coffee table as she made her way to the kitchen.

Frank had always brought work home with him, but she made a point of never getting involved, never asking too much. But this case was different, even Irene could see that. She had no intention of reading any of it but couldn't help catching a quick look at the horrific images as she tidied the pages away. A series of empty, dead eyes staring back out at her.

She shuddered, despite the heat of the water in the washing-up bowl. She knew the case well, everyone did. Frank had lived and breathed it back in 1998, and although he had never discussed the case with her at home, she read enough in the newspapers at the time to know how bad things had been. Then she'd witnessed first-hand the toll it had taken on him as the months passed by and Frank had failed to find the killer.

Failed.

For that was how he had viewed it — a failure on his part; nothing more, nothing less. And no matter how many times Irene would try to reassure him that it wasn't down to him, that it wasn't his fault, she knew he would take the blame with him to his grave.

Unless he was able to help Jack MacIntosh with his current investigation. If they managed to find the Central Line Killer after all this time, Frank might die a happier man. Maybe *happy* wasn't the correct word — *contented*, perhaps. But was it going to be worth the emotional turmoil to get to that point? Irene certainly didn't want Frank's last few days, weeks or months taken up with so much soul-searching, constantly beating himself up about what he did and didn't do back then. Neither of them knew how much time he had left — the doctors equally unsure. Cancer was a cruel enough disease, but it was made all the worse by the uncertainty of the prognosis. They were acutely aware of the final destination, just not how long it would take to get there. Would it be today? Tomorrow? Next month? Whatever the uncertainty, Irene didn't want their precious time together swallowed up with such traumatic memories. What if the case was all he thought about before he died? That his last thoughts were of murder, torture and his own failings as a police officer? She desperately wanted to create some happy memories with her husband before he was no longer with her and resented the feeling that she was losing him back to the job all over again. A job that had already taken so much from him.

She knew she was being selfish — *again*.

Stacking the remaining dishes on the draining board, she watched the water disappear down the plug hole. Wiping the tears from her blotchy cheeks, she placed a well-practised smile onto her face and turned her attention to making something for lunch when Frank stirred. No matter what turmoil she felt within, she couldn't let him see she was struggling.

* * *

Time: 2.40 p.m.
Date: Saturday 11 April 2015
Location: Metropolitan Police HQ, London

Jack had spent the last hour collating all the relevant documentation from the current investigation, plus those from the 1998 cold case, ready to send through to Rachel Hunter. He decided not to cloud the issue with the '96 and '97 sexual assaults just yet.

DS Cassidy had shown him, not for the first time, how to scan and save what he needed to a folder on his laptop, and now he was compiling the accompanying email. As promised, Cassidy had taken on the task of sending the paperwork for the Yorkshire sexual assaults over to Frank Tyler, organising a courier so he had hard copies to work with rather than having to open numerous email attachments. Cooper was busy dealing with re-submitting all the forensic evidence to the lab, and Daniels was glued to the computer monitor still analysing the CCTV.

Although the lab was always snowed under with work, Cooper being in a relationship with Jenny Davies — the head of Central London Laboratories — could sometimes work in their favour; at least, Jack hoped it might. If they could get the testing rushed through as a priority, it would help the case enormously.

The bill would no doubt be horrendous, but Jack didn't care — he wasn't intending to ask first, having long been of the view that it was easier to seek forgiveness for something than permission to do it in the first place. Justice had no price tag in his opinion, and if he got into deep water because of it, then so be it. Shit happened. It wasn't like it would be the first time — he was used to swimming with the sharks by now.

Which just left submitting the evidence to Rachel. Jack didn't want to go into too much detail about where they were with the case. From what he'd learned about Rachel since she'd first advised on one of his cases, she much preferred to come to a case cold.

Just present me with the facts, Jack — I'll do the rest.

He didn't quite know how she did it — getting inside the minds of some of the most depraved people to walk the planet, trying to establish what made them tick, what made them who they were and do the things they did. She often warned him that getting inside a killer's head was the last place anyone should want to be, not for any length of time anyway, but it was a place she frequently went herself. She had a cool and unflustered way of handling the most disturbing of cases, often with a good measure of dark humour thrown in, too. It was a coping mechanism many of them in the job used.

Jack turned his attention back to the email, deciding to keep it brief and merely list the attachments he was sending through — then it would be up to Rachel. Reading it through one more time to check for the stubborn typos that his one-finger typing invariably threw up, he simply signed it "Jack" and hit the send button.

Almost immediately, an "out of office"' reply flew straight back into his inbox.

I am out of the office on a conference in Atlanta until 18 April. All urgent enquiries please forward to Martin Hedges on extension 7764.

Bugger.

Sighing, Jack leaned back in his chair to rub his eyes. What the hell was he meant to do now? He wasn't sure who else he could trust as much as he did Rachel. It had taken him this long to warm to the idea of using a criminal psychologist in the first place — so the thought of involving someone else that he'd never met before wasn't appealing.

Before he could contemplate the next step, the door opened, and Cooper peered around the doorframe. "Jenny says she'll fast-track what she can on the forensics, boss, and I'm back looking at the CCTV while Trev follows up on the Tube worker angle."

Jack raised his eyebrows. "Anything much on that yet?"

Cooper shrugged. "Not a lot. He's just trying to track everyone down again, then see what they can remember."

Jack nodded. "See if we can establish where they've all been since 1998 — and, more importantly, where they are now."

"Will do, boss."

"Cheers for that, Cooper." Jack noted the detective hovering in the doorway and knew there was more to come. "I take it there's something else?"

CHAPTER ELEVEN

Time: 3.00 p.m.
Date: Saturday 11 April 2015
Location: Cracknell Street, London

Jessica Fleming snapped her head around. She was sure she'd heard a noise, but each time she looked behind her there was nothing but an empty street. Chastising herself for being so on edge, she carried on along the pavement. Tony had told her often enough about how neurotic she could be — one of the many reasons he cited for their two-year on/off relationship now being at a permanent end. It hadn't come as too much of a surprise to her, if she was being honest; when she found out he'd been sleeping with her best friend, she'd come to that particular conclusion fairly rapidly by herself. But her reaction to it had surprised her. She'd expected to feel upset, maybe even angry, but definitely to have at least felt *something*.

Instead, all she had felt was empty.

But it wasn't an altogether unwelcome feeling. Being free of Tony meant she could now do as she pleased, maybe even put herself first for a change. Tony took great relish in calling her quick-tempered and highly strung — but was it any wonder? Nothing she did was ever good enough for him — he would criticise or find fault in everything she did.

But no more.

Now she was free.

Pulling her bag up onto her shoulder, she continued along the path. It felt like this was the first day of the rest of her life, with plenty of good times yet to come, which was partly why she had decided on a change.

Visiting New Wave hair salon as boring old Jessica, she had left an hour and a half later as Jess. Reinventing herself had cost her more than she could really afford, but she didn't begrudge a single penny. She was worth it, *and* she deserved it — Tony had made her miserable for far too long.

Losing the long blonde locks that she'd cherished for more years than she cared to remember felt invigorating, and as each tress fell to the tiled floor she felt lighter — both physically and mentally. Before leaving the salon, she deleted Tony from her contacts list on her phone and blocked him on all her social media apps. Her new-found lightness continued in abundance with every step that she took.

She didn't need anyone to hold her hand any more — and she definitely didn't need someone as toxic as Tony Kingdom; it had just taken her this long to realise it. Walking along the street now with her new haircut, and the new jacket she'd treated herself to last week, there was a renewed vigour in her step.

Just as her stride began to lengthen, a satisfied smile crossing her newly glossed lips, she felt the first tell-tale spots of rain hit her cheeks. Squinting skywards, she saw the ominously dark grey clouds bunching together overhead. More raindrops started to splatter onto her face, bigger ones this time.

The unusually warm days had been welcome after such a long, cold winter, but they inevitably triggered sporadic torrential downpours in the afternoons. The topsy-turvy weather wasn't all bad — it brought with it the most spectacular rainbows. Mother nature could be a beautiful thing.

More raindrops pelted the ground as a crack of thunder made her jump. Tutting beneath her breath, Jessica realised she'd forgotten her umbrella. She could see it now, hanging on the back of the kitchen door in her one-bedroom flat. Pulling the collar of her jacket up as far as she could, she swung the shoulder bag up onto her head. It wouldn't help much, judging by the sheets of water now falling from the sky, but it was better than nothing.

Her quickened step soon turned into a jog as she continued along the rapidly darkening pavement. Although only mid-afternoon, the light was beginning to fade, and her previous good mood and buoyant thoughts about the future were deflating along with it. Reaching the end of the path, she burst out onto the main road and charged in the direction of the bus stop.

* * *

Time: 3.00 p.m.
Date: Saturday 11 April 2015
Location: Metropolitan Police HQ, London

Jack resumed the seat that he'd vacated only twenty-four hours before. Receiving a second summons to see the chief superintendent wasn't unusual, but that didn't necessarily mean it wasn't disconcerting. Dougie King had asked for daily updates, and he seemed to be sticking to it.

"I went to see Frank Tyler this morning." Jack thought he would get his position in early. "And the team are already analysing the previous investigation. We're covering a lot of old ground, but it needs doing. And regarding the body found yesterday, we're looking at CCTV from close to the scene and around White City Tube station. I'm also arranging to send everything through to Rachel Hunter."

"No ID yet, I take it?"

Jack grimaced. "No. Missing Persons was a dead end. But on the back of the press release yesterday, we've had some calls come in with potential names — DS Cassidy is following those up."

"And what about the journalist angle?" Dougie King handed Jack a mug of his finest Colombian coffee. "How are you handling that now it's reared its ugly head again?"

Jack's eyebrows twitched as he took hold of the mug. "You were aware of the journalist being involved in Frank's investigation?"

King nodded. "I was one of the select few, yes. There weren't many of us trusted with the information outside of the immediate investigation team." He took a sip from his mug. "What are your thoughts? Any misgivings at all?"

Jack hesitated, taking the opportunity to hide behind his coffee mug for a few moments and gather his thoughts. "Misgivings, sir? In what way would I have misgivings?"

"Just wondering if you'd given any thought to why she's been specifically targeted — again." The chief superintendent gave a faint shrug of his broad shoulders. "It's an unusual set of circumstances."

"It is that, sir. To be honest, I'm not quite sure what to make of it — I'm hoping to have another chat with Frank once he's had a chance to review all the paperwork."

"Frank's a good man. Is he well?" Dougie King relaxed back in his swivel chair, the leather creaking beneath his weight. "And his wife — Irene, isn't it?"

Jack paused, once again glad of the mug to hide his reaction. He wasn't quite sure how much other people knew about Frank's current state of health — cancer could be a particular lonely and personal journey, and he didn't want to speak out of turn. "He's doing OK, considering. Irene looks after him well."

"That's good to hear."

Jack eyed the chief superintendent over the rim of his mug, then took a surreptitious glance at his wrist. As much as he enjoyed Dougie King's company — and his coffee — he had places he needed to be, things he needed to be doing. Finding a suitable stand-in for Rachel Hunter being one of them. "Forgive me, sir, but I really should get going. Unless . . . ?" Jack caught the senior officer's eye, letting the man know that he wasn't daft. He hadn't been summoned here to talk about Frank Tyler's health or, indeed, the involvement of Lorna Henshaw. An update on how the new investigation was going could be done just as easily via email. There was something else on Dougie King's mind — Jack could see it buried between the lines on the man's forehead.

Chief Superintendent King placed his coffee mug down on his desk before he spoke. "There's been a development in the investigation into the Christchurch explosion."

Jack's eyebrows shot up. The Christchurch explosion? The one that had sent him tumbling to a fractured foot not three months before. Instinctively, he stretched his leg out beneath Dougie King's desk and flexed his toes. "Development? What kind of development?"

King paused for a beat, a concerned look crossing his face. "I've asked them to contact you direct, Jack — keep you in the loop, so to speak. If you don't already have an email, then expect one before the day is through."

"OK." The earlier intrigue in Jack's tone was now joined by an element of trepidation. "Any clue forthcoming? An email from who exactly?"

"I don't really think it's my place, Jack. You'll know about it soon enough. All I ask is that you don't let it sidetrack you — you need to focus on Operation Quicksand. If we have a second chance at getting this Central Line Killer — or whatever he's called these days — off the streets, then you need to concentrate on that."

"Naturally, sir."

As soon as Jack had drained his coffee, he made his excuses and headed back to his office. Once behind his desk, he woke up the computer monitor and noted there were thirty-seven new unread messages since the morning. He immediately dealt with fifteen by way of the delete button and, out of the remainder, he soon saw the one the chief superintendent had been referring to. It had come in just before midday, from Simon Peterson, the SIO down in Christchurch in Dorset who was heading up the investigation into the explosion at the Old Mill Road flats.

Jack skimmed through the first few paragraphs — merely Simon checking in with him and asking about his foot. It was the fourth paragraph that caught Jack's attention where Simon gave him a brief résumé of the forensic tests being carried out on the material used to detonate the bombs inside the flats.

Early tests suggest that the remote detonator and the explosive materials used at Old Mill Road were of the same type and consistency as previously seen in an explosion in 2010. Enquiries continue.

Jack scrolled down to the next paragraph, eyes widening as he digested the rest of Simon's message. The final paragraph summed it up.

The vast majority of the explosive material at Old Mill Road failed to detonate — a fact that we are at present keeping from the media. The official story is one of demolition material at the site being accidentally triggered. This will be the official line while we continue to investigate any connection with the earlier 2010 case. Your discretion is appreciated while the case is transferred to MI5. A case officer will no doubt be in touch.

Wow.
MI5.
Resting back in his seat, Jack tried to make sense of it all. He hadn't had much to do with the spooks before, but if what Simon was suggesting turned out to be true, then this could put a whole new spin on things.

One thing he did know for sure was that he needed to speak to Rob.

* * *

Time: 3.00 p.m.
Date: Saturday 11 April 2015
Location: HMP Wandsworth, London

Lindsay Jenkins rolled out of the bottom bunk. Although the walls of the Victorian jail were thick, he could easily hear the yells and jeers from the other inmates travelling along the landing; the wing was getting tetchy. It was day four of the enforced lockdown and a nervous unrest was building once more.

Jenkins tuned it out; he was too old and cranky these days to want to get involved, and experience told him it wouldn't bring about the end of the lockdown any quicker — in fact, it was more likely to extend it if things carried on the way they were. He knew the best course of action was to keep his head down.

Stepping across to the other side of the cell, he flicked the switch on the kettle. Scooping two large teaspoons of instant coffee into a plastic mug, he waited for the water to boil. Although he preferred to have sugar in his coffee, their stash was currently hidden away from prying eyes. Magee had been the one to find the false bottom in the desk drawer — and it made the perfect hiding place.

Sugar was a valuable commodity on the inside, more so now that smoking was banned. Cigarettes were still traded, of course, ban or no ban, alongside the seemingly inexhaustible supplies of cannabis and heroin. Drugs and prison went hand in hand. Spice or mamba was fast becoming many prisoners' method of escapism. But drugs and tobacco still needed to be smuggled in, which had varying success rates.

Sugar, on the other hand, was freely available. A surprisingly small backhander into the right palm could secure you a decent quantity from the prison kitchen. In itself, sugar was fairly innocuous — but in the hands of the right kind of prisoner, it could be lethal.

Napalming.

All you needed was boiling water and a quantity of sugar, and you had yourself your very own napalm bomb.

Jenkins tipped the boiling water onto the cheap coffee granules and stirred with a plastic spoon. He had witnessed several episodes of "napalming" back in Belmarsh and it was never a pretty sight, the victim's skin literally disintegrating before the eyes. As a consequence, many prisons limited the amount of sugar inmates could keep in their cells, performing unannounced cell searches from time to time — hence the more than healthy stash in the false-bottomed desk drawer.

As he stirred the murky brown liquid in his mug, Jenkins' gaze slid across towards the desk, a smile twitching at the corners of his mouth. As a seasoned prisoner — having spent more years than he could remember incarcerated in one prison or another — he always made a point of checking out the competition whenever he arrived somewhere new. Better to be forewarned as to the pecking order on the wing — find out who was in charge, who not to make an enemy of, and who to avoid. Magee's name had been fairly close to the top of all three lists, but Jenkins wasn't entirely sure why.

The man wasn't built like a mountain as some of the others were, although he did carry a few extra pounds more than he should. But he did have an explosive temper when the right buttons were pushed — which Jenkins had managed to do not long after being assigned the same cell. He touched his nose, the fracture now healing but the memory as vivid as ever.

The letters.

Abandoning his coffee, Jenkins pulled open the desk drawer. Magee had told him in no uncertain terms that the letters were out of bounds. Quite why that was, Jenkins didn't know and was in no position at the time to ask, with the blood still pouring from his nose.

Pulling out the bundle, held together by an elastic band, he sat the letters down on top of the desk. What was the man afraid of? Who cared if he had a bit of skirt on the outside that maybe the current girlfriend didn't know about? As far as Jenkins was aware the man wasn't married, so was free to do as he pleased. Maybe he had a string of pen pal lovers, all convinced that they were "the one". Or maybe it was boyfriends. Either way, Jenkins couldn't care less.

But it still intrigued him as to why the letters were off limits. The more he thought about it — and he'd had plenty of time to think about it during the extended lockdown — the more he wondered if there was something inside that he could exploit, something he could use to his advantage.

With at least another two hours until he might be taken out for some exercise, Jenkins was bored. And Magee was away seeing the quack with some cock and bull story about injuring his hand. Jenkins wouldn't put it past the man to have made it up just to get some extra time outside the cell.

Mind made up, Jenkins swallowed the rest of the cheap coffee and flicked off the rubber band. He slid the first letter out of its envelope and began to skim-read the contents. It didn't seem to be all that sensational, just someone checking in with him after Magee's trial. Jenkins felt a little deflated. He replaced the letter and pulled out the second. It was from the same person, someone who signed off with just the letter X. A quick check on the front of all the remaining envelopes revealed the same uniform handwriting. Maybe Magee didn't have a string of lovers after all; maybe it was just the one.

The contents of the second letter made his brow twitch, the third made it frown. By the time he had read all fifteen his eyes had almost popped out of his head. Knowing Magee could be back any second, he stuffed the letters back inside their envelopes, rebound them with the elastic band, and placed them back inside the drawer.

A grin crossed his unshaven face as he spooned more cheap coffee into his mug, mind racing. He had always known his cellmate to be a bit of a dark horse, but he'd never suspected him to be quite this dark.

Right on cue, the cell door opened, and Magee stepped back inside, hand bandaged. Jenkins took his coffee across to his bunk, stretching out on the thin mattress and turned to face the wall. He had no intention of confronting his cellmate with what he had just seen; there would be time enough for that.

But as he lay there, staring at the grey brickwork, all he could think about was . . . who was X?

***

Time: 3.05 p.m.
Date: Saturday 11 April 2015
Location: Cracknell Street, London

He wasn't sure he liked her hair that way, preferring the long blonde locks that had brushed her shoulders. He had watched her disappear into the hair salon with a pensive look on her pretty face, only to reappear ninety minutes later transformed.

And it wasn't just the hair.

There was a smile on her face that hadn't been there before, a lightness to her step. His gaze trailed her as she made her way out onto the main road. No doubt she would be making her way towards the bus stop on Beyton Road, just like she usually did. Rain splattered heavily against the van's windscreen just as he noticed her quicken her stride. It made him smile, watching her pull the bag up onto her head to ward off the downpour. With no umbrella and just a flimsy jacket on, she would be soaked through within seconds if she didn't find shelter.

He followed her at a distance — enough so she wouldn't sense his presence, but close enough not to lose sight of her. As predicted, she dashed out into the main street and without hesitation darted across the road in the direction of the bus stop.

Perfect.

He could see, even from this distance, that she was shivering. She would be putty in his hands.

Leaving her just enough time to reach the shelter, he pulled the van out into the slow-moving traffic, windscreen wipers on full to deal with the torrent of rain falling from the skies. He maintained a steady speed as he stopped at a set of traffic lights, glancing towards the passenger seat where the grey bandana lay next to the coil of thin wire. Not taking his eyes from the road ahead, he reached over and placed both items in the glove box while heading towards the bus shelter.

CHAPTER TWELVE

Time: 3.35 p.m.
Date: Saturday 11 April 2015
Location: Metropolitan Police HQ, London

DC Daniels replaced the phone's handset and shook his head. "I've managed to speak to three Tube workers from the 1998 investigation so far — but I can't find anything that they failed to tell DI Tyler and his team back then. None of them raised any red flags for me. Of those that I did manage to speak to, one was a train driver who'd been employed by the Underground for eighteen years. He had several medical issues which forced him to take early retirement. I can't detect any animosity about the end of his employment." Daniels pulled out another sheet of paper from the pile on his desk. "Another was dismissed for poor performance, bad timekeeping and failure to adhere to safety regulations."

Jack moved closer. "Any grievance at the dismissal?"

Daniels shook his head. "Nothing. He wasn't exactly complimentary about Transport for London, but I don't feel he had any deep-seated animosity that would lead to murder. He'd only worked on the Underground for a little over nine months, and quickly found a better job in another part of the country. He was quite open that he hadn't really given the Underground network much thought since."

Jack nodded. "OK, that sounds like a dead end."

"The last one I spoke to was very similar. Dismissed for gross misconduct but seems happy enough where he is today — I can't see it being a factor." Daniels tapped the sheet of paper in front of him. "There are a couple more I've left messages with, but the rest are proving difficult to trace after all this time."

It had been a long shot, but Jack was secretly hoping for better news, or at least a glimpse of a new line of investigation. But the tunnel seemed as dark as ever, no suggestion of a light at the end of it. "Good work, Daniels, at least it's a box we can say we've ticked. By all means follow up on any outstanding members of staff, but I think we can probably safely shelve that part of the investigation. Don't try to grow flowers in the desert." He turned towards the rest of the team. "There's an updated press release going out later this evening, so I have a feeling the calls to the hotline will multiply as a result. Amanda? What have you had so far?"

Cassidy swallowed another mouthful of her peppermint tea. "It's slow going at best. Most are crank calls as far as I can tell. Some people's idea of fun." She grimaced and sipped more tea. "But the next call could be the one we need."

Jack sighed, thinking of better ways the detective sergeant could be spending her time — but acknowledged she was probably right. The next call could be the one they'd been waiting for, steering them towards an ID for the victim. Without an ID, progress would be slow. "For the time being, I think you'll have to." He glanced up at the wall clock. "Time is getting on, though. Don't feel you need to stop all night. We can start again bright and early tomorrow."

Cassidy pulled her notepad towards her. "I'm happy to stay for a while, field some more calls."

"And I'll finish looking at the statements of the Underground staff," added Daniels. "It shouldn't take long."

"What about you, Cooper? How's the CCTV looking?"

DS Cooper swallowed the last of his energy drink then tapped his keyboard. "I've been logging registrations of cars and vans seen in the vicinity of Wheeler Street and White City Underground. Trying to see if any appear in both locations."

Jack's eyebrows hitched. "Anything?"

Cooper shook his head. "Not yet, boss, but there's a fair few more to cross-check. I'll stay on a bit tonight, now I'm on a roll."

Jack nodded his gratitude. He knew he should volunteer to stay late too, but the early start to go and see Frank Tyler was starting to catch up with him. Operation Quicksand looked to be stalling before it had even got going. The irony of the choice of name wasn't lost on him — they were on unstable ground, all right. He just hoped it wasn't going to suck them under.

About to resign himself to a couple more hours with the team, the chirp of an incoming text kicked that thought into touch.

* * *

Time: 4.10 p.m.
Date: Saturday 11 April 2015
Location: Manor Farm Road, London

Jessica stared wide-eyed up toward the ceiling of the van, heart pounding. What was happening? When she had come round, it had taken a moment or two before the fear hit her — then she found her hands bound behind her back, her feet strapped together at the ankles.

The van lurched around a corner, causing her to roll sideways. Panic-stricken, unable to move, she tried to regulate her breathing, made all the more difficult by the tape secured across her mouth. When the van straightened out again, she tumbled back and came to rest up against a roll of carpet. It smelled damp and musty.

How could she have been so stupid? Getting into his van like that? Did she have no sense? Only a short time before, she'd been almost skipping along the pavement towards the bus stop, revelling in her new-found freedom and release from his vile clutches. It had taken a while for it to register, but she now realised what a calculating manipulator he was. She'd had so many warnings up to now, choosing to ignore them all. Her sister had been right all along. So why had she let him suck her in again? Why had she let him give her a lift?

If she hadn't, she wouldn't be here.

Every fibre of her being screamed at her to ignore him when he'd pulled up at the bus stop — to tell him to leave her alone. But then she'd looked up at the sky and seen the thunderous clouds overhead, the sheets of rain already pelting the pavement — and the bus wasn't even in view yet. As much as she hated to admit it, the van looked warm and dry — and Tony could drop her much closer to her front door than the number 44 could. Plus, she had her new haircut to think of.

So, against her better judgment, she had let him talk her into it and she'd got in.

Tears pricked at the corners of her eyes as the van lurched around another corner. If only she could scream, kick out with her feet, bash her fists against the side of the van. Anything to alert someone to her predicament. But she was trussed up like a Christmas turkey, unable to make a sound.

It hadn't taken long after climbing into Tony's van for the argument to spark. He just couldn't help himself. Asking her where she'd been lately. Who she was seeing. She could see the jealous venom in his eyes intensifying by the second.

And then the atmosphere had changed — just as she knew it would.

If only she hadn't got into his van.

CHAPTER THIRTEEN

Time: 6.45 p.m.
Date: Saturday 11 April 2015
Location: Kettle's Yard Mews, London

"Beer?" Jack handed across the bottle of Peroni without waiting for a reply.

"Cheers." Carmichael took the beer and headed for the sofa, grinning when he saw Marmaduke curled up next to one of the cushions.

"Good to see the little fella still making himself at home. I always had you down as a cat man, Jack."

Jack didn't fancy asking what constituted a cat man, so decided to change the subject. Back at the station, he'd left the team finishing up with the CCTV and Tube worker investigations, and Cassidy still trawling through the crank calls about a potential ID for their victim. Jack didn't envy her job one bit.

The text from Rob suggesting a beer couldn't have come at a better time, the email from Simon Peterson still playing on Jack's mind. Seeing no reason to put it off, he decided to come straight to the point. "I'm guessing you heard the same news that I did — about the explosion?"

Carmichael gave a nod, taking a long pull on his beer. "I did. Still not quite sure what to make of it all, to be honest."

Jack had had to read the email from Simon several more times before it started to make any kind of sense — if it even did.

Early tests suggest that the remote detonator and the explosive materials used at Old Mill Road were of the same type and consistency as previously seen in an explosion in 2010. Enquiries continue.

Jack was well aware what enquiries the email was referring to, and no doubt Carmichael did, too — the 2010 car bomb that ended the life of the head of MI5, Charles Tindleman, Rob's adoptive father. Jack remembered the case well. The terror threat alert was immediately raised to the highest possible level — critical, which meant that an attack was highly likely in the near future — something that placed the whole country on a knife edge. The fact that the victim was Charles Tindleman added another complex layer to the subsequent investigation. This was no random target, no drive-by shooting or suicide bomber targeting the masses. This was deliberate; this was targeted — someone had wanted Charles Tindleman dead.

And then, it seemed, five years later they had tried to do the same to Jack.

"Since the shit hasn't yet hit the fan, I'm guessing those in charge are no closer to finding out who it was that wanted to blow you up?" Carmichael had already drained his first bottle, getting to his feet and heading to the kitchen for replenishments.

"Not yet."

Jack was prepared to lie to most people when the situation warranted it, but one person he couldn't lie to was Rob. The man had stood at Jack's side on plenty of occasions in the past and he deserved better than that. So, Jack had come clean about what led to the Old Mill Road explosion — telling Carmichael all about Ritchie Greenwood over a pie and a pint in a country pub as they made their way back from Knowles Farm earlier that year. Jack had still been hobbling around in his protective walking boot, still partially deaf from the force of the explosion. At the time, Carmichael had taken it all in his usual, unflustered stride.

The detective sergeant placed a second beer in front of Jack. "You planning on giving them a clue anytime soon? Mentioning Greenwood by name?"

It was a question Jack had asked himself plenty of times over the last three months. He'd known the minute it happened that Ritchie was responsible for planting the explosives that almost killed him, but the news that he was also connected to the car bomb that terminated the former head of MI5 was something new. If Jack passed on that kind of intelligence, it would lead to an avalanche of delicate and unwanted questions. The resulting can of worms that would be ripped open wasn't an enticing thought.

Ritchie Greenwood was a scalp the Met had been hunting for some time. Now the boss of the capital's biggest organised crime gang, if Jack's close affiliation with the man became common knowledge, his career would be on the line. Again. It wasn't something that necessarily concerned him — but this time it could be Rob's career at risk, too.

Jack eventually shrugged. "I don't plan on confessing all just yet, mate. But I might see if I can find him — Ritchie, that is. He's gone quiet since it happened, which isn't like him. He's not stupid, so I'm guessing he's keeping his head down somewhere. He must have known someone would make the connection to the car bomb eventually." Saying out loud that he intended to actively try and find Ritchie Greenwood almost put Jack off his beer.

Almost.

Instead, he sank the rest of his bottle and reached for the second. "I'll let you know if I hear anything. You intending to mention anything to Barbara?"

Carmichael grimaced. "I don't think that's my call, mate. She's done so well since Dad died. I remember the first few months after it happened, maybe even the first year — she was just so lost, a shadow of the woman she used to be. Losing him like that hit her really hard." He took an extra-large gulp from his beer. "But slowly she started to rebuild her life — a life without Dad. And she's so much stronger now. Her life has a purpose where it didn't have one before. Even so, I'm not sure she's strong enough for this kind of news. Not yet."

Jack had to agree. "Well, she won't hear anything about it from me, Rob. The spooks are taking over, so it'll be a closed shop from now on anyway."

Placing his beer bottle down, Carmichael pulled one of the pizza boxes across the coffee table, flipping open the lid and scooping up a slice of pepperoni. "Do you really think that was him at the farm?"

Jack and Carmichael hadn't really discussed what had happened at Knowles Farm, but Jack had thought about it numerous times since. "Do I think those pigs were feasting on James Quinn's remains?" He paused, giving a shrug as he picked up a slice of pizza. "Logic tells me it has to be him."

"That's not what I asked. You're not a hundred-per-cent sure?" Carmichael washed a mouthful of pizza down with some beer. "Quinn might still be out there?"

Jack could only shrug again. If Quinn wasn't dead, then it had been an elaborate ploy to make it believable. The man he knew had killed his mother in 1971, eaten by pigs. It was a fitting end — *if* it was true.

Jack decided to let the question lie for a while and, for the next fifteen minutes, they ate in silence, Jack surprised as to how hungry he was, happily devouring his share of the pizza. Stomach full, he settled back against the cushions, Marmaduke still slumbering next to him. Carmichael suggested another beer, but Jack waved the offer away. "I need a clear head for tomorrow, mate. Early start in the case."

Carmichael nodded and reached for his third. "I've booked leave for Monday, by the way."

"Monday?" A quizzical look crossed Jack's brow before it dawned on him. "The funeral. You're going, then?"

Carmichael gave a reluctant nod. "I wasn't going to, but then I thought maybe I should. Not to pay my respects or anything like that, you understand — that particular ship sailed and sank a long time ago. But I just thought maybe I should be there. At the end, so to speak."

"Makes sense."

"Plus—" Carmichael flipped the top off his beer bottle — "I might take the opportunity to see if I can have a poke about and track down Genete while I'm there. It's a long shot, I know, but . . ."

"No luck with the solicitors, then?"

Carmichael grimaced. "No. Client confidentiality or some such crap. They wouldn't tell me anything, very tight-lipped. Wouldn't even tell me if she was still in Liverpool."

"Well, it sounds like they probably have an address for her — they just won't tell you what it is. It's a start. It might mean she's traceable in other ways."

Carmichael nodded. "That's what I thought. I've put in a few calls to some of my social services contacts — and they in turn are putting in a word or two for me with their colleagues in the North West. I just want to know if I'm barking up the wrong tree."

"I take it you've done a trawl on socials?" Jack hated social media with a passion and steadfastly refused to be a part of it, but acknowledged it had its uses. Tracking people down was one of them.

"Done the usual, yes. If she's on there, she's not using the surname Carmichael. But Genete isn't a very common first name and I'm still coming up with a blank. I've a feeling she might have changed it completely."

"That makes things a bit tricky."

"You could say that. So, I thought what the hell — I'll go up and see what's what. Even if nothing comes of it, it might be good to go back and revisit a few memories. Put a few demons to bed at the same time. I've not been up that way for years."

Jack's own dalliance with revisiting his past hadn't ended all that well — the visit to his childhood home resulting in him being blown up and left for dead. He hoped Carmichael had better luck.

* * *

Time: 11.30 p.m.
Date: Saturday 11 April 2015
Location: Freemantle Buildings, Addison Street, London

As he pulled the ligature tighter, the woman's throat made a series of gurgling sounds as she fought to suck in air. It was a pointless exercise, he knew that much, but he always liked to see them try. If he hadn't already tied her hands together behind her back, she would be desperately trying to grasp the tight wire that was circling her neck. Instead, she was rendered helpless.

He smiled and tightened his grip further.

It surprised him how willingly they allowed him to bind their wrists and ankles, often putting up little or no resistance. It was the fear that did it; fear was such a potent emotion. He could see it in their eyes as they pleaded with him, as they begged him to let them go. One after the other, they would promise to do as he asked, allow him to do whatever he pleased — in the vain hope that he would spare them their lives.

The smile grew broader beneath his balaclava. He was never going to let them go, not from the very minute they crossed his path, no matter how much they pleaded or promised to please him. But they weren't to know that, and it amused him to think they had such a futile glimmer of hope to cling to.

The woman's gurgling had lessened a little, but he could still feel her body jerking against him — so he tightened the

125

ligature again. The wire was cutting into her pale skin now; the more she thrashed, the deeper it went.

It had crossed his mind on more than one occasion that he could drug them to make their bodies more pliable. That way he could take his time and do whatever he wanted to them, without risking them fighting back. But where was the fun in that? He wanted to feel them struggle beneath his grip, feel them lash out and try to wrench themselves free. The very thought made his breath quicken.

Pulling her body in close, he inhaled the scent of her shampoo, which reached him even through the thickness of his woollen balaclava. He wanted to see her face, now they were close to the end; needed to see the look in her eyes as the life was finally snatched away. It was a sight he never tired of.

It hadn't taken much to tack the jagged piece of mirror to the wall.

Pulling the woman tightly against him, he lifted his gaze to stare into his reflection, just as her pale, bulging face breathed its last. Eyes wide open in horror, the light within them eventually dimmed.

She was gone.

Breathing hard, more from excitement than physical effort, he lowered her slumped body to the floor. Beneath the thick balaclava, his skin felt hot and sweaty, but he knew he couldn't take it off just yet. He'd been doing this long enough to be careful about the traces he left behind.

Having already tied the rope in a loose hangman's knot, he slipped it easily over the woman's head and around her slender, limp neck. Removing the gag from her mouth, he tucked the fabric inside his pocket. There was no risk of a scream escaping her lips now — that, along with the air in her lungs, had been silenced forever.

Resting back on his heels for a moment, he savoured the peace. Death was usually a quiet affair; there was an oddly pleasant tranquillity that immediately followed the brutal act of taking the life of another. It was the act of dying that could sometimes be noisy.

Pulling on the rope, her limp body soon swung from the pole above the window. As much as he wanted to linger, now that the act of killing was over, he knew he needed to leave. There was one more place he needed to go before the sun came up. He'd chosen to make the kill here, this time, and not in the back of his van like the others; it was a departure from his usual routine that he wasn't entirely sure he was comfortable with. But sometimes change could be exhilarating.

The camera flashed in the dimness of the empty office space. Another one for his collection. Satisfied, he pulled the jagged piece of mirror from the wall and checked around for any sign of his presence. There was none. With one last, lingering look at her limp body as he left, he took the stairs two at a time and stepped out into the night.

CHAPTER FOURTEEN

Time: 4.15 a.m.
Date: Sunday 12 April 2015
Location: Rougham Street, London

Predictably, sleep had evaded her once again. Even a herbal sleeping tablet along with her night-time hot chocolate had failed to help her to drift off. Each time she closed her eyes, all she could think about was *him* — and when the next missive would appear on the doormat. Which was how she found herself sitting halfway down the stairs in the early hours of the morning, waiting.

From her vantage point, she had a clear view of the front door.

And the letterbox.

She couldn't see anything through the mottled glass, outside still dark with the sun not yet risen. And she knew watching the doormat was a bad idea, only feeding her anxiety, but she couldn't stop herself. Was this going to happen every night? Would she toss and turn for hours, unable to close her eyes for fear of what she might see in her dreams?

Another envelope.

Another victim.

Shivering, Lorna pushed herself to her feet. She willed the strength to return to her limbs, making her way along the hallway towards the kitchen, where she leaned up against the worktop. There was no point returning to bed now — she was exhausted, but sleep wasn't the answer. Blinking through the tiredness, she reached forward to switch on the kettle. A cup of strong coffee was what she needed. Maybe more than one.

As she busied herself getting a cup and saucer from the overhead cupboard, she wondered if she was worrying over nothing. Perhaps she had overreacted and there wouldn't be any more white envelopes. The first might have been a one-off, just a copycat trying their luck — the killer might not strike again.

With her new-found sense of inner calm, Lorna popped two slices of bread into the toaster while the kettle boiled. She may as well start her day, not let the disrupted start to the morning go to waste. As the weather reports for the coming day weren't very promising, with a risk of heavy, thundery showers striking at any moment, she decided today would be a day to get things done indoors. There was a list of jobs as long as her arm that needed doing, and with nothing else to distract her, she set about preparing a plan while she got butter and jam from the fridge.

After a round of toast and jam she felt better and, even though it was still only half past four, she decided to tackle the first job on her list — cleaning out the fridge. She had been retired for some time now, which gave her plenty of free time, but there were always some jobs that never seemed to get done, no matter how much time you had on your hands — cleaning out the fridge being one of them. In the end, it wasn't all that bad and didn't take long. She threw away some out-of-date pâté that had been lurking at the bottom of one of the salad drawers, and discovered a packet of feta cheese that she'd forgotten was there.

After cleaning the fridge, she set about changing the batteries in the kitchen wall clock. For the last five weeks it had been nine fifteen all day long. It was such a simple job, but another she had continually put off.

With two jobs now deleted from her mental to-do list, she poured herself another cup of filter coffee and savoured the velvet texture as it slid down her throat. She resisted the urge to glance back over her shoulder and check the doormat. She couldn't allow herself to be held to ransom like this — it had already ruined one night's sleep, she couldn't let it haunt her all day, too. The police had yet to return to install the cameras — maybe when they did, she would be able to relax a little.

Energy and purpose renewed, she pulled the egg basket toward her and had a peek inside.

Six eggs. Perfect.

Flicking on the radio, Lorna hummed along to James Bay's "Hold Back the River" while getting the rest of the ingredients out of the cupboards. She fancied a spot of baking — maybe a sponge cake and then a quiche to use up the feta she'd found in the fridge earlier.

She had barely started weighing out the ingredients when she heard the letterbox flap.

* * *

Time: 6.05 a.m.
Date: Sunday 12 April 2015
Location: Herne Bay, Kent

Jack had been true to his word — hard copies of the 1996 and 1997 investigations had arrived late yesterday afternoon. Frank had started to study them as soon as the courier had left, but tiredness soon got the better of him. So, instead he'd risen early and taken himself downstairs to the conservatory while Reenie slumbered on.

He often woke early these days, the painkillers only good for a short period overnight, so he took his usual position in the recliner, swallowing some more tablets as he started reading. It hadn't taken long for him to begin to recall the detail surprisingly well — a series of sex assaults across Yorkshire, spanning ten months. He remembered the team had weighed up the potential link to the Central Line Killer case at the time but had just as quickly discounted it. The exact reason for that escaped him right now, but it filled him with unease just the same.

The ferocity of the sex attacks in Yorkshire were similar in nature to the murders in the capital but, unlike the Yorkshire attacker, they had no physical description of the Central Line Killer — there had been no survivors, no witnesses. A crude E-fit had eventually been circulated, from a very dubious sighting, but it bore little resemblance to the Yorkshire sex offender.

Frank felt an unwelcome chill that had nothing to do with the open kitchen window. They had clearly come to the conclusion that it wasn't the same person, but had that been a startling error of judgment on his part? Had it merely led to more attacks, and then ultimately more murders? Frank swallowed, his throat dry, and continued reading the file.

He remembered contacting the DI heading up both investigations in Yorkshire — a man by the name of Gareth Bell. Although they'd never met in person, Frank wondered if the man shouldered the same heavy burden that he himself did — the weight of a failed investigation.

The first sexual assault took place in September 1996 and the perpetrator was almost caught in the act. He fled the scene after getting disturbed — the woman's screams bringing residents out of their houses nearby.

The second attack was in November in Huddersfield. A third followed in December in Hebden Bridge. There was then a break until early February of the following year — a young woman attacked in Harrogate. Two assaults in Ripon followed in April and May, with the final attack recorded in July in Whitby.

It took Frank the best part of two hours to finish reading all the summaries, witness statements and other evidence that had been collated, after which time Irene appeared with a plate of toast and honey, plus one of his build-up milkshakes — along with his morning medication.

Placing the paperwork on the floor by the side of the recliner, he took hold of the plate and glass. From the aroma, the milkshake was banana flavour this time. He felt his stomach recoil. He didn't have the stomach for breakfast these days, but knowing Irene worried about him when he didn't eat, he nibbled at a slice of toast to please her.

The bread stuck in his throat, so he washed it down with some of the milkshake. Dropping the half-eaten toast back on his plate, he leaned forward and scooped up the 1998 papers for the Central Line Killer. He was increasingly sure the answer had to be buried in there somewhere. Jack might have been full of praise about the quality of the investigation, but Frank knew it hadn't been pristine.

And if there was indeed a mistake hidden in among the paperwork, Frank wanted to be the one to find it. He might be rather skinny and weak these days, the cancer eating away at him day by day, but he would shoulder whatever burden came next. He could take the criticism if it came lumbering his way — what was the worst that could happen? He was dying anyway.

With a renewed burst of energy, he opened the 1998 file once again, feeling that he owed it to each victim to pull the case apart at the seams, getting to the bottom of it once and for all — even if it was the last thing he ever did.

Sadly, he knew it probably would be.

* * *

Time: 8.20 a.m.
Date: Sunday 12 April 2015
Location: London

Pinning the freshly printed photograph onto the wall, he stepped back to admire his work. This one had given him a lot of pleasure, that unmistakable thrill when the last breath was squeezed from her body. Seventeen years had only deepened his desires, which were now reawakened from their enforced slumber. He felt the familiar yearning for the thrill of the kill more than ever.

Settling into the solitary armchair in the corner of the sparsely furnished room, he reached for the glass of whisky he'd already poured, savouring the taste as it hit his tongue. It was early, but time meant nothing to him right now. He needed a palate cleanser, something to refresh him before moving on to the next.

Knowing he had a while to wait, he poured another generous couple of inches into the base of the tumbler and, as he did so, his eyes strayed to the bundle of letters stacked up next to the bottle. They'd been stowed away in the cupboard beneath the stairs for some time and he wasn't altogether sure why he'd chosen now to dig them out again. Placing the tumbler back on the side table, he pulled the bundle onto his lap.

An odd feeling fluttered in the pit of his stomach. There were twenty-three letters in total, the first arriving in late January 1998. That first letter stuck in his memory so fiercely he could almost recite it word for word. A second followed not long afterwards, and then a third. Each one feeding his ever-increasing desires. For the first six months of that year, the letters still came. Three in March, two in April, three more in May and then four in June.

Then there had been nothing for what seemed like an eternity, but it could only have been a matter of weeks. He remembered the mixed emotions that raged through him as he waited, the anxiety building and threatening to overwhelm him.

When the next letter arrived, relief flooded in — but his elation was short-lived when he realised it was nothing more than his own letter returned to him, recognising his own neat handwriting on the front in an instant. Wondering if it had been a mistake, an error at the sorting office, he'd written another, carefully printing the name and postal address on the front.

Then he'd waited — again.

The letter was returned to sender eight days later.

So, he'd sent another — and the same thing happened.

And another.

And another.

Four more letters were returned, the final one landing in December that year.

He then struck up the courage from somewhere to make the call — only to be told by a disinterested voice on the other end of the line that sending more letters would be a fruitless exercise and he should stop.

That had been early 1999 and he'd spent much of the next twelve months in limbo. The compulsion to write more letters was almost too much, but he knew he couldn't take the disappointment if they were returned to him unopened.

The idea for the murders had come to them towards the end of 1997, over a drunken Christmas alcohol binge. A meticulous plan soon developed, using London Underground stations as a smokescreen. The stations themselves meant nothing; nothing more than a way to tie the police, and the media, up in knots. When Ellis was arrested, the man had assumed the plan would be incarcerated alongside him.

He gave a throaty laugh as he sunk a mouthful of the whisky. Ellis being imprisoned had given him the surge in confidence he'd needed to go it alone. He didn't need the man any more, and he certainly proved that once he'd started to put the plan into action.

And here he was, seventeen years later.

He remembered the millennium coming and going, nothing more than an overhyped damp squib in the end. The world had kept on turning just as it always had, and the next fifteen years all seemed to roll into one. To begin with he'd wallowed in his own self-pity, feeling bereft; it really felt like a bereavement. The lack of contact had forged a massive hole in his life, a hole that he'd done his best to fill with a mixture of drink and drugs.

To some extent he was successful. But as the years passed by, drink and drugs were no longer enough for him — the hole slowly deepening each day. After a while he'd left it all behind.

To begin with, the Spanish coast had done well to satisfy his complex desires. By targeting those that wouldn't be missed — itinerant workers or solo travellers — his growing hunger was sated. As his confidence grew, he widened his net to Southeast Asia. Managing to survive on a handful of cash-in-hand jobs, it didn't take long for any number of solo backpackers to cross his path.

One such backpacker had been Imogen. A pretty thing, full of life and wonder at what the world had to offer. As soon as he'd heard her name, memories of his time at Great Easton Secondary School had cascaded uncontrollably through his head. They'd had the same sandy blonde hair, the same peppering of freckles on unblemished skin.

Perfection.

He'd enjoyed ending her life the most, adding another picture to his growing gallery, but the call to return home that followed soon became too great.

Home.

Now he was here, he knew he needed something bigger to satisfy him; the desires infiltrating his thoughts on a daily basis, sparked by Imogen and the memories she stoked, were becoming much harder to control.

He tossed the bundle of envelopes back onto the side table and swallowed the rest of the whisky. It was no use going back over old ground; that was the past. He was the master of his own destiny — making his own choices, his own decisions.

And now he was back, he felt stronger than ever.

Glancing back up at the wall opposite, he caught sight of the time from the wall clock and smiled.

It was still too early, but he could wait.

His time would come.

* * *

Frank rested his head back against the recliner and sighed. As far as trips down memory lane went, this wasn't one he'd enjoyed all that much. During the last few months, when he and Reenie had finally acknowledged that his time left on this planet was limited, they'd started to reminisce about the past — dragging out photo album after photo album, reliving times gone by captured on film.

The albums were abundant with memories — notably their wedding day, the births of their children, then the christenings and birthdays that inevitably followed. Page after page of Christmas celebrations and summer holidays caught on camera, each set of pictures bringing a smile to their faces, and occasionally the odd tear, too. He knew Reenie had found it hard, her face damp with salty tears by the end of the evening.

But thinking back to 1998 had been a wholly different affair, with certainly no smiles to be had.

Frank had picked apart the investigation several times now and was reassured that they hadn't missed anything blindingly obvious. Every step had been detailed, every lead followed through. They just hadn't had a break.

Then he'd turned his attention back to the Yorkshire sexual assault cases, again questioning whether he had been right to dismiss a connection so quickly. As he read the evidence through once more, he still couldn't see it. There had been a piece of wire found close to the attack on Trace Manning in Harrogate, and the attacker had made a crude attempt at strangulation. But that was it. The wire couldn't be linked to the victim and gave up no forensic detail. Similarly, the piece of grey material found close to Gail Colman, the Central Line Killer's first victim in 1998, couldn't be forensically connected. It could have come from anywhere — the crime scene was a disused warehouse, after all. So, rightfully or wrongfully, Frank had shelved that line of investigation.

The question now raking through his head was, was he right to do so? But if the case landed on his desk again today, in the absence of any forensic evidence linking them together, he was sure he would end up making the same decision.

It didn't exactly offer him much comfort.

He could still be wrong.

Reaching for the painkillers left out for him, he washed them down with the remains of the milkshake. The tablets often made him drowsy, but the pain was eating into him more and more now, and he needed to rest.

As he swallowed, he thought about the other matter that had pricked his conscience as soon as he'd begun re-reading the paperwork.

Lorna Henshaw.

The killer's use of the journalist in 1998 had been unusual to say the least. Frank hadn't seen anything like it before, nor since. Quite why she had been involved hadn't made much sense to him back then, and it still didn't now.

With the painkillers duly swallowed, he reached over to the small side table and picked up his notepad. He'd been listing all the things that sprung into his mind as he read the case notes again, the issues that bothered him, things he wanted to talk to Jack about.

One such item was Lorna Henshaw.

Frank took a pen and wrote her name down in capital letters, underlining it twice.

* * *

Time: 2.30 p.m.
Date: Tuesday 8 September 1998
Location: Metropolitan Police HQ, London

"She's downstairs in interview room three." DC McGregor held the incident room door open. "I've given her a coffee. She's quite shaken up."

Detective Inspector Frank Tyler nodded, slipping on his jacket as he followed the detective constable out into the corridor. "OK, I'll go and have a chat with her. While I'm gone, can you and DS Trafford go out and arrange to speak with the family of Lynn Jaggard again? There's a couple of follow-up questions I'd like to ask. Trafford has the details."

"Sure, will do."

With McGregor heading in the opposite direction, Frank made his way down the two flights of stairs to the row of interview rooms on the ground floor. A dull ache began to pound at his temples, not helped by the three black coffees he'd consumed for breakfast that morning, one after the other. Reenie had offered to make him something more nutritious, but he'd waved the offer away and told her to go back to bed. A 5 a.m. start for one of them was enough.

Frank pushed the door of interview room three open and tried to plaster his face with a suitably welcoming smile. It wasn't easy. Lorna Henshaw was starting to unnerve him.

"Miss Henshaw," he breezed, shutting the door behind him. "Good afternoon. Good of you to come back."

Lorna Henshaw smiled hesitantly, her hands circling a polystyrene cup of mud-coloured liquid. "It's no problem, Inspector. I want to help in any way I can."

Frank pulled a plastic bag from his pocket, setting it down on the table before taking a seat opposite. "Talk me through again how this one came about." He turned the bag to face the journalist, noting how the woman's hands trembled as her eyes lowered to the table.

Inside the evidence bag was the latest communication from what the media were now calling the Central Line Killer. There were now five such missives on the evidence log, including this one — and five dead women. Frank and his team were working fifteen-, sixteen-hour days, seven days a week, and they had precious little to show for it — something that the bosses up above were haranguing Frank about at every available opportunity.

The pressure was on to find the killer before five dead women became six, but Frank had run out of ideas. He couldn't just pull a suspect out of thin air, as much as he might want to. The case was breaking him, beating him even, and it wasn't a feeling he enjoyed. No matter how many hours they spent sifting through the evidence, re-evaluating every item, the identity of the killer remained elusive, out of their grasp. Frank couldn't even use the excuse that the trail had gone cold — there had never really been a trail to follow in the first place. Other than the connection to the Central Line, there appeared to be nothing linking the victims to each other. Nothing that they could latch on to and see where it went.

Nothing, that was, except for Lorna Henshaw.

For some reason, a reason they had yet to work out, the killer had chosen her to be involved.

The question hammering inside Frank's skull was: *why?*

He watched the journalist prise her fingers away from the coffee cup, tentatively drawing the plastic evidence bag towards her. Wide eyes, a little red-rimmed, blinked downwards. Frank shifted a little in his seat, watching the woman's every move. Most people had heard of Lorna Henshaw — she was a relatively well-known name in the murky world of investigative journalism, but it wasn't until this case that their paths had crossed. And she wasn't quite what Frank had expected — smaller and quieter, maybe even timid. Certainly no Kate Adie.

As Frank continued to observe her from his side of the table, she seemed to shrink before his eyes. "Take your time," he nudged. "There's no rush." *Except there is*, he wanted to add. Time was something they really didn't have. "Anything you can tell us could potentially be helpful."

Lorna glanced up and attempted a smile, but Frank soon noted her bottom lip starting to quiver.

"Sorry," she breathed. "This is all so horrifying. I don't really know where to start." She paused, lip quivering some more. "I think I've told you everything I can."

Frank settled back in his seat, arms folded across his chest, not taking his eyes from her for a single second. "Tell me again."

* * *

It was true — Lorna Henshaw had given them quite a detailed account of how each of the five envelopes had so far ended up on her doormat. But what she hadn't given them was a credible explanation as to why.

Frank didn't believe in random coincidence or chance. Not when it came to police work — and definitely not when it came to murder. The journalist's apparent stalling was starting to niggle him. He had spent enough time in the interview room by now to trust his instincts — and he could see Lorna Henshaw was feeling uncomfortable. It could, of course, just be the setting — the situation she found herself in — but, right now, Frank didn't feel as though he entirely trusted her.

"Of course," she replied, lowering her hands to her lap. "This one arrived, like I said before, on Friday morning. I got up in the night for a glass of water, and it wasn't there then. When I went back downstairs at eight o'clock, there it was." The journalist frowned. "But you already have the camera footage, don't you? The cameras set up outside the house?"

Frank nodded. "We do. It shows the Royal Mail van outside your property on Friday morning, the postman delivering a bunch of letters at 7.32 a.m."

"So . . . ?" Lorna frowned again. "I'm not sure I understand what else I can tell you. As soon as I saw it on the mat, I called you. I didn't open it — I didn't even touch it."

"And you're sure there was nothing else before this — no other contact from the killer? No suspicious phone calls? No one hanging around your house or following you home? No contact other than these envelopes?"

The journalist shook her head. "No, nothing. Just the envelopes."

"Have you given any more thought as to who might want to target you? I know we've touched on this before. Any articles or investigations that might have sparked someone's interest in you?"

Lorna sighed, her lip still trembling. "I've thought of nothing else. I gave you a list of all the high-profile investigations

I've been involved in in recent years, but it would be impossible to prise apart every single one."

Frank had to agree. One line of enquiry they had been working on was looking for someone Henshaw may have offended during the course of her reporting career — but the team had very quickly become bogged down in a media quagmire. Lorna Henshaw was a prolific investigative journalist, and the very nature of her job meant she stamped on quite a few toes, grinding many into the dust. It was a line of enquiry they had quickly abandoned, which then led Frank to the more unnerving conclusion — that maybe the journalist wasn't being entirely truthful.

"Have you ever worked on a story involving the London Underground? Or any other metro service anywhere in the world?"

Lorna puffed out her cheeks and exhaled. "Nothing that really springs to mind, no. I did do a small article on the sarin attacks in Tokyo in 1995 — then followed it up with a series of smaller articles investigating whether London's transport network would ever be susceptible to a similar attack. Would that count?"

"Possibly. Were you critical of the Underground system at all? Point any fingers at anyone?"

"Not to my knowledge, no. As I recall, my conclusion was that although any transport network had its flaws, London's was safe in comparison to many."

"No other articles in relation to London?"

The journalist shrugged. "I did do a small piece as a junior reporter on the ten-year anniversary of the King's Cross fire. So that would have been in 1997. But it was just straightforward journalism. I didn't say anything controversial — at least nothing that wasn't already being mentioned by all the other newspapers at the time."

Frank nodded, making a mental note to check up on both. It was another long shot and, if he was honest, he was becoming less convinced that Henshaw's media background had any part to play in this. "What about your personal life? Anything we need to be aware of?" It had occurred to him that maybe they were looking at this from the completely wrong angle — and that the victims weren't the intended targets. They were merely collateral damage. Maybe the *real* target was sitting right in front of him.

"My what?" Lorna's eyebrows shot up.

"Personal life," repeated Frank. "Husband? Lover? Anyone jilted at the altar?"

Colour flooded the journalist's cheeks. "No jilted lovers, Inspector — I can assure you of that. I've never been married and haven't been in a relationship with anyone since 1994. Does that answer your question?"

Frank detected an edge to Henshaw's tone. "More than adequately, thank you."

"Well, if that's all, I really need to get back to work."

"Of course." Frank plastered another smile onto his face as he got to his feet. "Don't let me keep you."

Once he had shown the journalist out of the building, Frank bounded up the stairs, two at a time, and burst into the incident room. DC McGregor looked up, somewhat startled.

"McGregor, get the rest of the team together. I want to establish how feasible it might be for our journalist friend to have sent those envelopes to herself."

* * *

Time: 9.15 a.m.
Date: Sunday 12 April 2015
Location: Herne Bay, Kent

Frank prised open his eyelids, squinting at the early morning sun that was now trying to slant in through the patio doors. His mouth still felt dry, his throat a little tender — no doubt he'd been snoring as he napped. Returning the recliner to its upright position, he reached for the glass of water Reenie had set out for him while he'd been asleep. Glancing at his watch, he noted he'd only been out for half an hour or so. Blinking away the tiredness, he swallowed the water.

Lorna Henshaw.

The bloody woman was haunting him in his dreams now.

Frank recalled asking his team to dig further into the journalist's background, including whether she could have sent the envelopes to herself, but nothing bore any fruit. He still struggled with the feeling that she was more involved than she was letting on but, after a while, he tried to put it down to his general mistrust of most people that crossed his path. It was a personality trait only Reenie seemed to fully understand.

But here he was again, some seventeen years later, having the same thoughts.

Sighing, he replaced the glass and let his gaze travel back to the stack of paperwork on the coffee table. All he had were a bunch of suspicions, and mostly unfounded ones at that. The idea that the Central Line Killer was active again was affecting him more than he was willing to let on. Although he knew it was irrational, he couldn't shake the feeling that he was partly responsible. He had failed to find the killer back in 1998 — that was a fact — and although it didn't sit right with him, he had learned to come to terms with it over the years, to come to terms with his failings as a detective. Nobody was perfect, and that included him.

But now another woman had died.

Once again, Lorna Henshaw's face sprang to the forefront of his mind. Before he could talk himself out of it, he reached for his mobile and scrolled down to Jack's number. He might have let the killer slip through his fingers the first time around — he wasn't prepared to let it happen again.

CHAPTER FIFTEEN

Time: 8.30 a.m.
Date: Sunday 12 April 2015
Location: Rougham Street, London

Jack took the small piece of folded paper in his hands. Another Underground map — this time with Mile End Underground circled. "And this came when?"

"Just before five thirty this morning. By courier, I think." Lorna Henshaw's face was ashen. "They'd gone by the time I reached the door, but I think it was a motorbike — I heard what sounded like one, but I can't be sure. It was still dark."

Jack slid the map back inside the envelope. "We're already checking out the vicinity around Mile End Underground."

"There's more." The journalist bit her lip, and if her face could have drained of more colour then it would have. "This came, too." She pulled another piece of paper out of her pocket, her hand shaking. "It told me not to tell the police . . . but what am I supposed to do? I don't want to be involved in this any more. Why is he targeting me like this?"

Jack cast his eyes down to the second piece of paper.

Article in the Daily Courier by 16.00 — or she dies.

Jack's eyes widened. "This is new, right? You didn't get this type of message with the others back in 1998? Or the one two days ago?"

The journalist shook her head. "No. Nothing like this before." She swallowed and looked away, voice quivering. "I don't want to be involved," she repeated.

"I appreciate that, Miss Henshaw, but I'm afraid that you are." Jack was aware his tone sounded harsher than he would have liked. Rob had left at a reasonable hour last night, but Jack had still slept poorly. Not only had the current investigation been coursing around inside his head, he also couldn't stop thinking about Ritchie Greenwood and his involvement in the murder of Charles Tindleman. The revelation about the explosives used at Old Mill Road had sat uncomfortably with him since reading Simon's email. The resultant recipe had been another sleepless night.

At 5 a.m. he'd joined Marmaduke on the window ledge for a morning coffee and had arrived at the station an hour later. The early morning briefing left the team continuing to follow up on possible IDs for their victim and working through more statements from disgruntled Tube workers from the 1998 investigation and also CCTV. Jack wasn't convinced any of it would help.

He tried to place a more sympathetic look on his face but knew he had failed. "Sorry, I know it's not exactly what you want to hear."

Tears streaked the journalist's cheeks. "How can I possibly publish an article? I'm *retired*. I don't want this poor woman's life in my hands like this."

Jack took a breath and tried to inject some reassurance into his tone. "Please don't think you're responsible for any of this. This woman — whoever she turns out to be — I'm really sorry to say it, but I feel it's already too late for her. What you choose to do, or not to do, will likely have no real impact."

"She's *dead*?" The horror in Lorna's voice made it tremble.

Jack nodded, solemnly. "That's my feeling, yes. I'm sorry."

The journalist's face began to slacken. "I'm not sure that makes me feel much better."

"Possibly not. But we're already following up on this, don't worry." He waved the envelope in the air. "If she *is* alive, we'll do our best to get to her in time."

"So why involve me at all? What does he *want*?"

"Of that I'm not too sure." It was an unusual step for any killer to take, especially a prolific one like the Central Line Killer. But Jack had no answers. "It could simply be the killer wanting to get inside your head — trying to get someone to sympathise with him. He might want you be his voice." He gave a shrug. "I'm hypothesising. I really have no idea."

"So, what should I do about the note?" Lorna gestured towards the paper still in Jack's hand. "The article, I mean? Shouldn't we act on it to make him think he's in control, calling all the shots?" She gave a sheepish look, a small amount of colour returning to her cheeks. "Sorry — I clearly watch too many crime dramas on TV."

Jack started to head towards the door. "We might need to consider going down that route, yes. It won't be easy, though — you don't work for the *Daily Courier* any more."

"You're right." The journalist followed Jack along the hallway. "*I* don't work for them — but I know someone who does."

* * *

Time: 8.45 a.m.
Date: Sunday 12 April 2015
Location: London

He knew he should probably be doing something more constructive than just sitting and waiting, staring at his phone — but the whisky had dulled his senses a little now. There were still some hours to go until the four o'clock deadline he'd set, but maybe the article would go out earlier than planned. The thought gave him a renewed thrill and he refreshed the news feed for the popular twenty-four-hour news channel of the *Daily Courier* once again.

He had no reason to suspect the journalist wouldn't do as he'd instructed. She'd been a useful pawn in his games up to now — why would that suddenly change? Of course, there might be another scenario — they might find the woman before the paper had a chance to print the story. And if they did — would they still publish his carefully chosen words?

With the bottle now empty, he leaned back in the armchair and gazed once more at the collection on the wall opposite.

His girls.

He owned them.

Possessed them.

Maybe he loved them in his own way, but love was a concept he knew little about.

When he'd read the various newspaper reports that flooded the press, it did nothing but fascinate him. Details about the families they'd all left behind, the friendships left in tatters, relationships torn apart. They had all led such intricate lives, with so many people touched by their disappearance.

It wasn't something he could easily relate to. He had no family of note — none that he wished to acknowledge anyway — and no one who would readily notice his absence. He had parents, obviously — but whether they were alive or dead he didn't much care; his mother left when he was just a baby. And he'd had no siblings. So, it was always only ever himself; just him, alone in the world.

Always alone.

Except for Ellis Magee.

Ellis was the only person he ever came close to calling a friend. No one else; just Ellis.

School had been particularly difficult, never a place where he'd felt truly comfortable. If the other kids had left him alone, he would have navigated it a lot better — but, of course, they didn't leave him alone for a second. The overweight, glasses-wearing weird kid with no friends, who wore third-hand clothes and lived on the wrong side of town — they were like bees around a honey pot.

He could handle it when it was just the name-calling — able to shut it out, pretend it wasn't happening. He'd experienced it before at other schools for as long as he could remember, so it wasn't exactly a surprise, but then the seasoned school bullies got wind of him — and the verbal taunting soon turned physical.

If it hadn't been for Ellis, he wasn't sure how things might have turned out.

* * *

Time: 10.45 a.m.
Date: Monday 16 March 1987
Location: Great Easton Secondary School, North London

The kicks came thick and fast now, most of them landing on his sides and back, the occasional one connecting with his sprawling legs. He tried his best to draw his knees up to his chest, to curl up tightly into a ball and cover his head with his hands, but he was fighting a losing battle. He felt the blood start to trickle from his nose, his ears ringing from the repeated blows.

Then, as if that wasn't enough, along with the kicks came the jeers.

'Fatty.'
'Four-eyes.'
'Weirdo.'
'Spotty.'
'You stink like a pig.'

He didn't really know why they picked on him. He might be a little overweight, but there were plenty of other kids in the school that were fatter than he was. He wore glasses — so what? So did some of those who were standing there kicking the living daylights out of him.

Did he smell? He wasn't sure. Maybe he did, especially when he'd had one of his accidents, but he washed every day — mostly — and his father dumped him in the bath every Sunday, whether he needed it or not.

More kicks, more taunts.

Clasping his hands together over his head, he scrunched up into an even tighter ball and willed the onslaught to end. He knew it would eventually — even bullies had a limit and usually an even shorter attention span. But the kicks and punches seemed to go on forever and, just when he thought he couldn't stand it any longer, the unmistakable sound of the bell for the end of morning break rang out.

A sudden welcome silence filled his ears where, only moments ago, they'd been bursting with the thudding sound of boots on flesh. As he tried to regain control of his ragged breathing, wondering how many fresh bruises and cuts he would have to explain away when he got home, he heard a voice speak.

"Stop whimpering, fatso, and get up."

To begin with he wasn't sure what to do. The voice didn't sound all that friendly, and his first instinct was to curl up some more and brace himself for the next round of kicks and thumps. But before he could make a decision, he felt a hand on his shoulder pulling him up into a sitting position.

"Big kid like you should be able to take care of yourself."

Squinting through half-closed eyelids, he recognised the round face staring back at him. Ellis Magee — one of the most notorious bullies Great Easton had to offer. He swallowed, a fresh wave of trepidation building. He wasn't sure what was worse — facing Ellis on his own with no one else around to come to his aid, or the baying crowd of cowards that had been here just moments before.

Ellis's hand was still gripping his shoulder, and moments later he felt himself being dragged to his feet.

149

"There you go — wasn't so bad, was it?"

"N . . . no." He didn't know what else to say. "Thanks."

The bully brushed the compliment aside. "You need to toughen up, mate. These kids are a pain in the arse, but you let them walk all over you. Let them do it once, they'll do it again. You need to show them who's boss."

"But . . . how . . . ?" He felt Ellis's hand on his elbow, guiding him across the playground towards the main school building.

"Do exactly what I say, and they'll never bother you again."

So, without much option, he'd done just that.

* * *

Time: 8.55 a.m.
Date: Sunday 12 April 2015
Location: London

Ellis Magee.

He looked once again at the pile of letters on the side table. The boy had saved his life, no question about it, and from that day on, things were different at Great Easton Secondary School. But they were an unusual pairing — the biggest, hardest school bully that ruled the corridors and play-grounds, with the socially awkward overweight kid who barely said boo to a sparrow, never mind a goose.

But no one ever dared to question it.

The other kids still picked on him — Ellis couldn't be with him every second of the day, especially as they were never in the same classes — but it was never with the same intensity as before. Everyone feared Ellis Magee and didn't want to beat the living crap out of his new best friend, however odd the twosome appeared to be.

Opening a fresh bottle of whisky, he poured another drink and glanced once more at his phone. Still way too early. He rose from the chair and moved across to the map. It excited him to see so many places already circled — but equally he knew there were so many more still to come. Anticipation started to build, which he tried to dampen with a mouthful of the cheap whisky. He hoped Ellis would approve of his methods, even be proud of his achievements. But, at the same time, he cared little these days.

He turned his attention back to the map. He could try and take her tonight — he knew exactly where she would be, and when. But it would mean deviating from his plan and relying on an element of luck instead.

No — tomorrow would be soon enough.

Tomorrow she would be his.

* * *

Time: 8.55 a.m.
Date: Sunday 12 April 2015
Location: Rougham Street, London

Jack sat in the driver's seat of the Mondeo, teeth clenched.

I should have known.

The minute Lorna Henshaw said she knew someone who could help them out with the article, Jack knew exactly whose name would be on her lips.

Jonathan bloody Spearing.

Stamping on the accelerator, Jack pulled the Mondeo sharply away from the kerb. He couldn't let Spearing get under his skin like this. He needed to concentrate on the job in hand; namely, the hunt for the next victim — for a victim she surely was by now. Trawling through the paperwork for the 1998 murders told him that much — but if there was the tiniest of chances she *was* still alive, they would flood the area around Mile End with as many bodies as they could in an effort to locate her.

The wheels were already in motion in that regard, teams mobilised the moment the journalist had made the call. Jack had checked before leaving for Rougham Street and, as yet, nothing had been found — but there was still a lot of ground to cover. While they waited for news either way, Jack knew he would have to turn his attention to the killer's additional request, the newspaper article. Jack hated dancing to the killer's tune, but what other option did he have?

As galling at it sounded, Lorna Henshaw was right. They had to try and keep the killer onside somehow. If he was willing to communicate with the journalist, then they had to seize the opportunity to keep that channel open. If they did that, there was an outside chance the man would slip up — and it would take something like a slip-up to give them the break they so desperately needed.

So, Jack knew he would need to swallow his pride and accept Spearing's involvement, whether he liked it or not. Which he didn't.

But *Jonathan Spearing*?

Spearing had all but hung Jack out to dry at the beginning of the year, circulating that video the way he had, and it was something that had almost cost Jack his job. So the pair had unfinished business, with all pleasantries now well and truly off the table — if there had been any there to begin with.

Jack was like an elephant.

He didn't forget.

CHAPTER SIXTEEN

Time: 10.30 a.m.
Date: Sunday 12 April 2015
Location: Freemantle Buildings, Addison Street, London

PCs Paddy Harper and Ben Lomax pulled up part of the way along Addison Street. It was the fourth location they'd been sent to since the call had come in earlier that morning — and the tension was mounting. Other teams had been dispatched to other potential locations around Mile End and the clock was ticking far too quickly. No one had even considered this to be a prank call; it was merely a question of which building the poor soul would be found in — and when she was found, whether she would still be alive.

PC Lomax had only been in the job three months and had yet to see the true depths of depravity that some human beings could sink to, and the levels of violence they could direct against their fellow man, but PC Harper was a seasoned officer. He had resisted the call for promotion when it came knocking, enjoying having his boots on the ground too much. He'd seen a lot in his twenty years on the job, but this one made even his skin crawl.

"Come on, Ben," he grimaced, exiting the patrol car. "Let's go and see what we've got."

The building was at the bottom of a narrow, one-way side street — stretching around the corner and out of sight. Harper felt a familiar stirring in the pit of his stomach. It was almost identical to the building where they'd found the first victim just two days before.

They were told that the building had lain empty for the last eighteen months. The last business to inhabit it had been a media company specialising in sports broadcasts; before that, a financial services company and then a recruitment agency. None seemed to last that long — rental prices in this part of the city no doubt curtailing their ambitions and sending them off to newer, cheaper pastures elsewhere. There had been several reports over the last six months of antisocial behaviour, local youths using it as a place to congregate in the evenings, racing their whining 50cc motorbikes up and down the one-way street outside. Harper was sure he'd been called out here at least twice before to move them on.

Walking around to the back, Harper saw a metal sign nailed to the brickwork above the rear entrance. *Croasdale Media Services*. Windows on either side of the entrance were already boarded up, graffiti tags covering every available space. Away from the main road and a five-minute walk from the Tube station, the area had an eerie quietness to it, even at this time of the day on a Sunday. It didn't feel like London at all.

Heavy cloud cover was starting to build, snuffing out the morning sunlight, with just the occasional rumble of far-off thunder threatening rain. Harper stretched his gaze skywards, taking in the four-storey building. From the outside, everything appeared to be in order. The rear entrance was closed, and didn't look as though it had been opened in a good while. Apart from the boarded-up windows on the ground floor, each window retained its glass; whoever had smashed the ones lower down had either tried and failed higher up or decided it wasn't worth the effort. Behind him was a brick wall, approximately eight feet high with thick metal spikes punctuating the top to no doubt discourage unwelcome trespassers. The wall curved round to meet the far side of the building, ending in a wooden side door.

A wooden door that was hanging off its hinges.

"Shit."

* * *

Time: 10.40 a.m.
Date: Sunday 12 April 2015
Location: Metropolitan Police HQ, London

Jack stared at his phone.

Frank's call had caught him on the hop just as he'd arrived back at the station. There had been two missed calls from the retired detective while he'd been at Lorna Henshaw's house, but he'd managed to answer the third call just as he ran up the stairs to the incident room.

Lorna Henshaw.

Frank hadn't beaten about the bush, coming straight out and saying that he felt something wasn't quite right with the journalist's involvement; and that he'd had misgivings back in 1998, although nothing concrete had come out of it.

Misgivings.

Hadn't that been Dougie King's choice of phrase before?

Jack made a mental note to look at the paperwork again for himself because, if he was being completely honest, Lorna Henshaw was starting to niggle him, too. As soon as he'd heard Frank utter the words "I couldn't help but think she might have been involved", Jack's own concerns redoubled. What purpose had involving the woman actually served? It led the investigation team to discovering the bodies, but there were numerous other ways of achieving that aim which wouldn't have needed her input at all. So why her?

155

As he entered the incident room, he noted a quiet hum of activity. Slipping his phone back in his pocket, he turned his attention to the team.

"As you know, Lorna Henshaw received a second envelope earlier this morning. She believes it was delivered by motorbike around five fifteen."

"I take it we don't have the cameras in place yet, boss?" Cooper looked up from his computer monitor, having recently consumed a breakfast bacon roll, if the smear of brown sauce on his chin was anything to go by.

"Not yet," confirmed Jack, "but it's something I'll be chasing up today. See if you can get us any CCTV cameras in the vicinity that catches that motorbike."

Cooper nodded, wiping the sauce from his chin as he turned back to his computer.

Jack pulled the envelope from his jacket pocket and went to hand it to DC Daniels. "Make sure this gets put into evidence, and a copy makes its way up onto the board. It's another Underground map with Mile End circled. Are there any reports of anything being found yet?" As his eyes swept the room, nothing but blank expressions and shakes of the head greeted him. Damn. "Let me know as soon as you hear anything. There was another development with this one, though." Jack pulled the second piece of paper from his pocket. "This time our killer wants his fifteen minutes of fame with an article in the *Daily Courier* later today."

"He wants to be in the news?" Daniels' eyebrows hitched as he took hold of the second missive. "That doesn't sound like our normal psychotic killer."

"Indeed it doesn't," Jack grimaced. "But I feel we might have to indulge him, so I'm arranging to see another journalist to set that in motion." Jack didn't want to utter the words *Jonathan Spearing* out loud, so decided to move on. "In the meantime, anything positive from the potential IDs of our first victim?"

Cassidy pushed herself up from her seat and went across to the whiteboards. "Surprisingly, yes. I found three calls that stood out as potentially being our victim — right age range and physical appearance. I've now managed to narrow it down to just the one — a Keeley Saul, age twenty-four from North London." Pausing, she wrote the woman's name onto the whiteboard. "The call was from her best friend, who told me that Keeley didn't show up at work yesterday, and then failed to keep an arrangement to go to the cinema later that evening. She isn't answering her phone and doesn't appear to have been home. The press release Friday evening made her friend concerned, so she called us."

"Sounds promising," agreed Jack. "Do we know anything more about her?"

Cassidy nodded. "She gave me Keeley's parents' contact details, and I spoke with her mother this morning. She confirmed she hadn't seen her daughter since Thursday last week when she dropped off her three-year-old son — which fits with our victim having had a caesarean in the past. Keeley also hasn't returned a voicemail, but Mrs Saul wasn't overly concerned about that. She wasn't due to see her daughter until tomorrow — Keeley was apparently having some time to herself, and her son was staying with Mr and Mrs Saul. Speaking to me, however, prompted Mrs Saul to visit Keeley's flat, which isn't far from the family home, and all she found was her daughter's cat, which appeared not to have been fed and the litter tray not cleaned for a couple of days. I've literally just got off the phone with her again — the description matches, even down to the clothes she was wearing, so she's agreed to come down to the mortuary to confirm." Cassidy's face went slack. "But I really don't think there can be any doubt."

Jack instantly thought about Marmaduke and who would feed him if Jack never made it home. It was a feeling that sat strangely with him, a feeling he wasn't used to. "Good work, Amanda. Assuming it's her, start building up a background. Where she works, who she socialises with, past relationships, that kind of thing. We need to establish where she might have crossed the path of our killer."

"On it, guv," confirmed Cassidy, heading back to her desk.

"While Amanda is following up on our first victim — Daniels, I've got another job for you." Jack pulled up a chair, settling down next to where DC Daniels was staring intently towards his computer monitor. "Somewhere in the 1998 paperwork should be something regarding Frank Tyler's suspicions about Lorna Henshaw." Jack saw the young detective's eyebrows twitch. "I take it no one's come across it yet?"

There was a shake of the head from Daniels, followed by negative murmurings from Cassidy and Cooper in the background.

"In that case, I'm sorry but I need you to go through everything again. Somehow, we've missed it. I've no idea how much documentation there will be — I suspect not a lot — but take a look and report back as soon as you can."

"Any particular type of suspicions?" Daniels started tapping his keyboard.

Jack gave a shrug. "I'm not sure. Just a general feeling that all was not as it seemed."

"Will do, boss."

"And assuming there's nothing more from the Tube worker line of investigation, shelve that for now and concentrate on this." Jack turned towards Cooper. "Anything yet from Jenny?"

"Not yet, boss. She worked late last night so we may get something later on today. She's putting everything we sent through as a high priority."

"Thanks, Cooper. It's appreciated."

"Any news on Dr Hunter?" Cooper wiped his chin with a serviette. "We have a profile yet?"

Jack grimaced. He had meant to sort out getting the papers sent to another psychologist, but the task had slipped down his mental checklist. "Rachel Hunter is unavailable — off on some jaunt across the Atlantic. I haven't yet sent the papers anywhere, but I'm working on it." It wasn't exactly the truth, and he knew he couldn't stall for much longer.

Dougie King would be wanting his daily update before long. Checking his Fitbit, he sighed and made his way back towards the door. "If anyone needs me, I'll be downstairs in one of the interview rooms." He paused while shrugging back into his jacket. "I don't expect to be long."

CHAPTER SEVENTEEN

Time: 11.10 a.m.
Date: Sunday 12 April 2015
Location: Metropolitan Police HQ, London

"Don't make this any harder than it has to be — for either of us." Jack paced up and down by the door of interview room one. "All I need you to do is pen the article as suggested. That's the limit of your involvement — *finito*."

Jonathan Spearing grinned as he rocked back in his chair, the look on his face telling Jack he was enjoying every minute of the detective's discomfort. "What's in it for me?"

Jack's eyes darkened as his pacing came to an abrupt end. "Nothing. What the hell were you expecting?"

Spearing raised his arms theatrically. "Hey, I'm just asking. You came to me, right? I'm just wondering why I would want to get involved in something like this."

Jack approached the table where Spearing sat, leaning on it with clenched fists.

"Because you've been asked. *Nicely*." Against his better judgment, Jack had had to tell the reporter all about the envelopes delivered to Lorna Henshaw — including those from

1998. He didn't trust Spearing as far as he could chuck him, but there was no other option open to him. And, on top of that, the man now appeared to be gloating. "Call it your civic duty — I don't really care, to be bloody honest. I just want you to do it. And believe me, if there was another way I would be taking it." Jack paused, the words starting to catch in his throat. *I can't believe I'm actually going to say it.* "But the investigation needs your help."

There, he'd done it — and he hadn't been immediately struck down by a lightning bolt direct from on high. As Jack fixed the reporter's jubilant face with his customary stony gaze, he realised very quickly that something more was going to be needed if he was to get what he wanted. Simply asking for his help wasn't going to be enough for Spearing. Sighing, Jack pulled out one of the chairs opposite and sat down. With a clenched jaw, he added, *"Please* — I really need you to do this."

"Well, well, well." The smile on the reporter's face transcended into a full-on smirk. "As you've clearly taken the time to ask me so *nicely* — of course, I'd *love* to help. Just tell me what to do."

Jack ignored the sarcasm. He still couldn't quite believe he was doing this, but there was no credible alternative right now — and time was rapidly running away with them. "All I need you to do is write and submit an article as dictated by Lorna Henshaw. You need to write it word for word, unabridged — or whatever it is you people call it." Jack paused, irritated by the smirk still plastered across Spearing's face. He leaned in closer. "And I need you to take this seriously — a woman's life may depend on it. Maybe more than one."

Spearing's eyes widened and his eyebrows shot skywards. "Someone might die?"

Jack sighed and rubbed his eyes. "Just write the bloody article, will you? Leave the grown-up stuff to us." Pushing himself up from his chair, he headed for the door. "Lorna will be in touch. Let me know when it's done — it must go live by four o'clock this afternoon. And your lips remain sealed. If I get even a sniff that you've been gossiping, it won't be pretty."

Jack pulled open the interview room door, hesitating in the doorway. He shot a dark look back over his shoulder.

"And don't think I've forgotten about that video."

* * *

Time: 11.30 a.m.
Date: Sunday 12 April 2015
Location: London

Taking out the small Underground map, he circled Shepherd's Bush Underground and slotted it inside the next envelope. He thought about including another instruction for a further news article, but felt the one that was due to hit the headlines later today would have the required impact. Maybe he would treat them to another message when it came to number four.

Gloves on, he sealed the envelope and placed it on the table next to the map. When he'd delivered the second envelope in the early hours of the morning, he was sure there was no sign of a camera. But he was equally sure the police would hurry along setting up the surveillance of the journalist's house. They were slow off the mark in '98, but they would have learned their lesson by now.

Not that a camera would deter him. It just made the whole thing more interesting.

Although he wasn't planning on taking her until tomorrow, he always liked to plan ahead. As he placed the grey bandana and black balaclava next to the envelope, he wondered just how long the journalist had been sat by her front door, watching the letterbox. It gave him a peculiar thrill to think he had managed to invade her headspace once again. Was she having trouble sleeping, waking up every hour in a cold sweat? Although he knew it was cruel — he wasn't quite so detached from humanity not to understand — he couldn't help but smile.

162

He hadn't always had this mean streak in him; at least, he didn't think he had. He was certain he hadn't been born with these thoughts. Babies weren't usually born bad, everyone knew that. Cruelty had been instilled in him as he'd grown, as he'd been nurtured by society. He couldn't pinpoint exactly when or where, but Great Easton Secondary School had been a major factor, he was sure of that. He may have started out as a quiet, maladjusted weird kid but by the time he left the school, it, and Ellis Magee, had turned him into a cold-blooded killer.

But he didn't need Ellis now; he didn't need anybody. This was all his own work, every last bit of it. The last seventeen years had passed by in a drug-and-alcohol-infused fog, so much so that he barely remembered much of it. He had moved abroad after a while, taking his talents to a distant land — but it wasn't the same, and London eventually lured him back.

And London would be where he stayed.

CHAPTER EIGHTEEN

Time: 12.30 p.m.
Date: Sunday 12 April 2015
Location: Freemantle Buildings, Addison Street, London

Jack pulled the elasticated cap over his head and followed Elliott Walker along the corridor. Once again, they were on the second floor, heading towards a window at the rear that overlooked a deserted access road.

"Body was found at around ten forty-five this morning by two patrol officers. They called it in after spotting a rear entrance had been forced open." The crime scene manager nodded to where the body of a young woman, dressed in a pair of pale blue jeans, navy T-shirt and cropped black jacket, lay face up next to the floor-to-ceiling window. "Body was cut down by PC Harper but on examination it was clear to him that there were no signs of life. Appropriate calls were then made, and the body hasn't been touched since." Elliott stood to the side, allowing Jack and DS Cooper to step ahead of him.

The scene was remarkably similar to the one at the offices on Wheeler Street some forty-eight hours ago. "You getting a sense of déjà vu here, Cooper?" The similarities were striking.

Apart from this building being a little more abandoned than the one before, it had all the hallmarks.

"Afternoon, Jack." Dr Philip Matthews was kneeling by the side of the body, his head cocked to the side. "I'll be with you in a second or two."

"No rush, doc," replied Jack. *She's not going anywhere.*

A few moments later, the pathologist straightened up. "Thin ligature mark to the neck with signs of manual compression. Bruising consistent with restraint to both upper arms."

"Same as before?" Jack gestured towards the window. "Dead before being strung up?"

Dr Matthews nodded. "Almost certainly, but I'll know more once I get her back to the mortuary."

"Killed here or elsewhere? And any idea as to when?"

The pathologist took a moment to consider both questions. "On balance, I would say the victim was killed here this time. Even without removing the clothing, liver mortis can be seen in the lower limbs and feet. This would suggest she has remained upright for some time after death. As for rigor mortis and the time of death — difficult to be precise without further examination, but it wasn't long ago."

"Thanks, doc."

"I understand we may have a positive identification for the young woman brought in on Friday?" Dr Matthews stepped to the side. "Perry is going to handle the viewing with the mother this afternoon. A very sad business."

Jack nodded. "Well, subject to a positive ID at the mortuary, we now have a name, yes." He let his gaze stray back to the body lying on the floor a short distance away, wondering how long it would be until they had a name for this poor soul, too. "Which obviously helps, but we still have a long way to go."

"Then I'll get out of your way." The pathologist gave a wave of the hand as he began to make his way towards the exit. "I'll be in touch about the PM, Jack."

Once Dr Matthews had disappeared from view, Elliott reappeared. "The two officers who found her are still here if you need them. Downstairs, I believe."

Jack nodded his thanks. "We'll pop down and have a word on our way out. Anything else I should know about?"

"Not that I can see. It's not as clean a crime scene as the previous one — this place has been derelict for some time, and I understand there's been a few issues with break-ins and criminal damage in recent months. It'll make evidence retrieval a little more challenging, but we'll do what we can. I'll be in touch when we have anything."

"Sure." Jack watched the crime scene manager cross the floor to where two of his investigators were waiting, then gestured for DS Cooper to join him over by the window. "What do you see here, Cooper?" He nodded towards the floor-to-ceiling glass.

"Similar to the one before, boss. Quiet access road at the back. Not overlooked. The only potential witnesses are some way away — there's a building over there which looks like an office block, but I'm guessing it's unlikely to have anyone inside on a weekend."

"I'm inclined to agree with you, Cooper, but we'll follow it up anyway." Jack led the way back toward the stairs. "We also need to find out what the significance is of the window. It can't be just a coincidence."

"Aye, boss." Cooper pulled out his notebook. "First victim in '98 was found in a disused warehouse, hanging next to the only window in the whole place. Second victim was found in a block of flats under renovation, again by one of the windows. Third victim was hanging in the window of a restaurant, the fourth in an old car showroom. Victim five was found in the window of a disused motor spares shop on an industrial estate, and the last one in '98 in an office block not dissimilar to this one."

"All of which makes me feel these locations must mean something to our killer, Cooper — we just need to work out what that something is."

The detectives reached the bottom of the stairs, where PCs Harper and Lomax were waiting. Jack recognised them from before.

"Elliott tells me you were the first on scene again. That's tough luck."

PC Harper grimaced. "It is that. Let me show you where we think he got in — it's just around the back." He led Jack and Cooper out of the front entrance and along the access road at the side.

When they reached the rear, Jack noticed the main door looked to be intact, but saw PC Harper was pointing towards a brick wall at the side. Set into the wall was a wooden door hanging off its hinges.

"Leads through to a rear courtyard and, by the cigarette butts on the ground, it looks like some kind of smoking area. As no one's worked here in a while, it's most probably kids. There's been a spate of antisocial behaviour reports around here recently. But you can see the fire exit door from here, clearly forced open."

Jack and Cooper poked their heads through the wooden door to see the courtyard — and then the fire exit door with clear damage to its frame.

"The forensics team are coming down soon to process it." PC Harper followed the two detectives back around to the front of the building where PC Lomax was waiting by the patrol car. "You need us to stay around any longer?"

Jack shook his head. "No, you can get yourselves off. If I need anything that's not in your statements, I'll be in touch."

Once PC Harper had headed back to the patrol car, Jack turned to his sergeant.

"I think we might just be getting a better picture of our offender here, Cooper, what do you reckon?"

"Aye, boss." Cooper followed Jack back to the Mondeo. "What our man's doing is risky, but he's not a risk-*taker* — not in the usual sense, anyway. He's choosing locations that are secluded, even in the middle of a city like this, and he's making sure he's not seen or disturbed. Take here, for example.

He could take his own sweet time getting in that fire door, no one can see him. He's cocky. Confident." Cooper slipped into the passenger seat. "Our killer has thought about this — he's thought about this a lot."

Jack grinned as he slid the keys into the ignition. "Good man. We'll make a profiler out of you yet."

* * *

Time: 1.00 p.m.
Date: Sunday 12 April 2015
Location: London

He wondered if they'd found her yet.

There was nothing in the news, but he didn't expect there to be — not yet. He knew how the police worked, limiting the information they revealed until they were ready. It was like some intricate game of chess. Tactical. Planned. The thought excited him. He liked playing games — especially games that he had created.

Just like this one.

The news article wouldn't hit the online platforms for another three hours, if the journalist had done as he requested. Her involvement had never hit the headlines before, which was why he had decided to force her hand this time around. Nervous energy competed for space with the excitement already fizzing through his bloodstream. It was a tantalising mixture.

He poured himself another whisky and turned back to the map, his mind focused on the next one for his collection. He knew who she was, where she would be, and also where he would display her. A lot of thought went into the locations and, so far, each one had been perfect. But it wasn't really the building that mattered.

It was all about the window.

* * *

Closing his eyes to block out the searing rays from the hot summer sun, he clenched his teeth until they started to ache. Sweat trickled from his scalp, finding its way from the back of his neck to eventually pool beneath the collar of his school shirt. At least he'd had the foresight to loosen his tie.

Giggles and sniggers rippled around the rest of class 3C. He was glad he had his back to them — at least he didn't have to witness their gleeful faces, their eyes shining with laughter. If he did, he wasn't quite sure what he would do. He knew what he *wanted* to do — he wanted to grab hold of their scrawny little necks and choke the living daylights out of every one of them, making the others watch until it was their turn. That's what he wanted to do, but it wasn't yet time.

Despite the discomfort from the overbearing heat, he began to smile.

Although he wasn't allowed to move, not even look at his watch, he guessed he'd been standing there for at least thirty minutes, maybe even longer. His leg muscles were starting to ache, his calves twitching. And the stuffiness of the biology classroom wasn't helping either, making his head feel fuzzy.

Opening his eyes, he tried to focus on something outside — anything to stop himself from swaying. As he blinked through the salty droplets of sweat now dripping into his eyes, he willed the light-headedness to recede. The last thing he wanted to do was faint in front of the whole class.

It was bad enough that he'd wet himself.

Again.

The smell of the concentrated urine that had soaked through his trousers now reached his nostrils, the musty aroma making him feel sick.

More giggles.

More sniggers.

Now he could hear whispering, too.

"*God, you stink!*"

"*What a baby! Wetting yourself!*"

"*Do you need a nappy?*"

Clenching his fists by his sides, he tried to shut the voices out; the whining little voices that grated on him, day after day. What would he give to shut them up once and for all? A strong hand around their throats would soon sort that out. They would stop their pathetic giggling then.

It was the girls who were the worst. He hated them with a passion; hated them all for what they did to him. He could hear them now, whispering and sniggering behind his back. It made his blood boil. But he could hear Mr Ronson's monotone voice bouncing off the walls, too. Today's lesson was all about cell division and the creation of life. As he swayed by the window, he heard words like mitosis, mitochondria and chromosomes circulating, but right now all he wanted to do was *end* life, not create it. The lives of Imogen, Amber and Julia most of all.

This wasn't the first time Mr Ronson had made him stand by the window in front of the whole class. It was the second time this week alone — and it was only Wednesday. It was the biology teacher's favourite form of punishment — and one seemingly reserved just for him. No one else was made to stand by the window, in the full glare of the sun and the whole class. Everyone else got away with murder. They talked incessantly, chewed gum, threw scrunched-up paper notes at each other — and Mr Ronson barely batted an eyelid. Instead, the man saved all his punishment and ridicule for *him*.

With a fresh trickle of sweat making its way down his neck, he tried to stare through the glass and ignore the jibes that were still rippling their way around the classroom behind him. As he did so, he became aware of movement outside. Although it wasn't break time yet, three girls were making their way across the playground.

The playground.

His stomach began to tighten. If Ronson didn't let him step away from the window soon, punishment over, afternoon break time would begin, and he and his urine-soaked trousers would be in full view of half the school within seconds. Clenching his teeth, he focused his gaze on the broad oak tree on the far side of the playground. He just needed to get through the next few minutes — and then maybe the girls wouldn't see him, especially if he didn't move to spark their attention.

He knew it was futile but tried anyway. As they crossed his line of vision, he couldn't resist a quick glance towards them. He knew he shouldn't, but he did it anyway. His stomach churned when he recognised the taller of the girls.

Imogen Baxter.

Why did it have to be her?

Before he could look away, their eyes locked — and it didn't take long for the grin on her face to follow. All he could do was watch as she tugged the arm of the girl next to her — and then there were two pairs of laughing eyes taunting him. It took seconds for the third girl to turn her gaze towards him, too.

Although he couldn't hear what they were saying through the thick glass, he could certainly see how hard they were laughing.

At him.

Now they were pointing, too.

Laughing and pointing.

Pointing and laughing.

All he could hear inside his head was their mocking tones taunting him, getting louder and louder by the second, until he couldn't hear anything else, not even his own heartbeat. They even drowned out the monotone drivel from Mr Ronson. Sweat pooled in the small of his back as colour flooded his cheeks. He felt breathless, his head swimming as the three girls swam in and out of focus. Feeling faint with the heat from the sun and the burning shame, his legs crumpled beneath him.

* * *

Time: 1.30 p.m.
Date: Sunday 12 April 2015
Location: London

Stirring from his memories, for a brief moment he thought he could still smell the stale urine.

He didn't have as many issues now — not in the same way they had plagued him in his teenage years — but he did still have the odd "accident" from time to time. It was usually when he felt excited or aroused. Ellis never teased him about it the way the others had. He just accepted it for what it was. So long as the smell didn't get too bad.

Girlfriends had come and gone. He had never really been able to hold down any kind of relationship for long — so now he didn't even try. He didn't need anyone anyway.

He already had his girls.

CHAPTER NINETEEN

Time: 2.25 p.m.
Date: Sunday 12 April 2015
Location: Metropolitan Police HQ, London

Jack led Cooper into the incident room, feeling immediately buoyed by the grin on Cassidy's face.

"We've had a call from the lab while you've been out, guv. I think you might want to hear this one."

Collapsing into one of the vacant chairs, Jack winced as his foot reminded him that he'd been on his feet for too long. "Go on — we could do with some good news."

Cassidy turned back to her computer monitor. "They've been working on the evidence for the 1996 and 1997 sexual assaults — in particular, semen samples found on some of the victims' clothes."

"And?"

Cassidy's grin widened. "They've managed to extract a full DNA profile from all samples tested so far."

Jack felt his heart jolt, the discomfort in his foot forgotten. "You're kidding? A full DNA profile?"

"Exactly that. Just shows you how techniques have improved over the years, guv. It's being run through the database as we speak."

"That's excellent news, Amanda." Jack looked across the incident room to spy DS Cooper already plucking the last apple pie from the Mr Kipling box. "Thank Jenny for expediting everything for us, Cooper. Do you know what else she's working on?"

Cooper took a mouthful of pie before heading towards his desk. "From what I remember, there's still more clothing to be tested from the Yorkshire assaults. And then there's everything from the 1998 murders. I'll bring up the evidence log so we can check, but I'm sure she'll let us know the minute they get any more results. I'll ask her when I get home tonight, anyway."

"This could be the break we need, guv." Cassidy went across to perch on the edge of Cooper's desk, peering over his shoulder and brushing away stray pastry flakes from his tie. "If the DNA is a hit, we could get our killer."

Jack gave a hesitant nod. "You're right, it could — but let's not get our hopes up too much. Back in the late nineties, the database was still in its infancy. Not all offenders were swabbed as routinely as they are now. It was only in 1999 that Lothian and Borders Police started to take DNA samples from all its offenders, the first ones to do so. Down here, we were still only taking samples from the most serious offences. And don't forget, if our killer hasn't come to our attention subsequently, then his DNA won't appear on the database, no matter how much we might want it to."

Cassidy's face fell a little. "But it's a start, surely? A step forward at least?"

Jack gave an appreciative smile. "It's certainly that, Amanda. Don't get me wrong, it's good news. Even if we don't get a name from the database, it puts us in a position to be able to rule people out. Let me know when any more results come in."

"Mrs Saul should be at the mortuary now." Cassidy pushed herself away from Cooper's desk and returned to her own. "She's going to ring me once it's done."

"Assuming it's a positive ID, we'll need to release the name to the press and start finding out as much as we can about her background. Can I leave that with you, Amanda? Once she calls, let the PR department know. And while you're at it, start cross-referencing her with Lorna Henshaw. Do the same for the 1998 murder victims, too. And also, the sexual assault victims. I want to know if she can be linked, however tenuously, to any of them."

Cassidy resumed her seat. "I'll get onto it right now, guv. Do you really think she might be involved in all this?"

"I have no idea, but we need to check it out. There's still something about her that isn't quite right. Frank Tyler thought so in 1998, and I feel it now. Daniels, have you managed to get anywhere with the background checks on her? Anything interesting to report?" The look on DC Daniels' face didn't fill him with much confidence.

"I did find some references to her in the 1998 papers, but there wasn't a lot. If they did suspect her of involvement, then they must have discounted it quite early on, or at least moved on to other lines of enquiry."

"Just give us what you have. If we need to dig deeper, we will."

Daniels pulled several pieces of paper across his desk. "DI Tyler ordered a trawl of all articles Henshaw was involved in that mentioned the London Underground. All he managed to find was a piece written ten years after the King's Cross fire. It didn't really say a great deal that wasn't already in circulation at the time — there were already a few recommendations from the resultant enquiry to make the Underground safer and prevent such a disaster happening again, but she didn't really stir the pot that much."

"Go on." Jack hoped there was more, his foot beginning to ache again.

"Then Tyler ordered a wider trawl, this time for any mention of Underground systems around the world, not just limited to London. There were a couple of articles she wrote about the safety of women on the Paris Metro, and then another series of articles about the sarin attack in Tokyo in 1995."

Jack raised an eyebrow. "Tokyo? Remind me about that one?"

Daniels selected another piece of paper. "In March 1995, five members of a religious cult launched a coordinated and deadly attack on the Tokyo subway system, releasing a quantity of sarin — a particularly nasty nerve gas. They used bags of liquid sarin which they pierced with the tips of their umbrellas before making their escape. Thirteen people died. Lorna Henshaw wrote several articles on how susceptible London would be to a similar attack — the last one was penned in 1996."

"And what was her conclusion?"

Daniels shrugged. "That there were inevitable flaws in the system, that some London Underground staff were unsure what the emergency protocol would be in such a situation."

"A damning report? Did she ruffle any feathers?"

Another shrug followed, then a shake of the head. "Not exactly. The overall conclusion was that no metro system in the world could be one hundred per cent safe, but London was one of the safer ones. I'm not convinced what she said would be enough to spark off something like this. And to be honest, it's all quite tame in comparison to some of the investigative reports she did afterwards."

"You're probably right, Daniels, but let's keep it in mind. Some people have long memories. Let's get a full background check repeated on her. I want to know where she's worked, where she's lived, any relationships she's had, failed or otherwise." Foot protesting, Jack pushed himself to his feet and headed for the whiteboards, swiping up a marker pen on the way. "The second body found this morning was at a very similar location to our first victim on Friday, with the same thin ligature mark around her neck. She was also strung up in front of a window. Although Dr Matthews can't be sure, he feels she was killed at the location this time. Cooper, do the usual CCTV trawl in and around the building and the Tube station. Compare it to the first location, see if you can find anything in common." Jack added the sparse details to the board, then turned around. "Amanda, can you do the usual with Missing Persons? And Daniels — as well as looking into our journalist, try and figure out the relevance of the window. See if it crops up in any other unsolved cases."

Daniels nodded and shuffled closer to his desk. "Will do."

Jack's shoulders sagged as he tossed the marker pen back down. A quick glance at the wall clock told him they still had an hour or so until the deadline for the article in the *Daily Courier*. Would Spearing do as he was instructed? There was a first for everything, but Jack still didn't quite trust the man.

"I'm heading back to my office. Let me know if anything else comes in." Jack was well aware he was overdue with Dougie King's daily update, but felt a suitably worded email would suffice this time around. Once the news article was out, things could get tricky, and Jack didn't particularly fancy being in the chief superintendent's firing line when it did.

He needed to keep his head down.

* * *

Time: 3.35 p.m.
Date: Sunday 12 April 2015
Location: Westminster Mortuary, London

Perry Musgrove remained standing at the entrance to the Westminster Mortuary as Mr and Mrs Saul's VW left the car park. Viewings were always difficult — it was difficult not to feel as though you were trampling all over someone else's private grief — but this one had been especially so.

Keeley had just turned twenty-four — only a year younger than himself, with so much to live for. It was a phrase that was often dragged out in situations like these — "she had so much to live for" and "cut down in the prime of her life" — but that didn't make them not true. Keeley did have so much to live for, and now she wouldn't get to do any of it.

Perry could see a range of emotions ebbing and flowing across Mr and Mrs Saul's faces as they dealt with the horrendous task of identifying their daughter's body; no parent should ever have to do that. To begin with it had been raw emotion that flooded their faces, their eyes already red and swollen, their cheeks blotchy and damp. Lips trembled; haunting cries escaped from their mouths. Then more tears had flowed.

Dr Matthews had once sat Perry down, not long after he'd started working at the mortuary, to instruct the young pathology technician about the various stages of grief. It wasn't something young Perry had spent much time thinking about up to that point. Some said it was five stages, others seven. Dr Matthews had been of the view that it depended on the person.

'Grief is as individual as you and I are, Perry,' the man had said. 'There's no right or wrong about it.'

Mr and Mrs Saul were very clearly in the denial stage when they first walked into the mortuary. The hope in their eyes told Perry that they wanted the body beneath the white sheet *not* to be their daughter, that this was all just some horrible mistake. Perry had even heard Keeley's mother whispering to herself, "*It can't be her, it can't be her,*" as they were taken through to the viewing room.

Denial would then very quickly transform into the second stage — anger. Anger at a life lost, anger at the sheer brutality of death. It was at that point that Perry noticed the change in both parents' eyes — the pain of sadness and sorrow being joined by a fiery revulsion at what their daughter had been subjected to.

Perry had handled many a viewing now and knew when the right time came to step back and leave the family with their newly emerging grief. One time he had lingered too long, the family then turning to him for answers.

Why did this happen? Why her? Why? Why? Why?

As Perry turned away from the entrance, heading back inside, he hoped Mr and Mrs Saul had managed to obtain some degree of comfort from their visit. It would be a while before they stumbled their way through to the next stage of the grieving process — bargaining, when they would inevitably seek to blame themselves in some way. Depression then followed close behind, before acceptance was finally achieved. It would be a long and rocky road.

Sighing, Perry made his way back towards the examination room. And the rest of the afternoon list that lay ahead.

* * *

Time: 4.05 p.m.
Date: Sunday 12 April 2015
Location: London

And there they were — every single one of them. *His words.* The journalist had done what he'd asked, printing everything as he'd dictated.

It gave him a curious thrill to see it there in black and white.

> *I am the Central Line Killer —* the one you are all searching for. *And believe me when I say this:* I am your worst nightmare. *I am the man sitting next to you on the bus. I am the man queuing behind you at the checkout.* I am the man walking towards you in the park. I am everywhere. And you will never catch me, I can assure you of that. For I will not stop. I can hear you asking me why I do it. I do it because I can. Because I must. *For far too long people have treated*

me like dirt, like something to be stamped on then scraped
from the sole of their shoe. You all *take responsibility for*
what I have become. You all *made me this way. So, you* all
deserve this. Like I say, I will never stop, just like you didn't
stop with me. You want someone to blame for this? Take a
long hard look at yourselves. You are *all* to blame.

He would never have classed himself as a wordsmith,
leaving school long before his exams were done — but even
he thought the article had been well written. He'd left school
before the end of term, taking nothing with him to show for
it other than a kaleidoscope of bad memories. But he hadn't
let it hold him back. He could get his point across more than
adequately — he didn't need a grade C in English to do that.
Everyone was reading his words today, listening to what he had
to say. Just like they never had before. Today everyone would
sit up and listen, his words reaching all four corners of the
country in a flash.

They might not have known it at the time, but his school
days had prepared him for the adult world, just not in the way
everyone expected.

* * *

Time: 12.10 p.m.
Date: Thursday 8 December 1988
Location: Great Easton Secondary School, North London

The last day of school was still some six months away, but he
had no intention of spending another day inside its four walls.
He wouldn't be staying for his exams next summer — what
would be the point? Mum and Dad wouldn't care — *if* they
even noticed, that is. Sometimes he wondered if they even
realised he was breathing half the time.

He would be sixteen next month — *sixteen* — and the day
couldn't come quickly enough. At last, he would be able to

make his own decisions; do whatever he wanted. *Be* whoever he wanted.

Even with Ellis as his friend, life at Great Easton had been a misery from the first day he stepped over its threshold as a spotty twelve-year-old. The whole experience had been a walking, living, breathing nightmare. If it wasn't the repetitive chanting and relentless taunts of Imogen Baxter and her cronies, then it was the teachers themselves, especially Mr Ronson. The biology teacher had been his form teacher for the last three years and had made no attempt to step in and put a stop the bullying. If anything, he seemed to encourage it — quickly introducing his own special form of humiliation.

The window.

Just thinking about the window now made him shudder.

In his head, he had already killed every one of his tormentors a thousand times over, finding the most painful and humiliating way to end their pathetic little lives. If he could do it for real, then he would in a heartbeat.

The idea made him twitch.

The mannequin had come from the English department. With the drama group putting on a Christmas play, there were hundreds of props and other useful items crammed into the storage cupboards. He didn't know what the play was, much less even cared, but the props would definitely come in useful.

Of the few people he'd passed in the corridor, no one questioned why he was carrying a full-sized mannequin towards the science block. One advantage of being the school weirdo was that people questioned nothing.

He let himself into Mr Ronson's biology classroom, the man himself either squirrelled away in the staff room or patrolling the grounds to pounce on anyone out of class without a valid reason. He disliked most teachers at Great Easton, but he disliked Ronson the most. The man looked down on everyone with a haughty, sneering look on his face — a pair of weak, watery eyes set deep in his pallid, slack face. When any of the girls whispered "*fatso*" or "*weirdo*" or "*flubber-boy*", even if well within his earshot, Ronson would let it go — a faint, mocking smile plastered onto his thin lips.

Which made him the perfect target.

Although he detested his classmates for how they treated him, they were just kids — old enough to know better, for sure, but they were still kids, nonetheless. Kids were naturally brought up like pack animals, all too willing to follow the crowd, conform to the masses; to behave as sheep. But a teacher? Teachers should be above all that, stamping out bullying and setting an example. He laughed to himself as he closed the classroom door behind him. Hell would freeze over before Mr Ronson showed him any support.

Setting the mannequin down on the floor by the window, he started to hum as he worked, the exquisite sense of anticipation building with each second that passed. Lunchtime was in twenty minutes, so he had just enough time to perfect his creation. From his backpack he pulled out a number of additional items he'd managed to acquire from the drama group's stash of props. A pair of dark brown corduroy trousers, a checked shirt, a tan-coloured zip-up cardigan with imitation leather patches on the elbows. It wasn't an exact match, but it was close enough.

It couldn't be any more perfect.

The school had a strict uniform policy — boys and girls were expected to wear shirts, ties and blazers all year round — but teachers seemed to be allowed to turn up in all manner of creations. Mrs Jones, one of the art teachers, wore long flowing dresses in the summer, dungarees with a thick jumper in the winter. Mr Carter, head of the maths department, wore a variety of different-coloured chinos and polo shirts. PE teacher Mr Callaghan was never seen in anything other than a tracksuit but had a startling number to choose from.

Ronson, however, was a slave to routine — always a pair of dark brown or grey corduroy trousers, a checked shirt and his favourite cardigan, day after day, come rain or shine. Which made the dressing of the mannequin all the easier.

Once appropriately attired, he popped a wig on its head — a messy bird's nest of curly black hair. He then took the water bottle from his backpack and threw half of it at the mannequin's trousers, letting some of it pool on the floor beneath. Then he took a thin rope and tied it around the mannequin's neck. Dragging one of the biology class's metal chairs across to the window, he climbed up and threw the rope over the wooden curtain pole above.

The mannequin was light, so it didn't take much effort to haul it several inches off the floor, leaving it to hang in front of the window. Securing the rope, he pulled a black marker pen from his back pocket and gave the mannequin a thin moustache.

Mr Ronson. Unmistakable.

Glancing at his watch, he saw there was less than ten minutes before the lunchtime bell sounded, sending hundreds of children out into the playground. He couldn't help but smile.

For a finishing touch, he pulled two lengths of coarse string from his backpack and proceeded to tie the mannequin's wrists and ankles together.

Done.

Leaving everything where it lay — he wasn't bothered who found his backpack now — he slipped out of the classroom and into the corridor. He didn't mind who saw him, either — so was content to saunter along, quietly humming to himself with a grin on his satisfied face. He *wanted* people to know what he'd done, *needed* them to. And, in about seven minutes' time, they would.

Letting his grin spread, he jogged out of the science block and across the playground towards the school gates. With a final glance over his shoulder at Mr Ronson hanging in front of his own classroom's window, he laughed as he skipped out of the school grounds for the very last time.

* * *

Time: 4.15 p.m.
Date: Sunday 12 April 2015
Location: London

Placing his phone down, he rose from the chair and crossed back over to the map. The bandana and balaclava were still waiting.

Soon it would be time, but not yet.

He wanted her right now — so incredibly hungry for the next kill. She was tantalisingly close; he could almost taste her blood on his tongue, feel her life in his hands pulsating as he ended it. He momentarily wondered if this was what it felt like to be a wild animal, hunting for prey.

But he knew he needed to wait. Ellis had taught him that.

She would be his soon enough.

Just like all the others had.

* * *

Time: 6.00 p.m.
Date: Sunday 12 April 2015
Location: Metropolitan Police HQ, London

Jack eyed his desk phone, willing it to stay silent. He'd sent Dougie King an email containing a brief résumé of the day's progress fifteen minutes ago and, so far, it had elicited no response. No response was good in Jack's book — but now the four o'clock deadline had well and truly passed, he knew it was only a matter of time before the proverbial hit the fan.

Using his phone, he scrolled to the end of the online news article which had gone out at one minute past four o'clock. Jonathan Spearing had, it seemed, done exactly as he was asked. It was all there, word for word, just as the killer had instructed; but somehow the words had taken on a new meaning now they were there for the whole world to see, and Jack knew he was in trouble before he'd even got to the end of the first paragraph.

184

With the discovery of the second body earlier that day, getting the article published to save her was largely a moot point now, and Jack had always known it would be. The killer wasn't bargaining with them; he wasn't offering them a deal. It was purely a game. A game that the killer was in control of.

The article hadn't been cleared with those above — and Jack fully expected Dougie King to request his presence before long to explain himself. But the chief superintendent would have to find him first. Rubbing his eyes, Jack knocked the desktop handset from its cradle and switched his mobile to silent. He wasn't going to make it easy. But before he could consider what next step to take, the office door burst open, and DS Cooper rushed in.

"Boss — we've had a breakthrough!"

Less than a minute later, back in the incident room, Cooper had activated a series of CCTV images, bringing them up onto the interactive whiteboard. "We can clearly see our victim making her way along Beyton Road towards the bus stop."

Jack and the rest of the team watched the woman running through pelting rain, her right hand pressing a bag to her head as she flew along the pavement. Cooper then slowed the images down to half speed.

"The clothing is identical to that of our second victim, and when she turns to cross the road towards the bus stop, we get a brief glimpse of her face. It's definitely her." Cooper let the recording play on for a few more seconds before freezing one of the frames. The woman turned to the side, as if she were looking back over her shoulder towards the camera, and there could be no mistake.

It was her.

"What happens to her next, Cooper?" Jack inched his chair closer to the whiteboard as the detective sergeant restarted the film.

"You'll see she crosses the road here and looks to be heading for the bus shelter. Whether it's her intention to board a bus or just shelter from the rain, I can't tell."

The team continued to watch in silence as the woman darted across the road to the sanctuary of the bus stop, taking a seat beneath the shelter.

Jack frowned. "I take it we don't see her get on a bus, then?" Buses, as a rule, had surprisingly decent CCTV cameras these days, so if their victim boarded one, they would get a very clear picture of her — and maybe even a clue as to her movements afterwards.

"Unfortunately not — see for yourself." Cooper restarted the images at normal speed, and moments later a high-sided white van came into the foreground, parking illegally at the side of the road outside a discount electrical store. The recording then showed the driver exiting the van and heading straight into the shop, leaving the van's hazard lights flashing.

Jack immediately saw the problem. "Bugger."

"The van completely obscures our view of the bus stop, boss. The driver is gone for exactly seventy-nine seconds — I've counted — and when he emerges to drive away, our victim is gone." Cooper played the images on, showing the now empty bus stop. "No buses stopping during that time, either."

"Shit. And we don't pick her up anywhere else? Cameras in surrounding streets, maybe?"

Cooper shook his head. "Nothing yet, but there are a few more cameras still to check. My gut feeling is she didn't walk away from that bus stop."

Jack sighed. "Which means she must have got into another vehicle in the seventy-nine seconds she's gone from view."

Cooper closed the CCTV images down. "I'll continue looking through the cameras for surrounding streets, logging vehicles in the vicinity during that seventy-nine second window. It's a busy time, and a busy junction. We'll have a fair few registrations to follow up on."

Despite the disappointment, Jack knew it was still a good shout and a tiny step forward. "Keep at it. She must have got into someone's car or van — she can't have just bloody disappeared into thin air." He stood up and glanced at the wall clock. "But I'm mindful of how long this might take. Anyone desperate to stay on tonight?"

"I'll stay a while, boss. Get stuck into that CCTV." Cooper was already turning back to his monitor. "Jenny will be late home anyway, so I might as well."

"I've got a training run tonight, boss." Daniels shifted in his seat. "But I can cancel?"

Cassidy got up from her chair, depositing an empty cereal bar wrapper in the bin. "I'd stay but I need to get home sometime soon as I've a couple of people coming round to look at the flat."

Jack shook his head as he shrugged into his jacket. "No problem — you go on your training run, Daniels, and you get back to your flat, Amanda. Cooper can cope here. How's the flat hunting going, anyway?" Jack was aware Cassidy intended to move out of her small one-bedroomed flat, in the same accommodation block as Daniels, but with the housing market the way it was, she was finding it difficult.

Cassidy grimaced as she reached for her jacket. "Not so good. Everywhere is so expensive these days, I think I'm going to have to look for a flatmate."

Jack reached the door. "Let me know if you find anything more on the CCTV, Cooper — but otherwise don't make it a late one. I'll be here for a while longer, but I don't plan to stay all night."

"What about the news article, boss?" Cooper gestured towards his computer screen. "We've all seen it."

Jack made a face. "It is what it is, Cooper. Although I don't usually like giving the killer a voice, I feel it was a step that needed to be taken."

"You expecting some flak?"

"A shedload, Cooper, but nothing for you to worry about. It was my decision, and mine alone. Just stoking the fire, and all part of the plan." Jack hoped he sounded more convincing than he felt. "Might be an idea to keep your heads down for a while, though. Let the dust settle. Maybe don't answer the phone."

As he went to grab the door handle, the familiar chirp of an incoming text sounded. Instantly wary that it might be the chief superintendent on the warpath as the nuclear fallout from the *Daily Courier* article began, Jack relaxed when he saw it was only his brother.

CHAPTER TWENTY

Time: 7.15 p.m.
Date: Sunday 12 April 2015
Location: Kettle's Yard Mews, London

Leaving Cooper studying the CCTV, Jack welcomed the peace and quiet of the flat. As soon as he'd collapsed onto the sofa, Marmaduke had leaped up and made himself at home. With the stirrings of another headache beginning to throb at his temples, joining the ache in his foot, Jack tossed a couple of painkillers into his mouth and dry swallowed.

He tried to force all thoughts of the Central Line Killer and Dougie King from his mind, needing some time away from both; but he knew paracetamol probably wasn't going to be enough. Just as he rested his head back against the cushions and closed his eyes, the sound of the intercom for the communal door downstairs buzzed.

Marmaduke jumped down from Jack's lap, a disgruntled meow following.

"Sorry, mate." Jack pulled his eyes open and heaved himself to his feet. The text he'd received at the station earlier had been from Stu, warning him about an impending visit.

Sorry, bro, the message had said, followed by a smiley face emoji. *Isabel insisted. Act surprised!*

During the time that Jack had been laid up after Ritchie Greenwood had tried, and failed, to blast him skywards, Isabel had taken it upon herself to go into full-on mothering mode. Every day for the first fortnight she had turned up with bulging shopping bags and cleaning products. She had insisted on staying to prepare his meals, clean the flat, and then undertake any other odd jobs that Jack didn't feel really needed doing — but he let her get on with it just the same.

"*It makes her feel useful,*" had been his brother's explanation. "*I'd leave her to it if I were you — it's less trouble that way.*"

It got to the point that Jack eventually handed over his spare key so Isabel could let herself in and out, saving him the time and effort of opening the door. After the initial two weeks, she'd reduced her visits to every other day for another six — and he started to get used to the intrusion, even welcoming it on occasion.

Pulling open the door, he greeted the pair by putting on his best surprised look. "Wow, this is an unexpected treat. Come on in." Jack caught his brother's eye, and they exchanged a knowing grin.

"I hope you haven't eaten yet," breezed Isabel, immediately heading for the small kitchen area at the back of the flat and heaving two carrier bags up onto the work surface. "Because I've brought dinner."

"Not yet, no." Jack thought of the leftover curry he'd been planning to devour sitting in the fridge. "Good timing."

"And I hope you're hungry too, because I've brought plenty." Isabel flashed a smile over her shoulder. "Why don't you both take yourselves over to the sofa and watch some TV or something while I prepare? Mac — get your brother a beer."

"Best do as you're told, bro," muttered Mac, running the gauntlet to the fridge to grab two bottles of Budweiser. "Trust me, it's less painful in the long run."

Jack headed back to the sofa, Marmaduke returning to resume his position. Mac grinned as he handed Jack a beer. "See, I told you you should keep him!"

Jack made a face but carried on rubbing the ginger tabby cat behind both ears. As Isabel busied herself in the kitchen, he flicked through the TV channels. The final day of the Masters golf tournament was underway, but Jack had little interest in the game. His brother was more of a football fan and spent ten minutes telling Jack all about the strengths and weaknesses of the current Chelsea side, and then their hopes of securing the Premier League title. Jack made suitable noises where appropriate, but football wasn't his thing either.

If he chose to watch anything, it would be rugby. He'd enjoyed watching a lot of the Six Nations matches in recent weeks — the upside of recovering from a fractured foot was having extra time on his hands. It had been a thrilling contest, England only losing out on the final day on points difference to Ireland. The final round of matches had seen a record-breaking 221 points scored across just three matches, the most ever in a single weekend. And Jack had lived and breathed every one of them.

Muting the TV, he left it on a twenty-four-hour news channel. Even without sound, Jack knew what the lead story would be — the Central Line Killer. Another press release had gone out, naming the first victim as Keeley Saul following the positive ID at the mortuary. But now the article penned by the killer himself was making headline news. It had even pushed the Hatton Garden jewellery heist from the top spot, something that had been in the news continuously since the beginning of the week. The robbery had been unprecedented, and the capital was still reeling from the sheer audacity of it.

Until the Central Line Killer came along.

"That one of yours?" Mac gestured with his bottle towards the TV.

Jack nodded. "It is. I hoped we might avoid the shit hitting the fan, but . . ." A non-committal shrug followed. He knew he'd left the station's PR department holding a ticking time bomb, and he was glad he'd had the foresight to switch his phone off.

"Such a nasty business," commented Isabel, appearing with three plates of homemade curry. "Makes you scared to go out on your own at night, what with that and the jewellery thieves still out there."

"It's a tricky time, for sure." Jack cleared space on the coffee table for the plates. "But we're doing all we can on both cases." As a response it sounded pathetic, something he was all too aware of.

Isabel settled down on the sofa next to Mac, adding a plate of warm naan bread to the table. She nodded towards the food. "Freshly made chicken jalfrezi — much better for you than the takeaways you seem to live on, Jack. So many hidden calories and salt — not good for your arteries or your intestines. And don't try to deny it, I've seen the contents of your fridge *and* your kitchen bin. The evidence is irrefutable."

Jack reached for his plate, a suitably contrite look on his face. "I wouldn't dream of it. This smells delicious, thank you. I'm sure my digestive system and blood pressure will forever be in your debt."

"I've also brought you a selection of spices, plus some lean cuts of beef and pork so you can whip up a quick curry when you get in from work at night — it doesn't take long and so much healthier for you."

Jack grinned, tearing off a portion of naan bread. "Thank you, I can't wait." He exchanged another knowing look with his brother before stuffing the warm bread in his mouth. "You're too good to me. Both of you. I don't deserve it."

The rest of the evening passed by pleasantly enough, and Jack even managed to temporarily forget about Dougie King and the potential nuclear fallout heading his way. They'd switched off the news and put on some music instead — Mac and Isabel both making fun of Jack's eclectic tastes.

As enjoyable as the evening had been, Jack wasn't sad to close the door behind them and have the flat to himself again when the time came. With leftover chicken jalfrezi stashed away in the fridge, he reached for another beer before switching his phone back on. He could quite happily have kept it silenced all night but wondered if Cooper or anyone else had been trying to get in touch with him. Slap bang in the middle of a case, he shouldn't be going AWOL. Taking a deep breath, and an even deeper swig of the Budweiser, he braced himself for the onslaught.

And he wasn't disappointed.

Five texts from Dougie King.

And two voicemails.

But it was the one from DS Cooper that caught his attention.

* * *

Time: 10.45 p.m.
Date: Sunday 12 April 2015
Location: Metropolitan Police HQ, London

After taking a taxi to the station, Jack shot up the stairs two at a time. Bursting into the incident room, he was more than a little surprised to see Cassidy and Daniels there, too.

"Trevor and I thought we'd pop back and help out," explained Cassidy in response to the inquisitive look on Jack's face. "Trevor's run got cancelled and my flat hunters didn't show."

"I'm no' sure I believe them, boss." Cooper grinned from behind a burger wrapper. "I think they came back to check up on my eating habits."

Jack eyed the empty crisp packets and energy drink cans in the bin next to the detective sergeant's desk. "They could have a point." He switched his gaze to Cooper's computer screen, which was already angled towards him. "Show me what came in on the DNA."

Cooper scrunched up the burger wrapper and swivelled his chair back round to face the monitor. "Notification came

193

through about an hour ago. A hit on the database for the DNA found at the Yorkshire sexual assault scenes."

Jack's mind churned. As soon as he'd seen Cooper's message he'd jumped in a taxi and headed straight over. *They had a name.* And if the Yorkshire sex assaults were the work of the Central Line Killer, then Operation Quicksand had just been dealt an unexpected boost.

A name.

Cooper made way for Jack at his desk. "Two semen samples from the '96 and '97 cases are a match to Ellis Magee."

Jack squinted towards the monitor. "What else can you tell me?" He noted Cooper's pensive expression, the same expression on Cassidy and Daniels' faces, too. The hairs on the back of Jack's neck began to prickle, his stomach tightening. Something wasn't right. "What's wrong?"

"As soon as we got the match, I did a search for Ellis Magee on the system. Found a match to a forty-three-year-old male originally from Hackney."

"And?" Jack scoured the faces of his team once again. Why weren't they more excited? This was a breakthrough they hadn't expected to get — surely they should be bouncing off the ceiling? He squinted back towards Cooper's computer. "What is it you're not telling me?"

Cooper cleared his throat. "Ellis Magee was convicted in Sheffield Crown Court in September 1998 for a series of robberies across South Yorkshire, one of which resulted in the death of a security guard. He was given a life sentence with a minimum tariff of twenty-seven years. He was arrested on the third of January of that year and held in custody until his trial date. He's currently at Wandsworth, not due for parole until 2025."

Jack felt his shoulders sag, his body deflate, as if someone had just stabbed him with a pin, and a rusty one at that. It didn't take a genius to work it out. If Magee had been arrested on 3 January 1998 and remanded in custody until his trial in September that year, then there was no way he could have been the Central Line Killer. And, as he was still languishing in prison now, he wasn't their current killer either.

Shit.

Suddenly, the beer and chicken jalfrezi from earlier shifted uncomfortably in the bottom of Jack's stomach. This wasn't the kind of breakthrough he'd been hoping for. He gazed up at the whiteboards. "OK, so it looks like the links to the '96 and '97 attacks really were a red herring after all. All we can do is move on and concentrate on what we do know."

"Mrs Saul phoned me again after the visit to the mortuary." Cassidy's face looked glum. "She's understandably distraught but wants to be kept up to date with everything to do with the investigation. I've told her we'll arrange a family liaison officer to be with them."

Jack nodded. "Yes, we'll get that sorted first thing tomorrow." He glanced at the clock. "It's late. I think we all need some sleep before we crack on with this again in the morning. Cooper, I want you to stay with the CCTV tomorrow. Amanda and Daniels — find out all you can about Keeley Saul."

CHAPTER TWENTY-ONE

Time: 8.45 a.m.
Date: Monday 13 April 2015
Location: Metropolitan Police HQ, London

Jack had made it into the office at a little after six. As delicious as the chicken jalfrezi had been, it had continued to swirl uncomfortably in his stomach as he tossed and turned throughout the night. The revelation about the DNA hit had dealt them an unexpected blow. In the small hours of the morning, he'd drummed up the courage to read Dougie King's text messages, and then listen to his voicemails, and had been pleasantly surprised as to their content. There was no swearing, at least, which Jack took to be an encouraging sign. He knew he would have to face the chief at some point today but intended to put it off as long as possible. After hiding in his office for as long as he dared, finding time for an early morning call to Dr Matthews at the mortuary, he decided to brave the journey to the incident room.

His mood was instantly buoyed when he saw DS Cooper's face sporting a broad grin.

"We've got a name, boss — for our second victim."

Jack strode across to the detective sergeant's desk, eyeing the mound of empty crisp packets and energy drink cans littering its surface. "I thought I told you to go home, Cooper? You've not been here all night, have you?"

Cooper grinned again but shook his head. "Not quite. I came in early as I wanted to crack on with the rest of the CCTV. After logging all the registrations for vehicles in the area around the bus stop, I decided to try and find out where she might have come from."

"And?" Jack pulled a chair over to Cooper's desk.

"I managed to track her back to Cracknell Street, where she went into a hairdressing salon just before one thirty. She came out ninety minutes later." Cooper angled the computer monitor in Jack's direction and started playing the images. "We see her leaving there at three o'clock and heading towards Beyton Road."

A series of jumpy, grainy shots showed a woman heading along a narrow side street. The figure then held a bag over her head and broke into a jog as the heavens opened above. It was unmistakably their victim.

"I've just got off the phone to the manager of the salon. Woman by the name of Sherri Jeffery — seems to know our victim relatively well, a regular customer. She told me the girl's name is Jessica Fleming."

"Good work, Cooper. We have an address, too?"

Cooper nodded. "I also got her mobile number."

"Any idea if she lived alone? Had a partner?"

Cooper paused the CCTV just as the woman disappeared from view. "The manager told me that Jessica had recently split from her long-term boyfriend, a chap by the name of Tony. She doesn't know the guy's surname. They lived together for a while but, after the split, he moved out."

"Any other family?"

Cooper shook his head. "Unclear at this stage. We'll do the usual checks and see what comes up."

"Keep digging. See if you can find us some next of kin, then we can take a run out to her home address later on today. Are the others around somewhere?"

"They've just nipped up to the canteen to get us breakfast."

"What about our friendly journalist?" Another reason Jack had been unable to sleep last night had been Lorna Henshaw and the niggles Frank Tyler had mentioned. "I still want to know more about her background."

Cooper nodded and pulled his notebook towards him. "Trevor's been working on that. From what he's managed to pull so far, she's always been involved in journalism in one way or another since leaving education. She studied English and drama at university then, after a couple of temporary admin jobs, she secured a place at a local newspaper. Seems to have worked her way up from the bottom. Stayed with that newspaper for four years, before landing a junior reporter role with one of the bigger tabloids. She joined the *Daily Courier* in 1997 and took a step back from the job last year." Shrugging, Cooper caught Jack's eye. "That's about it. She's never been married and isn't on any form of social media."

Jack sighed. "Any known links to any of our victims?"

"I think Trevor's still working on that angle. But we got sidetracked with the CCTV this morning."

"Well, I'm reliably informed that cameras have now been installed at Henshaw's property. Have we had any joy at trying to locate that motorbike courier from Sunday morning?"

"Next on the list, boss."

Jack jumped as the incident room door swung open, but it was only Cassidy and Daniels armed with paper plates. He breathed a sigh of relief as he got up from the chair. Dougie King had yet to track him down.

"I'm heading back to my office for a bit. I spoke to Dr Matthews earlier and the PM should happen sometime this morning. Daniels, can you head over there and manage that one alone today? I need Amanda and Cooper digging into both our victims' backgrounds and keeping with the CCTV angle." Jack could tell by the eager expression on Daniels' face that he didn't mind at all.

"Of course," replied the detective, placing a paper plate with two bacon rolls on it next to DS Cooper. "Leave it with me."

Jack noticed the relieved expression on Cassidy's face as she was spared another trip to the mortuary.

"And as for Lorna Henshaw, I'm still not done with her. Keep cross-checking for links with *any* of our victims, including the 1998 murders. There must be something somewhere."

* * *

Time: 10.15 a.m.
Date: Monday 13 April 2015
Location: Liverpool Lime Street Station

The further north he travelled, Robert Carmichael noted the weather steadily improved — leaving the heavy skies and thunderstorms behind in London and replacing them with much clearer and calmer conditions. As he exited the station to track down a taxi, the Liverpool sunshine warmed his skin.

The hotel was a walkable distance, but he didn't want to rely on his navigation skills when the funeral was due to start in less than two hours. There would be plenty of time to walk the streets later if he fancied reliving his youth and embracing nostalgia.

As the taxi pulled away into the morning traffic, Carmichael stared out of the window. On the journey up he'd tried to think how many times he'd been back to the North West since leaving aged eight. It could only be a handful of times at best. With no family to speak of other than Genete, there hadn't been a reason to.

Fleetingly, Carmichael had considered coming by car — the journey could be done in under four hours on a good run — but he'd opted for the train for several reasons. The first one was that his car was currently making all sorts of odd noises, noises that he couldn't quite put his finger on. He'd put off getting it looked at by the garage, but it would be sod's law that as soon as the tyres hit the motorway something disastrous would happen.

That in itself was a good enough reason to take the train — but it wasn't the only one.

The main reason was that he didn't quite trust himself to go through with it.

He could book the hotel, fill the car with petrol, even plan the route he would take in the minutest detail — but that didn't mean he would actually arrive. There were countless places along the way where he could turn the car around and go back home, plenty of service stations offering him an easy way out.

But getting onto a train was a different matter altogether. Once those doors slid shut behind you, changing your mind and heading back home seemed much more of a challenge.

So, he'd boarded one of the earliest trains from Euston and hadn't looked back.

By the time the taxi dropped him off at the hotel, he only had twenty minutes to check in and get changed before needing to start making his way to the crematorium. He'd put his one and only decent suit into the dry cleaners and even polished his good leather shoes; he wasn't sure why. She was his mother, granted, but the woman hadn't cared about him during her lifetime, and he was sure as hell she hadn't at the time of her death. So he didn't really owe her anything — not even his respect, if he was being brutal about it.

But something else was compelling him to come here.

And that something was Genete.

If there was even the outside chance that she would be there, the trip would have been worthwhile. But would she turn up? Would he even recognise her if she did? It had been over thirty years, after all. Doubt started to creep inside Carmichael's head as he was shown to his room on the top floor.

Glancing at his watch, he saw that he had precisely ten minutes to make the short walk to the crematorium, so he pulled his suit from the protective suit carrier, pleased to see that it had survived the journey relatively crease free, and changed into a fresh shirt.

The map on his phone told him the crematorium was only a twelve-minute walk away in a more-or-less straight line from the hotel. With the morning bright and clear, showing no hint of the thunderstorms plaguing the south-east of the country, Carmichael pulled out a pair of sunglasses and set off.

After a few minutes, a sign told him to bear left, and Carmichael soon found himself walking through a leafy park complete with duck pond. Several young mothers were standing by the side of the water, keeping a firm hold of their excitable toddlers while they threw in a selection of crusts for the ducks to feed on.

Carmichael frowned as he passed the pond. With sunglasses shielding his eyes from the bright sunlight, a distant memory tugged at his brain. Hadn't he and Genete fed the ducks somewhere like this? Somewhere close to their home? The memory sharpened — he could almost hear the sound of Genete's excited squeals as she watched her big brother throw the stale bread into the water. It felt so real.

Carmichael was aware that feeding bread to ducks was sometimes frowned upon these days, depending on who you talked to — but, growing up, it had been something every child had done at least once.

Leaving the duck pond and excitable children behind, he continued through a gate that led him out into a large parking area. Right before him stood the crematorium — a small, understated brick building with a flat roof.

Feeling oddly nervous, Carmichael approached the entrance and stepped inside.

* * *

There was barely the whisper of a knock at the door before DS Cooper burst into Jack's office. "Sorry, boss — but I think you'll want to hear this."

Jack raised his gaze from the stack of emails he was wading through. He had successfully avoided Dougie King so far, although the silence was starting to unnerve him. He'd used the time to check in with Elliott, and given Frank Tyler a call, too. If he tied up the desk phone for long enough, then Dougie King's PA would have a hard time getting through. It was a feeble way to go about things but Jack was out of other options. "Go on."

"Jessica Fleming's boyfriend. The manager at the salon told me his name was Tony. I've just been taking another look at the vehicle registrations lifted from the CCTV close to the bus stop where we last see her. And guess what I found? A van registered to a Mr Anthony Kingdom."

"And we think that's the ex-boyfriend?" Jack's eyebrows hitched. "Anthony is a common enough name."

"That was my initial thought, too." Cooper paused, a smile emerging. "But the van is registered to our victim's home address."

"In that case . . ." Jack pushed himself up from his chair, grabbing his jacket. "He sounds like someone we need to talk to. We'll need to get a current address for him, though."

The detective sergeant's smiled widened. "That shouldn't be a problem, boss. The van caught on camera has his company details emblazoned across the side. Plus, his mobile number."

Jack swiped up his car keys. "Then let's arrange to go and have a little chat, shall we?"

* * *

Time: 11.00 a.m.
Date: Monday 13 April 2015
Location: Parkland Crematorium, Liverpool

"Stairway to Heaven" wasn't the song Carmichael expected to hear as his mother was brought into the crematorium. But, then again, what did he know? Maybe it was one of her favourites.

The building was like many a crematorium that he'd been to over the years. To the uninitiated they could look quite cold and bleak, both on the inside and out. But Carmichael liked their simplicity. When his time came, not that he wanted to think about it just yet, he wanted something unassuming like this. He didn't want an ageing church with stained-glass windows and choirs, uncomfortable pews and dusty hymn books. Plain wood-panelled walls and quiet carpeted floors were more than good enough for him.

But he would like a few more attendees, if he was being honest. Taking a look around, he was able to count those paying their respects to the recently departed Sheila Carmichael on the fingers of one hand.

And that included him.

The simple wooden coffin passed by, deftly deposited onto the wooden supports at the front. The smart-suited pall-bearers then stepped to the side, heads bowed as they respectfully and soundlessly edged away. Carmichael hadn't been asked to carry his mother's coffin, and he probably would have declined anyway, but he still wondered who they were — employees of the funeral directors, maybe?

It mattered not in the grand scheme of things.

The song petered out and was replaced with a heavy silence.

Carmichael soon started to wish he hadn't worn such a close-fitting suit. The warmth from the sun outside was filtering in through several high windows, causing sweat to gather around the inside collar of his new shirt. Shifting his stance a little, he glanced toward the mourners standing in the front row and wondered if any of them knew he was a relative of the deceased. But, then again, why would they? He had told the solicitors he wasn't interested in attending the funeral, and they hadn't replied to ask why. He guessed it didn't matter to them either way.

The funeral celebrant stood a short step away from the coffin and indicated that the small gathering should now be seated. Carmichael dutifully sat down on the fourth row behind the other mourners.

"Sheila was born right here in Liverpool on the twenty-seventh of July 1950 to parents Doreen and John. After leaving school aged fifteen, she began work at a textile factory in the city. Life wasn't kind to Sheila, but she always tried her best to succeed in everything she did."

Carmichael felt the back of his neck prickle, and it wasn't just because of the warmth of the building. His mother had been good at necking the gin; that was something he *did* remember.

The celebrant continued. "In 1973 she met Paul and became the proud mother of two children in the years that followed. She was a devoted mother to both children and they quickly became the centre of her world."

Carmichael clamped his mouth shut, feeling his temperature steadily rising.

Devoted mother?

Centre of her world?

It wasn't the childhood Carmichael remembered. Did they even have the right person in the box? Where was any mention of the cold flat, where ice formed on the *insides* of the windows? What about the empty fridge? The empty cupboards? Where was mention of the hand-me-downs that he and Genete were forced to wear, the damp patches on their bedroom walls, the freezing cold nights when they were left alone to fend for themselves while their mother drank herself into a stupor? Where were the bruised, tear-stained faces both children sported when the gin got too much?

That was the childhood he remembered — not this rose-tinted version floating out across the hushed crematorium.

"Sheila continued to be a loving mother as the children grew up, even though life continued to be hard on her." The celebrant went on to describe the idyllic life Sheila Carmichael had created for her two young children, but Carmichael found himself tuning out, having already heard enough. Where was the alcoholism? The neglect? The absent father convicted of murder and sentenced to life in prison?

He took a look towards the other four mourners, all seated on the front row. Could one of them be Genete? He hadn't seen his sister since he was taken in by the Tindlemans when he was eight and Genete had been almost six — but instantly knew neither of the two women there were her. Maybe they were from the solicitors, or the funeral directors, just making up the numbers.

He turned his attention back to the service.

"Sheila Carmichael — we honour your life and are blessed to have heard your laughter, seen your smile and felt your reassuring hand in ours. Our lives are richer for having known you and having shared the love you gave us and the love we felt for you."

If love came in the form of a slap, grimaced Carmichael.

"At the blowing of the wind, and in the chill of winter, at the opening of the buds and on the rebirth of spring, we will remember you. At the blueness of the skies and in the warmth of summer, at the misting of the leaves and in the brightness of the autumn, we will remember you. We honour your journey through life, and we remember with gratitude your deep love for your children, family and friends. We are grateful that you have been a part of our lives, but we now wish you well on the next part of your journey. May you travel safely and know that our love goes with you."

Carmichael swallowed the retort that threatened to leave his lips.

"You are no longer bound by this world, but a part of it. No longer tied to one place or time, but free. And so we ask that you go now, with all our love, as tenderly and reverently we yield your body to be cremated. Earth to earth. Ashes to ashes. Dust to dust."

Carmichael was familiar enough with the procedure at cremations to know what came next, and he wasn't disappointed — the red velvet curtains parting as the wooden coffin began its final journey. Interestingly, his mother's choice of exit song — or whoever it was who had chosen on her behalf — was "We'll Meet Again".

As the coffin disappeared behind the curtain, everyone stood up and Carmichael followed suit. He was glad there hadn't been any hymns or bible readings — the mother he knew would have been interested in neither.

And then it was over.

The other four mourners began to file out, not waiting for the velvet curtains to close, and Carmichael followed them to the side exit. The sunlight hit his eyes as soon as the door opened, making him scrabble to find his sunglasses again. Once able to focus, he saw an area directly in front of him called the Flower Terrace. He hadn't thought to bring any flowers with him, and didn't expect anyone else to have done so either. If the other mourners were indeed from the solicitors or funeral directors, then he was sure they wouldn't be wasting valuable funds on a bunch of carnations for a woman they didn't know.

Carmichael paused by the flower terrace, surprised to see several bunches of flowers left for his mother. Leaning forward, he peered through the tinted lenses of his sunglasses to read the small cards that accompanied them.

His attention was instantly drawn to one of them.

Rest in Peace, Sheila — from all at Cavendish House

Cavendish House?

Carmichael frowned and took out his phone, taking a quick snap of the card so he could research the place later. As he did so, he noted two of the mourners were also lingering at the terrace and, if he wasn't very much mistaken, their eyes looked moist.

"Did you know her?" He heard himself ask the question before he realised what he was doing. "Sheila Carmichael?"

Both women turned towards him, guarded looks on their faces, but eventually they nodded.

"Yes," spoke one of the women. "She was a resident with us at Cavendish House."

"Cavendish House? Where is that exactly?"

The women exchanged a hesitant look, Carmichael sensing their reluctance to answer. He tried a smile. "Sorry — let me introduce myself, I'm Robert. Robert Carmichael. She was . . ." He paused, searching for the correct word. "She was my mother."

CHAPTER TWENTY-TWO

Time: 11.30 a.m.
Date: Monday 13 April 2015
Location: Swansea Lane, London

Jack left the Mondeo parked around the corner, content to walk the final twenty or thirty metres on foot. A call to the mobile number on the side of the Kingdom and Son Carpets van, pretending to be interested in a quote for a new stair carpet, meant Jack and Cooper were expected.

As anticipated, Kingdom's van was parked outside the small, mid-terrace house. Jack led the way to the front door, Cooper bringing up the rear, and it only took one swift knock to bring the man to the door. Jack plastered his best welcoming smile on his face as it opened.

"Mr Kingdom? Anthony? We spoke on the phone earlier?"

A brief look of confusion crossed Tony Kingdom's face as he peered over Jack's shoulder to see Cooper loitering on the path behind. "Yeah — we did. Interested in a stair carpet, wasn't it?"

Jack saw no reason to beat around the bush and drew out his warrant card. "Well, yes, that is indeed what I said — I'm

Detective Inspector Jack MacIntosh from the Metropolitan Police. This here is my colleague, Detective Sergeant Cooper. Mind if we come in?"

Confusion now morphed into suspicion, and Jack immediately sensed the man's stance change — the door closing a little and one of Kingdom's booted feet edging forward to block entry.

Jack kept the neutral expression on his face. "It won't take a minute, I'm sure. And much better for all concerned that we do this inside, don't you think? Rather than conducting such a sensitive conversation out here on the doorstep. I mean, anyone could overhear, couldn't they?"

Jack could see the carpet fitter weighing up the consequences before finally taking a step back. "As you wish."

The hallway was narrow with aged wallpaper, the carpet somewhat faded and worn. Jack suppressed the smile that was threatening to emerge. A carpet fitter with a shit carpet. It wasn't a good look.

Tony Kingdom showed them into a small front room, the same dated wallpaper gracing the walls.

"You live here alone, Mr Kingdom?" Jack positioned himself by the window, his back to the curtains that he noticed were still closed.

Confusion returned to the carpet fitter's face. "Why? What's that got to do with anything?" He paused, then seemed to relent. "It's my dad's place, I'm just stopping here for a while — I'm in between places at the moment."

"I see. You used to live with your girlfriend, Jessica Fleming, is that right?"

"*Ex*-girlfriend," corrected Kingdom, an edge of hostility entering his tone. "We split up."

"I'm sorry to hear that, Mr Kingdom. Do you happen to have contact details for any close family she may have? Parents? Siblings? I take it that she didn't have any children?"

"Look, I don't mean to be funny . . ."

"And I'm not laughing, Mr Kingdom." Jack noted Cooper discreetly stepping to the side, positioning himself between the carpet fitter and the door to block off any potential escape route. He gave the detective sergeant an appreciative nod. "I'm afraid I have some bad news. We have reason to believe that Jessica was found dead yesterday morning." He waited for the man's reaction, but Kingdom's face remained stony. "She has yet to be formally identified, hence we need contact details for her family. But we are quite sure it's her."

Eventually the carpet fitter responded. "Dead? How?"

"I'm afraid I can't divulge that at this stage, but we're treating the death as unexplained at present. Can you tell me the last time you saw her?"

Kingdom briefly glanced towards the now blocked-off exit. "Ages ago. Like I said — we split up."

"How long ago is 'ages ago', exactly?"

Kingdom shrugged. "I dunno. A month, maybe. I don't keep a diary."

"So, you wouldn't have seen her at all this week — specifically on Saturday?"

The carpet fitter shook his head. "Nope."

"What about Cracknell Street? When was the last time you would have been in that part of the city?"

A shrug this time. "Again, ages ago. I don't go out that way much."

"Not this week at all?"

"Nope."

"How about Beyton Road?"

Another shrug, followed by a further shake of the head. "Not been there in ages."

Jack exchanged a quick look with Cooper. There was the first lie right there.

"And what about family? Do you know where we might find her next of kin? Her parents, for example?"

Kingdom's jaw tightened. "I never met them."

I wonder why, mused Jack.

Once again, Kingdom's eyes darted toward the door.

"Just a few more questions, Mr Kingdom, then we can leave you in peace. What about other family?"

The carpet fitter sighed. "She has a sister, works in a shop on Tottenham Court Road. I've never been introduced. And her parents I think live down in Sussex somewhere. Her dad's an architect. But, like I said, I've never met any of them."

"That's certainly a shame — they've missed out on your sparkling wit and personality."

The muscles in Kingdom's jaw tensed. "What are you trying to say?"

"Absolutely nothing at all, Mr Kingdom. You're being most helpful. One last thing — I don't suppose you know of anyone who might want to do Jessica any harm, do you? Any enemies?"

"No one I can think of."

"How long were you together?"

"Two years, on and off."

For Jessica's sake, Jack hoped it was mostly *off*. "And how is business these days? There a lot of money in carpet fitting?"

A guarded look entered the man's eyes. "Business is all right. I manage."

"Is it just you? You run the business by yourself?"

Kingdom gave a hesitant nod. "Just me. Took over from my dad when he gave it up a couple of years ago."

"And you've always lived and worked in London?"

The carpet fitter slowly shook his head. "We came up from Dagenham 'bout ten years ago."

Jack filed the information away in his head then plastered another plastic smile on his face. "In that case, we'll leave you to the rest of your day, Mr Kingdom. Thank you for your time."

"That's it?"

"For now." Jack began to walk towards DS Cooper and the door. "If I think of anything else, I'll be in touch. Don't go disappearing anywhere, just in case."

Tony Kingdom followed the detectives out into the hallway. "So, you're not wanting that quote for a carpet, then?"

* * *

"Not the sharpest tool in the box, Cooper." Jack fired the Mondeo's engine into life. "But we know he's told at least one porky in there."

Cooper nodded. "Aye. His van was definitely in the vicinity of the bus stop."

"But if we confront him now, I'm sure he'll concoct some cock and bull story about it not being him driving — so let's see if we can track the van's movements elsewhere that day, see if we can't actually see the driver."

"You think it's a coincidence the van is seen at the exact location Jessica disappeared from?"

"Not a chance — but we'll let him stew for a bit while we check out the van. Then I want to bring him in for a more formal chat. In the meantime, let's see if we can locate the sister and the parents."

The journey back to the station would take around twenty minutes, and Jack found himself zoning out for much of it. His head was cluttered with thoughts about Tony Kingdom. Had they just stumbled across the Central Line Killer? A carpet fitter from Dagenham?

Coming to a stop at a set of traffic lights, Jack glanced out of the side window. A split second later, hands still clamped to the wheel, he wrenched the Mondeo sharply to the right, crossing the carriageway and coming to an abrupt stop on the other side of the road. A cacophony of car horns blasted in his wake, plus an angry shout from a startled Lycra-clad cyclist Jack had missed by inches.

"Boss?" Cooper braced himself against the passenger door. "Everything OK?"

Without a word, Jack threw open the driver's door and hurtled across the pavement in a matter of seconds. "Where is he?" Jack grabbed hold of the man's upper arm, yanking him backwards and almost sending him crashing to the ground. "Where's Ritchie?"

Rhys Williams cried out, his voice edged in pain and not a small amount of fear. "What the fuck, man?"

Jack used his other hand to pin Rhys up against the out-side wall of a mobile phone shop. "I'll ask you one more time — where is he?"

Jack had recognised Rhys the minute he set eyes on him, the man sauntering along the street without a care in the world. But the lad clearly hadn't seen Jack's impression of Bruce Willis, dodging the traffic and cyclists in order to apprehend him.

"I dunno who you mean — get off me, man."

Jack stood firm. If anything, he put more weight behind his grip. "Don't lie to me, Rhys. It's not big and it's definitely not clever." Pausing, he held the young man's gaze in his. "You don't recognise me, do you?"

Rhys held the stare, confusion and defiance vying for dominance. Then his eyes widened, and his mouth slackened. "It's you, isn't it? You're the geezer that came to the pub with that doctor fella."

Jack slowly nodded. "And the penny finally drops." He again tightened his grip. "So, I'll ask you again, Rhys. Where's Ritchie? And don't tell me you don't know because, believe me, I'm not in the mood today."

Rhys's eyes darted fearfully from side to side as if looking for an escape route, but Jack soon felt the young man's tense shoulders relax. "Honestly, I don't know. They shipped out from the pub — had to go somewhere else sharpish, but I don't know where. They don't tell me nothin' — not until they want me to do something for 'em."

Jack regarded the young man for a second, figuring he had to be nineteen at the most. Just how had someone like him ended up in the clutches of Ritchie and his gang?

"OK." Wariness edged Jack's tone as he released his grip a little. "Say I believe you . . ."

"Honest, I swear! I don't know where they are!"

"You all right, mate?"

Jack turned toward a voice coming from over his left shoulder, coming face to face with a burly-looking thug lock-ing eyes with Rhys.

"This tosser bothering you?"

Despite being outweighed by at least four stone, and the man's fingers sporting a number of rings that could inflict a fair amount of damage if they were on the tail end of a punch, Jack's patience was wearing thin. "Just fuck off, mate." Pinning Rhys to the wall with one hand, Jack fumbled in his jacket pocket for his warrant card. "Unless you want to see the inside of a police cell in the next five seconds, I suggest you move along." He flashed the warrant card plus a dark look in the man's direction. "*Now* would be good."

The would-be Samaritan didn't need asking twice, his hands already raised in surrender as he backed away. Jack turned his attention to Rhys. "OK, I'll believe you for now. But I want you to tell me the minute you know where he might be."

The look on Rhys's face told Jack that might be a step too far — so he decided to sugar-coat it a little. "And who knows — you keep me in the loop regarding Ritchie, then maybe I can do the same for you sometime. Give you help when you need it. Think about it."

Jack released his grip and, before the lad had time to take to his heels, he pressed a business card into his sweaty palm. "Remember, the minute you know where he is, I want to know."

* * *

Time: 11.45 a.m.
Date: Monday 13 April 2015
Location: Swansea Lane, London

Tony Kingdom watched the detectives disappear from sight before letting the net curtains fall back into place. Then he'd stood at the shrouded window for the next ten minutes, disquiet mounting.

Fuck.

Jessica fucking Fleming.

He was under no illusion that this would be the end of it — he knew the police would be back before too long, hammering at his door once more.

Fuck.

Mind made up, he grabbed his phone and started searching.

"Who was that at the door? It sounded important." Tony turned to see his father standing in the doorway.

"Just business, Dad. Nothing to worry about." The look on the old man's face told the younger Kingdom that his words hadn't had the desired effect. "Seriously — just let me deal with it."

Dennis Kingdom shrugged and started to back out of the room. "No argument from me there, son — but just see that you do. I know a police officer when I see one and I don't take too kindly to that filth knocking at my door at all hours. If this is a sign of things to come, maybe it's time you moved on."

Tony was about to say that the middle of the day wasn't exactly "all hours" but decided against it. Some battles weren't worth pursuing. Instead, he waited for his father to disappear before resuming his Google search.

Does bleach remove traces of DNA?

* * *

Time: 11.50 a.m.
Date: Monday 13 April 2015
Location: The Duck Pond Café, Liverpool

After the short service, the walk back through the park and past the duck pond hadn't taken them long. He'd chosen a table inside, tucked away in a corner to give them some privacy — but as the café's only customers it was largely a moot point. Carmichael placed the tray down and handed out the mugs.

"Who were the other two at the service? The two men in your row, both dressed in suits."

Judith Farrow took her hot chocolate and wrapped her hands around the warmth. "They were from the solicitors. They came to Cavendish House not so long ago to help Sheila with her will."

Carmichael sat down, placing a plate of three generous slices of fruit cake into the centre of the table. Even though he hadn't felt like eating anything, it seemed the right thing to do in the circumstances — tea and cake. Or in this instance, coffee and hot chocolate. "They wrote to tell me she'd died and told me I was a beneficiary, but also said there was virtually nothing in her estate. If she didn't have anything to leave behind, it begs the question why she would need to employ solicitors like Houghton and Sandford to write a will for her. I'm quite sure they don't come cheap." Carmichael had researched the firm before boarding the train — they were one of the most exclusive, and expensive, solicitors in the North West.

Judith exchanged a look with her colleague, who had introduced herself earlier as Tessa.

Carmichael immediately sensed the uneasiness. "Look, I have no axe to grind here. Far from it. I last saw my mother when I was five. I'm not interested in anything she may have had. I certainly don't need or want her money. I'm just intrigued."

Judith's face relaxed a little and she took a sip of her hot chocolate. "Sheila did have some money at the time of her death, but not a lot. What she did have she wanted to split between Alcoholics Anonymous and Liverpool Women's Refuge."

Carmichael's eyes widened over the rim of his coffee cup. "Really?"

Judith nodded. "She was quite insistent that whatever she had left went to them. She instructed us to bring in solicitors to make it official when she knew her time was limited."

Carmichael wasn't sure he wanted to know the answer to his next question but found the words tumbling from his mouth just the same. "What did she die of? The solicitors didn't tell me anything." *And I didn't ask.* For some reason, he now felt curious.

Judith reached for a slice of cake. "Liver cancer. She was quite unwell towards the end." The care worker looked up from her plate and reached across the table for Carmichael's hand, giving it a soft squeeze. "I'm sorry."

"It's OK." Carmichael gave a faint shrug. "Like I said, we weren't close. To be honest, I never really knew her. Today was quite surreal, listening to everything being said about her. It felt like I was sitting through the funeral of a total stranger." He tried to keep the bitterness from his tone, but knew he'd failed. "None of what I heard had a grain of truth to it. Loving mother? Do you know what she did to me and Genete?" Carmichael took a mouthful of his coffee to swallow the acid lacing his voice. Then he tried another smile. "Sorry, that was uncalled for."

"You don't need to apologise." It was Tessa who spoke this time and reached for Carmichael's hand. "I knew your mother quite well, probably better than anyone else at Cavendish House. When she came to us, she was quite unwell with alcoholic psychosis. I don't think we got to see the real Sheila until she'd been with us for some time. I could sense that it was in there, buried deep within, but her illness would often spiral out of control. She spoke about you, though, in her more lucid periods."

Carmichael's eyebrows hitched once again. "Really?"

"Yes," nodded Tessa. "You and Genete. She spoke very fondly of you both."

Carmichael stared down into the black liquid of his coffee cup, eventually sighing. "Sorry, I find that quite hard to believe. The mother I remember abandoned us when we were no more than five and three, preferring the bottle to being a parent. Our father was already serving a life sentence in prison for murder, so we spent three years in various foster care settings before I moved away down south." He broke off and gave a sad shrug. "I don't really have much more to say."

"I understand." Judith rejoined the conversation, nibbling at the edge of her cake. "In your shoes, I would feel exactly the same, believe me. But try not to think too harshly of her. She really did struggle at times. It was the alcohol, you see. It really got a hold of her. But despite what she may have done in the past, what choices she may have made, she never forgot about you."

"No?" Carmichael did his best to hide the derision in his voice resurfacing, but again failed. He afforded the two women another faint smile. "Sorry — again. I don't really know why I came up here, to be honest."

"You don't need to explain yourself to us." Judith put the cake down. "Everyone needs the chance to say goodbye, no matter what has happened in the past. It's a chance to close that chapter of your life for good."

"Maybe, but I still feel I should offer some explanation. You don't know me from Adam and here I am being rude. I didn't know her, you're right — certainly not in the same way that you both did. The mother that I knew was wholly different to the person you're speaking about. And it feels strange even calling her that — my mother. She was never a mother to me and Genete — not really. I appreciate the problems she may have had — I'm a police officer, I see it all the time — but . . ." Carmichael exhaled a frustrated breath. "Who abandons their kids and never gets back in touch?"

Carmichael caught the look that passed between the two care workers and pushed away his rapidly cooling coffee. "What? There's something else?"

There was another glance exchanged before Judith spoke. "Look, I don't know if I'm supposed to tell you this but . . ." She glanced towards Tessa and shrugged. "I don't see why you can't know. Not now that Sheila is no longer with us."

"Know what?" Carmichael felt his stomach tighten, nudging the plate of fruit cake a little further away. "What don't I know?"

Judith took another sip of her hot chocolate and fixed Carmichael with a pair of kind eyes. "Your mother was in contact with Genete — your sister. And she had been for quite some time."

"Genete?" Carmichael didn't bother trying to hide his surprise. "When? How?"

Judith lowered her gaze and took another fortifying sip of her drink before replying. "I can't really say when it started — but it was a while ago now. I walked into the day room one morning to see your mother sitting by the window. She used to like sitting there watching the world go by, it was her favourite place. Usually she would sit alone, but this time she had a young woman with her."

"Genete?"

Judith gave a slow nod. "Although I had no idea who she was at the time, I only found that out later. She became quite a regular visitor to Cavendish House over the next few years."

"Years?" Carmichael's brow creased. "How long ago are we talking about?"

"Like I said, I'm not really sure. At a guess I would have to say about three or four?"

"*Three or four?*" Carmichael's eyes widened. "You're saying she was in touch with Genete for four *years?*"

"I really can't be sure, but it must be about that, yes. I'm sorry." Judith tried a half-smile. "If it helps, I don't think there was any planning involved — Genete just happened to turn up one day. I'm not sure how the two of them got talking. I suspect she was there to see another resident and she just stumbled across your mother."

"What other resident?"

Judith shrugged. "I have no idea. It was most likely to do with her job."

"Her job?" Carmichael suddenly realised he knew as little about his sister as he did about his mother. "What did she do?"

"She was working for the university at the time — in their psychology department. As far as I know, she still does."

Psychology? Genete?

"Which university would that be?" Carmichael's brain began to whirr. He'd thought his search for Genete would

219

be like looking for the proverbial needle stuck in the largest haystack in the North West, but maybe that haystack had just shrunk a little.

"The one in the city — Liverpool University. I take it you're not in touch?"

Carmichael shook his head. "No, we lost touch when we were separated." Suddenly finding his appetite, he took the final slice of cake from the plate. "But now I think I just might be able to find her."

* * *

Time: 11.55 a.m.
Date: Monday 13 April 2015
Location: Lark Road, London

"You OK, boss?" Cooper looked warily across to where Jack had slipped back behind the wheel of the Mondeo.

"All good, Cooper. All good." The engine was still running, so it took Jack a matter of seconds to pull the car back into the traffic. "But if anyone asks, you didn't see what just happened back there."

"See what, boss?"

Jack smiled. That was what he liked about his team, their unswerving loyalty.

On the way to the station, he thought back to the impromptu run-in with Rhys Williams. It wasn't like Jack to rough someone up like that, get so physical with them — and certainly not in public — but the case was getting to him more than he wanted to admit. Or maybe it was Ritchie that was getting to him. Whatever it was, he was getting older and crankier by the day — maybe even by the hour. Rhys was small fry, Jack knew that. The lad would barely be on the fringes of Ritchie's empire, but he'd looked frightened when Jack had found him bleeding out from a stab wound to the abdomen in the back room of the Hanged Man last January.

No, not frightened — scared out of his bloody wits. And at barely nineteen, who could blame him? The chances of Jack being able to turn the boy, get him to inform on Ritchie and his gang, were slim — minuscule even — but if there was even the slightest chance, he owed it to Rob to do whatever he could. Jack would quite happily never clap eyes on Ritchie Greenwood again as long as he lived, but if it meant Rob got the closure he needed after the death of Charles Tindleman, then he would seek the man out in a heartbeat. The detective sergeant had been robbed of his childhood, then lost the only father figure he'd ever known in one of the most traumatic ways possible. If Jack could do something to help heal that pain, then he would die trying.

Noting the time, Jack cast a sideways look at Cooper as they progressed through the early lunchtime traffic. "What do you say about a quick pit stop on our way back? Hungry?"

CHAPTER TWENTY-THREE

Time: 12.15 p.m.
Date: Monday 13 April 2015
Location: Liverpool University

Genete Hill pushed her half-eaten sandwich to the side and glanced at her watch. Surely it must all be over with by now? Part of her had wanted to go — the crematorium wasn't that far from the university, and she knew she wouldn't be missed. She could have paid her respects and been back behind her desk in the same amount of time she had spent nudging the chicken salad sandwich half-heartedly around on her desk.

But she'd made a promise — and felt she was obliged to abide by it.

Her diary was clear for the rest of the day — she had orchestrated it that way on purpose, *just in case*. Although there was a pile of work to get through to keep her busy, none of it was particularly urgent, and her heart wasn't in it anyway. Lifting her gaze to the window, she saw a beautifully crisp blue sky and considered taking a walk around the park to stretch her legs. The fresh air would help clear her head.

But before she could make up her mind, the desk phone rang. Sinking back into her chair, she lifted the handset from the cradle.

"Genete Hill, Behavioural Sciences. How may I help?"

To begin with, Genete wondered if the caller had hung up, as nothing but silence filled her ear.

"Hello?" she repeated. "Can I help you? You're through to the Behavioural Sciences department at the university."

It was then that she heard the caller clear their throat. "Yes, sorry. It's me, Rob." The caller paused while Genete frowned. "Robert Carmichael. Your brother."

* * *

Time: 12.20 p.m.
Date: Monday 13 April 2015
Location: Westminster Mortuary, London

Dr Matthews leaned forward and rubbed his eyes. It wasn't often that cases got to him. He could count on the fingers of one hand the number of times he'd been rendered speechless by what he saw in the post-mortem room. He'd seen it all by now — bomb blast victims, horrific mutilations, decapitations, ritualistic murders and much more besides. But nothing had quite prepared him for how he felt after examining the body now resting in the chiller.

It wasn't that the body was horrifically mutilated — it wasn't. Apart from the deep purple contusions around her neck, she looked almost at peace. But the pathologist knew the last moments of her short life were likely to have been anything but peaceful.

It wasn't the condition of her body that had struck a sombre chord with him; it was more the fact that this was the work of the Central Line Killer. Not that it was any more abhorrent than that of any other killer, it just struck home that little bit more deeply when it was on your own doorstep.

The Tube stations circled on the maps pulled from each victim's mouth were all stations Dr Matthews was familiar with, as were many millions of Londoners. He used the Central Line frequently when the Volvo was off the road, and he had to trust Transport for London to get him to and from the mortuary. During the Central Line Killer's frenzy in 1998, he remembered persuading Mrs Matthews to take taxis whenever she needed to get around the capital or wait for him to be free to take her himself. She had looked at him quizzically at the time but accepted the advice with good grace.

Reaching for the freshly brewed coffee Perry had left for him, Dr Matthews woke up his computer monitor just as the office door opened and the man himself entered.

"We have another priority case listed for this afternoon." Perry handed over the revised schedule for the rest of the day. "Suspicious death in Croydon."

Dr Matthews took the sheet of A4 paper and scanned it. Another life lost. Another body to persuade to give up its secrets. After more than thirty years in the job, it didn't get any easier.

"Thank you, Perry. Has young Detective Constable Daniels left for the station yet?"

Perry nodded. "He has, but I could call him back if you need him for something? He won't have got very far."

The pathologist smiled but waved the suggestion away. "No need, Perry. I'll give Jack a ring in a bit. Why don't you pour yourself another coffee and take the weight off your feet for a while?" He nodded towards the coffee machine. "We've got some time before needing to start our next case."

Perry hesitated, seeming to wrestle with the decision before relenting and slipping into a vacant chair with a mug of the pathologist's finest Costa Rican coffee. "Don't mind if I do, actually. I was up late last night studying."

"And how's that all going, Perry?" Dr Matthews knew the mortuary technician was considering embarking on a full medical degree, hopping over to the dark side to become a fully-fledged forensic pathologist. In the twenty years Dr Matthews had been at the Westminster Mortuary, Perry had been his best technician by far. It was a strange job that didn't suit everyone. Often people liked the idea of it, maybe even visualised themselves working in the role, but when they actually had to do it for real, they discovered that they just couldn't. The job was physically and emotionally draining, and not everyone had the resilience to see it through.

But Perry was different. Dr Matthews had known that the minute the slightly built lad from Doncaster had stepped through the mortuary door. And if he decided to move on and get his degree, then the boy would make an excellent pathologist.

"All good so far, thanks." Perry took a gulp from his coffee. "But I'm still not a hundred per cent sure it's what I want to do."

Dr Matthews sat back in his chair, nursing his coffee in his lap. "If I can offer any advice at all, it's not to rush. You have years ahead of you, Perry, you don't have to decide now. You're doing exceptionally well here as a technician, don't forget that. It's an important and varied role, which you've mastered just about as well as anyone can. I would certainly miss you if you decided to leave — this place only runs so smoothly because you're at the helm. But I will also never stand in your way, *if* it's what you want to do."

Perry sighed, his face remaining tense. "That's exactly it. I'm just not sure at all. I like the idea of it — but then I see what I've achieved here, how much I enjoy what I do, and I feel I'd be mad to even contemplate changing that."

"Like I said — there's no rush. You'll always have a job here, certainly so long as I'm in charge, anyway. Maybe keep up with the studies and keep your options open for now?"

The mortuary technician nodded enthusiastically. "That sounds like a plan." He made to get up, his coffee half drunk. "I'll start prepping for the afternoon session." When he reached the door, he paused and turned. "How do you deal with this, day after day?"

Dr Matthews instantly knew what Perry was asking without the need for any further explanation. How did you deal with witnessing what one human being could do to another? How could you see it, one case after the other on some morbid conveyor belt, and not let it affect you?

All the pathologist could do was give a slow shrug and what he hoped was a reassuring smile. "On balance, Perry, I feel most human beings are good people. Never lose sight of that. Those that commit these crimes, they are in a small minority. Minuscule, even. It's just that we get to see it every day. Don't let it cloud your judgment or faith in humanity."

"But how do *you* manage to do it, though? Keep so level-headed, I mean." Perry rested a hand on the door handle. "You always appear so calm and collected. How do you stop what you see affecting you?"

"I have a good woman at home, Perry. She keeps me grounded and sane. It enables me to leave what I see on the mortuary slab right here — where it belongs."

Perry gave a rueful smile and pulled open the door. "Maybe that's where I'm going wrong. I only have Oscar the cat waiting at home for me."

"Cats can make great company too, Perry, don't forget. Your time will come, I have no doubt. You just wait — someone will cross your path when you least expect it. In the meantime, why don't you pop out to that nice new sandwich shop around the corner and get us some decent sandwiches? I'm feeling rather peckish."

* * *

Time: 1.15 p.m.
Date: Monday 13 April 2015
Location: The Duck Pond Café, Liverpool

Carmichael recognised her straight away. The elfin shape of her head, accentuated by the short, cropped hairstyle; it was the Genete he'd known as a boy. After quickly returning to the hotel to freshen up, he'd then headed back to the park, and in that short space of time his head had been flooded with memory after memory — the age-old dam bursting the moment he heard her soft voice on the other end of the phone.

Genete.

He couldn't help but smile as he approached. She was sitting at an outdoor table, just like she said she would be, nervously playing with a laminated menu. Carmichael felt his heartbeat quicken. He couldn't quite comprehend the events of the day — he'd cremated his mother and found his long-lost sister all within a matter of hours. It was insane.

As he neared, Genete looked up. Their eyes locked for a split second before the pensive look on her face relaxed.

"Hey, Tig." Carmichael wondered if she would remember the childhood nickname he'd given her during their time together in foster care. She had been obsessed with *Winnie the Pooh*, and Tigger especially. From the look on her face, she did.

"Hey, yourself." The familiar smile beamed out at him. "You gonna sit down or carry on making the place look untidy?"

Carmichael grinned, pulling out one of the metal chairs at the side of the table. "You haven't changed, then — still as bossy as ever." As he sat down his grin extended. "It's great to see you."

"Likewise."

Just then, a waitress appeared by their side. "You two ready to order or do you need a few more minutes?"

Carmichael took hold of the laminated menu, suddenly aware of how hungry he felt. The chunk of fruit cake he'd sampled right here only a short time ago had barely touched the sides. "I'll have one of your sausage sandwiches — with chips. And a black coffee, please." He fancied something a lot stronger than coffee but figured it might not be so wise on an empty stomach.

The waitress scribbled the order down on her notepad. "And for you?" She looked up expectantly at Genete.

"I'll have what he's having, but a Diet Coke instead of the coffee."

"Sure thing, won't be long." The waitress scuttled away, leaving Carmichael and Genete in a comfortable silence. It was Genete who broke the ice.

"How was it? The funeral?"

Carmichael considered the question for a moment. How was it? He wasn't altogether sure when he thought about it, his brain still scrambled. He hadn't been all that sure what to expect, and finding Genete certainly hadn't been on his radar at all. It was something he'd wished for, obviously, but he was a realist at heart and knew how much of a long shot it had been. But the shot had unexpectedly hit the bullseye.

"It was OK, I suppose," he eventually replied. "To be honest, I'm not really sure why I went. Last time I saw her I was five. The woman they were talking about this morning . . . ?" He gave an exhausted shrug. "That wasn't the mother I remembered."

Genete nodded. "I get it."

"You chose not to come?"

Genete hesitated, then shook her head. "Part of me wanted to, felt like I should, but she'd asked me not to. Mum, that is. Said she wanted me to remember her the way she was." She gave a shrug. "Maybe I should have gone."

The waitress chose that moment to reappear with their drinks and an assortment of cutlery. "Food will be about ten minutes."

Once the waitress was out of earshot, Genete continued. "I guess you know that I met her a while back — and I've been visiting her on and off for the last few years or so?"

Carmichael nodded, tipping two sugar cubes into his coffee, needing the energy hit. "Two care workers from Cavendish House told me today. I met them at the crematorium. I was a little surprised, I'll admit. I had no idea you two were in touch." He tried his best to hide the bitterness from his tone. He didn't really feel bitter when he thought about it — if his mother had got in touch with him to suggest that they meet, would he have gone? Probably not — which spoke volumes.

"I wouldn't exactly call it being in touch. I stumbled across her by accident. I was up at Cavendish House seeing a patient when someone called out her name. Sheila. Sheila Carmichael." Genete took a breath, and a sip from her Coke. "It was a name I hadn't heard for a long time, and it made me stop in my tracks. I had no real reason to think that it was her, there must be so many other Sheila Carmichaels around, but when I saw her, I just knew. I just knew it was her." Genete broke off for another sip of her drink, her face slack. "A few discreet questions to the staff confirmed that it was Mum."

Mum.

Even the word sounded alien to Carmichael. "How often did you see her?"

"Not much to begin with. It would only be if I was up at the house seeing a patient. There was maybe a period of about eighteen months where I hardly saw her, but then . . ." Genete broke off, a haunted look crossing her face. "Then I started going a little more frequently, and not just when I had an appointment. It was after they told me of her cancer diagnosis — probably about two years ago." Genete paused again. "I'm not really sure why, but she looked so vulnerable. So frail. I felt she needed someone."

Carmichael was about to say *so did her children*, but he stopped himself with a sip of his coffee. Genete didn't need his catty remarks.

Genete carried on. "You never tried to find her?"

Playing with the teaspoon resting by the side of his coffee, Carmichael shook his head. "No. I didn't feel the need. Barbara and Charles took such good care of me, so it was never something that crossed my mind." Carmichael stopped, wondering how much he should talk about life with his adoptive family. During their phone conversation earlier, Genete had told him how she hadn't been quite so fortunate as her big brother, being brought up in a succession of short-term foster placements, so he didn't want to rub salt in any wounds. "It took me a while to settle in with them, but I never once thought about contacting Mum or even trying to find out where she was. The more the years went by . . ." Carmichael left the rest unsaid.

Genete nodded. "I don't think I would have — tried to find her, I mean. I really didn't go looking for her."

"What was she like?" All Carmichael could hear were the alien descriptions banded about during the cremation service. None of them sounded like the woman he remembered.

The waitress arrived with their food order, depositing two sausage sandwiches and two bowls of chips in front of them. "Enjoy!" she breathed, placing bottles of mayonnaise and other sauces onto the table. "Let me know if you need anything else."

After the waitress had left, Genete picked up one of her chips. "It's hard to say, really. She was on a lot of medication towards the end — even when I met her, actually. She suffered from a variety of mental health conditions that only deteriorated more when she got the cancer diagnosis. A lot of the time I wasn't sure she really knew who I was."

"And towards the end?"

Genete nibbled at a chip. "Towards the end her attitude towards me changed a little. She would hold my hand and recount stories of when we were little. Or at least she would talk about us when we were little — a lot of it I didn't remember. She could have been talking about anyone. She rambled a lot. At times I didn't know if she realised I was her daughter."

"What kind of stories?"

"Just silly little things, really. Trips to the park. Holidays. Christmas. Like I say, I don't know if any of it was true, as I don't remember a lot of it."

Carmichael bit his tongue. He certainly did remember his childhood and there were precious few holidays and Christmas celebrations. "Did she ever mention me?"

Genete popped another chip into her mouth and then picked up the sausage sandwich. "She did. Certainly towards the end, anyway. She would have this funny look in her eyes when she spoke about her son — *the copper*."

"She knew I was a policeman?" Carmichael's eyebrows lifted.

Genete shrugged. "I guess she must have."

Carmichael picked up his own sandwich and decided to change the direction of the conversation. "Tell me about your work. How long have you been at the university?"

They spent the next twenty minutes telling each other about their respective careers while devouring their food. Carmichael's stomach growled in appreciation.

"You must have handled some fascinating cases." Genete swirled her last chip around the bowl, scraping up the last of the mayonnaise. "Who would have thought — my big brother a detective!"

Carmichael laughed and swallowed the last of his sandwich. "Trust me, it's not as glamorous as it sounds. There's a lot of paperwork, a lot of hanging around waiting for things to happen, especially if you're in court. It's not like it is on the telly."

"Yeah, but still. A detective! I think it's brilliant." Genete's eyes shone. "You've done really well for yourself."

"Likewise." Carmichael wiped his mouth with a serviette. "My little sister the psychologist. How cool is that? I think your job is far more interesting than mine. And you say you're specialising in criminal psychology?"

Genete nodded. "We've got a brand-new department at the university — Behavioural Sciences. It's being led by Dr Schneider — he's just about the best criminal psychologist there is out there. I'm really lucky. I'm learning so much from him."

The next forty-five minutes passed by in a flash, brother and sister slipping easily back into each other's company. Eventually Genete announced that she would have to get back to work, but that she was on leave as of tomorrow for two weeks. Tentative arrangements were made for her to travel down to London.

Carmichael found a new spring in his step as he walked back to his hotel.

CHAPTER TWENTY-FOUR

Time: 1.15 p.m.
Date: Monday 13 April 2015
Location: Metropolitan Police HQ, London

"While you were out, the press statement about Jessica has gone live." DS Cassidy took the cardboard tray of takeaway coffee cups from Jack's outstretched hand. "Obviously not her name yet, as we're still trying to find her next of kin."

"Well, our friendly carpet fitter tells me her parents live down in Sussex — her dad's an architect. There's also a sister who works in a shop on Tottenham Court Road. See what you can do with that."

Cassidy nodded and plucked her chai latte from the tray. "Thanks, guv."

Jack waved the compliment aside. "This was Cooper's treat, wasn't that nice of him?"

Jack and Cooper had called in at Isabel's Café on Horseferry Road on their way back to the station — not because Jack was particularly hungry, but he wanted to thank Isabel for the curry last night. Although more than happy in his own company, he'd welcomed the pair dropping by.

"Is he a suspect, guv?" Cassidy resumed her seat by her computer. "Tony Kingdom?"

Jack frowned as he took a gulp of his plain black coffee. "I'm not sure. There's definitely something about him I don't like. He's shifty, and he didn't seem all that upset at hearing of Jessica's death. On top of that, he lied outright about being in the vicinity of the bus stop on Saturday." He pulled out a chair and sat. "We need to firm up on where that van was in the moments prior to it being seen on Beyton Road. See if we can categorically prove that he was behind the wheel. Then we'll go back and have another chat." After another gulp of coffee, he sighed. "Anything else of note while we've been away?"

DC Daniels cleared his throat. "I've been looking into the relevance of the window. Unfortunately, I can't find anything in unsolved cases that could help us, so I turned my attention to looking at the cameras in the streets around Lorna Henshaw's house. There aren't many out that way, and those I found haven't really shown anything useful. No suspect motorcycle couriers out early on Sunday morning. But there are plenty of roads not covered by cameras, so I don't think it tells us much."

Jack sighed again. He'd always known it would be a long shot. "OK. Just because we can't find a motorcycle courier doesn't mean there wasn't one. Leave the camera angle but stay with the journalist. There's still something not quite right. Dig deeper into her employment records and see if you can link her to any of our victims, however tenuously."

"Boss." Daniels trained his gaze back to his computer screen.

"And keep looking at the 1998 victims as well. Frank's team did a thorough job on their backgrounds, but just see if there's anything else you can find out."

"I've started building up a picture of Keeley Saul, too." Cassidy put her latte down and sifted one of the piles of papers on her desk. "She was twenty-four, lived alone with her three-year-old son, Ethan. Good support from her parents, who regularly looked after their grandson so Keeley could go back to work. She had a part-time job in a local supermarket, had worked there since she was eighteen. Ethan's father is no longer on the scene, but the split was amicable. He lives in Aberdeen and is currently in the middle of the North Sea on an oil rig. Keeley's phone hasn't been recovered — her mother can't find it in her flat — but we can see it was last active on Thursday morning."

"Good. See if there's any way she and Jessica knew each other." With another thumping headache brewing, Jack decided to take the remains of his coffee back to his office. Thoughts of Rhys Williams and Ritchie Greenwood were still bouncing around inside his brain and he needed to regain focus. Operation Quicksand was slipping away from them, and he could do without unnecessary distractions.

And he still had the delight of Dougie King to face as well.

* * *

Time: 3.00 p.m.
Date: Monday 13 April 2015
Location: Hazel Court Care Home, London

Sammy Hoskings zipped up her waterproof jacket and peered out the window. The heavens above had opened, and rain was bouncing off the tarmac of the car park. The weather didn't usually bother her, especially when it was at the end of her shift — she didn't mind the soggy walk home when there was a hot bath waiting for her at the other end — and, after the day she'd had, it couldn't come soon enough.

She loved her job at Hazel Court, more so than she'd expected to, but it could often be exhausting. It hadn't been her first choice of career, not even her second or third, if she was being brutally honest about it, but she had bills to pay and the advert had caught her eye. Initially she'd intended to do it for six months, maybe twelve at the most, but that was six years ago and she was still here. The hours suited, and the care home was only a twenty-five-minute walk from her flat.

She settled in almost instantly and soon became one of the residents' favourite carers — if they were allowed to have such things — but certain residents started to tug at her own heart strings, too. Take Nellie, for example. The ninety-two-year-old had moved to Hazel Court two years ago after the death of her husband, Ron. Ron had been Nellie's main carer and, with no extended family to speak of, she'd had to move to the care home. Sammy had gelled with her instantly.

Nellie was surprisingly quick-witted for ninety-two, with a razor-sharp mind, wicked sense of humour and eyes that sparkled whenever Sammy entered the room. She needed assistance with some of the basic daily tasks such as getting up and dressed, getting washed, her mobility declining as the years advanced, but she was otherwise the picture of good health.

And then there was Desmond. A bit of a charmer, Des liked nothing more than sitting in the day room next to the radio and serenading anyone who came within ten feet. He didn't always know all the words, and his dentures sometimes worked themselves loose as he crooned, but Sammy found it endearing all the same and made sure she spent at least some of her day sitting and chatting to him.

Turning away from the window, she winced as her new shoes reminded her there was still a wet walk home to come. She pulled the elasticated hood up over her head and started to walk towards the door.

"You're not walking home in this, are you?" Sammy turned to see Frances, one of the matrons, slipping behind the reception desk. "You'll get soaked right through."

Sammy gave a tired smile. "It's not so bad. I only have one more shift tomorrow morning before I have a whole week off. I'm going to celebrate with a long, hot bath and a glass of wine when I get home."

Frances chuckled as she grabbed hold of a ring binder and turned to go. "Well, you just be careful. I'll see you in the morning."

Sammy gave a wave as she pulled open the main door and stepped out into the wet. Although there was a bus stop over the road, and the number twelve would drop her a couple of streets away from her flat, at this time of day it would be packed. She didn't relish being squashed up next to soaking wet anoraks and dripping umbrellas — and it would be just her luck to have someone with a streaming cold breathing down her neck. With a week off work looming, she didn't want to get ill.

There was a Tube station a few minutes' walk in the opposite direction, but using the Underground right now filled her with unease. You couldn't escape the headlines that were bombarding the news channels, and there had been another live press report on the TV in the staff room just as she was getting ready to leave. Another body. And then there had been that creepy message from the killer late yesterday. A deep-seated ripple of fear was spreading across the city. The media had wasted no time in linking the recent murders to the Underground — and the Central Line in particular. Sammy had no intention of travelling on the Tube until the killer had been caught.

She shivered as she hurried down the steps. The light was fading fast even though it was only mid-afternoon, heavy thunderclouds blocking out any glimpse of the sun, and the wind was blowing fiercely, whistling through the trees that flanked the car park. Huge puddles had already formed underfoot, but Sammy splashed through them in her haste to start the journey home. She knew it wouldn't be long before the cold rainwater seeped into her socks, so she buried her hands in her pockets and barrelled towards the exit.

As she crossed the car park a set of headlights swept into view, causing her to momentarily check her stride. The van splashed through a series of deep puddles but, instead of passing her by, it slowed down to a stop, the driver's window down.

"Shocking weather out here, Samantha. Fancy a lift?"

Sammy bent down to peer in through the half-open window, rain dripping from the end of her nose. Inside looked warm and dry. A crack of thunder overhead made her flinch.

"Are you sure? It might be out of your way a little?"

"No problem. Can't have you walking home and getting soaked. You'll catch your death. Jump in."

* * *

Time: 3.00 p.m.
Date: Monday 13 April 2015
Location: Metropolitan Police HQ, London

Tossing his half-eaten sandwich into the bin, Jack collapsed back in his chair and let out a groan. Not only was Lorna Henshaw still a thorn in his side, now Tony Kingdom was proving to be, too. And since finding the hit on the DNA database for Ellis Magee, the investigation seemed be heading rapidly downhill. Frank Tyler had been right all along, kicking the potential connection with the Yorkshire cases into touch when he had. The piece of wire and the scrap of grey material looked to have been red herrings. It wasn't the same offender.

Which left them right back where they started.

Jack cursed beneath his breath. He knew there was still a positive to take from the news — Jane Telford would now have some new evidence with which to reopen the cold cases for the '96 and '97 sexual assaults, and Magee would eventually be brought to justice for the lives he had ruined. It was a comfort of sorts, but not a great deal more.

There was a brief knock at the door, DS Cassidy's head appearing around the frame seconds later. "Chris has asked Jenny to prioritise the rest of the resubmitted evidence from the 1998 cases, guv. You never know, we might get lucky again. Maybe get another profile?"

Jack nodded. "We might." He didn't really hold out much hope but admired the detective sergeant's optimism.

"Trevor is busy looking into every victim's background to see if there's a link to Lorna Henshaw. And Chris is conducting an ANPR trawl on Tony Kingdom's van, checking where it might have been lately."

Jack rubbed his eyes, tiredness fogging his thoughts. He could feel his foot throbbing beneath the desk. "What about next of kin for Jessica?"

"I've managed to speak with her parents now. Tony Kingdom was right, they live down on the coast in Sussex. The local force is providing a family liaison officer but they both intend to travel up to London tonight to formally identify her." Cassidy's face took on a pallid tone. "They know it's a formality — that we don't have any doubt that it *is* her."

"Thanks, Amanda. Let me know when you hear anything further from them."

"I've also managed to speak with Jessica's sister. I tracked her down to a computer shop on Tottenham Court Road. She filled in a bit of background for me, saying that Jessica worked part-time at the Crawfield Care Home, and as a receptionist at a local GP surgery. Interestingly, the sister had no time for Tony Kingdom and wasn't sad when she heard they'd split up. Although they'd never met formally, she knew enough about him to know he was a controlling and manipulative individual. Older than Jessica by quite a few years, he steadily cut her off from her friends and family. She thinks they were together about two years, and he had a very volatile temper. She often worried for Jessica's safety."

"That's good. Thanks, Amanda. Keep digging — the more we know about our victims, the greater the chance we have of finding out what happened to them. We need to know if any of them knew each other or have any other connection. Look for links to the 1998 murders, too. These attacks are too well planned for it just to be a matter of chance."

Cassidy slipped back out and left Jack with increasing aches in his head and his foot. Ripping open a fresh pack of paracetamol, he reached for his desk phone. It was a call he knew he couldn't put off any longer.

CHAPTER TWENTY-FIVE

Time: 3.15 p.m.
Date: Monday 13 April 2015
Location: Metropolitan Police HQ, London

"Take a seat, Jack."

It was a command, not a request, and Jack did as he was told. A mug of finest Colombian coffee landed in front of him, but he didn't dare take hold of it. Instead, he watched Dougie King manoeuvre himself into his leather swivel seat, trying to see from the man's expression just how much shit he was in. It didn't take long.

"No need to look so worried, Jack. You're not the condemned man — not yet, anyway."

Jack detected a small glint in the chief superintendent's eye and slowly reached for his mug, his mouth suddenly feeling dry. The coffee from Isabel's had been welcome, but the sandwich, although tasty, had stuck in his throat. "Thank you, sir." With this coffee still too hot to drink, he nursed it in his lap, feeling the burn through his suit trousers. Detecting Dougie King's unexpectedly relaxed tone, he decided to strike first. "We have IDs for both victims now, so we're picking apart their backgrounds, seeing if there's any common ground — including those from the 1998 investigation."

King nodded. "That's a positive step. And welcome, too."

"We're also looking into Lorna Henshaw's background a little more deeply — seeing if she has any connection to any of the victims. Frank Tyler did the same during his investigation, but we're giving it a fresh look."

"You think she might be the link?" Jack saw Dougie King's bushy eyebrows hitch a notch. "More than just a random reporter the killer lifted from the media?"

Jack could only offer a small shrug as he took a tentative sip of the boiling coffee. "Too early to say, really. There's nothing obvious, but I know she was on Frank's radar back in 1998. We'll keep looking into her history and also her current personal life, see what floats to the surface."

"You think she could be a credible suspect?"

"I wouldn't go that far — just another box to tick. Like I said, Frank had a few misgivings back in '98, but they came to nothing."

"And you have the same *misgivings*?"

There was that word again. Jack held his coffee mug in front of his lips while he considered the question, the rich aroma teasing his nostrils. Did he suspect Lorna Henshaw of more involvement than she was letting on? It wasn't a question he could truly answer.

There was definitely something linking her to both investigations, but he just didn't know what that something was. "Nothing tangible, no. But we do have a slightly more credible suspect who surfaced earlier today."

Jack spent the next five minutes outlining their visit to see Tony Kingdom on the back of his van being spotted close to where Jessica Fleming was last seen. "He swears blind he hasn't seen her for several weeks and was nowhere in the vicinity of Beyton Road or its bus stop. He's clearly lying, so I plan to bring him in for an interview under caution, but before we do that we're just checking where else his van has been seen, ensuring it was actually him driving that day, then seeing if we can tie him to any of the other murder locations."

"You think that's likely?" The chief superintendent leaned forward in his seat, elbows resting on the desk. "You've seen the press reports, Jack. This whole situation could spiral out of control very quickly. A credible suspect under arrest could be just what the city needs."

"We're working on it — that's all I can say right now." Jack went on to explain the DNA hit for the Yorkshire sexual assaults. "It means they aren't linked to either Operation Quicksand or Frank Tyler's 1998 cases, so it's an avenue we're no longer pursuing. Jane Telford will be working with the Yorkshire force to effect an arrest of the suspect in prison as soon as practicable." Mentioning Frank's name reminded Jack to tell the retired detective the news about the DNA hit before the day was out. The man had enough to worry about without the additional weight of potentially having made a career-ending cock-up on top of it all. It would come as a relief of sorts that Frank had made the right call. "We're still running tests on the 1998 forensic evidence, so something else might turn up."

"Well, that all sounds very promising." Dougie King settled back in his seat and held Jack in one of his infamous stares. Jack felt his insides start to squirm until he saw the smile break out on the senior officer's face. "Like I said, no need to look so scared, Jack. You're not about to face the firing squad just yet. I expect you think I've summoned you here to rake you over the coals about that article in the *Daily Courier*."

Jack found himself nodding. "Yeah, well, I can explain that . . ."

Dougie King held up a hand, the smile widening. "No need. I won't say that it hasn't caused a bit of a stir upstairs, but I for one think that you did the right thing."

Jack's eyebrows shot up. "You do?"

The chief superintendent sighed. "Don't forget, Jack, I used to be just like you once — more so than you realise.

If this was one of my cases and I was being handed a line of communication with the killer, I would do exactly as you have — keep that line of communication open. You have my full support."

Jack could barely keep the look of surprise from his face. "Just you, or . . . ?"

"Don't take liberties, Jack." Dougie King suppressed another smile. "My support is enough for you right now. The others might take a little more persuading, but I'm sure they'll come around when you catch the killer."

Jack took a gulp from his mug, feeling the heat singe his tongue. He wasn't so sure "when" was the word he would choose and knew his doubts must be plastered all over his face when the chief superintendent added, "And you *will* catch him, Jack. I have every faith. Carry on what you're doing and let me deal with all the flak — which leads me nicely on to the other reason for asking to see you."

Jack kept the mug hovering in front of his face. *Another reason?* What had he done now? "Oh?"

"A press conference, Jack. Now all this is out in the open, I don't feel we can put it off any longer, especially as we now have IDs for our two victims. It's set for six thirty this evening."

Jack glanced at his Fitbit. "I see, well, I suppose I could . . ."

Dougie King raised another hand. "No, Jack — I don't need you to be involved in this one. There will undoubtedly be some questions about the decision to give the killer a voice and I can't risk things boiling over again."

And by "boiling over" Jack knew precisely what the chief superintendent was referring to — Jack's tendency to enter into a slanging match with the assembled members of the press, sometimes even edging towards physical violence. On balance, Jack considered it a wise move.

"As you wish, sir — I'll stay away."

"Good man. And I would probably do better than just staying away, if I were you. In the nicest possible way, I don't want you anywhere near this conference — I don't even want you in the building. If you take my advice, ship yourself off home — continue working from there if you have to. But you can't be seen anywhere near this."

Jack nodded and risked a smile. "I'll be just like the invisible man, sir."

* * *

Time: 3.20 p.m.
Date: Monday 13 April 2015
Location: St Agnes Street, London

"Thanks for the lift." Sammy gazed out of the side window as the van made slow progress along the main road. They were crawling so slowly that she felt she would cover the distance in half the time on foot, but then saw the curtain of water falling from the sky above. It was as if someone had turned on a tap, water pummelling the van's roof. "I'd be drenched by the time I got home if I walked."

"No problem — it's not too much out of my way."

"What a stroke of luck you were there!" Sammy stretched her legs out in the footwell, her new shoes still pinching her toes. She couldn't wait to kick them off as soon as she got home.

"Isn't it?" he replied, smiling as the van negotiated the gridlocked street, windscreen wipers on their highest setting.

With the van's heater on full blast, Sammy began to feel her nose tickle. Damn. She'd started sneezing a few times earlier that day, and a dull headache was now threatening to make itself known. She felt her forehead with the back of her hand — not too warm.

"Are you OK?"

Sammy glanced over to the driver's seat, a tired smile following. "I'm fine. A little run down, I think. Tired — but aren't we all? I can't wait for my week off."

"Oh, you have some leave coming?"

Sammy nodded and stifled a yawn. "A whole week — after tomorrow. I can't wait."

"I bet. Doing anything nice?"

Letting her eyes half close, Sammy sat back while recounting her plans for her seven days free from work. Not usually such a slave to organisation, she wanted to make sure she didn't waste a single minute of her precious time off, so she had allocated an activity to each day — even if that activity was merely a Netflix boxset and chocolate.

It wasn't until she opened her eyes some five or so minutes later that she realised she must have nodded off and they had left the main road behind, taking a back street instead. Disorientated for a moment or two, she frowned and sat up a little straighter.

"I think I may have drifted off there for a while. Where are we? I don't . . ."

"Traffic was too backed up that way — I reckon there must have been an accident. I keep hearing sirens. We can cut down here, though — it's a little longer but at least we're moving."

Sammy gave a small shrug and settled back once more. Ordinarily she wouldn't have jumped into the van quite so readily — he was a bit odd and could make you feel uncomfortable if you spent too much time with him — but she really just wanted to get home. Feeling her eyelids drooping once again, her nose began to twitch. Blinking, she sighed and waited for the series of sneezes to follow.

It didn't go unnoticed. "Sounds like you might have a cold coming. Hang on, I've got something here somewhere." Pulling the van over to the side of the road, no other vehicle in front or behind to question the manoeuvre, he leaned across to the glove box.

Before Sammy knew what was happening, a large handkerchief covered her face.

* * *

Time: 5.00 *p.m.*
Date: Monday 13 April 2015
Location: Kettle's Yard Mews, London

For once, Jack had done as he was told and gone home, leaving the team with strict instructions to notify him if anything useful reared its head. Thinking back to his meeting with Dougie King, part of him had been surprised at the degree of loyalty the chief superintendent had shown — but the more he thought about it, the more he realised that was the man all over. In a time of crisis, Jack felt the man would have his back, and he hoped the feeling was mutual. There weren't many people Jack would stick his neck out for — but Dougie King was up there with Rob Carmichael.

Before finally leaving the station, Jack had taken a call from Dr Matthews — the pathologist informing him that the second post-mortem hadn't thrown up much by way of a surprise. The same ligature mark around the neck, the same scrunched-up Underground map in her mouth. And the poor girl's parents were on their way. Jack had then received a draft report from the man via email which he was now reading, along with a selection of other papers he'd grabbed on the way out.

After half an hour he needed a drink.

As Jack pulled a bottle of Budweiser from the fridge, his mobile chirped with an incoming message. Seeing it was from Carmichael, he slapped his forehead as he made his way back to the sofa. It was the funeral today and he hadn't even taken the time to ask how it went. With everything that had happened with the investigation, it had totally slipped his mind. What kind of a best mate did that make him?

On way back tomorrow morning. Lots to tell.

Sinking a third of the bottle, Jack wondered what "lots to tell" might mean. He hoped the funeral had gone well — if that was even a correct term to use — but then wondered if Rob's message was more to do with Genete. The man had been gone for less than twenty-four hours, so how likely was it that he'd managed to track her down in that short space of time? He made yet another mental note to catch up with Rob in the morning.

I must start writing these notes down, he mused as yet another reminder tweaked his conscience. *Not rely on the ageing brain matter quite so much.* He dialled Frank Tyler's number, which was answered on the second ring.

"Good to hear from you, Jack — I was just thinking about you, actually."

Jack rested back against the cushions, Marmaduke taking the opportunity to do likewise. "How's things, Frank? I hope it's not a bad time to call."

"Not at all. I'm just sitting here mulling things over, as it happens. Any news?"

Jack took another mouthful from his beer bottle. "Well, you could say that. I thought you'd want to hear as soon as possible. We got a full DNA profile for the attacker in the Yorkshire cases." He heard a sharp intake of breath at the other end of the line.

"A profile? And a name?"

"Yes. Which is kind of why I'm ringing. You were right, Frank. You were right all along not to make the link. The name we got from the DNA profile can't possibly be the Central Line Killer. He was behind bars from early January '98 — and still is. Thought you'd want to know."

Silence filled the other end of the line. Jack finished his beer and shifted his position on the sofa, much to Marmaduke's annoyance. "You OK there, Frank?"

A sigh eventually followed. "I'm good, Jack. I'm good. Just letting it all sink in. I had kind of resigned myself to the fact that I must have made a balls-up somewhere along the line. Missed the connection that could have brought an end to the case all the way back then."

"Well, I can categorically tell you that's not the case. No balls-up. I hope it allows you to sleep a little easier tonight."

246

"That it will, Jack. That it will. Thank you."

Jack could detect a slight wavering in the retired detective's voice, so decided to end the call. "I'll let you get on. It's getting late. I'll keep you up to speed."

"Cheers, Jack."

Placing the phone down, Jack felt a little lighter. He knew how much the failed investigation must have haunted Frank over the years, weighing heavily on his conscience when he didn't need it. He hoped the news went some way to offering a more peaceful night's sleep.

Knowing sleep was a million miles away for himself, Jack glanced up at the kitchen wall clock. The press conference would be under way soon and he was thankful that he was nowhere near it. At one time he would have welcomed the chance to cross swords with the capital's finest hacks, but in recent years he had become quite tired of the whole circus so was more than content to hand the reins over to Dougie King for this one.

Which left just one other thing on his mind.

CHAPTER TWENTY-SIX

Time: 5.00 p.m.
Date: Monday 13 April 2015
Location: Bridge Street, London

He'd pulled the van off the road, parking a few metres from the entrance to a one-way street. He already knew the area was free of cameras, and conveniently free of traffic, too. It was no more than a single-track lane, really — culminating in a dead end. After dark, it would be frequented by night-time traders — prostitutes bringing their punters to the relatively secluded road to earn their twenty or thirty quid a time. He had no idea what the going rate was these days, having never been a customer of theirs. It in no way appealed to him. He liked sex, of course he did; he was a man, after all. But he didn't want to pay for it.

His girls gave it to him for free. Albeit reluctantly.

Resting back on his heels, he looked toward her. She was beautiful. They were all beautiful — *his girls* — but this one was extra special. As he gazed at her, he felt the familiar loathing start to stir within him. Beauty, as he had learned to realise, was a double-edged sword. The girls at school had been part of the "beautiful crowd", the ones that everyone else craved to be accepted by. And they knew it.

His tastes had matured since his school days, but he still remembered the look of loathing they would give him whenever their paths crossed, the judgmental expression on their perfect little plastic faces.

Well, he was both judge and jury now.

And executioner.

Adjusting the bandana around his head, he ran a finger around the inside of the balaclava. His skin felt hot and sticky beneath the wool. He didn't really need to disguise himself — if she saw his face, it wouldn't matter any more. She wouldn't be alive for much longer. But it gave him a thrill to see the sheer terror in her eyes.

She was staring back at him, watching his every move. He saw that a lot towards the end — often wondering if it was a look of acceptance or just plain fear. He guessed he would never really know for sure, unless he asked them — but the tape across their mouths rendered them mute.

The handkerchief had done the trick once again. It was such a simple ploy, one he'd picked up from a bar in Valencia. After too many shots of tequila, he'd found himself sitting next to an anaesthetist from Madrid. As the alcohol flowed, the man's tongue loosened — enough to divulge the easiest and quickest way to render someone unconscious, and it was surprisingly simple. The doctor hadn't seemed to question his new friend's interest in the subject, readily accepting his payment for the information in shots.

Smiling at the memory, he turned back to the woman. She was gagged, just like the others had been, but it wasn't really necessary; they wouldn't be disturbed in this part of the city, and any sound they did make would soon be absorbed by the night. But he could do without the distraction as he went about his work. She was certainly attractive, and as his eyes took in her beauty, he began to feel a familiar stirring inside — quickly followed by an almost uncontrollable urge to empty his bladder. He shifted his position and instead picked up the camera, needing a distraction. Aiming the lens at her, he reeled off a series of close-up shots. She was particularly photogenic, with a symmetrical, heart-shaped face, full lips and smooth, clear skin; she would look good on the wall of his front room alongside the others.

He could tell she was trying to say something behind the tape stretched across her mouth, but he wasn't interested in her words. He needed her to be silent and let him do what he needed to do. The camera clicked as he completed the series of photographs, documenting this important part of the journey. More would come later when the final act had been completed.

* * *

Time: 7.30 p.m.
Date: Monday 13 April 2015
Location: The Hanged Man Public House

Jack slammed the door of the Mondeo.

What was he doing here?

It seemed to be a recurring question.

The darkness of the unlit car park swallowed the sound of his footsteps as he made his way across the weed-infested concrete that led to the front entrance. Although it had only been a few months since he was last here, he noted a fresh air of abandonment as he neared the crumbling red-brick building. Rhys's insistence that Ritchie and the gang had shipped out looked like it could well be true, but Jack needed to see for himself.

Approaching the door marked "Bar" he tried the handle, soon finding it was uncharacteristically locked. Frowning, Jack took a few steps to the side and peered in through one of the windows. Despite the grime, it gave a relatively clear view inside.

Squinting, he could just about make out the bar, but the recessed lights behind were extinguished. Everything looked dark and abandoned. Moving to the next window along, which gave a view of the rest of the pub, including the rather impressive inglenook fireplace at the end, Jack gave the glass a quick tap with his finger.

The sound brought no one out of the dark recesses, even when he tapped a little harder. Knowing there was a back entrance, Jack skirted the building and headed for the narrow door that nestled in among a curtain of rampant ivy. He didn't bother trying the handle this time — the shiny silver padlock told him it would more than likely be a waste of time.

Deciding he may as well head back to the Mondeo, Jack began to wonder where the hell Ritchie Greenwood and his cronies had decamped to. The Hanged Man had been their base for some time now, although that information wasn't widely known.

So, where the hell had they gone?

As much as Jack detested Ritchie and all that he stood for, he preferred having the man where he could see him. Not many people were welcomed into the gang's inner circle — even fewer actually wanted to be there. And he knew if anyone got wind of just how far he'd stepped over the line into Ritchie Greenwood's world, his feet wouldn't touch the ground on the way out.

And, so far, Ritchie Greenwood had been content with the arrangement. So, the man's apparent disappearance concerned Jack. Had the explosion at the Old Mill Road flats really been enough to drive him and the gang underground?

As he fired the engine and pulled out of the car park, Jack contemplated how he might track the man down. As distasteful as it sounded, he wanted to confront Ritchie face to face. He felt he owed that much to Rob. The discovery of the link between the explosives used to blow Jack skywards and the ones used to detonate Charles Tindleman's car wasn't a link anyone could ignore.

With the paperwork from Operation Quicksand calling him back home, Jack headed for the main road. Rhys might have been reluctant to divulge much to Jack in the street, but the lad had enough doubt in his eyes for Jack to think it worth keeping an eye on him. He was young enough to be turned, given the right incentive.

And he might be Jack's only way of getting to Ritchie — and the truth.

CHAPTER TWENTY-SEVEN

Time: 7.15 a.m.
Date: Tuesday 14 April 2015
Location: Metropolitan Police HQ, London

Jack made it into the station at a little after seven o'clock with three strong black coffees already inside him, but he wasn't alone in starting the day early. As he entered the incident room, he saw the team already hard at it.

DS Cassidy jumped up from her seat and set about fixing him coffee number four. "Morning, guv."

Jack gave what he hoped had a passing resemblance to a grateful smile as he took hold of the mug. "How's it all going? Anything much happen overnight? Any fallout from the press conference?" He had returned from the Hanged Man at just before nine and then found himself sitting up at the window with Marmaduke as the city slumbered around them. His head had been too full of Ritchie Greenwood and the car bomb that had ended the life of Charles Tindleman, not to mention the gallery of faces pinned to the whiteboards in the incident room, to allow him much sleep. He did manage to nod off in the early hours, waking up on the sofa with nothing but a stiff neck and a bad mood.

"I think it was quite brief, guv. But the calls have started coming in already."

By "calls" Jack knew Cassidy meant the usual waves of cranks that invariably flooded in once certain details were made public. He grimaced and stood in front of the whiteboards. "Have we managed to uncover any links to Lorna Henshaw yet?" He knew he was firing yet another shot in the dark, but he couldn't help feeling there was something they were missing. Something maybe Frank and his team missed, too.

"I was looking at that last night." DC Daniels got to his feet and approached one of the whiteboards where the Central Line Killer victims from 1998 were logged. "I looked at each murder victim from '98." He tapped the board with a marker pen. "Ages range from twenty-two to thirty-five. None of them lived particularly close to each other and not all were London born and bred. They didn't work in the same areas, those that had kids didn't go to the same schools or nurseries. DI Tyler pulled their bank records at the time, and I've gone through all of them again. It hasn't shown up anything we weren't expecting. They didn't go to the same restaurants, bars or cinemas. They didn't even shop at the same supermarket. With no social media around at that time, we can't do the usual checks there, but there's absolutely nothing to suggest they knew each other or had any friends in common. I can't find anything that would have caused their paths to cross. And none of them have any obvious links to Lorna Henshaw either."

Jack grimaced. It wasn't great news.

"So he *is* picking them at random," piped up Cassidy, opening a paper bag and pulling out a freshly baked muffin. "Even the journalist angle is a coincidence." She answered the frowns cast towards her breakfast with an exasperated sigh. "It's beetroot and carrot. You should try one, they're delicious."

Jack considered a reply, then decided against it, turning away from the whiteboard as well as Cassidy's unusual choice of food. "I don't think so. No killer is that random, not in my experience, and definitely not this one. Something links our victims together — and then something links them to Lorna Henshaw. We just haven't found out what it is yet. What about work histories?"

Daniels pulled out his notebook. "I've had a little more joy with that angle. The only link, and it's tenuous at best, is between Gail Coleman, our killer's first victim in 1998, and Sadie Bloomfield, his third victim. They both worked in care homes — well, one in a nursing home, one in a care home, to be precise. But the homes aren't anywhere near each other and are run by different care agencies. Gail left her employment two weeks before she died. Sadie was still employed at the time of her death."

Jack rejoined Daniels at the whiteboard. "What about the others from 1998?"

Daniels shook his head. "No links to the care sector for any of them, in their employment records at least. Cindy Benham worked in a shoe shop, Lynn Jaggard was unemployed, Christine Gooch worked for a medical supplier, and Becky Scott was a stay-at-home mum. The previous investigation team pulled their work histories going back beyond their current employment, but there's still nothing to suggest a link to the care sector for any of them."

Bugger.

Jack rubbed his unshaven chin. "OK. Keep digging anyway, there might be something in it. Get as much information as you can about the care homes Gail and Sadie worked at. If the homes are still in existence, see what records they have for visitors around that time. I appreciate they might be different homes and different care agencies, but it's the only link we have right now."

"Will do."

"We also have the link with Jessica Fleming. Amanda, you found out she worked part-time at a care home if I recall?"

Cassidy nodded, her mouth full of savoury muffin. "Yes. Part-time in a care home, part-time in a GP surgery."

Jack turned to one of the preceding whiteboards. "It might be tenuous, but it's a link all the same. What about Keeley Saul? I take it no link to a care home for her?"

Cassidy shook her head. "Not that her parents mentioned yesterday, no. I can always check again, give the family liaison officer a call? They just mentioned a supermarket — where she's worked since leaving school."

"Double-check anyway. And Cooper — dare I ask about the ANPR?" Jack eased himself into a vacant chair and took another mouthful of his coffee, savouring the strong, sweet flavour as it hit his tongue. Cassidy might have a poor taste in breakfast muffins, but she knew how to make a decent cup of coffee.

"I might have something here too, boss." Cooper shifted in his chair and angled his computer screen towards Jack. "I managed to track and log where our man Tony Kingdom went on the day in question. We already knew he was in and around the bus stop on Beyton Road where Jessica was last seen, but I've also managed to get him logged not a million miles away from Wheeler Street on Thursday evening."

"Expand on the 'million miles' bit, Cooper. How far away are we talking?"

"Three streets, boss."

Jack wasn't sure if it was the caffeine that sent a tingle up his spine, or the revelation that Tony Kingdom was potentially linked to their first victim as well. "Keep tracking that van. There's obviously no point trying to check it for the 1998 murders — ANPR was around back then but, with a 2005 registration, his van certainly wasn't. In the meantime, I'll get some uniforms to pull him in."

Cooper returned his gaze to his computer screen. Just at that moment, the incident room door opened, and a PC's head appeared.

"DI MacIntosh? There's someone downstairs who insists on seeing you. She says it's urgent."

* * *

256

Time: 8.15 a.m.
Date: Tuesday 14 April 2015
Location: Metropolitan Police HQ, London

Lorna Henshaw had been shown into interview room two. Jack knew it to be a particularly small and windowless room and, as she'd already been waiting inside for half an hour, he wondered what effect it might have. He didn't have to wait long to find out.

"Miss Henshaw. Sorry to have kept you waiting." Jack closed the door behind him but remained standing, leaning up against the wall by the journalist's side. "I hear you've got something for me?"

Lorna nodded and, with a trembling hand, handed Jack an envelope. "It came this morning."

Jack had already taken the precaution of wearing a pair of protective gloves, not that it was going to do much good. Tests on the previous envelopes had shown nothing of forensic value, just as the journalist had predicted. Before leaving the incident room, Jack had been alerted to the breaking news — there was a third body.

Or, at least, a third victim; the body had yet to be discovered.

Jack cast his eyes down at the envelope, pulling out the single piece of paper from inside — an Underground map with Shepherd's Bush Underground circled in red.

"He's not stopping, is he?" Lorna Henshaw dabbed her eyes with the sleeve of her cardigan. "He's just not stopping."

"No, he isn't," replied Jack, his voice matter-of-fact. "But we have teams out searching the area around Shepherd's Bush." He waved the map in the air before slotting it back into the envelope. "They'll find her."

"Alive?"

Jack knew a response wasn't really needed. Instead, he grabbed the only other chair in the room and pulled it across to the table. He afforded the journalist one of his fixed stares. "Why haven't you been in to make your statement?"

It was a valid question. On Jack's visit to the journalist's home on Friday he'd asked her to drop by the station to make a formal statement. Four days later and she still hadn't appeared.

Lorna's face slackened. "Sorry, I . . . I just . . . just haven't had the time."

Jack let the feeble response hang in the air longer than necessary. Lorna Henshaw was retired — it wasn't like she was run off her feet. She could have made the time if she really wanted to. "Well, now that you're here, perhaps we can get that sorted."

Lorna gave a faint nod and even fainter smile. "Of course," she whispered.

"And we'll get your cameras looked at, see if we can see anything for when the envelope was delivered."

"You don't need to bother with that."

Jack's eyebrows twitched. "No, why's that?"

"Because he went round the back this time. Slid the envelope under the back door." The journalist's jaw tightened. "He obviously knows about the cameras."

Of course he does.

They hadn't exactly publicised the fact that several surveillance cameras were installed at the reporter's home, but it wouldn't take a genius to work it out. The killer wasn't stupid. Jack immediately moved checking the camera footage down the priority list. Instead, he turned his attention to another line of enquiry. "Something else has been bothering me. How does the killer know where you live?"

Lorna frowned, deep-set lines now embedded in her forehead. "I'm not sure. But I haven't moved — I'm still in the same house I was in back in 1998."

"But how did he know back then? From my experience, and correct me if I'm wrong, most reporters — especially those involved in cutting-edge investigative journalism like yourself — would take steps to keep their personal details out of the public domain. Were you ex-directory?"

Lorna slowly nodded. "I was — and still am."

"So—" Jack held his palms up towards the ceiling — "how did he know where to target you? Surely it would have been easier to send the envelopes to the newspaper? But instead he chose your home address. If you were ex-directory, he would need to do some extensive digging to find out where you lived."

"I . . . I guess he would." The journalist's eyes widened. "What are you saying, exactly?"

Jack shrugged and got to his feet. "I've no idea, Miss Henshaw. Just mulling things over." He strode towards the door. "I need to get back to the investigation and get the ball rolling with this one." He waved the envelope in the air. "But if you don't mind, I'll send someone down to take a statement from you. Now you're here, it makes sense to put the time to good use — don't you think?"

On his way back up to the incident room, intending to leave the journalist stewing for a while longer, he found himself mulling over the most recent question to fog his brain.

Just how did the killer know where Lorna Henshaw lived?

CHAPTER TWENTY-EIGHT

Time: 9.35 a.m.
Date: Tuesday 14 April 2015
Location: Swansea Lane, London

Dennis Kingdom let the net curtain fall back into place before turning away from the window. He'd had doubts about letting Tony move back in after breaking up with that nice girl, and he was now being proved right.

Police.

This time they'd arrived en masse with uniforms, and Dennis could only imagine what the neighbours would be thinking. Especially that Mrs Croxton from number four — nothing got past her nosy beak. He bet she was already on the phone to the rest of them, spreading the evil gossip among all her equally nosy and irritating friends.

But — *the police*?

He couldn't care less what it was that they'd lifted Tony for this time — it mattered not to him; the boy was no angel, just like his father. It was most probably drugs — it always seemed to be drugs with the youngsters these days. But Tony wasn't his concern right now.

His overriding worry was that once the coppers started nosing around, and nose around they most certainly would, then they might just find out.

Bollocks.

After Tony had been hauled off in a police van, several officers had remained to guard the van outside and Dennis had caught the tail end of a phone conversation that talked of waiting for a low loader to arrive and take it away.

The bloody van.

Although Dennis had stepped away from the carpeting business a couple of years ago, he still used the van from time to time. Once they pulled it apart, they would undoubtedly find something — they always did. He'd tried to cover his tracks the best he could but . . .

The sat nav.

He swore under his breath as he went in search of a bag. Why hadn't he deleted the journey history on the sat nav? At the touch of a button, even the most inexperienced plod would be able to see everywhere the van had been.

Fuck.

Dennis knew an avalanche of questions would then follow, and he wasn't holding out much hope that Tony would stand up under intense questioning. The lad was bound to say something he shouldn't, let something slip. But it was too late to do much about that now. There was no way he would be able to get anywhere near the van.

All he could do now was run.

* * *

Time: 9.35 a.m.
Date: Tuesday 14 April 2015
Location: Metropolitan Police HQ, London

DS Cassidy had drawn the short straw and gone to take Lorna Henshaw's statement, leaving the team a beetroot and carrot muffin each.

261

"Try them — you might surprise yourself!"

Cooper had eyed the muffins cautiously before reaching for his customary bacon roll, oozing with a generous squirt of brown sauce. "I'm no' risking it, boss. Stick with what you know is my motto."

Jack was inclined to agree and poured another coffee instead. "You said you had an ANPR update, Cooper?" He took a seat next to the detective sergeant, who was already sinking his teeth into the soft white roll.

Cooper nodded enthusiastically. "Aye, boss. I think you'll like this one." He wiped a hand across his chin before pulling up a series of surprisingly good-quality camera shots onto his computer screen. "These were taken at a garage forecourt on the Goldacre Road." Cooper enlarged one of the images. "As you know, we've tracked Kingdom's van to Beyton Road with ANPR, but as I knew there was a petrol station not that far away, I took a stab in the dark and gave them a call. Then, hey presto." He angled the screen towards Jack. "Our Mr Kingdom stops for petrol at 2.49 p.m. — about fifteen minutes before the van is seen driving along Beyton Road towards the bus stop. You wanted proof that Tony Kingdom was driving the van that day — well, I think we've found it."

Jack's eyes widened as he watched Jessica's ex-boyfriend get out of the van on the garage forecourt and proceed to fill the vehicle with fuel. The camera footage was as clear as a bell — it was him.

"Well done, Cooper. I've heard our friend Mr Kingdom is now with us in the cells — we'll let him get comfortable before we go and have a chat." Jack made to get up from his seat, mind whirring. DC Daniels then caught his eye.

"Before you go, boss, there's something else here of interest."

Instead of heading for the door, Jack dragged his chair across to the detective constable's desk. "What have you got?"

"I stayed with the journalist angle — you said you still thought there was something not quite right about her? So I went back through the 1998 investigation, and I came across several references to another line of enquiry DI Tyler and his team looked into that year."

"Go on." Jack inched his chair closer.

Daniels pulled several pieces of A4 paper from the pile on his desk. "The fifth victim, Christine Gooch, was found in early September. Around the same time, Tyler began to question the involvement of Lorna Henshaw, beyond just receiving the envelopes. In particular, he posed the question as to whether it was possible that she could have sent the envelopes to herself."

Jack's eyebrows shot up. "To herself?" Although he had often questioned the journalist's involvement in the cases, he hadn't quite arrived at that scenario himself. "And did he come to a conclusion?"

Daniels gave a long-drawn-out sigh. "Difficult to be sure. The team certainly looked into it — analysed the timings of the envelopes being sent. All they really seemed to conclude was that, yes, it was possible — but not that it definitely had happened."

It was possible.

"No fingerprints were ever found," added Daniels, "other than her own. But she quite happily volunteered she was a big fan of crime programmes."

The journalist's voice came back to haunt Jack.

Sorry — I clearly watch too many crime dramas on TV.

Jack felt his insides shift. Was that what they were dealing with here?

"This is good. Keep at it, Daniels. Did they ever question how the killer knew her home address? She tells me she was ex-directory back then, so it's bugging me how he knew how to target her at home."

"I'll take a closer look, boss."

Jack nodded and pushed up from his chair. "I'm going to check in with the search teams soon. See if our third victim has been found yet. Then I think it's time Tony Kingdom explained himself."

Leaving the team to it, Jack headed back to his office after a brief detour to the canteen for a long overdue breakfast. He couldn't survive on a diet of black coffee for much longer, and DS Cassidy's savoury muffins didn't exactly float his boat. When he finally arrived back in his office, a freshly prepared ham and pickle sandwich in his hand, he found an unexpected visitor waiting for him.

"Hey, Jack. Bad time?" DS Robert Carmichael gestured towards Jack's rather dishevelled appearance and the sandwich half ripped out of its packet. "I can come back?"

"Not at all, Rob." Jack slipped behind his desk, taking a large bite out of the sandwich as he did so. "I'm about to interview a suspect but he can wait a while longer. Sorry I didn't get back to you yesterday, how was Liverpool?"

"Surprisingly good, as it happens. But don't let me keep you. We can catch up another time."

Jack swallowed his first bite and took another. "Now's as good a time as any to be honest, mate. What happened?"

Carmichael made no attempt to hide the grin on his face. "I found her. Genete."

Jack froze, sandwich hovering in front of his lips. "Really? That's incredible! How come?"

Carmichael's beam widened. "I can't quite believe it. There was a predictably small turnout at the service, but two women there knew Mum. Then I found out very quickly that they also knew Genete. Within a couple of hours, we met and had lunch. It's all still quite surreal."

Jack took another bite from his sandwich, stomach growling in appreciation. "I'm pleased for you, mate. I take it she's still living up there, then?"

Carmichael nodded. "Works at the university. But she plans to come down soon. We'll be keeping in touch."

"That's good news, Rob. Really good news." Jack stuffed the remains of his sandwich into his mouth then held a hand up in apology. "I'd really love to stay and chat some more, but I'd better round up Cooper and plan our interview strategy. We've got the ex-boyfriend of our second victim in custody."

Carmichael's eyebrows hitched. "You think it could be him?"

"We've placed his van close to where she was last seen, and also close to the location of the first crime scene."

"I heard there was another potential victim this morning, too?"

"I doubt there's any potential about it, Rob." Jack gave a sad shrug before nodding. "As much as it pains me to say it, I feel we're looking for another body."

"And this suspect is your guy?"

Jack paused, swallowing the rest of the sandwich and scrunching up the wrapper. "Of that I'm not too sure. But he certainly needs to answer a question or two."

Carmichael gave a slow nod. "You had a profile done yet?" The detective sergeant was well aware of Jack's usual reluctance to bring in the psychologists. "Has Rachel worked her magic?"

"Hit a bit of a roadblock on that one, Rob." Jack began to shrug into his jacket. "Rachel's off on some jolly across the pond — won't be back for a while. So, I'm none too clear who else to approach. Up to now, we've managed without."

Carmichael followed Jack towards the door. "That's interesting. How about you leave that one with me?"

"Eh?" Jack pulled the door open and stepped out into the corridor. "How do you mean?"

Carmichael paused before tipping Jack a wink. "Let's just say I might have a solution to your problem. Do you trust me?"

Jack hesitated for the shortest of seconds. "With my life, Rob. With my life."

CHAPTER TWENTY-NINE

Time: 8.30 a.m.
Date: Tuesday 14 April 2015
Location: HMP Wandsworth, London

"So, who's your secret admirer?" Lindsay Jenkins leaned up against the cell wall, arms folded across his chest. "I know you've got one, so there's no use denying it. I won't tell anyone. You can trust me to keep your sordid little secret." The ex-wrestler nodded towards the desk and the letters he knew were tucked away inside the drawer. "If we're gonna share a cell then we need to be upfront about these things, don't you think? Who is she?"

Jenkins detected a slight movement from the top bunk, the man's feet twitching. "None of your business," came the eventual curt reply. "And I don't appreciate you reading my personal stuff."

"Well, if it's so personal, why is it here? You practically flaunt those letters, out there on the desk. What's a man to do?" Jenkins knew he was treading on thin ice — stamping on it if the truth be told — and the man languishing in the top bunk could be pretty handy with his fists, something Jenkins had recent experience of.

But he still couldn't quite help himself.

"I mean, it has to be someone special, right? Who else signs their letters with a big fat kiss, eh?" Jenkins took a step back from the bunk and not a moment too soon, as Ellis Magee's hulking frame swung down from the mattress.

"Still none of your business. I've told you before about looking at stuff that don't belong to you!" Magee's voice was gruff, but had a keen, razor-sharp edge to it. "Keep on and it might prove detrimental to your health. You should watch yourself."

Jenkins locked eyes with Magee. The inference was clear, even to the uninitiated. *Leave it there.* But Jenkins couldn't resist and started to laugh out loud. "Hey, I'm just messin' with you, man! No need to get so jumpy. I couldn't care less who you're exchanging sweet nothin's with, just intrigued is all. I mean, I couldn't help but notice that they go back some way — and you've kept them all this time. Whoever they are, you must think quite highly of them. The one that got away, eh?"

Jenkins saw Magee's cheeks redden, his eyes narrowing as they took on a fierier look. The appropriate button had been pressed — all he needed to do now was step back to a safe distance and watch the nuclear fallout. Except in an eight-by-six cell, there wasn't much of a safe distance on offer.

"Keep your fucking nose out of stuff that don't concern you." Magee took a menacing step forward. "You don't scare me. I broke your nose once, I can do it again. And maybe not just your nose this time . . ."

Jenkins' grin widened. "You're so easy to wind up, mate! All I want to know is who this mysterious X is. Mr or Mrs? I mean, are we talking a major weirdo here? I've seen the news, I'm not stupid. But I'm prepared to keep my trap shut — for the right incentive. I can't say the same for anyone else around here. I mean, if word was to get out . . ."

Magee launched towards Jenkins, but the ex-wrestler was too quick for him and sidestepped out of the way just in time. Instead, the pair came face to face, muscles twitching.

"I told you once, and I'll tell you again," spat Magee. "It's none of your business."

Jenkins eyed his cellmate's fists balled at his sides, but the fire inside him had been ignited once again. "Well, I think it could very well become my business, judging by the newspaper headlines I've been reading. Your matey-boy, lover-boy, whoever the hell he is, seems to know quite a bit about them murders back in '98. A word in the right ear could earn me some extra Brownie points when I come up for parole. Might even get me a better cell. What do you think?" Jenkins grinned as he watched Magee's discomfort grow. He knew prisoner information was often handled with a liberal dosing of salt, and inmates informing on other inmates was a risky business — but it amused him just the same. He inched closer, his nose mere millimetres from Magee's so he could smell the man's foul breath. "What's it worth to keep my gob shut?"

* * *

Time: 9.45 a.m.
Date: Tuesday 14 April 2015
Location: Metropolitan Police HQ, London

Jack replaced the handset of the desk phone and sighed. It didn't come as any great surprise, but it still made his heart sink.

A third body.

He'd been on his way down to interview Tony Kingdom when the call came through. The location wasn't too far away — another audacious Central London spot which would be littered with cameras but, just like before, none likely to have captured their killer.

Elliott Walker and his team were already on their way as, no doubt, would be Dr Matthews. Just as Jack snatched up the keys to the Mondeo there was a tap at the door. He didn't try to mask the shock on his face. "Frank? This is a welcome surprise."

268

Frank Tyler edged into the office. "Morning, Jack, sorry to just land on you like this. But I've been up since before dawn — I've got itchy feet these days."

Jack wasn't sure if it was meant to be a metaphor or the truth, having no idea what side effects the drugs the man was taking would give him; itchy feet could well be one of them. "No problem at all, come on in. Take a seat."

Frank hovered by the side of the chair, but didn't sit. "Now I'm here, I'm wondering if it was such a good idea. You must be in the thick of it — I can see that you are." He gestured towards the array of paperwork strewn across Jack's desk. "I should leave you to it."

Jack saw the retired detective's narrow shoulders sag. "Don't be daft," he replied, slipping the car keys into his pocket. "Come and meet the team."

When Jack led Frank into the incident room, he saw the man's pallid face brighten, a new sparkle entering his jaundiced eyes. It was then that Jack knew why the retired detective had made the two-hour journey into the capital.

"This is the team. You've already met DS Cassidy. The two reprobates at the back are DC Daniels and DS Cooper. I'm guessing you've not set foot inside an incident room since you retired, Frank?"

Frank broke out into a genuine smile, making his way over to the bank of whiteboards on the wall. "You're spot on there, Jack. It's been over five years now."

"Things haven't changed all that much. Except for that monstrosity over there." Jack gestured towards the interactive whiteboard, currently standing idle.

Frank's eyes crinkled around the edges. "I bet that was a day you'll never forget — technology barging into your life uninvited."

"Much to my displeasure, Frank." Jack knew he was a bit of a dinosaur when it came to technology, but he felt he had a kindred spirit in the retired detective. The man was old school, and sometimes the old ways were still the best. "But I try to get by."

Frank picked up a marker pen, weighing it up in his hands. "Can't beat good old-fashioned detective work, though." He pointed the marker at a mound of paperwork stacked up on one of the desks. "Pen and paper."

"That's what I keep telling this lot, Frank, but do they listen? It's all iPads and WhatsApp with them these days." Jack grinned while checking the time on his Fitbit. "Look, feel free to stay here for as long as you want, Frank — or, if you feel up to it, maybe you'd like to join us? We've a crime scene to get to."

* * *

Time: 10.30 a.m.
Date: Tuesday 14 April 2015
Location: Pizza Palace, Fordham Lane, London

As Frank Tyler stepped out of the Mondeo and stared up at the frontage of the pizza restaurant, all manner of memories assaulted his senses.

Sadie Bloomfield.

It was like stepping back in time. It was 1998; the Backstreet Boys were still riding high in the charts, Harry Potter was only on his second book, and the cancer had yet to start devouring Frank's insides.

"You OK there, Frank? You can wait out here if you prefer?"

The retired detective heard the concern in Jack's tone as he continued to stand rooted to the pavement. Frank tore his memory back to the present and shook his head. "No, I'm good. Just having a bout of déjà vu, that's all."

Jack nodded. "Similar to Sadie Bloomfield, am I right?" He gestured towards the restaurant windows.

"Spot on." Frank accepted a protective suit and pair of overshoes. "It's uncanny." If the retired detective hadn't been convinced Jack was looking for the same killer that had wreaked havoc back in '98, then he was left in no doubt now. And inside was just the same, too.

Making their way into the restaurant, keeping to the metal stepping plates already spaced out on the floor, a strong arc lamp flooded the scene with light. Frank could feel the early morning milkshake stirring in his stomach as he neared the body. The woman's skin looked bleached white beneath the artificial light, except for the deep purple contusions around her neck. A pair of pale, glassy eyes stared skywards.

"Discovered earlier this morning by one of the search teams." Elliott Walker stepped forward. "Similar to before, she was found hanging in the front window." The crime scene manager gestured towards the vast floor-to-ceiling windows at the front of the restaurant. "Place has been closed for renovations for the last twelve weeks."

"This here is Frank Tyler, Elliott." Jack stepped to the side, raising a hand towards the retired detective. "Frank worked the cases back in '98."

Elliott gave a nod in greeting. "Nothing has been moved, other than the body — but, as you can see, there's not exactly much else in here."

Jack cast a gaze around the restaurant, noticing the chairs and tables stacked up at the rear, leaving the tiled floor clear of furniture. Many of the floor tiles were cracked or missing and, judging by the thick layer of brick dust covering most surfaces, the place looked like it wasn't reopening any time soon.

"I don't think any building work has happened for some time," added Elliott. "Maybe they ran out of cash."

Frank stepped forward to get a better view of the body. Although the poor woman's mouth was closed, he had no doubt about what would be found inside.

Another London Underground map. Just like before.

He straightened up and turned back towards Jack, his eyes sweeping the wall as he did so, another memory stirring.

"The wall, Jack. You need to take a look at the wall."

CHAPTER THIRTY

Time: 12.05 p.m.
Date: Tuesday 14 April 2015
Location: Metropolitan Police HQ, London

"Our killer likes to watch." Jack tacked a crime scene photo to the whiteboard. "I'm not sure it tells us much except our killer has a perverse interest in death, or at least the act of dying. But I want to know if anything similar was found at any of the previous crime scenes. Amanda, can you go through all the crime scene photos for the 1998 murders?"

Cassidy nodded. "Sure, guv."

"As you know, Tony Kingdom is in custody, awaiting interview. Cooper, let's get cracking on that one and see what he has to say for himself." Jack started to walk towards the incident room door.

"Before you go, guv." Cassidy picked up her notebook. "I got a call put through from Missing Persons while you were out. Someone contacted them earlier this morning, reporting a member of staff that hadn't turned up for work. Name is Samantha Hoskings. Sammy. She was due to start her shift at seven o'clock but didn't show. Her phone appears to be switched off. They put it through to me, just in case."

Jack frowned. "Have you managed to dig any deeper?"

"A little. I just got off the phone to a Mrs Maypole, manager at the Hazel Court Care Home. She confirmed Sammy was meant to start at seven this morning and it's most unlike her to just not turn up. She usually walks to work, taking her no more than half an hour, and has never been late before. She left work at around three o'clock yesterday afternoon, and no one has seen her since. Today is one of the residents' birthdays, and Sammy had been instrumental in organising a little celebration at the home. The manager feels there's no way she just wouldn't turn up, not after putting so much effort into it. She's tried Sammy's mobile, but no joy. Understandably, she was concerned about the recent headlines and called it in."

Jack felt a fluttering in the pit of his stomach.

Care homes.

"Daniels? Where are we on the potential links to care homes?"

"Visitor information has been requested for the homes Gail Colman and Sadie Bloomfield worked in back in '98. I haven't heard back yet so I'll chase it up."

"I think we might want to make it a priority now. If our victim *is* Sammy Hoskings, then we have yet another link to a care home. It might turn out to be nothing, but we shouldn't discount it too soon. And get back onto the manager. Ask what visitors they had in the twenty-four hours before Sammy was last seen. Get a full history. Also, see if they have next of kin details — we need to be sure it's her that we're talking about before we go much further."

"Will do, boss." Daniels turned back to his computer screen.

"Cooper?" Jack started towards the door. "Let's run through an interview strategy for our friend Mr Kingdom.

I'm told his van has now been removed and is being examined as we speak."

* * *

Time: 12.30 p.m.
Date: Tuesday 14 April 2015
Location: Swansea Lane, London

Elliott Walker had watched Dennis Kingdom jog down the short path that led to the road outside; there was no reason to stop him. The man's house was being processed, so it made sense that he made himself scarce. But Elliott hadn't been expecting him to pack a bag and leg it.

The crime scene manager had left a team at the pizza restaurant and made his way over to Swansea Lane to oversee the search there. He'd rung Jack on the way, letting him know he would call the minute they found anything.

The possibility that this could be the home of the Central Line Killer, and possibly the scene of the recent murders, meant they would be gathering every scrap of evidence they could. But the image of the father of their suspect legging it down the road still unnerved him.

The van had been picked up some time ago, the low loader taking it away for more detailed processing, and even from inside the Kingdoms' front room, Elliott could see various net curtains twitching along the street. All manner of salacious stories were no doubt now being concocted and passed along, like a game of real-life Chinese whispers — very little of which would be based on fact.

"Here."

Elliott's attention was drawn to the voice of one of his team in the hallway behind him. A familiar trickle of anticipation started to follow. If the Central Line Killer had been within these walls, they would soon find out.

* * *

Fuck.

Ellis Magee punched the thin mattress with a clenched fist, his knuckles connecting with the hard metal beneath.

Fuck. Fuck. Fuck.

He welcomed the stab of pain that shot up his arm.

Lindsay Jenkins was becoming an irritant and Magee's tolerance levels were famously short-lived at the best of times. The enforced lockdown had now ended, inmates allowed to go about their business — not that it made a lot of difference to Ellis Magee. But it did mean that Jenkins was out of the cell, giving Magee more time to think.

He wasn't concerned that Jenkins would shoot his mouth off about the letters — the man might look like he was built like a brick shithouse, but Magee had hurt him once before, so he could easily do it again. Jenkins was all talk, and Magee had had met plenty of cellmates like him in his prison career. The best course of action was to ignore him, and eventually the man would crawl back underneath whatever stone he'd emerged from.

But it still grated on Magee's frayed nerves.

The letters.

He'd always known they would come back to haunt him one day — and it looked like that day might be fast approaching. None of the letters contained anything that would directly cause him grief. At least the man had had the foresight not to sign his own name; that was something. Magee could plead ignorance over who it was — put it down to some crazed psychopath getting his rocks off sending unsolicited letters. He'd like to see a prosecutor try and prove otherwise.

And Magee prided himself on how careful his replies had been; he'd kept them suitably vague. And then he'd stopped replying altogether, tiring of the communication. It hadn't made him stop — if anything it seemed to spur the man on.

And now, after seventeen years, he was back.

Magee had no feelings for the fresh round of victims splashed across the newspaper headlines. He felt no desire or compulsion to tell the police what he knew about the killer. The system hadn't helped him, so he wasn't about to help it. The man would slip up eventually, everybody did.

In the meantime, Magee intended to keep his head down.

***

Time: 1.10 p.m.
Date: Tuesday 14 April 2015
Location: Metropolitan Police HQ, London

"The date is Tuesday 14 April, and the time is 1.10 p.m. This interview is being recorded and present in the room is myself, Detective Inspector Jack MacIntosh, and . . ."

"Detective Sergeant Chris Cooper."

Jack eyed Tony Kingdom across the table. "Your name for the tape, please."

"Anthony Kingdom. Tony."

"I must remind you that you have been arrested on suspicion of murder and are still under caution. You do not have to say anything, but it may harm your defence if you do not mention when questioned, something which you later rely on in court. Anything you do say may be given in evidence." Jack paused before launching into his first question. "Where were you between the hours of three o'clock yesterday afternoon and one o'clock this morning?"

A faint frown crossed Kingdom's forehead before he gave a slight shrug. "In the afternoon I would have been out in the van, I guess — then I stayed home all night."

"Anyone who can corroborate that? Anyone at home with you last night?"

Kingdom's eyes narrowed. "What is this? I thought this was about Jessica?"

Jack ignored the question. "Was anyone at home with you last night? It's a simple enough question, and as it was less than twenty-four hours ago it should be easy enough to recall."

Kingdom's stony gaze lowered to the battered wooden table in front of them. "There was no one home with me last night. I was alone all night."

"It's your father's house, isn't it? Where you live?"

The carpet fitter nodded. "I'm only there temporarily. I'm between places."

"So where was your father last night — if he wasn't at home with you?"

Kingdom's jaw tightened, his eyes darkening. "He went out for his usual cards night with some pals — stayed over."

"That's rather inconvenient, isn't it?" Jack took a few moments to shift some paperwork to the side before deciding to take a different tack. "How long have you had your carpet fitting business, Mr Kingdom?"

A wariness entered Kingdom's eyes. "My business?"

"Yes, Mr Kingdom. You supply and fit carpets, yes? Kingdom and Son Carpets, it says on your van. How long have you been doing that?"

"No idea. It was my dad's business before I got involved. What's that got to do with anything, anyway?"

"Where were you in 1998? Still living in London?"

Kingdom looked momentarily confused at the change of question. "In 1998? I was about twenty-two."

"And living in London?"

The carpet fitter frowned. "Back when we were living in Dagenham, yeah."

"Let's go back to Saturday just gone. Were you driving your van that day?"

Kingdom shifted in his seat, the wooden chair creaking, confusion doubling at yet another change in questioning. "Probably. I'm out and about most days of the week, visiting customers or suppliers. Have to make a living, don't I?"

"Indeed you do, Mr Kingdom. As do I. Did you happen to go anywhere near Beyton Road on your travels that day?"

The question was met with another lengthy silence.

"When exactly did you split up from your girlfriend Jessica Fleming?"

"Like I said before, a few weeks ago. Look, what is this? I never killed her, all right? I've seen the newspapers. You can't fit me up for it."

"I'm the one asking the questions, Mr Kingdom. And I've no intention of fitting anyone up, as you so eloquently put it. Did you see Jessica at all after you split up?"

"No."

"No? Not even once?"

An edge entered Kingdom's tone. "No."

"What about speaking to her on the phone?"

"Why would I want to speak to that bitch?"

Jack let the comment go. "So, you didn't see her at all on the day she disappeared — that would be Saturday the eleventh?"

"No, I already said."

"And you definitely weren't in the region of Beyton Road that day? You didn't stop to give her a lift home, maybe? It was raining quite heavily."

The muscles in Kingdom's jaw flexed. "No."

"Has Jessica ever been inside your van?"

A slight hesitation flickered across the carpet fitter's features. Eventually he replied, "No."

CHAPTER THIRTY-ONE

Time: 2.00 p.m.
Date: Tuesday 14 April 2015
Location: Metropolitan Police HQ, London

"Let's leave him to stew for a bit. We've got him lying on tape, which is good enough for now. Any news yet from the search at his house, or the van?" Jack asked the question even though he knew it was probably too early on both counts.

"Not yet, boss," confirmed Daniels. "They'll let us know the minute they find anything. However, I have had something back from the care homes." The detective constable edged to the side, making way for Jack to pull up a chair. "As I said before, there were two victims from 1998 who worked in care homes — Gail Colman and Sadie Bloomfield. I asked each home about their visitor records and, not surprisingly, they no longer keep them going that far back. But what *was* interesting was that they both still had records for contractors that visited. Something to do with keeping tax records."

"Contractors?" Jack frowned and inched his chair closer to the desk.

Daniels nodded and started tapping his keyboard. "Yes, people like catering suppliers, laundry services, voluntary services, medical suppliers and the like."

Jack raised his gaze to the computer screen, where Daniels was pulling up a series of emails.

"I got both homes to send me lists of contractors that visited the sites in the three months prior to the victims going missing. They appear to use the same services for catering, laundry and medical supplies." Daniels' hand hovered over the computer mouse.

"And?" Jack knew the detective constable well enough by now to know there was something more.

"I also found out that both homes had new carpets fitted by the same carpet supplier. Appleby Nursing Home, where Gail Colman worked, had carpets fitted in early January 1998, and Sunnydale Care Home, where Sadie Bloomfield worked, had theirs fitted in April 1998."

"And the carpet supplier was?" Judging by the grin on Daniels' face, Jack had a feeling he didn't really need to ask.

"A company called Kingdom Carpets — operated by a man called Dennis Kingdom."

"Which I bet later became Kingdom and Son Carpets." Jack jumped up from his chair. "Good work, Daniels. Keep digging. I want to know the exact dates Kingdom was on each site, and whether he could possibly have crossed the paths of our victims. Check if either home still has staffing records going back that far — let's see if our victims were working on the dates the carpets were fitted."

"Will do, boss."

"And check with Hazel Court as well. If Sammy Hoskings is our third victim, see if Kingdom happened to work on that site, too." Jack went to hover by DS Cassidy's desk. "And Amanda — start digging into the father, Dennis Kingdom. Where was he back in '98, and where is he now? We know he lives at Swansea Lane with his son, but I want to know specifically where he is right this minute."

"On it, guv. I'll give the crime scene guys a ring and see if he's still there."

Frank Tyler had been sitting at the back of the incident room, listening to the exchange. Jack noted the retired detective wincing as he stirred in his seat and went to check on him.

"You OK over there, Frank?" Jack knew pain when he saw it. "Can I get you anything?"

Frank gave a tired-looking smile and shook his head. "I came here on a whim, Jack, but now I think I need to leave you all to it." He waved his mobile in the air. "Reenie has been on at me to return home. And she's right. I've done what I came to do, whatever that was. I'm glad I was able to set foot back inside an incident room one more time, experience the cut and thrust of a live investigation again." Pain clouded the man's eyes. "It was something I needed to do. Before the end. Just see it, feel it for one last time. I'm not sure it makes much sense, said out loud, but I'm at peace with my past now. I can see the case is in very good hands and I know you'll catch him — you'll catch him where I couldn't."

Jack helped Frank to his feet, feeling the man's bones through the sleeve of his jacket. Jack was in no doubt that every inch of the retired detective's body was hurting right now, if the look on his face was anything to go by, but he'd still made the effort to come by, burying a few ghosts and demons along the way. Jack wondered if he would have the same level of courage when his time came. He shrugged the unpleasant thought off and guided Frank towards the door.

"Let me come down with you."

Frank patted Jack on the shoulder and shook his head. "No need, my boy. You've got plenty going on up here. I'll be fine."

As Jack watched the man shuffle along the corridor towards the stairs, he wondered if that would be the last time he saw Frank Tyler. He hoped not. He'd grown to like the retired detective even more over the last few days.

Turning back to the incident room, Jack caught Cooper's eye. "Let's go and have another chat with our friendly carpet fitter."

* * *

Time: 2.30 p.m.
Date: Tuesday 14 April 2015
Location: Walker Street, London

He knew he had to get as far away from home as possible — and as quickly as possible. The fact that Anthony was in custody didn't concern him, not as much as his own freedom and survival did, anyway. It sounded harsh, but that was the brutal truth of it. He wasn't built to be a parent — something he had told Karen on more than one occasion when she'd imparted the news that they were expecting all those years ago. It hadn't been planned — they were both barely twenty years old and clearly not ready for the responsibility that came with parenthood. But Karen had insisted.

After all that, she'd gone and left him for someone else anyway — leaving the baby behind. He'd made as good a job of it as he could — not as good as he should, he was sure of that, but that wasn't his fault, was it?

And Anthony was now a grown man, an adult; he could take whatever it was that was coming to him. But Dennis wasn't so sure about himself; his instinct to run was greater than ever. Police and forensic people were crawling all over his house, and he knew it was probably only a matter of time before they found something — after which his whole world would implode.

The van was a lost cause, he knew that much. He hadn't been careful — not as careful as he should have been — and it wouldn't take an expert to find it.

But the house?

Hitching the shoulder bag up onto his back he quickened his pace, continuing towards the park. They might find what

282

they were looking for, but he didn't need to make it easy for them.

* * *

Time: 2.45 p.m.
Date: Tuesday 14 April 2015
Location: Metropolitan Police HQ, London

"I must remind you that you are still under caution, Mr Kingdom." Jack settled back into his seat in interview room one. "And you still have the right to legal advice. Do you wish to avail yourself of the services of the duty solicitor?"

Tony Kingdom's jaw tightened, eyes hardening. "Done nothin' wrong, have I?"

"That remains to be seen. The question was whether you wanted a solicitor or not." Jack's foot was throbbing in tandem with his head, his nerves jangling from too much caffeine. It made for an uncomfortable mix. And he had little time for people like Tony Kingdom.

"No, I don't."

"In that case, we'll crack on. The time is now 2.45 p.m."

DS Cooper passed Jack a bundle of paperwork which Jack then placed face down on the table. Kingdom's eyes were immediately drawn to it, his brow creasing.

"Let's start with your work, Mr Kingdom. Carpet fitting, as I understand it?"

Tony Kingdom dragged his eyes away from the pile of papers. "Yes," he said cautiously. "I said before, it's no secret."

"Indeed, it's not. Kingdom and Son Carpets, no less. I assume the 'son' refers to yourself?"

The carpet fitter nodded. "Of course."

"You told us before that your father ran the business on his own, then you joined him and eventually took over. When did he start fitting carpets, Mr Kingdom?"

"My dad?" Kingdom's frown deepened. "Why don't you ask him?"

283

"Because I'm asking you. And he doesn't happen to be here arrested on suspicion of murder. So I'd keep your smart alec responses to yourself, if I were you." Jack felt a stab of pain cross his foot. "So, how about you answer the question?"

The frown turned into a scowl. "I don't know, exactly. He's always done it, since I was a kid. Does that answer your question?"

"Not really, but it'll do for now. When did the 'and son' get added? When did you start working with him?"

Kingdom's gaze narrowed. "I was about twenty-one, maybe twenty. So, about eighteen, nineteen years ago."

"Ever work up in Yorkshire?"

"No, why would I?"

"No particular reason, just a question. Did your father ever work up that way?"

Kingdom shook his head. "Not that I know of."

"Not that you know of. What does that mean?"

"It means I don't know."

"So, he could have?"

"Look, where's all this going? I thought you wanted to know about Jessica?"

Jack's lips thinned. "Oh, we'll be getting to that, don't you worry."

Just then, there was a sharp tap at the door and DC Daniels hurried in. "Just came through, boss." The detective constable handed over several sheets of A4 paper which Jack quickly scanned, a small smile twitching at the corners of his mouth.

Got you.

Jack nodded at Daniels as the detective left the room, placing the papers down in front of him. "Ever fit carpets in care homes, Mr Kingdom?"

The carpet fitter's eyes widened, confusion clouding his features. "Not that I remember. I'd have to check my records." He shrugged. "I've been to a lot of places. I can't possibly remember them all."

"I'm not suggesting you should, Mr Kingdom. But what about Hazel Court Care Home in particular?"

"Is that near St Agnes Street?"

Jack nodded. "One and the same."

"I think we might have fitted something there a few months ago. What of it?"

Jack ignored the dig. "Says here Kingdom and Son Carpets fitted three carpets there at the end of February this year. Would your father have been with you on that job?"

"I don't know. Maybe. He's stepped back from the business the last couple of years, and I've taken it over — but he helps out now and again if needed. I don't understand where this is all going."

"You said you didn't think your father ever worked up in Yorkshire. Would it surprise you to know that we have records of Kingdom Carpets undertaking work in two care homes, one in Harrogate in early '97, and one in Ripon in the summer of that year?" Jack picked up one of the sheets of paper.

Kingdom leaned forward, elbows on the wooden table, jaw flexing. "I told you before, I don't know. I don't remember that far back. I'd only just started working with him then."

"But it would have been his company, right? Kingdom Carpets. The invoice address was Dagenham."

The carpet fitter gave a faint nod. "That was where we lived back then."

"So, it looks like your father worked up in Yorkshire after all, doesn't it?"

"I guess." A guarded look entered Kingdom's eyes.

"But you weren't with him on either of those occasions?"

"No, like I said before — I've never worked up that way."

"Did he work away a lot, your dad?"

Another shrug. "Sometimes. He did what any decent man would do to put food on the table."

"So he *did* work away?"

"Probably. Dad had a number of commercial contracts back then — offices, care homes, restaurants. What of it?"

"You know of anywhere else he might have worked up in Yorkshire around that time?"

"Look, I'm not his bloody keeper — and I wasn't his boss back then either. He went where he wanted. Worked away a couple days from time to time, then came back. I never knew where. You'll have to ask him if you want the details."

Jack noted the hard edge to the man's tone. "And we will," he replied simply. Placing the paper to the side, he fixed the carpet fitter with one of his stares. "Let's go back to Saturday. You told us, on tape, that you didn't go near Beyton Road that day, and hadn't seen or spoken to Jessica. I think you said, 'Why would I want to speak to that bitch?' Is that true, Mr Kingdom?"

Jack watched the carpet fitter's face harden, the wariness returning to his eyes. But he remained silent, so Jack continued. "If you would be so kind, DS Cooper, to show Mr Kingdom the CCTV images."

Cooper flipped open the laptop he'd brought into the interview room, quickly navigating to the correct sequence of recordings. He then turned the screen around.

Jack kept his gaze fixed on the man across the table as Cooper hit play. "Mr Kingdom is being shown CCTV images from Saturday 11 April along the Beyton Road. As you will no doubt now see, Mr Kingdom, this series of recordings shows your vehicle being driven along Beyton Road at four minutes past three. We have another recording that puts Jessica at a bus stop on the same road at exactly the same time. Would you care to explain that, Mr Kingdom?"

The muscles in Tony Kingdom's jaw tensed but his mouth remained closed.

"You told us that you weren't in that area on that day, Mr Kingdom. But it seems you must be mistaken, does it not? Or was it just a downright lie?" At this moment, Jack was glad the carpet fitter hadn't availed himself of the duty solicitor — goading a suspect was usually frowned upon, much to Jack's displeasure. "You also said that you hadn't seen or spoken to

Jessica that day. Is that still the case, Mr Kingdom, or is that yet another lie?"

"You bastards," muttered Kingdom, a sneer crossing his lips as he slumped back in his seat. "You utter bastards. How do you even know it was me driving? I told you Dad sometimes still helps out with the business."

"Well, I think you've just told us right there and then. But we did think you might say that, so we had a look at some of the other cameras in the vicinity — and guess what we found." Jack nodded at Cooper to restart the recordings, this time one from the forecourt of the garage along Goldacre Road showing the carpet fitter filling his van with petrol at 2.49 p.m. "That *is* you, isn't it, Mr Kingdom? You don't have a twin?"

Kingdom turned his head away from the laptop, the sneer intensifying.

"Would you care to tell us why you lied?" Silence filled the stuffy interview room as Jack reached for another of the A4 sheets Daniels had brought in. "And, while you're at it, would you like to explain how Jessica Fleming's DNA has been recovered from the inside of your van? I seem to recall you telling us she hadn't *ever* been in the van — I think those were your exact words. But we can always check back in the recording. What do you say, Mr Kingdom?"

CHAPTER THIRTY-TWO

Time: 3.25 p.m.
Date: Tuesday 14 April 2015
Location: Metropolitan Police HQ, London

"We definitely have enough for a custody extension if we need one." Jack collapsed into one of the chairs in the incident room. Tony Kingdom had been returned to the cells, yelling all manner of expletives along the way.

"So, he definitely picked her up, then?" Cassidy poured hot water into a mug. "Jessica? He picked her up from the bus stop?"

Jack rubbed his eyes, feeling the grittiness beneath his fingertips. He'd managed to swallow a couple of painkillers after leaving the interview room, but the throbbing in his foot wasn't abating. It had been a long day already and showed no signs of coming to an end. They hadn't finished with Tony Kingdom by a long way.

"She's been in his van — the DNA evidence tells us that. But that's all we can say. There's no actual proof that he picked her up that day." Jack accepted the black coffee Cassidy placed in front of him. "Good shout on checking back with the Yorkshire sex assault cases, Daniels. I hadn't expected to find the care home link there. What made you look?"

DC Daniels cleared his throat, a small smile playing on his lips. "It was just something you said early on, boss. How we didn't want to make assumptions, in case we were wrong. I've always thought there was something about the Yorkshire cases, even though the DNA evidence points to Ellis Magee. I noted that DI Tyler and his team made note of two care homes when they looked at the Yorkshire assaults, and it just niggled me. So, I decided to contact them and see what contractor records they had."

Jack nodded. The cases hadn't sat right with him either. "Well, you were right to follow your instincts, Daniels. We've been led to believe that the two can't be connected — that the Central Line Killer isn't the same offender for the Yorkshire cases. But maybe we're missing something. Good work."

DS Cooper ripped open a bag of bacon-flavoured crisps and shoved a handful into his mouth, crunching nosily. "Maybe a night in the cells will encourage Kingdom to rethink his options. He might be more willing to talk once he's left to stew on it."

"But we have DNA evidence that Ellis Magee is the Yorkshire attacker, don't we?" Cassidy sipped her peppermint tea, frowning as Cooper emptied the remains of his bag of crisps into his mouth. "Could you make any more noise, Chris? You sound like a pig!"

"I'm sure I could," he grinned, scrunching the packet up and tossing it in her direction. "If you ask me nicely."

Jack heaved himself out of his chair and approached the whiteboards. "DNA tells us that Magee attacked the women in Yorkshire. And because he was locked up from the beginning of '98 he can't be the Central Line Killer. But are we right to say we're looking for the same killer today as they were in '98?" It was a rhetorical question, and Jack wasn't expecting an answer. "Where are we with any DNA for Operation Quicksand? And from the re-testing of the 1998 samples?"

Cooper went to retrieve his crisp packet from the floor. "Jenny says they're really backed up at the moment and one of the pieces of equipment went on the blink yesterday. I'll give them another call and see where we're at."

"What about the father?" asked Daniels. "We have evidence that Kingdom Carpets did fittings in two homes linked to the 1998 cases, and also at Hazel Court, which potentially links to our third victim. I've checked with each home, and it's entirely possible that Gail, Sadie and Sammy could have crossed their path while working. Staff records put them on site at the critical times that the carpets were being fitted. Then we have the two carpet fittings up in Yorkshire, both around the right time for the sex attacks. Maybe he's implicated — Dennis Kingdom — along with Magee?"

Jack remained by the whiteboards, frown increasing. "Could be, Daniels. It might be time to bring him in, too — make it a family affair. One thing we definitely need to do is find out if he knew Ellis Magee. Try and find out what you can about Magee before he went inside."

"Will do, boss."

"I've an update on Sammy Hoskings, guv." Cassidy looked sombre. "Bar a formal ID, I think it's quite conclusive that she's our third victim. I spoke to her mother, and she's sent in a relatively recent picture of Sammy. It's identical to the crime scene photo. She's going to make her way over to the mortuary once her husband comes home. She's utterly distraught. I wonder if one of us ought to be there?"

Jack gave a tired nod. "That could be a wise decision, Amanda. Daniels? How do you fancy a trip over to the mortuary? Dr Matthews could very well be doing the PM later today anyway — two birds and all that?"

Daniels nodded enthusiastically. "Of course."

Just then, Jack's mobile rang. Elliott Walker.

"Elliott — just the man. How's it going at the house?" Jack listened to the reply, nodding as the crime scene manager relayed the information to him. "Good, good. Let me know when you're done. Any idea where the father is? Dennis Kingdom? We want to bring him in."

As Jack took in Elliott's response, his face went slack. Sighing, he ended the call. "Elliott tells me Dennis Kingdom has gone AWOL."

***

Time: 3.40 p.m.
Date: Tuesday 14 April 2015
Location: Metropolitan Police HQ, London

Jonathan Spearing stopped outside the entrance and grimaced. It wasn't a place he enjoyed frequenting, unless it was to attend a press conference with the chance of seeing Jack MacIntosh lose his shit in front of the gathered media. *That* was always worth the effort.

But press conferences aside, he always tried to avoid rubbing shoulders with the police if he could help it. He always seemed to end up with a bitter taste in his mouth. And he was quite sure the feeling was mutual.

Hesitating on the top step, he wondered if he was making something out of nothing — his journalistic nose being overly sensitive. But equally he knew his doubts were just another excuse to put off the inevitable. Sighing, he pulled open the door and made his way over to the reception desk. There was no guarantee Jack MacIntosh would deign to see him anyway — the two didn't exactly see eye to eye at the best of times — but Spearing knew he had to at least try.

Contrary to what many believed, he did have a conscience of sorts. And his conscience was telling him all was not right with Lorna Henshaw.

***

291

DC Daniels stepped into the hushed mortuary. It was never usually a hive of activity, often having a tranquil feel even on the busiest of days, but this afternoon the quiet seemed to penetrate even deeper than usual.

Mr and Mrs Hoskings had already arrived, so he made his way along the corridor towards the viewing room. The carpet underneath his feet quietened his footsteps, the dim lighting on the walls adding to the sense of peace.

Daniels enjoyed visiting the mortuary — if *enjoyed* was the correct word to use. He found the whole process fascinating more than morbid; the human body was a remarkable thing. But he hadn't handled a viewing before. A slight nervousness rippled inside his stomach as he pushed open the viewing room door; he hoped it didn't show.

The soft carpeted floor continued inside, joined by neutral walls and diffuse lighting. Mr and Mrs Hoskings were seated on a two-seater sofa, hands clasped together. Perry Musgrove stood by their side and afforded Daniels a welcoming smile.

"Detective, good of you to join us."

Daniels nodded in response as he stepped closer. "It's no trouble." He turned towards the grieving couple. "I'm Detective Constable Daniels and I'm working on the investigation." He stopped short of saying "your daughter's murder". There was, of course, the remote possibility that the body lying next door wasn't Sammy Hoskings — so remote to be implausible — but Daniels stopped short of making it a fact right now. The couple would be faced with that particular truth in a matter of minutes.

"Thank you," whispered Mrs Hoskings, her face pale and wet from tears. Daniels saw her grip her husband's hand even more tightly. "Can we just get this over with?"

Daniels exchanged a look with the mortuary technician and nodded. "Of course."

Perry gestured for Mr and Mrs Hoskings to follow him into the room next door, Daniels remaining a few steps behind. The body was lying beneath a simple white sheet, a soft pillow supporting the head. Sammy's parents gathered at the side and waited. Taking hold of the sheet, the mortuary technician pulled it back to just below the chin then stood to the side, eyes averted.

Before joining Jack's team as a detective, Daniels had spent a good deal of time with the Traffic Division — and although he had never experienced a viewing before, he knew shock when he saw it. But the shock he saw on the faces of Mr and Mrs Hoskings was different to the type of shock he'd witnessed in the aftermath of a road traffic collision. Here it was infinitely raw; here it was intense and suffocating. In the confines of the small viewing room, there was nowhere for it to go.

Sammy's mother gripped her husband's hand, and Daniels saw her body start to shake. Perry quickly stepped around the bed and offered a hand, placing it on the woman's quivering elbow. No words were spoken, none were needed.

After what seemed like an eternity, Mr and Mrs Hoskings both nodded, Sammy's mother then reaching out to gently stroke the sheet that shrouded her daughter's body. Tears now flowed freely down her cheeks, and she didn't bother to brush them away. At her side, Sammy's father battled with his own emotions, his chin wobbling.

"I'm so sorry." It was all Daniels could think to say, and he wasn't sure if either Mr or Mrs Hoskings even heard him. With the viewing over, he began to step backwards and edge towards the door, but not before Sammy's mother managed to grab him by the arm as he passed.

"You'll catch them, won't you?" Her eyes were red raw. "Whoever did this to Sammy? You'll catch them?"

Daniels didn't hesitate. "We will, Mrs Hoskings. We will."

Once outside, Perry led Daniels back towards the front entrance, where they were joined by Dr Matthews on his way out.

"Thank you for handling the viewing, Perry." The pathologist nodded towards Daniels. "And you too, detective."

The mortuary technician held the door open as the pathologist stepped through. "Mr and Mrs Hoskings are still in with their daughter, I thought I'd give them a few minutes alone. I'll go back and check on them in a moment."

Dr Matthews gave a grateful smile. "That's very good of you, Perry." He turned towards Daniels and gave him a wink. "I hope Perry here has been looking after you. Don't forget I have that bookcase of textbooks in my office, if you're still interested?"

Daniels gave an enthusiastic nod. "Oh, I am, definitely. Just a bit pushed for time right now. Some other time, though?" He caught the mortuary technician's eye. "If you don't mind?"

"Not at all," replied Perry, his cheeks flushing a little. "Just let me know when you're free. I'd better get back to the viewing room."

Once Perry had left, Daniels followed the pathologist out into the car park. "I take it there was nothing new from the post-mortem?"

Dr Matthews paused by the side of his Volvo. "Very similar to the others — a thin ligature to the neck, resulting in asphyxiation. Similar defence wounds and evidence of manual restraint. Sexual assault evident once again. Swabs and bloods have been sent away to the lab. Tell Jack my draft report will be with him before the end of the day."

CHAPTER THIRTY-THREE

Time: 6.15 p.m.
Date: Tuesday 14 April 2015
Location: Metropolitan Police HQ, London

"Some lab reports are starting to come in now, boss." DS Cooper edged his chair to the side to make way for Jack. "Plus, we've a DNA profile isolated from the 1998 cases."

Jack grabbed a chair and dragged it across to Cooper's desk. "Is it good news?"

Cooper paused, bringing up the lab reports onto his computer screen. "Well, yes and no. The DNA profile isn't a match for Tony Kingdom."

Jack's heart sank. "Really?"

"But Kingdom's van does have plenty of carpet fibres in the back which are similar to those found in some of the 1998 cases."

"Carpet fibres in the back of a carpet fitter's van?" Jack sighed. "I'm not sure that's the discovery of the century."

"Maybe not, but the sat nav threw up something interesting."

"The sat nav?" Jack's interest was piqued.

Cooper nodded. "Analysis of the travel history tells us that the van has made several trips up to Yorkshire in the last eight weeks. Specifically, Harrogate and Leeds."

Jack frowned, peering more closely at the screen. "Yorkshire? What's Tony Kingdom doing up in Yorkshire? He's told us more than once that he's never been that way before."

"Could be his dad?" suggested Cooper. "He's mentioned Mr Kingdom senior sometimes helps him out. Maybe he borrows the van from time to time? And if Tony Kingdom's DNA isn't a match for the 1998 cases, then maybe Dennis Kingdom's is?"

Pushing himself up from his chair, Jack approached the whiteboard. "Let's bear that in mind if we manage to track him down. One or other of the Kingdoms is caught up in this, I'm sure. With the van seen close to both of our first two murder locations, and Jessica being inside the van at some point — it's too much of a coincidence for me. Unless I'm getting too suspicious in my old age."

"Maybe Tony Kingdom committed these murders, but not the ones in 1998?" Cassidy hovered next to Cooper's desk. "It would go some way to explaining the DNA and also the van."

Jack pressed a hand to the back of his neck, feeling an ache growing between his shoulder blades. "It would, granted." All of a sudden, the case seemed to be spiralling out in any number of different directions, each one adding to Jack's disquiet that something wasn't right; there was something they were missing. They might not be able to pin anything on Tony Kingdom directly, but there was no way Jack was prepared to let the man off the hook just yet.

"I've tried looking into Dennis Kingdom's background," continued Cassidy. "But there isn't much to go on. All I can find out is that they did live in Dagenham, as Tony Kingdom said."

Jack sighed, letting his eyes gravitate towards the whiteboards. His gaze came to focus on the name Lorna Henshaw. "What do we make of Jonathan Spearing's little contribution to the proceedings?"

While Jack and Cooper were interviewing Tony Kingdom, the *Daily Courier* crime correspondent had spoken with DS Cassidy.

"*I don't trust her*" had been the crux of the information he wanted to impart. "*I don't trust her one bit.*"

"He seemed quite genuine." Cassidy leaned up against Cooper's desk. "He didn't seem to have any particular axe to grind, said he didn't really know her all that well — there was just something about her that didn't sit right with him. He kept on repeating that he didn't trust her."

"That's rich, coming from Jonathan Spearing," scoffed Jack, his tone making it clear he still had no time for the reporter. "She niggles me, too — but I wouldn't pay too much attention to what Spearing has to say. Have we found anything more about her yet?"

Cassidy shook her head. "Trevor was looking into it but I don't think there was much to find. He should be back from the mortuary soon; he rang in to say Mr and Mrs Hoskings have formally identified the body as Sammy."

"OK — let's do the usual. Look into her background, friends and acquaintances, work histories. See if she in any way interacts or crosses the paths of our other victims."

Just then an email alert pinged on Cooper's computer, which immediately caught the detective's attention. "Whoa! This puts the cat among the pigeons!"

Jack and Cassidy went to peer over Cooper's shoulder as he opened the latest email from Central London Laboratories, their eyes widening as they read another result from the forensic examination of Kingdom's van.

"Bloody hell!" Cooper enlarged the forensic report. "Am I reading that right? They found a gun?"

Before Jack could begin to formulate a response, another email alert sounded. Cooper opened the attachment, this one showing the result of an analysis of Tony Kingdom's phone. The three detectives each scanned the contents, quickly followed by three sharp intakes of breath.

Cassidy was the first to speak. "Why in God's name is the man searching for how to get rid of DNA traces?"

Jack grabbed his jacket and made for the door. "DNA or no DNA, this man is caught up in this investigation somehow. He goes nowhere."

* * *

Time: 6.30 p.m.
Date: Tuesday 14 April 2015
Location: Bakewell Gardens, London

Pippa Moss peered at herself in the bathroom mirror. Her eyes looked puffy, her nose blotchy red, and she'd been sneezing like a trooper since getting up that morning. Right now, she would like nothing better than to slip back under the duvet with a hot lemon drink and watch some bad movies on TV, but she needed the money. London was an expensive city to visit, and an even more expensive one to live in — no matter which part of it you called home.

Reaching for another tissue, she blew her nose and groaned. Her head was banging and her throat felt like sandpaper.

But she needed the money.

And night shifts weren't all that bad. They were generally quiet, and with a bit of luck she might even be able to get her head down for a quick cat nap at some point.

Swallowing two paracetamol tablets with the last of her coffee — made extra strong and without milk to try and perk her up — she glanced at her watch. The Uber would be here soon. It was an expense she could do without — the new council tax demand had landed on the doormat a few weeks ago and had increased more than she'd wanted. Everything seemed to be going up these days — everything except her wages, that was. Which was why she had signed up to do the extra shift tonight.

Although the Uber was expensive, she didn't much fancy travelling on the Tube. Not only did she feel rough, and didn't

298

look forward to getting squashed up against someone else with a hacking cough or a runny nose to match her own, the headlines that had saturated the media recently made her shiver.

The Tube wasn't safe. The Uber was an expense, but at least it wasn't dangerous.

* * *

Time: 7.45 p.m.
Date: Tuesday 14 April 2015
Location: Kettle's Yard Mews, London

Jack had considered ringing Rob, suggesting a curry and a beer — but tiredness soon got the better of him once he'd stepped across the threshold of the flat. Marmaduke had greeted him in his customary way — mewing with increasing intensity until the tin of cat food was opened.

With the tabby cat now munching contentedly, Jack tipped a generous serving of single malt into a glass tumbler and collapsed onto the sofa. Once again, he had brought a selection of paperwork home with him, unable to sever himself from the investigation entirely. He already knew he would be bringing it home in his head, so he may as well bring the physical paperwork, too.

Dr Matthews had sent through the draft report on Sammy Hoskings' post-mortem, although it didn't throw up much by way of further clues.

Rubbing his eyes, he took a mouthful of the Macallan and let his gaze scan the documents spread out on the coffee table. In among that lot could be the key — the key everyone had missed so far, including Jack. The DNA results coming in were causing the investigation team to go round in circles. The link to Ellis Magee for the Yorkshire attacks was good news for Jane Telford and the cold case team, but not so helpful to Operation Quicksand. Initially it had been a welcome step — meaning they could shelve the '96 and '97 cases as being

299

unconnected to the Central Line Killer investigation and acknowledge that Frank Tyler had been right to discount it.

But now Tony and Dennis Kingdom were muddying the waters. Tony Kingdom was ruled out of the 1998 murders, but his van was connected to both Keeley and Jessica's murders, albeit loosely. Plus, they had evidence that Jessica had been inside Kingdom's van — not startling news when they were meant to be in a relationship, but Kingdom had quite vehemently denied it. Such denials always made Jack's investigative senses sharpen.

With the only plausible link between some of the victims being care homes, and those care homes having visits from Kingdom Carpets, the Kingdom family were slap bang in the middle of things. And Dennis Kingdom was nowhere to be seen.

And that was before the revelation that Tony Kingdom had been searching the internet on how to get rid of DNA traces, and also before the startling discovery of a weapon hidden beneath a seat in the van. Jack planned to confront Kingdom Jnr with both questions in the morning.

Swirling a mouthful of whisky on his tongue before swallowing, Jack relished the warmth that followed. Alcohol probably wasn't going to help him make sense of the mess the investigation was in, but it might help him sleep. He took another welcome slug from the tumbler. Jane Telford had rung just before he'd left the station, asking if he fancied a journey out to Wandsworth prison in the morning to go and pick up Ellis Magee. Jack had readily agreed. Something told him that Magee was still someone he needed to speak to despite the DNA saying otherwise. A brief background check on the man had thrown up little of substance — only confirming that he was from Hackney, went to school close by but didn't excel at anything; his life of crime began shortly after leaving the school gates. Something Jack did want to know, however, was if and when he'd ever crossed the paths of the Kingdoms.

Marmaduke, dinner completed, now joined Jack on the sofa, settling himself down on top of a stack of paperwork at Jack's side. Placing the now empty whisky glass down, Jack leaned over to gently nudge the tabby cat and rescue the papers from beneath. It took a few attempts before Marmaduke accepted defeat and begrudgingly edged to the side, mewing his discontent.

Jack tugged the papers free. They weren't connected with Operation Quicksand, but they were still adding to Jack's disquiet. The police accident report had been languishing in his desk drawer back at the station for long enough now, reminding him of its presence every time he rummaged inside for a spare pen or packet of painkillers. He knew he couldn't keep putting it off — but every time he thought about taking it out, another reason to keep it hidden from view surfaced.

So, he'd reluctantly listened to his inner voice and brought the report home. But tonight wasn't the night to tackle this particular minefield. Instead, he tucked the papers down the side of the sofa and placed a cushion over the top.

For now, he needed to concentrate on Operation Quicksand.

CHAPTER THIRTY-FOUR

Time: 8.20 a.m.
Date: Wednesday 15 April 2015
Location: HMP Wandsworth, London

As far as prisons went, Wandsworth had a reputation as being one of the hardest to do time in. With reports of repeated lockdowns, assaults on prison officers at an all-time high, episodes of self-harm among inmates at record levels — Jack was no expert in penal reform, but as a way of rehabilitating offenders, it didn't sound like it was working all that well.

The discussion had been had many times — were prisons there to punish or to rehabilitate? The system provided punishment by removing criminals from the streets and depriving them of their liberty, which also gave a degree of retribution to the victims of their crimes. But was that enough? If nothing further was done, would they just reoffend the minute their feet touched the tarmac on the other side?

But rehabilitation wasn't easy. Some institutions worked hard at it — offering inmates the opportunity to study particular trades such as carpentry or plumbing, while others studied for academic qualifications and sat exams. And some were surprisingly successful. Jack had his own opinions on the matter, although never much fancied the argument. When pushed for a response, however, he would often tread a fine line. In his opinion, rehabilitation was all down to the individual. You could offer all manner of opportunities to one inmate, give them a chance to change the direction of their life, show them the error of their ways — but if they didn't want to do it then it was a hiding to nothing, just an enormous waste of time and taxpayer's money.

Jack had long been of the view that criminals were just that — criminals. It was who they were, and who they would always be, no matter how many case workers, therapists and good-intentioned rehabilitation schemes were foisted onto them. It was just the way it was — which wasn't a particularly enticing thought.

"I don't believe I've ever been in your car before, Jack." Jane Telford released her seatbelt as they pulled into the visitor's car park.

"Not a lot of people have." Jack eyed the collection of takeaway wrappers and coffee cups in the passenger footwell. "If I'd have known I'd have tidied up a bit."

Jane grinned. "Don't mind me. This is nothing compared to some other cars I could mention."

"Oh?" Jack parked the Mondeo close to the security gate, eyebrows raised. "Anyone I know?"

"I couldn't possibly divulge such sensitive information, you know that." Jane gave a wink and zipped her mouth shut with her thumb and forefinger. Instead, she glanced through the windscreen. "So, how are we going to play this? We're going to go and get him out of his cell — do you want a quick word with him first?"

Jack nodded. As soon as Ellis Magee's DNA had shown up on the database in connection with the Yorkshire sex assaults in '96 and '97, Jane and her team had sprung into action to resurrect the cold case. But Tony Kingdom's revelations in interview yesterday had raised the question as to whether Magee had been acting alone. With Dennis Kingdom going AWOL, Jack's detective instincts were heightened. People didn't usually run unless they had something to hide.

Although Jack didn't really need to make the trip out to Wandsworth in person — he could just as easily ask his questions when Magee was brought back to the station for interview — he'd elbowed his way into the prison visit for two reasons.

One — he wanted to clear his head after a fitful night's sleep, and a change of scenery often worked wonders.

Two — he wanted to snoop around inside Magee's cell.

* * *

Jack stood in the doorway of the cell, two prison officers behind him. Jane Telford and three uniformed officers had entered first, and with five bodies now inside it was somewhat cramped.

Magee was lying on the top bunk, staring at the ceiling, hands clasped behind his head.

"Ellis Magee, I'm arresting you on suspicion of sexual assault and rape. You do not have to say anything, but it may harm your defence if you fail to mention when questioned something that you later rely on in court. Anything you do say may be given in evidence." Jane took a step to the side. "These officers will now transport you to a place where you will be interviewed."

For several seconds, nothing happened. Magee remained stretched out on the top bunk, hands cradling his head. Jack flashed a quick look towards Jane, who returned it with a small shake of the head. He'd met plenty of people like Ellis Magee before and had no doubt that the man would come quietly in the end. He didn't have a lot of options.

As if reading Jack's thoughts, Magee slowly pushed himself to a sitting position, then swung his legs over the side of the bunk. He dropped to the floor, narrowly missing bumping into one of the uniforms as he landed.

Smirk forming on his face, Magee held out his hands. "Go on then, make my day."

Ignoring the jibe, the nearest uniform secured the man's wrists with a pair of handcuffs.

"You'll be escorted out of the building and into a prison van." Jane started to follow the entourage to the door. "You will remain under caution for the entire journey."

Magee eyed Jane, the smile transforming into a wide grin. A wink then followed. "I know the routine. I have done this before, sweet cheeks."

Jack felt the hairs prickle on the back of his neck, taking an instant dislike to Ellis Magee. Swallowing his distaste, he remained standing in the doorway. "Just before you go, Mr Magee, I'd be grateful for a small word or two."

Magee's grin remained plastered to his face but at the same time a look of intrigue entered his eyes. "Oh, so what do we have here, then?"

"I'm Detective Inspector Jack MacIntosh, Metropolitan Police."

Magee's eyes crinkled at the corners. "My, my — they're bringing out the big guns this morning. To what do I owe this pleasure? You her boss or something?" He nodded towards Jane, causing Jack's hackles to rise even further.

"This won't take long," Jack continued. "I just need to ask a question or two before these lovely people take care of you."

"Oh?" Magee's scruffy eyebrows hitched. "Far be it for me to tell you how to do your job, mate, but shouldn't we be doing this in a nice cosy interview room with a cup of tea each?"

Jack held the man in a fixed stare. "Unfortunately, I don't have the luxury of time on my side. You're already under caution, Mr Magee. You don't have to answer my questions if you don't want to."

Another grin followed, revealing a row of brown, broken teeth. "Then ask away, my friend."

"Dennis Kingdom. He someone you know?" Jack watched for Magee's reaction to the name, concentrating on the man's eyes.

Brow flickering, Magee hesitated for a second or two before shaking his head. "Sorry, no. Never heard of the fella." He turned back towards Jane Telford, raising his restrained wrists into the air. "We good to go now? I could do with one of your lovely cups of tea — the water in this place makes it go all scummy on top."

***

Time: 8.45 a.m.
Date: Wednesday 15 April 2015
Location: Euston Station, London

As Genete stepped off the train, she felt another ripple of anxiety. What was she doing? The last forty-eight hours had passed by in a whirlwind. She had cremated her mother, albeit she hadn't been there to witness it in person, and then found her long-lost brother. And now she was here — in London.

It was crazy.

Rob was there, just like he said he would be, standing a good head and shoulders above everyone else on the other side of the exit barriers. She couldn't help but smile at his handsome face. She'd never really forgotten him, not in all the years they'd been apart. Big brother Rob. Although only five when they were separated, she could still remember the last time she saw him — being driven away from their foster home in the back of a silver-grey car. Rob's face had been pressed up against the window, with a look she now recognised as defiance mixed with bewilderment.

As she'd entered adulthood, she often wondered what had happened to him. Was he even still in Liverpool? It had crossed her mind once or twice to try and find him, but the idea soon ebbed away as life took hold. Instead, she adapted to her new life and looking for Rob had faded into the background.

But now he was here, and she couldn't help but grin.

"You made it, then?" Carmichael took hold of her bag, placing a hand on her elbow. "I'm parked out the front by the taxis."

Genete allowed herself to be guided through the hordes of passengers streaming along the concourse then out to the taxi rank, where a car was parked on a double yellow line.

"Do those signs actually work?" She nodded towards the laminated *Police Business* sign Carmichael was now retrieving from the inside of the windscreen.

"No idea. Probably not," he grinned. "But I've yet to get a ticket."

The journey to the station wouldn't take long, and as they drove Genete listened to her brother pointing out various landmarks as they passed. Some she was familiar with, others not so much. She let her head rest against the cool glass of the side window and closed her eyes.

"You OK?"

Genete nodded, eyes still shut. "I'm fine. Just tired. It was an early start, and I didn't get a lot of sleep last night."

"I'll shut up, then, but we're nearly there anyway. I can go and get you something to eat from the canteen if you're hungry? They do a really good all-day breakfast?"

Genete smiled, opening her eyes a little. "I'm fine but thank you. Maybe later. I'm a little too nervous to eat right now."

"Nervous? Why's that?" Carmichael slowed down at a set of traffic lights, flashing a concerned look towards his sister. "You don't have anything to feel nervous about."

Blinking, Genete sat up a little straighter in the passenger seat. "You don't think? I'm nervous about the whole thing. Meeting you. Meeting your colleagues. And, if I'm honest, I'm really nervous about saying that I could help you guys out with your criminal profile. I think I may have over-sold myself a little — I've never actually done any real profiling before."

Keeping an eye on the lights, Carmichael leaned across and gave Genete's hand a squeeze. "Trust your instincts. I'm sure you'll be amazing."

* * *

Time: *8.50 a.m.*
Date: *Wednesday 15 April 2015*
Location: *HMP Wandsworth, London*

With Jane travelling back to the station in one of the patrol cars, Jack took the opportunity to hang behind. Ellis Magee's cell was just like any other he'd seen over the years, especially in a Victorian jail such as this one. London had long outgrown the prisons built during Queen Victoria's reign, and new ones were few and far between. Belmarsh had been the capital's newest prison, but even that had long since reached capacity — and with the prison population throughout the country bursting at the seams it would only get worse as the years went by. Victorian jails like Wandsworth weren't designed for the twenty-first century prisoner.

Even without Magee in it, the cell felt cramped. The walls were a thick, cold brick that had been painted a dull, submarine grey, adding to the sense of confinement. The wing seemed curiously quiet to Jack, the communal walkways noticeably empty.

Inside the cell, Jack noted the heavy-duty metal bunk bed secured to the left-hand wall with a thin, stained mattress on each bunk. A desk was similarly fastened to the right-hand wall, next to a metal toilet. Some prison cells now had individual showers, but not this one. Jack sniffed the air — a mixture of body odour and urine greeting him.

A shelf above the desk housed the personal effects of the two inhabitants. It wasn't much, but not much was needed for a life inside. A quick rummage didn't throw up anything useful. A box of Sugar Puffs, a jar of cheap coffee, two plastic mugs that had seen better days and a packet of broken biscuits.

Jack quickly turned his attention to the desk below. There was a single drawer beneath which he pulled open and was immediately transported back to the hunt for the Bishop last year. Jack had searched the room of a patient at the New Green Psychiatric Unit and discovered several stomach-churning letters.

Letters.

Again.

Jack pulled out the bundle and set them on top of the desk. Each one bore the same uniform handwriting on the front. Opening them up, he started to read their contents. It didn't take long for a growing sense of disquiet to threaten to overwhelm him. Aware that he shouldn't really be there, Jack arranged the letters in chronological order and quickly took a snap of each, before replacing them where he found them and striding out of the cell.

CHAPTER THIRTY-FIVE

Time: 9.45 a.m.
Date: Wednesday 15 April 2015
Location: Metropolitan Police HQ, London

"Make yourself at home." Jack gestured towards a spare desk by the window. "Give me a shout if there's anything else you need."

Genete gave a nervous smile. "Thanks. That's great."

"All the paperwork is either on the computers or in among that lot over there." Jack waved a hand towards a table brimming with files. "If you're looking for physical paper-work, Cooper is probably your best bet. He can normally put his hands on most things fairly quickly."

Cooper raised a hand, sinking his teeth into his second bacon roll of the morning. "Yeah, no bother — just holler."

"If it's anything on the computers that you need, give Daniels a nudge."

Trevor Daniels lifted his gaze away from his screen and gave a lop-sided smile.

"Thank you, I'm sure I'll be fine." Genete slipped behind the desk and looped her bag over the back of the chair. "I hope I don't get in your way."

"You'll not get in anyone's way, I can assure you. I'm just really grateful for anything you can tell us. You're doing us a massive favour just by being here." Rob Carmichael had met Jack on his return from Wandsworth, a broad grin on his face as he introduced Genete.

Genete his sister.

Genete the forensic psychologist.

"What with Rachel Hunter otherwise engaged, I thought Genete might be able to help." Jack had almost bitten the detective sergeant's arm off.

Satisfied that Genete looked settled, Jack crossed over to DS Cooper's desk and dropped his phone onto a pile of folders. "Can you look at this lot for me, and then work your magic to get them printed off?"

Cooper picked up the handset, swiping through the collection of photographs Jack had taken in Ellis Magee's cell. "Sure. Won't take me a minute." He busied himself connecting the phone to his computer.

Jack hovered by the detective sergeant's shoulder. "You'll see the author of the letters used a PO box. Find out all you can as to any registered user, and any other correspondence address or contact details for them."

Cooper nodded, pushing the remains of the roll into his mouth as the images from Jack's phone started to populate his computer screen. "Will do, boss."

"Amanda, you're with me. Let's go and check in on Tony Kingdom and see if a night in the cells has loosened his tongue."

* * *

Time: 10.00 a.m.
Date: Wednesday 15 April 2015
Location: Herne Bay, Kent

Frank lowered himself back down into the recliner and closed his eyes. Yesterday's trip to the capital had taken much more

311

out of him than he'd expected. Reenie had been right — which, he had to admit, she usually was. When he'd finally returned, she'd greeted him with a smile and a hug — no "I told you so" or other recrimination. Instead, she handed him a dose of painkillers and set about making a cup of tea. He again reminded himself how incredibly lucky he was to have her in his life. He was dying, granted — and a lot sooner than he wanted or expected — but at least he was dying with Irene at his side. He was not alone.

This morning he'd slept longer than usual, only waking when Irene had placed his morning medication on the bedside table. Promising to take it easier today, he'd made his way downstairs to the conservatory to watch the world go by in the garden. As he waited for the painkillers to take effect, he thought back to his time in the incident room. He'd felt it almost immediately — the unmistakable buzz of a live investigation. It was like electricity, making the hairs on your skin stand end to end. There was nothing quite like it.

He was glad he'd made the effort to go, despite the exhaustion that followed. It had been good to catch up with Jack again, and Frank was more than reassured that the case was in capable hands. They'd spoken briefly about Lorna Henshaw on the way back to the station from the crime scene, Jack reiterating his own concerns about the journalist's involvement. Frank confirmed that he'd looked into the possibility the woman had sent the envelopes to herself, remembering it clearly, but had to conclude that, although, yes, it was certainly possible, there had been no way to prove it.

That had then sparked a "what if" conversation for the rest of the journey — *what if she had?*

Which soon led onto the *why*. If she *had* done it, what could have been her reasoning? What was her motive? She didn't seem to get anything out of it other than being involved in the case — but it was an involvement that was never made public. Would that have been enough? Would it have satisfied whatever perverse desire she might have had to feel important, to feel a valuable part of a murder investigation?

Jack wasn't convinced and Frank had to agree that neither was he but, by the time they'd returned to the station, they both accepted *it was still possible*.

And if it was possible back in 1998, then it was still possible now.

Frank was under no illusion about his visit to see Jack and the team; he wouldn't set foot in the building again. Maybe he wouldn't even make it into London again. But he was fine with that now. The itch had been scratched, the thirst quenched. He was at peace now — or at least a peace of sorts. He reached for the tea Irene had poured for him and savoured the warmth on his tongue. The only bonus now would be for the Central Line Killer to finally be caught.

Frank hoped Jack would succeed before his time on this earth ran out.

* * *

Time: 10.15 a.m.
Date: Wednesday 15 April 2015
Location: Metropolitan Police HQ, London

Jack made the necessary introductions for the tape recording, then settled back in his chair. "Ellis Magee." He could see from the pained expression on Tony Kingdom's face that the night in the cells hadn't been a comfortable one. Red-rimmed eyes stared out from a pale and wan complexion.

"Who?" The carpet fitter's voice was low and strained.

"Ellis Magee," repeated Jack. "You know him?"

Kingdom gave a slow shake of his head. "Never heard of him. Why?"

Jack ignored the question. "What about a PO box number? Do you ever use PO boxes for your carpet business? Your dad ever use one?"

Another blank expression followed, together with a frown. Kingdom reached for the polystyrene cup of murky-looking coffee he'd been supplied with. "No. Why would we?"

Jack again ignored the question. "Since your arrest, your father appears to have gone AWOL. Do you have any idea where he might have gone?"

The frown deepened. "Dad's gone?"

"Left the house with a bag, so I've been reliably informed. Does he have access to another vehicle, apart from the van?"

Tired eyes widening, Kingdom shook his head. "No, we had to sell the car a few years ago, tighten our belts. We only use the van now, share it."

"And places he might go to? You have any family around here, maybe your mother?"

A look of derision embedded itself on the carpet fitter's brow. "Now that's somewhere I know he would *never* go. He'd never willingly go anywhere near that bitch."

Bitch.

It was a term Kingdom had used twice now in relation to women — one for his mother, and one for Jessica Fleming. Jack slotted the information away for future reference. "Do you hate women, Mr Kingdom?"

The question appeared to take the carpet fitter by surprise but elicited no response.

"You don't seem to talk about them in a very endearing light."

Kingdom took a sip from the polystyrene cup, his face wincing at the taste. "Some of them *are* bitches, that's just a fact."

"And I take it one of those would be Jessica Fleming, am I right?"

"It's no secret that we fell out. Not a crime, is it?"

"No, but murder is — and so is concealing evidence in a criminal investigation. As is lying to the police." Jack's tone hardened as he gave a surreptitious nod towards DS Cassidy sitting by his side. "Detective Sergeant Cassidy here is going to show you, once again, images of your van close to the bus stop where Jessica was last seen."

Cassidy tapped the laptop's keyboard then turned it around to face the carpet fitter before hitting play.

"We know Jessica has been inside your van, Mr Kingdom, despite you claiming otherwise. The DNA evidence is quite conclusive on that score. We also know you were driving the van that day — you were seen at a petrol station only minutes before these images were taken. And—" Jack paused and held the carpet fitter in a firm gaze — "there is further evidence of a rather crude attempt to clean the upholstery inside the van. We found traces of bleach on the seat covers. Plus, you've been searching how to erase DNA evidence on your phone. Care to explain why?"

Jack watched the carpet fitter's face pale even further. The seconds ticked by, but Tony Kingdom remained mute.

"While you're thinking about that, how about what else we found in the van? Why did you have a gun concealed below the driver's seat, Mr Kingdom? Is this how you overcome your victims? Threaten them with a weapon?"

CHAPTER THIRTY-SIX

Time: 11.15 a.m.
Date: Wednesday 15 April 2015
Location: Metropolitan Police HQ, London

Jack jogged down the steps leading to the basement as quickly as his injured foot allowed. He was becoming accustomed to the almost continuous dull ache now, wondering if this was as good as it was going to get. It had only been three months, but his patience was growing thinner by the day.

Jane Telford was waiting for him at the entrance to the Cold Case Unit. "You didn't need to come all the way down here, Jack — a phone call would have sufficed. Not that it's not a welcome distraction."

Jack grimaced as he descended the final step. "It's fine — I needed to stretch my legs anyway. What's he said so far?"

Ellis Magee had been booked into the custody suite on his arrival from Wandsworth, and Jack had gleaned from the grapevine that the man had been interviewed about the Yorkshire sex attacks already.

"We've only conducted the initial interview, nothing too breathtaking. It didn't take long." Jane beckoned for Jack to follow her into the Unit's main office. "He wasn't exactly forthcoming. I get the feeling he likes to play games."

Games.

Jack was beginning to feel the same. Pulling out his phone, he passed it over. "Have a look at these images — they're from a bundle of letters I found in his cell. They're all signed by someone calling themselves X." He caught Jane's eye and knew the wily detective inspector would instantly be questioning the legality of the search — but he equally knew she would let it go; it wasn't her battle. Jack wasn't afraid to get his hands dirty from time to time, and if the information led them to the identity of the Central Line Killer, then he would risk the wrath of a few defence barristers down the line. "There's nothing in them that directly implicates Magee to the 1998 murders, the letters are clever, but whoever this X is clearly knows something. *'Another one down.' 'Who's next?' 'Working to the game plan.'* It's all there. They even name the Tube stations."

Jane narrowed her gaze as she scrolled through the images. "I see what you mean. But any half-decent defence lawyer would have a field day with this lot if it was all you had."

Jack nodded. "Which is why I need to know who this bloody X is."

"And I take it you want me to ask him in interview?" Jane raised her eyebrows as she handed the phone back. "I can try, but it won't exactly be easy. He's been arrested on suspicion of the Yorkshire sex attacks, not the Central Line murders. As soon as we bring these letters into the interview the duty solicitor will come down on us like a ton of bricks. Or at least they should. You'd have to explain how you came by them and what relevance they had. I think we'd struggle on both counts there."

Jack knew Jane was right, but that wasn't what he was asking. Not yet anyway. "I wouldn't put you in that position — all I want to find out is whether he knows of Tony Kingdom or Dennis Kingdom. See what his reaction is — if any. I know I asked him in his cell, but I'm not convinced

317

that was the best place. Let's see what he says when he's under interview conditions."

Jane's eyebrows hitched a little higher. "That's all? Just Tony and Dennis Kingdom?"

Jack nodded. "For now." He thought he could detect a small smile playing on her lips. "If you wouldn't mind, that is."

"Then consider it done. We're due to resume his second interview as soon as the detectives from Yorkshire CID arrive, which should be soon. But I think we'll leave it there — I don't think I want to ask you why you want to know; the less I know the better, I feel." The smile lingered.

"Probably wise," agreed Jack, turning for the door. "But thanks. It could help us enormously."

Jack said his goodbyes and headed back to ground level, then up to the incident room. As he entered, DS Cooper jumped out of his seat.

"More lab results have started coming in, boss. All three victims — Keely, Jessica and Sammy — show traces of carpet fibres on their clothing."

"Carpet fibres?" Jack headed towards Cooper's desk. "Any chance that can be narrowed down?"

Cooper tapped his keyboard and brought up the series of reports on his monitor. "So far, all that's been confirmed is that all three have the same type of dark red or maroon fibres. Analysis shows it to be a polyester and nylon mix. Pretty standard for a carpet."

"Carpet fibres give us another link to Tony Kingdom," added DS Cassidy, joining Jack at Cooper's desk. "Or even Dennis Kingdom."

Jack ran a hand over his chin as he sighed, feeling the stubble prick his fingertips. "It does. But wrapping a body up in a carpet is pretty standard stuff. We still need some way to link it to their van. But I agree it's a step forward. Pop it up on the board."

"The lab is cross-referencing the fibres with other samples they've taken from the van. They'll let us know if they get a match." Cooper closed the lab reports down.

"Anything more with Tony Kingdom's phone?" Jack turned towards DC Daniels. "Can we place the phone at or near any of the crime scenes?"

"Cell site data isn't back yet, boss." Daniels turned towards his computer screen. "I can chase it up, though. In the meantime, I've gone back over everything surrounding Lorna Henshaw."

"Oh?" Jack grabbed a chair and pulled it towards Daniels' desk. "What have you found?"

"Unfortunately, still no links with any of the victims — including the 1998 cases. There's no evidence I can find that any of them even read the same newspapers, no one subscribed to the *Daily Courier*, and no evidence any of them accessed news reports online. Lorna Henshaw didn't live anywhere near them, and there's no evidence she interacted with any of them. I think it's a dead end, boss."

"Nothing else at all?" Jack tried to keep the deflation from his tone.

"I looked deeper into her employment records. Outside of the media, just a few temporary jobs after leaving college. Nothing suggests any link to our victims."

Jack nodded. He didn't like dead ends. Lorna Henshaw still bothered him, for reasons he wasn't quite sure of. On the drive back to the station from the crime scene yesterday, Frank Tyler had again voiced his own concerns about the woman. They had then discussed the idea of her being more involved than she was letting on, but that was all it had been. An idea. There was nothing even remotely concrete to go on. And there was Jonathan Spearing's veiled warning about the journalist, too. Jack may not like Spearing, but the man wasn't stupid.

"Good work anyway, Daniels. Let me know about the cell site data when it comes in. Regarding Lorna Henshaw — maybe have a look at those temporary jobs before she got bogged down in the media. What was she doing and where? See what else you can find."

Daniels nodded and turned back to his computer screen.

"I've managed to take a look at the crime scene photos for the 1998 murders, guv, like you asked." Cassidy pulled her notepad towards her. "Shards of a broken mirror were found at the car showroom where Lynn Jaggard was found in July 1998, crudely tacked to the wall. The owners of the building confirmed it didn't belong to them, so the only conclusion was that the killer must have brought the mirror with them. No mirrors found at the other crime scenes, although there was mention of evidence of something on the walls at three other sites. Some sort of sticky substance. Might be evidence that the killer tacked something up there — could be a mirror?" Cassidy gave a half shrug. "The investigation team didn't spend too much time on it, the lead seemed to peter out."

Jack nodded. "Well, it at least backs up what I'm beginning to feel about our killer. He likes to watch, for whatever reason that might be." Thinking about the killer's psychological make-up made Jack think about Genete. Carmichael's sister was huddled over her desk in the corner of the incident room, concentrating hard on what she was reading. He didn't feel it necessary to disturb her so turned his attention back to his team.

"Tony Kingdom is starting to panic — I can feel it. We've confronted him with the DNA evidence about Jessica being in the van, the search results on his phone about destroying DNA, and also the gun found beneath the driver's seat. We'll leave him to stew for a while before we interview him again. I have a feeling he's starting to appreciate what position he's in."

* * *

Time: 11.30 a.m.
Date: Wednesday 15 April 2015
Location: Ashcroft Nursing Home, London

Pippa yawned. The shift had been busier than she'd anticipated, with three members of staff ringing in sick with what sounded like the same bug she was suffering from. Maybe she should have cancelled her extra shift, kept her germs to herself — but then she thought about the money again.

With another yawn, she made her way along the corridor that led to the back door. She should have left three hours ago, but she'd reluctantly agreed to stop on for a while longer as they were short-staffed. They were due deliveries from both the catering suppliers and the laundry services, and Pippa had volunteered to oversee both.

It was an aspect of the job some of the others disliked, but she welcomed the distraction. It gave her the chance to have a natter with someone else for a change. And, as a rule, she got on well with the delivery drivers. There were a couple of oddballs, for sure, but you could find them in any job if you looked hard enough. One of the drivers for the catering suppliers would catch her eye on occasion, silently looking her up and down. He would never say anything, just plaster a weird smile on his face as he unloaded the van. To start with it had unnerved her, but now she barely noticed. If it was him on the delivery run today, then she was sure she would cope.

Some of the other drivers were less odd, passing her a tasty treat while she waited. Nursing home food was a lot better these days than people imagined — gone were the days of lumpy mashed potato, gristly meat and watery, tasteless vegetables. Now everything was healthy and nutritious, and surprisingly well cooked, almost up to restaurant standard.

And they did the most divine desserts, not the traditional sticky semolina or rice pudding. Pippa hated both with a passion — most probably because of being force fed them at school until she was sick — but she did have a sweet tooth. She quietly hoped chocolate mousse was on the menu today, or maybe even apple crumble.

Reaching the back door, her stomach rumbling in anticipation, she pushed the fire door open, grateful for the blast of fresh air that followed. The home was kept warm, so it felt good to feel the cool air on her skin. As she stepped out into the car park she noticed the familiar catering van heading in her direction. Her stomach rumbled even more as she thought about the tasty desserts on board.

She just hoped it wasn't the weird guy in the driving seat.

321

CHAPTER THIRTY-SEVEN

Time: 11.50 a.m.
Date: Wednesday 15 April 2015
Location: Metropolitan Police HQ, London

Genete flexed her neck and took a sideways glance out of the window. Clouds were gathering and there was a rumble of thunder threatening rain. Was she really up to this? A real, live investigation? Pulling the headphones from her ears, she rubbed her eyes. Her stomach shifted as she again questioned whether she had bitten off far more than she could chew. She'd never done anything like this before, not even close.

After booking a fortnight's annual leave several months ago, she hadn't envisaged spending the beginning of it cocooned inside a stuffy London police incident room. Instead, she'd had visions of taking long walks around the Lakes, interspersed with cosy duvet days on the sofa catching up with a whole host of box sets she'd earmarked on Netflix, recharging her batteries, feeding her soul.

But instead of Netflix she was here, looking at post-mortem reports and delving into cold cases.

The team had been great, welcoming her into the fold instantly. Cooper had even gone to the canteen and brought

322

her down some food, while Cassidy had kept her well hydrated with peppermint tea. The tuna sandwich had been lovely, but it now swirled uncomfortably in her stomach alongside the tea.

The names of each victim from the 1998 murders were now listed in her notebook, together with a comprehensive background ranging from their family and employment histories to their movements on the day they were last seen. Then she had added the three victims from the current investigation. As she looked back down at her notes, the overwhelming feeling of imposter syndrome come crashing back in.

What if she got it all wrong and merely made everything worse?

Rubbing her eyes again, she tried to focus on her notes. *Of course* she could do this. She'd been taught by one of the best forensic psychologists in the world and gained top marks in all her exams. She could do this standing on her head, in the dark, with one hand tied behind her back; all she needed was some self-belief.

Taking another mouthful of the cooling peppermint tea, she started going through each of the bullet points in her notepad once again. Somewhere on these pages was the one clue to help the team find the killer — she just had to find it.

She'd had the incident room to herself for a while now, the others off doing whatever it was they were tasked with. She hadn't asked, not feeling it was her place to question their comings and goings. She hoped they weren't just staying away to give her space, but at the same time she welcomed the peace and quiet within which to work. Back in Liverpool, she had her own office within the Behavioural Sciences department, and although it was small — barely more than a cupboard, in reality — it meant she could work uninterrupted. She wasn't used to being part of a team. She just hoped she didn't stick out like a sore thumb.

Having studied each of the victims of the 1998 murders, and also the current cases in Operation Quicksand, Genete turned her attention to the sexual assaults in Yorkshire. Jack had informed her that the potential link to the Central Line Killer had been discounted due to DNA evidence — but something was drawing her back to it. DNA was a wonderful invention in modern science, a game changer in analysis and detection, but nothing was ever quite that cut and dried. Dr Schneider at the university always urged her to look for the unexpected.

She admired him immensely. The man's office was a haven to the workings of the human mind. A staunch Sherlock Holmes fan, several framed book covers and quotes littered his walls.

'There is nothing more deceptive than an obvious fact — just because a fact is obvious doesn't mean the correct conclusion to be drawn from it is.'

Was this what they were looking at here? The DNA evidence being accepted as an obvious fact and not challenged any further?

On the face of it, the Yorkshire offences were markedly different — none of the sexual assaults resulted in murder, for a start — but Genete knew every killer had to begin somewhere. For the next hour, she immersed herself in the attacks in Halifax, Harrogate, Huddersfield, Hebden Bridge, Whitby and Ripon. The towns were relatively close to one another, easily accessed by car. Serial offenders would often stick to a familiar patch, somewhere they felt comfortable and able to operate without standing out. Yorkshire seemed to do just that for this particular offender.

As she worked, she again made comprehensive notes in her notebook on each victim — their backgrounds, their personalities, and the circumstances of each individual attack. With the '96 and '97 cases, Genete had the advantage of being able to hear from the victims themselves, something they didn't have for the Central Line Killer victims. She read each of their witness statements several times over, making bullet points as she went.

As she read, she could almost feel the pain seeping out of the paperwork as each victim relived the single worst moment of their lives.

But at least they weren't dead.

One of the victims — Trace Manning — had said exactly that during the course of one of her interviews.

"At least I'm not dead."

It was a heart-wrenching statement to read. As terrifying as it was, Trace Manning was fully aware it could have ended very differently. Genete shivered and inched her chair further towards the radiator beneath the window. She wasn't sure she would have been as brave as these women had been.

Rob had popped his head into the incident room a while ago, checking she was getting on all right and promising a curry later. She'd smiled and sent him on his way. Thoughts of a curry right now turned her stomach.

With a heavy heart, she reached for the pile of witness statements once again and started to read.

* * *

Time: 12.45 p.m.
Date: Wednesday 15 April 2015
Location: Kettle's Yard Mews, London

Isabel negotiated the stairs up to Jack's second floor flat, the shopping bags banging against her calves as she climbed. She knew it wasn't strictly necessary any more; the man was more than capable of going to the supermarket himself now and running the hoover around. But she enjoyed it — she liked feeling useful, needed. It gave her a sense of purpose.

Since inheriting a large sum of money on the death of her parents, the initial elation and then excitement had started to wane. Having enough money — *too* much money, if she was being honest — shifted your priorities somewhat, even if you didn't realise it. She loved working in the café, but she didn't

325

need it to make the same kind of profit that she had before. She had enough cash to pay off her debts, and didn't owe anyone a single coffee bean any more, which consequently meant that the urgency to succeed was no longer there.

The café was still turning over a profit — Isabel was a shrewd businesswoman if nothing else — but knowing that it didn't really *need* to took some of the satisfaction out of it, and inevitably the money had lost some of its shine.

Sighing, she rested the bags on the floor by Jack's front door and fished around in her pocket for the key he'd given her. Maybe she would leave the keys behind this time — make this the last visit, the last time she mollycoddled the poor man. Mac often teased her about how she scurried around doing odd jobs when Jack was more than capable of doing them himself. Maybe he was right.

The minute she stepped across the threshold, Marmaduke came trotting over from where he had no doubt been asleep, yawning and peering up at her through sleepy cat eyes. Isabel grinned, placing the bags down again and bending to give the ginger tabby a tickle under the chin. Once the cat had had his fill of attention, he turned away and Isabel took the shopping through to the kitchen.

She'd been to the market that morning to get some fresh vegetables. From the time she'd spent in Jack's flat over the last few weeks, she'd quickly learned that he wasn't quite meeting his five-a-day target — probably not even five a week.

Opening the fridge, she moved the stash of beer bottles to the side, along with the half-eaten takeaway containers, and filled the space with fresh carrots, red onions, broccoli, green beans and multicoloured peppers. She'd already decided not to cook him anything for later, having no idea when he might be home and fully aware that she needed to let him look after himself — so she decided to just do the washing up and have a general tidy instead.

Once the kitchen was gleaming, with all the washing-up put away in the cupboards, she moved on to the living room.

There wasn't a lot to do — just a few stray coffee mugs on the table — so she took a cleaning cloth and some spray cleaner and began to wipe down the TV unit and shelves opposite. One advantage of Jack living such a minimalist lifestyle was that tidying up didn't take that much time at all. Knowing that he kept a small vacuum cleaner in a cupboard next to the bedroom, she pulled it out intending to give the carpets a quick going over before leaving.

She removed the cushions from the sofa to give them a shake before replacing them, brushing wayward crumbs onto the carpet. As she placed the last cushion back, she noted several sheets of paper tucked down the side of the sofa. Wondering if it was something important to do with Jack's work, she pulled them out to place on the coffee table before resuming her vacuuming.

But that was before her eyes had inadvertently strayed to the first page.

Isabel had given up French at the earliest opportunity at school, something she later regretted when her wanderlust took her travelling, but even she knew enough of a smattering of the language to have a decent stab at what it said.

And not all the words were in French.

One word in particular stood out.

Faraday.

* * *

Time: 1.00 p.m.
Date: Wednesday 15 April 2015
Location: Metropolitan Police HQ, London

Jack hovered by the whiteboards.

"Do you believe him, guv?" DS Cassidy perched on the edge of her desk. "Tony Kingdom?"

Jack's lips thinned. "I'm not sure what to believe right now, Amanda, but I'm edging towards thinking he might be telling us the truth. Or at least a version of it. He's at least admitted that Jessica Fleming had been inside his van after all."

"Well, he had to really, didn't he, boss?" Cooper tapped a biro against his chin, leaning back in his seat. "I mean, we have DNA evidence. He couldn't really deny it much longer."

"Indeed, Cooper. His explanation might stretch the imagination, though. We'll need to see if we can corroborate any of it."

When Jack and Cassidy had resumed the interview, Tony Kingdom had eventually agreed that he *had* picked Jessica up in his van that day, admitting that he'd followed her from the hair salon to the bus stop.

"*I just wanted to know what she was doing, who she was seeing. I never killed her, though.*"

Jack folded his arms and leaned up against the incident room wall, taking the weight off his throbbing foot. "Do we believe him when he says he stopped at the bus stop, seeing it was pouring with rain, to offer her a lift home? Does that fit with what we know about him?"

"He hasn't had anything nice to say about her so far," chipped in Cassidy. "Calls her a bitch. Seems to loathe her. Why would he stop and give her a lift?"

Jack sighed. "And if we *do* believe he had a moment of overwhelming compassion, do we then believe that he turfed her out less than ten minutes later after another of their famous arguments?"

"I can try and go through the CCTV again, boss." Cooper inched his chair closer to his desk. "Widen the net and see if we can catch her leaving his van?"

"We need to do something to either prove or disprove it." Jack pushed himself away from the wall. "He doesn't have much of a link to our other two victims. Or the 1998 murders."

"But the carpet fitting company does. We still have them fitting carpets in two of the 1998 cases, and two of the sexual assault cases." Cooper looked up from his screen. "Surely that's enough of a link — it can't just be chance, can it?"

"It's a link, yes." Jack rubbed his eyes and slumped down into one of the vacant chairs. "But not to everything. I'm wondering if we're taking a giant leap down the wrong rabbit hole, here."

"Do we believe him when he says he doesn't know Ellis Magee?" Cassidy sipped her peppermint tea. "He didn't hesitate to deny it."

Jack sighed. "He's lied in interview before, he could be lying again. The truth is, I don't know."

"Maybe he's our Mr X? Could we get a handwriting sample analysed, see if we can link him to the letters?"

Jack saw the pound signs multiplying before his eyes. "We could. Let's see if we can get anything more from forensics first. Have we any DNA from Operation Quicksand yet?"

Cooper reached for the phone. "I'll ring Jenny."

"Where's Daniels?" Jack's question was answered by the detective constable rushing through the incident room door, a sheaf of papers under his arm.

"I think I might have found something, boss." Daniels hurried over to his desk, depositing the paperwork on top. "As we know, back in 1998 we have Gail Colman and Sadie Bloomfield working in a care home and nursing home, respectively. And Sammy Hoskings from yesterday. I've looked at all the paperwork again and found more links to other care homes." Pausing, he pulled out a sheet of A4 paper covered in his neat handwriting and slipped back into his seat. "Cindy Benham — she worked at a shoe shop, but there is mention in her background checks that her father was resident at Cedar Lodge nursing home at the time of her murder. For Lynn Jaggard, similar checks on her background and next of kin show an uncle resident in Forest Glade Care Home. Christine Gooch worked for a medical supplies company that serviced many of the nursing and care homes in and around London, and Becky Scott — the last victim in 1998 — worked as a volunteer at two nursing homes in the capital. I did a cross-check and none of these places had any record of having carpets fitted in the months prior to the murders. I'm wondering if the carpet fitting link is a red herring — but there *is* still a link to the homes themselves, that this is where our killer interacts with his victims." Daniels sat back, an expectant look on his face. "What do you think?"

Jack had already made his way over to the detective sergeant's desk, peering over his shoulder. "You could have something there, Daniels. Keep with the care home and nursing home angle. If it wasn't carpet fitting, look into the other contractors again and see who else might have crossed our victims' paths."

"Already started, boss." Daniels pulled another sheet of paper out of the pile, his grin extending. "Remember Frank Tyler and his team interviewed various disgruntled Tube workers, thinking there might be a link that way?"

Jack's eyebrows hitched. "The Tube workers? I thought we'd discounted that?"

"We had — sort of." Daniels handed Jack the sheet of paper. "That's a record of an interview with Spencer Kershaw, sacked from his job with the Underground in late 1996. Although his interview doesn't ring any alarm bells, I noticed the statement mentioned his current employment. He works for a catering company that supplies most care homes in London."

* * *

Time: 1.00 p.m.
Date: Wednesday 15 April 2015
Location: Ashcroft Nursing Home, London

Pippa hovered outside the open doors of the van, then glanced up at Spencer Kershaw's grinning face.

"Go on, help yourself."

Pippa tried a smile in return. When she'd seen it was him behind the wheel of the van as it pulled up outside the nursing home's back door, her stomach had dropped. She was tired and grouchy, her nose congested and her throat scratchy; Spencer Kershaw she could do without.

"Just my sodding luck," she'd muttered to herself as she'd descended the steps to meet the van. Her head was banging, despite the paracetamol she'd swallowed half an hour ago. She wished she hadn't agreed to stay on for these extra few hours now, yearning for her duvet and some chicken soup. She already planned to call in sick for the remainder of the week, to try and kick these bugs into touch before the weekend.

But she still needed to get through the next hour or so, and that included dealing with Spencer Kershaw.

"I know there's some of your favourite in the back — chocolate mousse, isn't it?"

Pippa edged closer to the open doors. She could really do with a sugar hit right now, and the mousse *was* extremely good. Before she could make up her mind, Kershaw stepped forward, hand outstretched to help her take the step up into the rear of the van. Quickly sidestepping his sweaty clutches, she grabbed hold of the door and pulled herself inside.

"It's OK — I can manage."

* * *

Time: 1.35 p.m.
Date: Wednesday 15 April 2015
Location: Metropolitan Police HQ, London

Stretching out his leg beneath the desk, Jack willed the painkillers to take effect. He'd left Daniels the task of tracking down Spencer Kershaw from the catering suppliers. After a brief look back through Frank Tyler's investigation, Jack saw that the former Tube worker had been interviewed twice, but Frank seemed to have discounted him as a suspect.

Jack felt the all-too-familiar disquiet once again at potential leads possibly being sidelined prematurely. He'd given Frank a call, but there'd been no answer. Just then, there was a faint knocking at the door and, seconds later, Genete's face appeared around the frame.

"Genete?" Jack pulled a smile onto his tired face. "Come on in. Take a seat." As Genete slipped into the vacant chair opposite, he noted the familiar Carmichael look of doggedness and determination on her face. "How's it all going?"

"Good, I think." Genete bit her lip as she sat, then held up a small sheaf of papers that she'd had tucked under her arm. "I just wanted to run something by you."

Jack leaned forward, pushing several files to the side of his desk to make space. "Sure. Show me what you've got."

Genete handed the papers across. "I was taking a look through the Yorkshire attacks from '96 and '97. I know they've been discounted as being connected to the Central Line Killer due to the DNA evidence and the perpetrator being behind bars, but . . ." She frowned. "Then I noticed something."

Jack's eyebrows hitched. "You think they might be linked after all?"

A pensive look joined the frown. "I'm not sure. But reading the statements from the victims in '96 and '97, I'm convinced that attacker wasn't working alone. It's a relatively uncommon phenomenon, certainly in sexual assault cases, but it's not completely unheard of." Genete nodded towards the papers. "The statement on top — from Gemma Howie. She mentions the smell of stale urine at the time of the assault, but not coming from the attacker. The statement underneath, from Colette Burgess, also mentions stale urine, but she also thinks she heard the attacker speaking to someone else before running off. A third, Mandy Steed, mentions hearing another voice at the time of the attack." She paused and gave a faint shrug. "It might be nothing, but . . . what if this second person is your Central Line Killer?"

CHAPTER THIRTY-EIGHT

Time: 1.40 p.m.
Date: Wednesday 15 April 2015
Location: Metropolitan Police HQ, London

Genete took up her position in the incident room, standing in front of the whiteboards, and pressed her fingernails into her palms. She wasn't a great public speaker, more at home ensconced in her office and communicating with others via email and reports. She didn't mind speaking with patients, more comfortable that it was a one-to-one with no pressure to "perform", but make her stand up in front of others and her legs would turn to jelly in a matter of seconds.

"Genete has some news." Jack stood by Genete's side and gave her what she took for an encouraging smile. It didn't make her feel all that much better, but she tried a smile in return. She hoped it didn't seem too much like a grimace.

Looking out at the expectant faces of the investigation team, she felt her mouth become curiously dry. Unclenching her fists, she reached for the folder on the table by her side. The folder would give her something to do with her hands, so long as she didn't drop the bloody thing. Her hands shook as she pulled out the first sheet of paper. Clearing her throat, she wished she'd taken Jack up on his offer of a glass of water.

"Hi, yes — th-thank you," she stammered, cheeks immediately pinking. "I have a few things I'd like to bring to your attention."

And then she was off.

As she began to read out the salient points she'd gleaned from the evidence, her confidence grew. Her voice became stronger, her throat no longer dry or tight.

"The three investigations are connected: the sex attacks up in Yorkshire in '96 and '97, the 1998 murders in London, and the three murders making up Operation Quicksand." Genete's eyes roamed the room, catching the surprised looks on the detectives' faces as they listened. "I know what you're all thinking — that DNA evidence from the Yorkshire attacks led to a suspect who was in prison at the time of the murders. That may still be true, but it doesn't mean that the cases aren't connected."

"He had an accomplice?" DS Cassidy inched her chair closer, intrigue crossing her face.

Genete inclined her head. "That's my view. Let me explain why."

For the next ten minutes, Genete recounted extracts from the statements given to Yorkshire police that suggested the existence of a second perpetrator.

"Gemma Howie says . . ." Genete pulled out another sheet of A4 paper from the folder. "'*I could smell urine — as if someone had wet themselves and let it dry. But it wasn't on him. It wasn't on the man who raped me. He just smelled of body odour, cigarettes and stale alcohol. He didn't smell of urine. But it was there, somewhere near . . .*'" Genete looked up. "It may be that the case detectives dismissed it, thinking it was referring to the location of the attack. We've all been to those delightful communal corridors and lifts that seem to smell like a toilet, right?"

A variety of murmurings and nods of heads rippled around the incident room. Genete continued. "But I think it was more than that. The smell of stale urine is mentioned in another witness statement, and two more describe the attacker as possibly speaking to someone else during the attacks or shortly afterwards." She selected another sheet from the folder. "'*Take this,*' one of the victims recalls hearing, as if the attacker was passing something to someone else. Another remembers hearing, '*Let's go.*' Those two statements in isolation may not seem like much, but I feel it suggests the presence of a second person." Genete paused, taking in a deep breath. "Although the piece of wire and section of grey cloth haven't been linked forensically, that doesn't mean a link doesn't exist. We know the same kind of wire was used in the 1998 murders. And we also know that the Yorkshire sex attacker wore a grey bandana. I know it's a bit of a leap, but what would you say if I suggested that the second person present during the sex attacks in '97 and '98 could be your Central Line Killer?"

Genete could see from the expressions on the rest of the team's faces that she had their attention. She pressed on. "And then you tie that in with the letters found in Ellis Magee's prison cell. All letters signed by X, all clearly from someone who knows Magee well and knows about the murders. They have relationship, a connection with Magee. We know Magee is your Yorkshire sex attacker — that, I don't think, is in any dispute — but what if the person corresponding with him was present for the Yorkshire attacks and is now the killer you're all hunting?"

"The Central Line Killer," breathed Cassidy, slowly nodding.

"I feel the Yorkshire sex assault cases *are* linked to your current case — albeit it's not the same main offender." Genete looked up just as she flipped over the last sheet of paper from the folder. "I've also drafted a basic profile for your offender, based on the paperwork I've seen today." Briefly pausing to take a breath, she started to reel off the bullet points.

"Your offender is a white male, current age range of forty-one to forty-nine. Seventeen years ago, he would have been twenty-four to thirty-two. My own view is that he is most likely to be on the lower end of those scales. He is local to London or at least knows it well. He is well travelled in and around the city, and uses public transport, in particular the Underground. He is a cool and calculated person. He is unlikely to have completed further education and may even have left school early. He is a planner. He is not a risk-taker. He likes order and routine, and he is patient. To others he will appear insignificant. He won't be remembered by people that meet him, and he won't have many close friends or work colleagues. He will be single and will never have married. He is unlikely to be in a current relationship, and any relationships he has had in adult life will have been short-lived. Former partners may have complained about controlling and coercive behaviour. He will have a medical or psychological condition linked to the urinary system, leading to him suffering from bouts of incontinence. But he won't appear unkempt, and his personal hygiene will be acceptable. He is likely to be estranged from his family. He has an obsessive personality. In 1996 and 1997 he was content to play a supporting role in the attacks, but in 1998 he took control. The 1998 murders were extremely well thought out and he will have been working to an agreed plan — similar to those occurring this week."

"Why change his MO?" DS Cooper leaned back in his chair. "Why go from sexual assault and rape to murder? And why the gap from 1998 to now? Why leave it seventeen years?"

Genete shrugged. "Something happened between the last sexual assault offence in '97 and the first murder in '98. Something profound that sent him off on a course of killing rather than raping."

"A natural progression?"

"Not necessarily. Not all sex offenders make the leap to murder. Some do, obviously, but they tend to be the ones who commit the more violent and sadistic rapes. Having said that, motivations to rape and motivations to murder are entirely different for most offenders. But something happened to your offender to turn him."

"Maybe the incarceration of his mate," added Cooper. "Leaving him on his own, to his own devices?"

Genete gave another nod. "Most likely. The two would have had an unusual bond. It could, of course, always have been their plan to move onto murder, or it could have been something your killer adapted to in early '98. I'm inclined to believe it was the former."

"So, it was always the plan?" Jack rubbed his chin. "The pair of them together?"

Genete put the folder back down onto the table. "Difficult to say, but your offender likes routine, he likes to follow orders and rules. As for the gap of seventeen years — he could very well have been abroad, or merely gone undetected for that period of time. But it will always have been his plan to resume this pattern of killing."

"If Magee had an accomplice, my bet is on our Mr X." Jack got to his feet and ran a hand through his hair. "Which means we need another chat with him. I'll ask Jane what the plan is for his interviews. Cooper, anything to report on the PO box for those letters?"

Cooper scooted his chair back to his desk. "Not really, boss. The address hasn't been in use for some time — last activity was the butt end of 2000. It's an inactive account and no one can tell me yet who was behind it. They're still digging."

"There's something else, too." Genete caught Jack's eye. "It's about the involvement of the journalist."

Jack felt his stomach clench. *The bloody journalist.* He gestured for Genete to continue.

"As I said before, your offender has a controlling and obsessive personality. Anyone who enters his world will soon find themselves subject to his obsessions. He is a manipulative individual. He gets people to do his bidding. If anyone refuses, that will anger him — hence not being able to maintain close relationships. But I feel the involvement of the journalist is different. He uses her and controls her — gets her to do what he wants. In 1998, he uses her to lead the investigation teams to the bodies. In your current investigation, he is going one step forward and using her to give him a voice. He is pulling the strings all the time — pulling *her* strings."

"What are you saying exactly?" Jack had an uncanny feeling he already knew.

"He knows her," Genete replied simply. "She isn't some random person he picked. The two have met before and interacted on some level. It may not necessarily have been a deep interaction but, whatever it was, it had a lasting effect on him. For whatever reason, he remembers her."

Jack sighed again and ran another hand through his hair. *The bloody journalist.* "I knew there was something about her. We need to have another chat, and soon." He started towards the door. "Thanks, Genete, you've given us real food for thought here. As well as Lorna Henshaw, I'd like to have a chat with one of the victims from the Yorkshire assault cases. Amanda, can you find me one who might be willing to talk?"

"I'll get onto it right away, guv." Cassidy sprang into action and shot back to her desk.

"And Daniels — any luck on tracing this Spencer Kershaw?"

Daniels shook his head, eyes still trained to his computer screen. "Not yet — I've called the catering company and I'm just waiting for them to get back to me."

"Chase it up. And get that journalist back in."

CHAPTER THIRTY-NINE

Time: 2.45 p.m.
Date: Wednesday 15 April 2015
Location: Putney, London

Colette Richards gave Jack a weak smile as she stepped back to let them in. "Please come through. Sorry, the place is in a bit of a mess. I've not been feeling great this week and I'm a little behind on the housework."

"Not a problem, Mrs Richards." Jack edged into the hallway, closely followed by DS Cassidy. "Thank you for seeing us at such short notice. It's very much appreciated."

Colette Richards had been Colette Burgess at the time of her attack in 1996. Cassidy's quick phone call to her earlier confirmed that she'd married seven years ago, becoming Mrs Richards, and the couple had then moved to Putney. Colette had explained that Yorkshire no longer felt safe, and she'd needed a new beginning.

Colette led the detectives through to the front room. Although it was light and airy, almost all the floor space was covered in an array of toys and games. "Like I say, I'm a bit behind on the housework. And children make such a mess, don't they?"

"How many children do you have, Mrs Richards?" Cassidy stepped over a large teddy bear.

Colette gave another weak smile. "It looks like I have a troupe, doesn't it? But I only have the one. Thomas. He's two. And a mini whirlwind, as you can see." She gestured towards the wall by the side of the window. "He's at the finger painting and drawing on walls stage."

Cassidy smiled. "He must bring you a lot of joy."

Colette nodded, tucking a strand of hair behind her ear. "He does. It took me a long time to learn to trust a man again, hence I came to motherhood later in life than most. A lot later than I had imagined. I was thirty-seven when I had him, but he's a sweetheart, a real darling. I can't imagine ever being without him."

Jack cleared his throat. "I'm sorry we have to revisit this again for you, Mrs Richards. But it could help our current investigation." He saw the woman's eyes stray towards the folded copy of the *Daily Courier* sitting on a side table, her face tightening.

"Of course," she breathed, a resigned look entering her eyes. "Please, take a seat. If you can find room." She gestured towards the sofa. "Would you like something to drink? Tea? Coffee?"

Seating himself on the edge of the sofa next to a stack of washing, Jack shook his head. "We're fine, and we really don't want to take up too much of your time. We just have a few questions to ask you, based on your previous statement."

"Is it him?" Colette nodded towards the newspaper as she edged further into the room. "The same man who attacked me? He's killing them now?"

Jack detected the fear in the woman's voice. "No, it's not the same man. As you will no doubt know from the newspaper headlines, our current investigation is being linked to a series of murders in 1998. We now believe that the attacks in Yorkshire in '96 and '97 are also connected, although it's not the same perpetrator." Jack saw a look of confusion join the fear on the woman's face. He pressed on. "We just have a couple of things to ask you, based on your previous statement." Jack nodded towards Cassidy, who handed over three sheets of A4 paper. "This is the statement you gave to officers up in Hebden Bridge back in December 1996."

Colette took the papers, her face whitening by the second. Jack and Cassidy watched as she spent the next few minutes reading them through, her hands trembling. Once finished, she looked up, eyes moist. "I think that's how I remember it. What else do you want to know?"

"I'm interested in the possibility of a second attacker." Jack saw no reason not to dive straight in. Time was not on their side. "You hint in your statement that there may have been two men there, not just one. Could you expand a little on that?" If Jack had any criticism of the Yorkshire team's investigation, it was that no one seemed to pick up on several of the victims suggesting a second person was present.

Colette lowered her eyes to the paperwork once again. "Yes, I remember. I also remember that the officer who took my statement seemed to want me to focus more on the man who . . ." She took a breath, hands still shaking. "The man who raped me."

Jack nodded. "I can understand that, but I'd really like to know more about why you felt there was someone else there." He flashed a look at Cassidy. They had discussed a vague interview strategy in the car on the way over, agreeing that Jack should be the one to head up the questioning. Cassidy had taken some time to coach him on the appropriate things to say — and, more importantly, what not to say. He took another breath and carried on. "I appreciate how traumatic this might be for you. Please accept my apologies, but it could be really important."

There, he'd done it. Got in touch with his softer side, just as Cassidy had taught him to. But he did truly feel sorry for Colette, it wasn't purely an act. The woman had been through a terrible ordeal that he couldn't even begin to imagine. He couldn't empathise with her, but he could try and sympathise. She came across as a sensible and stoic kind of person, but Jack was fully aware that such impressions were often a smokescreen. He suddenly felt very inadequate. But before he could assassinate his own character any more, Colette spoke.

"Do you think he's the killer?" Colette's eyes widened. "The second man who was there at my rape — he's gone on to kill all these poor women?"

Jack found himself nodding. There was no point in denying it. "It's possible, yes. So, it would really help if you could tell us everything you remember about him. I appreciate it was some time ago."

Colette looked back down at the statement she still held in her hands. "I've relived every second of that night over the last nineteen years, I can assure you. I play it over and over inside my head; it never goes away." She paused for breath. "And each time I do that, I'm certain there was someone else there."

"Can you tell me anything more about him?" Jack edged forward on the sofa. "No matter how small."

Colette took in a shuddering breath. "He smelled. That much I do recall. I tried to convey that to the officer who took my statement at the time, but I can see here that it isn't really mentioned. But I can smell him, even now. It was urine." Colette paused, giving a small half-laugh. "And I can assure you that I'm an expert in pee at the moment — I'm trying to potty train Thomas and it's a bit hit and miss."

"I'm sure. Carry on, you're doing really well."

"The man who raped me didn't smell. Well, he did — just not of urine. He smelled of cigarettes and alcohol, like I mentioned. And bad breath. Body odour. But the smell of urine was away in the background. And it moved, as if the person was moving around. But he never got too close, and he never touched me."

"Anything more you can tell us about him?"

"I heard him speak — the man who raped me. Towards the end, he spoke to someone, I'm sure of it. Something like, '*Let's go.*' That's all I can remember."

Jack gave what he hoped was an encouraging smile. It was what he had expected but didn't really take the investigation on that much further forward. All the same, he was glad they had taken the time to come. Colette would make a good witness.

342

Having agreed to resurrect what must have been very traumatic memories, a past that she was trying to forget, Jack felt the woman deserved the truth.

"We think we have the person who raped you and committed the other attacks during 1996 and 1997. He's currently in custody and being interviewed."

Colette's eyes widened, her bottom lip starting to tremble. Absent-mindedly, she grabbed the sleeve of her cardigan and began twisting it in her fingers. "Really? You have him?"

Jack nodded. "We think so. It's early days but we're confident it's him. This does mean that, if and when we charge him, and the case goes to court, you may have to give evidence. Will you be OK with that?"

Colette's lip trembled some more, but then she straightened up and wiped her blotchy cheeks with the back of a hand. "You just try and stop me."

After thanking Colette for her time, Jack slipped back behind the wheel of the Mondeo. Colette hadn't recognised the names of Ellis Magee, or Tony or Dennis Kingdom, and Jack believed her. But he was increasingly convinced they had just taken another step towards finding the Central Line Killer. The man had been Ellis Magee's accomplice in the Yorkshire sex attacks and the author of the letters found in Magee's cell, the man signing himself the mysterious Mr X.

They just didn't know who he was.

Yet.

* * *

Time: 2.50 p.m.
Date: Wednesday 15 April 2015
Location: Isabel's Café, Horseferry Road, London

Isabel nervously bit her lip. She'd left the café in her employees Dom and Sacha's capable hands and retreated to the flat upstairs. Her pidgin French hadn't been enough to translate very much of the six-page document beyond the word *Faraday*, which appeared multiple times, but then she had seen the date.

26 September 1986.

It was a date that had been seared into her memory for almost thirty years.

26 September 1986 was the day her parents had died.

She'd taken a series of hurried snaps of the paperwork in Jack's flat, before rushing back to the café. Dominic had been a sweetheart and volunteered to translate it for her. With a love of languages, it hadn't taken him long.

The A4 sheet of paper trembled in her hand.

It's not a complete word-for-word translation, as there was quite a bit of repetition, but it gives you a broad idea.

Isabel had smiled her thanks and shooed Dominic back downstairs. Now the knots in her stomach were tightening once again as she lowered her gaze to the paper.

"Accident mortel de la route" — *fatal road traffic accident.*

On the night of 26 September, a vehicle left the road 25 km from Lyon, plunging down an embankment. The vehicle exploded on impact, killing both occupants — British nationals Christopher and Elizabeth Faraday from Surrey, England. The evening was wet, the road surface slippery in the vicinity of the accident. There were no markings on the road to indicate braking or a prior collision having occurred. The road in question has seen thirty-two accidents in the last five years with fifteen fatalities. It is an unlit section of road with sharp bends.

Both occupants of the vehicle were wearing seatbelts and were restrained inside the car on impact. Injuries sustained were consistent with the vehicle hitting the bottom of the embankment at speed. Separate post-mortem reports confirmed the cause of death was multiple trauma.

There were no witnesses to the incident. The first person on the scene was a family friend of the Faradays — Mr Clive Bentley. Mr Bentley was able to positively identify the deceased.

Isabel let the paper drop from her hand.
Clive Bentley.
Uncle Clive.

* * *

Time: 3.15 p.m.
Date: Wednesday 15 April 2015
Location: Metropolitan Police HQ, London

"You know who he is." Jack tossed a copy of the *Daily Courier* onto the wooden table, almost sending the half-drunk plastic cup of coffee flying. "Tell me."

Jane Telford had been good enough to pause the interview with the man to allow Jack to ask his questions. The team from Yorkshire had arrived, making use of the Met's facilities to try and elicit a confession out of Ellis Magee for the assaults in '96 and '97. So far, the man wasn't saying much. Jane had offered to stay but Jack had quietly advised that she might want to go and get herself and her Yorkshire colleagues a bite to eat in the canteen, as it would be getting busy before long. Jane knew Jack well enough by now to understand the inference.

"You don't want to be there, Jane. It won't be pretty."

"Shouldn't we be recording this?" Magee nodded towards the tape recorder, and then at the video recorder high up on the ceiling, both standing idle. A smirk covered the convicted prisoner's face. "I mean, I'd hate for anything to happen in here that might suggest maltreatment of a prisoner." The smirk lengthened.

Jack kicked the spare chair away and leaned across the table, his face inches from Magee's. "Oh, believe me, I'd love to ram my fist down your throat right now, but apparently that's an interview tactic frowned upon these days."

"And then I'd do you for assault, Inspector. That wouldn't look so good on your disciplinary record, you know."

Jack gave a faint laugh and leaned in closer. "I don't think you quite understand how things work in here, sunshine. Prison has obviously made you soft." Pausing, he straightened up a little, a smile emerging on his lips. "You'd be surprised how many people fall off the chairs in interview rooms these days. Do themselves all manner of damage. Surprisingly careless of them, don't you think?"

The smirk that had been on Magee's face slipped a little. "You can't do that."

"I wouldn't be doing anything. Like I said, the chairs in here are death traps. And it's so unfortunate that most of the time it seems to happen when the recording equipment isn't working either." Jack's tight smile disappeared. He didn't usually get this animated with a suspect, but Magee was pushing his buttons in all the wrong ways. And his foot was aching. Pissed off was an understatement. "So how about we cut the crap and you just start by telling me who this is. Just tell me. Stop protecting him."

"Who says I'm protecting him?"

"I do. You're protecting him by omission."

"That's not a thing."

"It is if I say it is. Want to take the risk? I guarantee I know more people in this building than you do." Jack held Magee in a tight gaze. "Tell me who your accomplice is."

346

CHAPTER FORTY

Time: 3.45 p.m.
Date: Wednesday 15 April 2015
Location: Metropolitan Police HQ, London

After handing Ellis Magee back to Jane Telford and the Yorkshire detectives, Jack was informed that Lorna Henshaw had arrived.

"Thanks for coming in." Jack knew he needed to say the T word, although he felt anything but thankful right now. People were holding out on him — Lorna Henshaw included. "It's just a couple of questions to help us clear up a few inconsistencies."

"Inconsistencies?"

Jack thought he detected an element of concern in the journalist's tone. He pressed on, seeing no point in dragging it out. "Do you know someone called Tony Kingdom or Dennis Kingdom?" He watched Lorna's brow twitch.

"No, I don't. Why? What have they done?"

Jack flashed her an irritated look. The paracetamol he'd taken to stave off the pain in his foot had yet to take effect.

"Sorry," the journalist added, trying what looked like a forced smile. "Force of habit. Investigative journalism never quite leaves you."

"What about Ellis Magee?"

The same blank expression followed. "No, sorry. I don't think so . . . why?"

Jack took a breath, well aware that he needed to get through this as quickly as possible. Time was marching on relentlessly. The killer wasn't waiting for them to play catch-up — he may have already killed his next victim for all they knew. "We think our killer knows you — and you know him." Jack watched closely for a reaction, and he didn't need to wait long.

"What? You think I *know* him? How?" The journalist's voice hitched up several notches, along with her eyebrows. "How could you think that?"

"Quite easily, actually." Jack pulled out a chair and sat down, more to rest his foot than for emphasis. "This is getting serious now, Miss Henshaw — think again for me."

"I . . . I don't understand what you mean. How could I possibly know who he is? He never gave me his name."

Jack noted the journalist's face had paled. "We need to know why he wants to target you in this way. Our forensic profiler tells us he's a manipulative individual and well versed in getting people to do what he wants. And she's convinced you are known to each other."

Lorna visibly flinched, her eyes bulging. "But it . . . it can't be true. It just can't be."

"Trust me, it is. Now, I need you to cooperate and tell me who he is."

* * *

Time: 3.45 p.m.
Date: Wednesday 15 April 2015
Location: Ashcroft Nursing Home, London

Sitting behind the wheel of the van, he smiled as the breaking news report played out on the radio.

"*Man arrested in connection with a series of sex assaults in Yorkshire during 1996 and 1997.*"

348

The words made the hairs prick at the base of his neck. Although no further detail was given, *he knew*.

He knew it had to be Ellis.

The brief news report mentioned further evidence had come to light — and more hairs began to prickle. He bit his lip to suppress the smile as various scenarios raced through his mind. Ellis would keep his mouth shut, he was sure of that. The man wasn't stupid. Seventeen years or more of silence had to count for something, surely.

Ellis had abandoned him, at a time when he needed him the most. Each time one of his former friend's letters was returned, each time he'd collected them from the PO box, it drove another spike through his heart.

He turned the heater up in the van and tried to push thoughts of Ellis Magee from his mind. He didn't think about the man much these days — but whenever he did, it invariably led him to think about Great Easton Secondary School. Ellis may have been the only *pupil* to give him the time of day during his time there, but there had been someone else.

* * *

Time: 11.45 a.m.
Date: Tuesday 12 May 1987
Location: Great Easton Secondary School, North London

He could feel his underpants clinging to his skin as he sat, his school trousers thin and cheap. He didn't want to imagine how many other children had worn them before his mother picked them up from the charity jumble sale. They didn't really fit — pinching at the waist and three inches too short. Another reason for the others to pick on him, as if they needed any further excuse.

And today had been no different, the jeers and taunts starting almost as soon as he walked through the school gates. Ordinarily, he could cope with it, tuning it out as best as he was able to — but today had been different.

For today he had wet himself.

Again.

At fourteen he should be over this, he knew that, which made it all the more embarrassing when it happened. The school had urged his mother to take him to the GP after the first few accidents occurred, as surely there had to be something wrong. It was a request she had reluctantly followed through, and a variety of GP and hospital appointments had followed. The resultant prodding, poking and intrusive questioning had culminated in a series of x-rays and scans — the conclusion of which was there was no physical cause for him to wet himself at age fourteen.

So, there was only one explanation left — it was all in his head.

Psychosomatic.

At which point his mother had lost interest.

It was the third time in the last four weeks that he'd found himself sitting outside the school office, wet underpants seeping into his trousers.

"I'm sorry, but we don't have any spare trousers in the lost property this time."

The woman had a caring face, concern etched around her wide, pale green eyes. Out of all the staff in the office, he liked her the most. Although she wasn't really a woman, no more than a girl really — what could she be, early twenties at the most? He nodded and lowered his gaze to his lap, colour burning his spotty cheeks. He knew he was starting to smell, she was just too kind to say so.

The other women in the admin office always kept their distance from him — exchanging disapproving glances anytime he shuffled in. But this one was different; she seemed to actually care.

"That's OK," he muttered, cheeks even redder. "If I'm excused, I'll just go home."

Home.

All that would be waiting for him there would be another slap for turning up with foul-smelling clothes again. Instead, he would go to the park and use the public toilets — there he could clean himself and at least try and dry his damp clothes under the hand dryer. It would take a while, but he had nothing better to do.

"Are you sure?" A pensive look crossed the woman's face.

He shrugged a response. "I'll be fine."

His tone must have told her otherwise because, after a quick look at her watch, she patted his shoulder and turned towards the inner office. "Wait here." Crossing over to the door that separated the foyer from the office within, she pushed it open and popped her head inside. "I'm just taking an extended lunch break — I need to do something in town. I'll be back by two."

And then they were off.

The woman's house was in a nice part of the city, not too far from the school as it turned out. As the car turned into her street, he saw litter-free pavements, neatly presented front gardens and colourful window boxes. There were no overflowing dustbins here, no cracked windows, no peeling paintwork. His cheeks reddened when he felt her looking at him.

"It's my parents' house," she explained, releasing her seatbelt. "They left it to me when they died. I wouldn't be able to afford to live here otherwise."

"It's nice," he replied simply, following the woman's lead and unbuckling his seatbelt.

Without another word, they left the car and made their way up the short path to the front door. Self-consciously, he glanced around again while she rummaged in her handbag for the front door keys. The smell of concentrated urine had filled the car on the short journey over, and he'd noticed the driver's window being surreptitiously opened a few inches as they made their way through the lunchtime traffic. He didn't blame her, of course; he stank to high heaven.

351

Which was another reason why he liked her. She was actively going out of her way to help him when she didn't really have to. He could count on the fingers of one hand the number of people who'd shown even the tiniest amount of humanity towards him. Maybe it wasn't one hand at all.

Maybe it was just the one finger.

A strange sensation rippled inside.

"Here." With a smile, she pushed the door open and gestured for him to follow her inside. "If you want to pop in there, I'll find you something fresh to change into." She gestured towards a door on the left as they entered the hall.

The bathroom was always cold and damp at home, no matter what time of year it was. Mould encased the solitary cracked window, creeping along the walls and causing the plaster to fall away in chunks. It wasn't until he started school that he realised hot water usually came out of bathroom taps, having never experienced it before. Some days, he would linger at the school sinks, his hands submerged in the hot water until they turned pink. Yet another reason he was marked down as the class weirdo.

He peeled off his damp trousers and underpants, placing them into the sink. He smiled at the green plastic frog attached to the plug. The water came out hot and fast and he quickly whipped up a soft, creamy lather from a bar of rose-scented soap. Once he'd rinsed and wrung out his clothes, he washed himself down.

Now fresh and clean, he peered outside the bathroom door to find a pile of clothes on the carpet. A pair of grey jogging bottoms, boxer shorts and a fresh pair of socks. Conscious of his own nakedness, he hurriedly pulled them on, inhaling the fresh scent of washing powder. Now suitably dressed, he gathered up his damp school clothes and stepped out into the hall.

The aroma of frying beef burgers hit his nostrils, and he made his way towards it.

* * *

Time: 3.50 p.m.
Date: Wednesday 15 April 2015
Location: Ashcroft Nursing Home, London

What would he give right now for the taste of a homemade burger? He still remembered it to this day. It had been thick and juicy, with thick-cut chips from the deep-fat fryer. She'd even allowed him to drown it all in as much tomato sauce as he'd wanted. He'd devoured the whole plate in a matter of minutes.

The memory was so vivid, he could almost taste it on his lips right now.

Pushing the thought of food from his mind, he placed a coil of rope next to the bandana and balaclava already sitting on the passenger seat. There would be plenty of time to satisfy his hunger later. Right now, there was a completely different craving he needed to feed.

***

Time: 3.50 p.m.
Date: Wednesday 15 April 2015
Location: Metropolitan Police HQ, London

"I really don't know — you have to believe me."

Jack had lost count of the number of hours he had spent inside interview rooms over the years — it had to be thousands — and he could usually spot a liar a mile off. But was Lorna Henshaw lying to him? He still couldn't quite tell. Time was ticking, as was his patience.

"Just think back. It might have been some time ago. Anyone who befriended you, anyone who might be capable of something like this." Jack had brought a copy of the *Daily Courier* with him, the latest murder splashed across the front page.

"I . . . I really don't know." The journalist's face was beyond pale now. "Honestly."

353

Honesty and journalism weren't a combination Jack was familiar with, so he pressed on. "Think again. Anyone you might have interacted with over the years, someone who might be capable of something like this. Just give us the name of anyone who ticks these boxes."

"And like I said . . ." Lorna's voice took on a keen edge. "I *can't* help you. I never wanted to be caught up in this. I didn't back then, and I don't now. I never asked for it. I don't want to be involved."

"Well, that's just tough, isn't it? Because you are." Jack knew his tone was bordering on the unacceptable, but he was beyond caring right now. "I need to find this man. This Mr X. And if you don't choose to help me then, quite frankly, I feel that says a lot more about you than it does about me."

Jack pushed up from his seat and headed for the door, exasperation flooding every cell of his being. He was done here. It was a dead end and a time-consuming one at that.

"Hold on." The journalist's voice was barely above a whisper. "What did you just say?"

Sighing, Jack rested his hand on the door handle. "What did you think I said? Have you even been listening? We're looking for a particularly sadistic killer here, and it's someone who seems to know you. All I want you to do is help us find him. I *need* your help. But you don't seem to be too concerned."

"No, I mean what you said just now. About Mr X."

Jack frowned, turning around to face the journalist. If it was possible, the woman's face had paled even more. Prickles started to stab him at the nape of his neck. "We think that's what he calls himself. We found some letters relevant to the investigation, signed 'X'. Why?" Jack took several steps back towards her. "Do you know him?"

CHAPTER FORTY-ONE

Time: 4.10 p.m.
Date: Wednesday 15 April 2015
Location: Metropolitan Police HQ, London

"Spencer Kershaw's van was tracked back to the catering company's depot about twenty minutes ago, boss." DS Cooper placed the telephone receiver down. "As far as they know, he's still on site. And while I remember — I managed to find CCTV of Jessica around the time Tony Kingdom claims she left his van. She's seen walking along Beaumont Street, and the area and timing suggests Kingdom was telling the truth."

Jack shook his head, rubbing his eyes. "Thanks, Cooper. I think we can put Kingdom to one side for now — and we can also forget about Spencer Kershaw. He's not our man."

Jack had bounded up the stairs from the interview room as fast as he dared, his foot protesting at the exertion. Lorna Henshaw had finally come clean about her time as an admin assistant at Great Easton Secondary School — and how her path had crossed that of the elusive Mr X.

"*He gave me a card,*" she'd eventually disclosed, once the shock had receded. "*To say thank you — thank you for helping him. He signed it 'From X'.*"

"Luke Naylor." Jack turned to face the team. "*This* is our prime suspect for the Central Line Killer, and the accomplice in Ellis Magee's sex attacks up in Yorkshire."

"We know anything more about him, boss?" Cooper was already entering the name into his computer.

Jack grimaced. "Not much. But let's stay with the care home angle — I still think that's how he targets his victims. Check with the catering company again — see if they have any record for Naylor. If that doesn't bear fruit, cast the net wider. We might be running out of time."

* * *

Time: 4.10 p.m.
Date: Wednesday 15 April 2015
Location: Ashcroft Nursing Home, London

The end of the double shift couldn't have come soon enough for Pippa Moss. She'd been crazy to agree to stay on for an extra stretch while they found agency staff to cover the staff sickness. Her throat had gone from scratchy to sore, making her wince every time she swallowed. She'd dosed up on paracetamol throughout the day, but she didn't feel much better for it. Each minute had dragged, and she repeatedly questioned whether the extra money was even worth it.

Sighing, she pulled on her jacket and hoisted her bag up onto her shoulder. Her neck ached, her head pounded, her eyes felt puffy and swollen. Even her teeth throbbed. She had no other thought in her head than crawling back under the duvet with a hot water bottle. She prayed the neighbours were quiet and would let her sleep.

The thought of fighting her way through a crowded bus didn't appeal to her, and neither did the Tube. Everyone had been talking about the Central Line Killer in the staff room today, and none of them were prepared to take the risk of travelling on the Underground. The thought of being squashed into a packed Tube train didn't appeal much at the best of times, and definitely not now a killer was on the loose, streaming cold or no streaming cold.

She'd thought about another Uber, but she didn't really want to waste the extra cash she'd worked so hard to earn. So, when Luke had offered to give her a lift home, she had almost kissed him.

Almost.

He was a little bit odd, but not odd enough to refuse the offer of a warm and comfortable journey back home. He told her he would be waiting out in the car park, so she said her goodbyes to the day staff and hurried out of the door before anyone could talk her into staying even longer.

The van was parked just where he said it would be, underneath a bank of trees. As Pippa left the building, she jogged down the steps and pulled her jacket closely around her. The unseasonably warm temperatures they'd been enjoying recently had dipped overnight, leaving a crisp feel to the air.

"Thank you, Luke," she said, pulling open the passenger side door and slipping inside. "It's really kind of you to give me a lift."

Luke smiled, turning the key in the ignition. "No problem at all. It's my pleasure, I can assure you."

CHAPTER FORTY-TWO

Time: 5.30 p.m.
Date: Wednesday 15 April 2015
Location: Metropolitan Police HQ, London

"It's not catering suppliers, boss." DS Cooper waved Jack over to his desk. "I think it's laundry."

As Jack approached, all he could think about was James Quinn's prison escape at the beginning of the year, the breakout assisted by a prison laundry van. The manhunt was still ongoing, but Jack wasn't sure it would come to much. Did he really believe the man had been reduced to nothing but pig food at Knowles Farm? He certainly wanted to — but he knew the man had faked death once before. He pushed the unwanted thought from his mind. "Tell me more."

"Care homes often have controlled parking in their car parks — trying to stop locals or commuters using their property to park in for free. Which means vehicles must log their registrations to gain access." Cooper paused and pulled a document up onto his computer screen. "I went back through the contractor details I got earlier. I started with the victims from Operation Quicksand — Crawfield Care Home and Hazel

Court Care Home. They both use the same laundry services company and gave me the vehicle registrations for the delivery vans they used. I've been putting them into the ANPR system."

Jack felt his stomach tighten. "Just tell me the good news, Cooper — if there is any."

Cooper grinned. "One registration visited the homes in the time immediately prior to each victim disappearing and is also seen in the vicinity of each of our three crime scenes over the last week."

"When you say vicinity, how close are we talking about?"

"One or two streets away, boss. And not just that. I had a look at the 1998 investigation as well." Cooper opened another window on the computer. "Chestnut Laundry Services supplied laundry to Appleby Nursing Home, Cedar Lodge Nursing Home, Sunnydale Care Home and Forest Glade Care Home. Basically, all of the homes we know are linked to the victims. It might have been a different vehicle back then, but it's still the same company. My bet is it's the same driver."

"Do we have a name for him?" Jack knew his luck would run out soon. "Or an address?"

Cooper shook his head, but the grin remained. "No name or address, boss — but I do know where he's going to be at six thirty this evening."

* * *

Time: 6.45 p.m.
Date: Wednesday 15 April 2015
Location: Birchwood Care Home, London

It wasn't ideal. By now he should be well on his way across the capital, putting the final pieces of his plan into place.

Instead he was here.

He'd spent more time than he wanted inside the building — there was some issue with the paperwork, which, for some reason, needed his presence inside to sort it out. Usually, he would open up the doors of the van and merely let them deposit the laundry inside for themselves. He wasn't keen on getting his hands dirty if he could avoid it.

Pippa had been easy enough to overcome. It always surprised him how simple it could be. He knew he didn't have the social skills that others did — but was it any surprise after what he'd had to contend with while growing up? He was ostracised at school, ostracised at home; it didn't take a genius to work out that some damage might ensue. But despite his idiosyncrasies, no one really considered him a threat.

Which he used to his advantage. He may not have finished school, but he wasn't stupid.

He started the engine and licked his lips. Pippa was safely secured in the back of the van, concealed by a roll of carpet. He knew the tape across her mouth would silence any screams she might want to release — and the restraints around her wrists and ankles would keep her immobile. His chosen location this time wasn't too far away, but he had to contend with the evening traffic, which may lengthen the trip.

But he didn't mind; he knew what was coming.

Sometimes the greatest pleasure came in the waiting.

* * *

Jack swore under his breath. It had seemed like a good idea at the time. He blamed Rob Carmichael.

Once Cooper had established where Luke Naylor and his van were due to be that evening, Jack had embarked on what might be construed as a rather reckless undertaking. It was a good job Dougie King seemed to have left him alone; the man would hit the stratosphere if he knew where Jack was right now.

Which was in the back of Luke Naylor's van.

It had been a quick decision — and, in his defence, Jack hadn't had time to fully weigh up the pros and cons. Rob had popped his head into the incident room at the critical moment — and taken it upon himself to offer to tag along. Naylor had been scheduled for a laundry collection at Birchwood Care Home, and Jack had had just enough time to hot foot it over. The problem was the backup he'd requested hadn't, something about an incident closing the main road.

So, there they were — just Jack and Carmichael, and a killer.

Carmichael had taken charge, informing Jack that his colourful past could be used to their advantage. Full of caffeine and paracetamol by this time, Jack was open to any offers to help them catch Luke Naylor. But, not for the first time, he was now questioning his choices.

"*Ask no questions, Jack. Before Barbara and Charles took me in, I led an interesting life.*"

As it turned out, that interesting life enabled Rob to break into the back of the waiting Chestnut Laundry Services van while its occupant was inside the care home, and where Jack now found himself.

Shit.

Now inside the van, he wasn't quite sure what he was meant to do.

Pippa looked like she was OK. She was conscious, if a little confused at seeing Jack hurl himself into the back of the van. Her feet were tied together at the ankles, her hands behind her back, and she was wrapped in a roll of old carpet.

Jack had indicated that she should remain quiet — a somewhat unnecessary instruction, given her mouth was secured with tape. Wide-eyed, she had nodded.

But quite beyond that, Jack wasn't sure.

Carmichael had remained outside in the Mondeo, on the lookout for the promised backup, but before Jack could contemplate what his next step should be, he heard the driver's door slam and the engine roar into life.

Double shit.

Within seconds the van started to move, Jack feeling the vehicle bouncing over the surface of the car park of the

Birchwood Care Home. He'd already silenced his mobile to vibration alerts only, as now would not be the time for an unsolicited call from an insurance company. Thinking quickly, he climbed behind a tall stack of laundry — thankful that Naylor seemed to have had a busy day and visited a fair number of care homes.

Pippa was wedged up against one side of the van, the carpet that concealed her body covered in yet more bundles of dirty laundry. Jack had positioned himself on the other side. There was nothing for him to do now but wait.

CHAPTER FORTY-THREE

Time: 7.30 p.m.
Date: Thursday 16 April 2015
Location: Duke of Wellington Public House

"My round." Jack got up and headed towards the bar. The last twenty-four hours had been a whirlwind and Jack was struggling to deal with the fallout. They had eventually apprehended Luke Naylor with the assistance of a stinger. The use of the devices was controversial; it was a new addition to the Met's armoury and there were many critics. Jack was firmly in the positive camp — he didn't want to contemplate what might have happened if the Chestnut Laundry Services van hadn't been stopped when it had.

Pippa had been understandably traumatised by the experience — but she was alive. It was something she wouldn't appreciate until much later when the events of yesterday had truly sunk in.

Dougie King had stepped up to the plate and fielded the questions that had invariably filtered down from above, stressing the fact that Jack's team had played an instrumental part in solving three investigations, two of which were cold cases. The news had satisfied those above for the present — but Jack knew he faced an uphill battle to convince everyone his actions had been within the realms of acceptability.

With a tray full of drinks, Jack made his way back to the table by the dartboard.

"Cheers, boss." Cooper accepted his pint of lager, eyes shining. "I've been dreaming about this."

"Jenny still banning alcohol?" Jack handed round the rest of the drinks.

Cooper gave a grunt in reply as he took his first sip. "She allows spirits — apparently, they don't have carbs. But I really miss beer . . ."

"Well, I think you've earned it, Chris." Cassidy gave a smile as she sipped her slim-line tonic. "I won't tell if you don't." She got up from her seat and headed back towards the bar, calling over her shoulder. "I'll get us some crisps."

Jack and Cooper exchanged a look — the unexpected compliment, and offer of further banned food, surprising them both. Jack slipped back into his seat by the window. "Ellis Magee has been charged with seven counts of rape and sexual assault for the 1996 and 1997 Yorkshire cases. We don't know yet what plea he'll enter — I'm hoping he pleads guilty and spares the witnesses the trauma of giving evidence at a trial, but we'll have to wait and see."

"Has he been asked about Luke Naylor?" Cooper took another long sip of his beer. "The two were clearly in it together."

"I'm being told that he was quite tight-lipped during interview when Naylor's name was mentioned." Jack took his first sip of lager, savouring the taste. "But we'll have to wait and see what happens. He may change his tune when he realises what he's up against. Naylor has been charged with six counts of murder from 1998, and three further counts for Keeley, Jessica and Sammy. He's also been charged with the abduction of Pippa Moss. I'm told the detectives from Yorkshire are still investigating his role in the rapes."

"Confession?" Cooper sank another mouthful of lager. "I guess that's too much to hope for."

Jack made a face over the rim of his pint glass. "He didn't say a lot in interview either. More lab results have come in, though, matching his DNA to samples found on all three of our victims, plus various further samples from 1998. Fibres have also been found in the laundry services van that match the balaclava and bandana. As if that wasn't enough, photographs of all the victims from Operation Quicksand, and also from the 1998 cases, were found during a search of his home address — photographs of them alive *and* dead. He hasn't provided any explanation or defence as such — we'll have to see if his position changes as the case moves forward."

"How did the pair of them end up in Yorkshire?" Cassidy returned to the table, dropping six packets of crisps next to Cooper's pint glass. "It's a long way from home for both of them."

Jack reached for a packet of cheese and onion. Not usually a fan of crisps, he suddenly felt famished. "The papers for Magee's 1998 trial for robbery showed him as living in the area as a jobbing electrician. My guess is Naylor went up to join him at some point — the man seemed obsessed with him for some reason — but when Magee was arrested, Naylor returned home to London. Magee served the first few years of his sentence in Doncaster but was later moved down to Wandsworth after becoming a bit of a handful up there. I'm also told that investigations are starting into potential offences Naylor might have committed abroad. Checks have shown he left the country sometime after the first Central Line Killer murders, before returning to the UK and starting his killing spree again."

Cassidy slid back into her seat next to Jack. "I've been in touch with the family liaison officers for Keeley, Jessica and Sammy." She gave a sigh. "The families are all still coming to terms with what's happened."

"I don't doubt that for a second, Amanda." Jack ripped open his crisp packet, tossing another across the table towards Cooper. "No bacon, I'm afraid, Cooper. Beef is as close as you get."

Cooper caught the packet in mid-air. "Beef's just as good. I'm stoked that the care home angle paid off in the end, though. It was just a tenuous link at the start."

"Sometimes that's all it needs, Cooper — and it was a good spot. Even if the victims didn't all work in care homes, there was a link to one in there somewhere, and that's where they could have crossed Naylor's path. Keeley was the only one we struggled with for a connection — but it turns out she had an elderly aunt in care. It's all there, Cooper. We just had to take a chance and dig for it."

Cooper ripped open the bag of beef-flavoured crisps. "And Lorna Henshaw? She just had the misfortune to cross Naylor's path as a teenager? She didn't play any part in the murders?"

Jack considered the question while he sank another third of his pint. Lorna Henshaw still bothered him, but he wasn't too sure why. "As far as we can tell, that was it. Wrong place, wrong time. For some reason, Naylor remembered her. Henshaw recounted an incident shortly before Naylor left school where she took him back home for a change of clothes after he'd wet himself — apparently, he had a medical condition that made him susceptible — so we think that's how he knew where she lived. That was always something that bugged me. I won't lie, though — I did think she was more involved than she was letting on. As did Frank Tyler." Jack gave a small shrug. "I guess we were wrong on that front."

"So, what about Tony Kingdom?" Cassidy waved away Cooper's offer of a crisp. "And his father?"

Jack tipped the rest of the cheese and onion crisps into his mouth, already eyeing up a second packet. "Dennis Kingdom was picked up trying to board a ferry at Dover. His prints are all over the gun found beneath the driver's seat of their van.

However, I believe Tony Kingdom is guilty of nothing more than being a rather unlikeable individual. We found a small quantity of cocaine and amphetamines in his room, but it's unclear at this stage if it was just for personal use or whether he was involved in dealing. I believe him when he says he wasn't aware of the gun."

Cassidy raised an eyebrow. "So, the gun was Dennis's?"

Jack nodded. "So it would seem. Regarding the 'card games' Tony told us about in interview — it seems the people Dennis Kingdom rubs shoulders with are known to the police as low-level criminals. The gun is being sent for additional tests, but it's suspected it could have been used in several raids on shops and other businesses across the capital in recent months."

Cassidy nodded. "And Kingdom was telling the truth when he said he picked Jessica up from the bus stop, only to throw her out a short time later?"

"Aye," replied Cooper. "So it would seem. I managed to find some camera footage that showed Kingdom's van stopping at the side of the road, and Jessica getting out. Once we knew it was Luke, a fresh CCTV trawl showed his laundry van in the same road at the same time."

After the team worked their way through the rest of the crisps, and Jack bought a second round of drinks, the door swung open to reveal Rob Carmichael and Genete.

"Pull up a seat, Rob — the boss is in the chair." Cooper grinned as he reached for another packet of crisps. "Get your order in quick."

Carmichael grinned back as he headed for the bar. "I'll get the next round in. Same as before for everyone?"

After fresh drinks were placed on the table, plus more crisps, Carmichael and Genete took their seats.

"How long are you staying?" Jack edged his stool to the side to make way. "In London, I mean."

Genete took a sip of her gin and tonic. "Just a few more days. Rob says he'll show me the sights before I head back home."

"Well, I hope it's not the last time we see you. You really helped us with the case." Jack gave an appreciative smile. "We couldn't have done it without you." Jack wasn't one for banding around compliments, but when it came to Genete he had nothing but praise. Rob had told him some more about his sister after the case reached its climax last night — how she used her last foster family's name of Hill, and didn't do any form of social media, which was why Rob had found it so hard to track her down — and Jack liked her instantly.

"Where's Daniels?" Carmichael glanced around the table as he sank the first third of his pint. "Out on one of his training runs?"

Jack shook his head. "Not tonight. I'm reliably informed that he's over at the mortuary being given a lesson in livor and rigor mortis, and all other things delightfully post-mortem."

Carmichael's eyebrows hitched over the rim of his glass. "Really? That sounds a bit heavy for a Thursday night. He's not thinking about a change of career, is he?"

Jack smiled into his pint glass. "I'm not so sure it's the subject matter that's the attraction — maybe more so the teacher." His grin widened at the questioning look on the detective sergeant's face. It was Cassidy that piped up to give an explanation.

"Perry — Dr Matthews' young mortuary technician — has taken quite a shine to our Trevor." She giggled into her tonic water. "It's all quite sweet. He's a lovely lad."

After the third round of drinks had been supped, Jack got up to buy another.

"Not for me, guv." Cassidy got to her feet and pulled on her jacket. "I've another couple coming round to view the flat. Fingers crossed they turn up this time."

"Before you go, Amanda—" Cooper scrunched up his fourth crisp packet and popped it into an empty pint glass — "I've been meaning to ask you something. It's been bugging me for a while. What do you think — do more people die from falling coconuts or falling pineapples?"

Cassidy hovered beneath the dartboard, a frown forming. "What do you mean?"

Cooper gave a shrug, hiding a grin behind his pint glass. "Just interested in what you think. What would be more common — falling coconuts or falling pineapples?"

Jack rounded up the empty glasses. "Just ignore him, Amanda, he's jesting with you. Pineapples don't grow on trees."

"Sure they do, boss." Cooper's grin stretched further. "Black Lace wouldn't lie to us, would they? 'Agadoo' and all that?"

Jack made his way towards the bar, taking Cassidy by the elbow as he did so. "Just google it, Amanda — and then ignore him."

Cassidy cast a glance over her shoulder as she headed towards the door. "I don't know what to say, Chris. I sometimes feel sorry for Jenny if this is what she has to put up with."

* * *

Time: 9.45 p.m.
Date: Thursday 16 April 2015
Location: Kettle's Yard Mews, London

Jack had returned from the pub in a relatively good mood. Ellis Magee and Luke Naylor would face what was coming to them — Jack just needed to hand the case over to the CPS now and let them handle the prosecutions. It was always a tricky time — the team had lived and breathed this case for the last six days, but now it had reached a conclusion they needed to move onto other live investigations, of which there were plenty.

The couple of hours in the pub had been good — Cassidy had disappeared to oversee her flat viewing, and Cooper had slipped away not long afterwards as Jenny had announced she was on the way home. Jack and Carmichael had enjoyed another round of drinks, Genete nursing her second gin and tonic, not wanting another.

And then Jack had arrived at Kettle's Yard Mews alone. As usual. But it was a position he was more than comfortable with. Marmaduke had greeted him with a deep-throated purr, and the pair had settled down on the sofa while Jack surfed the headlines. He was quietly satisfied that the news the Central Line Killer had now been captured was the lead story, hopefully instilling some degree of confidence into the city. Time would tell.

Weighing up the advisability of pouring himself a small measure of single malt to finish the evening, Jack was, instead, disturbed by a text message.

Jack — please tell me about the crash that killed my parents.

He instantly knew who the message was from without needing to look. *Isabel.*

I know Clive was there. I just want to know why.

Jack sighed, wishing he had poured himself that single malt.

It was a conversation he knew he needed to have — he just didn't realise that it would have to be now.

THE END

MESSAGE FROM THE AUTHOR

There are many people I need to thank for helping get *No Red Lines* onto the bookshelves.

First, I must thank Detective Inspector Steve Duncan and Police Sergeant Rebecca McCarthy once again for their help throughout this book. As always, it is very much appreciated. If there are any remaining procedural inaccuracies, then I can assure you that they are mine and mine alone, and they are there for entertainment purposes only!

Thanks also go out to many of my colleagues at the West Suffolk Hospital in Bury St Edmunds who have loaned me their names for use in this book — namely, Sadie Bloomfield, Keeley Saul, Sherri Jeffery, Colette Burgess, Christine Gooch, Cindy Benham, Becky Scott, Trace Manning, Lynn Jaggard, Laura Eldridge, Gemma Howie, Marie Owen, Gail Coleman, Jessica Fleming and Kristel Turner. Thank you!

My good friend Sarah Bezant once again deserves a very special mention — your brilliant attention to detail when reading my early drafts is invaluable. I honestly couldn't do any of this without you.

And, of course, I must thank everyone involved at my publishers, Joffe Books — and especially Kate Lyall Grant for continuing to believe in me and making my writing the best it can possibly be.

And, finally, it is you — the readers! Without you, none of these books would ever see the light of day. I thank each and every one of you.

To keep up to date, there are various ways to get in touch:

www.michellekiddauthor.com — join my author newsletter for information on future releases and special offers. I also give away free downloads, content not available anywhere else!

Facebook: michellekiddauthor

X @AuthorKidd

Instagram @michellekiddauthor

THE JOFFE BOOKS STORY

We began in 2014 when Jasper agreed to publish his mum's much-rejected romance novel and it became a bestseller.

Since then we've grown into the largest independent publisher in the UK. We're extremely proud to publish some of the very best writers in the world, including Joy Ellis, Faith Martin, Caro Ramsay, Helen Forrester, Simon Brett and Robert Goddard. Everyone at Joffe Books loves reading and we never forget that it all begins with the magic of an author telling a story.

We are proud to publish talented first-time authors, as well as established writers whose books we love introducing to a new generation of readers.

We won Trade Publisher of the Year at the Independent Publishing Awards in 2023 and Best Publisher Award in 2024 at the People's Book Prize. We have been shortlisted for Independent Publisher of the Year at the British Book Awards for the last five years, and were shortlisted for the Diversity and Inclusivity Award at the 2022 Independent Publishing Awards. In 2023 we were shortlisted for Publisher of the Year at the RNA Industry Awards, and in 2024 we were shortlisted at the CWA Daggers for the Best Crime and Mystery Publisher.

We built this company with your help, and we love to hear from you, so please email us about absolutely anything bookish at feedback@joffebooks.com.

If you want to receive free books every Friday and hear about all our new releases, join our mailing list here: www.joffebooks.com/freebooks.

And when you tell your friends about us, just remember: it's pronounced Joffe as in coffee or toffee!

* 9 7 8 1 8 0 5 7 3 0 8 9 7 *